Scoundrel for Hire

"I know this is just a lark to you," she whispered fervently. "But my whole world will come crumbling down if you don't pull off this role."

Those pewter eyes held her spellbound. For a moment, she forgot that one poorly timed lie, one spiteful wisecrack, and he could destroy every happiness she'd ever known.

"This is the point of no return," he said softly.

His words sizzled along every nerve. He was right, of course. "Don't tell me you've suddenly developed a conscience," she chided tartly.

"Nothing so drastic." A smile teased the corner of his mouth. "But I trust I'll be a busy man in the nights to come. And I was noticing how much you seem to . . . admire me."

"Admire you?" *Good Lord.* She wanted to crawl under a potted fern. Was she that transparent?

"Come now, Silver." His voice lowered to a murmur. He shifted, his lips parting above hers in the most hypnotic way. "You would much rather I lavished my kisses on you."

ADRIENNE de WOLFE

SCOUNDREL for HIRE

AVON BOOKS  NEW YORK

AVON BOOKS, INC.
1350 Avenue of the Americas
New York, New York 10019

Copyright © 1999 by Adrienne Sobolak
Inside cover author photo by Wild at Heart
Published by arrangement with the author
Library of Congress Catalog Card Number: 99-94462
ISBN: 0-380-80527-8
www.avonbooks.com/romance

First Avon Books Printing: December 1999

AVON TRADEMARK REG. U.S. PAT. OFF. AND IN OTHER COUNTRIES, MARCA REGISTRADA, HECHO EN U.S.A.

Printed in the U.S.A.

WCD   10 9 8 7 6 5 4 3 2 1

To my agent, Laura Tucker,
the greatest champion a writer ever had.
Thanks for believing.

Prologue

December, 1870

The cemetery was windswept and barren, a landscape of ice.

In all his fourteen years, Raphael Jones had never seen anything bleaker, not even during the war, when Jedidiah had burned furniture to keep the family warm. That year, Rafe believed he'd never see a worse Christmas Eve.

Then yesterday Mama had died.

The ground was so frozen that the gravediggers had used axes to hack at the earth. Their torches sputtered and hissed in the snow that whooshed down from Kentucky's Pine Mountains. Standing alone to watch, Rafe had braved the sting of that storm, his limbs warmed by the rage that still seethed through his veins. The only part of him that could never be thawed was his heart. Finally, stripped of his last ounce of hope, he'd been forced to accept the raw truth: God didn't care about him or his prayers.

Rafe's four-year-old sister stood beside him. One mittened hand holding his, the other clutching Mama's prayer book, Sera gazed toward the icicles on the oak guarding Mama's grave. She was too young to understand. Perhaps that was why she hadn't cried during the memorial service, not even after Jedidiah had barked, "Not another word, Seraphina. Not another word about ghosts, you hear me?"

"Not ghosts, Papa," she'd piped up in childish innocence. "Angels. Beautiful angels with golden wings. Mama's dancing with them by the tree. Can't you see?"

But Jedidiah Jones hadn't seen. Preacher Jones never saw anything unless it was blasphemous. Angels might not be, but Sera certainly had been when she'd spoken of her dead mother and dancing. At least, that's what Jedidiah had raged in front of the mourners who'd shivered in his church, waiting impatiently for his eulogy to end so they could hurry home to their cheerful fires and Christmas hams.

Rafe knew he should be used to his adoptive father's ways, but today, Jedidiah's lack of compassion had made Rafe sick. As cold as it was, Rafe had bundled up Sera and six-year-old Gabriel and shepherded them outside. They'd hurried past the black-plumed horses of the hearse, to the frozen mound that marked their mother's final resting place. Here, he'd thought, his kid brother and little sister could say good-bye the way they wanted to, without Jedidiah's scorn.

Unfortunately, Rafe was no longer sure he'd done the right thing. Beneath her ribboned baby cap, muff, and cape, Sera was shivering, even though he'd wrapped his scarf around her shoulders. Gabriel, when he wasn't coughing, was stamping his boots in his hated knickerbockers and ribbed wool stockings.

"Gabriel, you should take Sera inside now," Rafe said, his voice thick from unshed tears. "It's getting dark, and you look cold."

"I'm not cold," Gabriel said quickly, belying the

evidence on his too pale face. Despite the radiance that never left his eyes, Gabriel wasn't a healthy child. Jedidiah always said that radiance came from Gabriel's fevers. Mama used to say it was the mark of a servant of God. Personally, Rafe thought that gleam came from mischief, since Gabriel was happiest sneaking frogs into the house or tying Sera's shoelaces in knots.

"Rafe?" Sera was tugging on his hand. "Do we have to go inside? I want to stay out here with Mama."

"Me too." Gabriel coughed for a moment, then sniffed. "Do you reckon Mama knows we're here?"

"Of course she does," Sera answered brightly. "Angels always watch over children."

"Yeah?" Gabriel didn't look convinced. He reached down to fondle the ears of his spotted hound. "Say, do dogs go to heaven?"

"Sure." Sera parroted Mama. " 'God loves all creatures great and small.' Right, Rafe?"

Sure. Rafe's chest heaved. *Every creature but me*, he thought bitterly. He tore his eyes from his sister's guiltless face. He had no illusions about the disgrace he'd caused his mama, much less the shame he'd caused his family.

So why don't you get it over with, God? Why don't you strike me down so I can't destroy anyone else who loves me?

Before God could oblige, saving innocents like Sera and Gabriel from the malignance in Rafe's soul, an angry young man called out from the church. "Sera! Where are you?"

Sera caught her breath, and Rafe stiffened, recognizing his older brother's voice.

"Gabriel?" the young man called this time. "Answer me!"

Both Sera and Gabriel shrank closer to Rafe.

"Uh-oh. Michael sounds mad," Gabriel whispered behind his palm. "Should we hide?"

Sera nodded, her eyes as round as moons. Together, they glanced around the cemetery, more worried about a spanking than pneumonia. Rafe watched, uncertain what to advise, until they spied the icy steps of a tomb. When their faces lit up like twin candles, Rafe envisioned broken bones.

"Hold on," he warned, grabbing their coat collars before they could run. Unfortunately, the oldest Jones sibling rounded the corner in time to see Rafe restraining the children.

"When they didn't answer, I should have known you were to blame," Michael Jones called across the churchyard. "Never mind that it's Christmas. Or that Mama was laid to rest today. You just can't let a single minute go by without sinning, can you?"

The old guilt ate at Rafe's gut. He neutralized its acid with anger. Let Michael and every other hypocrite in his father's congregation say he was spawned by Satan. Now that Mama was gone, the gossip couldn't hurt her.

Michael threw open the cemetery gate and stomped inside, making the children squirm. He was a tall, broad-shouldered boy for his sixteen years, weighing a good twenty pounds more than Rafe. To see them together—Rafe with his tawny locks, Michael with his blue-black curls—most folks had a hard time believing they were brothers.

Maybe that's because they weren't, Rafe thought resentfully. Not full brothers, anyway.

Jedidiah had suffered the proof of Mama's adultery

like the Christian martyr he was, deigning to raise her bastard as his own son. In his heart, though, Rafe knew Jedidiah had fed and clothed him only because he'd wanted the pleasure of watching Mama repent every day. Jedidiah Jones hated Rafe.

And Michael was his father's son.

Hastily wiping away the proof of his grief, Rafe straightened his spine. He wasn't going to let Michael catch him in a weak moment. No one, not even Jedidiah, had a tongue that lashed like Michael's. Most folks figured Michael would follow in his father's footsteps and become a shepherd of the Lord.

Rafe just knew his brother would grow up to be a hanging judge.

Halting two paces from the children, Michael planted his fists on his hips and glared at Rafe. "Well? What do you have to say for yourself?"

"I don't answer to you."

"That's your trouble, Raphael. You don't answer to anyone."

"Yeah? Well, I reckon I'll just go to hell then."

"Not if Papa has anything to say about it. You're woodshed-bound, boy."

Turning his shoulder in dismissal, Michael next faced his youngest brother. Gabriel hastily put his hound between them. In spite of the child's defiance, Michael's blue eyes softened. "You were coughing all night again, Gabriel. I don't want you getting any sicker. Let's go." He held out his hand.

"I'm not sick like he is," Sera said, tossing her dark ringlets. "I'm staying here with Mama."

"You can't, Sera. Mama's dead. She's underground," Michael added, as if to soften the reminder.

"No, she's not. She's over there." Sera waved at the tree. When she blew it a kiss, Michael pressed his lips together, much like his father always did.

"Papa told you not to talk that way. Now come on. You're coming with me and Gabriel." With his free hand, he tugged the prayer book out of her grasp.

"Hey!"

"You know Mama's prayer book's not a toy."

"Give it back!" Her soprano voice shrilled in panic. "I can't see Mama any more. I can't see the angels!" She threw herself after the treasure, but when Michael held it out of her reach, she started to sob, jumping up and down and grasping at thin air. "Mama, where are you? Mama, come back!"

Rafe took a stiff step closer. "Give her the prayer book, Michael."

Wrestling with both children now, Michael glared daggers at him. "This is more of your influence, I'll wager."

"Saints don't wager," Rafe flung back. "Or maybe you've been led astray by those dime novels you've been hiding in your Bible."

Michael's cheeks mottled. The prayer book dropped, and the children dove after it. But Michael didn't notice. He was too busy clenching his fists.

"Profligate."

"You don't even know what that means," Rafe retorted, rallying the sass everyone had come to expect from him. "You just heard *him* say it once, and you figured it was bad."

"Yeah? Well, I don't need Papa to tell me what bastard means. You're not fooling anyone, Raphael. *She* wasn't fooling anyone."

"You leave Mama out of this," he warned, taking a step closer and clenching his own fists.

"Out of what? The truth?" Michael's lip curled. "You came into the world, and you ruined her."

"I did not!"

"Mama could have gone to heaven if it wasn't for you. I don't know how you can stand to live with yourself."

Rafe reeled at this nearly mortal blow. Was it true? Was his beloved mother burning in hell because of him?

"You're lying," he choked. "Mama is too in heaven."

"Whores don't go to heaven," Michael growled, his eyes narrowing in accusation.

"No!" Rafe grabbed his taller brother's coat lapels. "You take that back. Mama is not a whore!"

"Take your hands off me, filth!"

Michael shoved, and Rafe swung. In the next instant, they toppled onto the grave. Kicking and punching, cursing and howling, they fought like Cain and Abel. Rafe could see little more than the hail of dirt and snow as his fists rained down on his brother's mouth. His only thought was to silence that lashing tongue forever.

Michael fought back, though, more devil than saint. Tearing at Rafe's hair, jabbing at Rafe's nose, he landed blow after ear-ringing blow as they rolled, locked in mortal combat. Fourteen years of bitter rivalry for their mother's affection were unleashed in that explosion of rage. Rafe thought he might have killed his brother if he'd had the size and strength to stay on top. The thought scared him—scared him enough to miss a punch. Michael's gloves promptly closed over his windpipe.

"Raphael!" Jedidiah's horrified cry pierced the pounding in Rafe's ears. "Raphael Jacob, unhand your brother at once!"

Rafe's shirt collar twisted, jerking him back with

such force that he nearly strangled in the noose of his tie. For a moment he wheezed, flailing backward through steam clouds of breath; in the next instant, he slammed shoulder-first into a fence post.

"Michael!" Jedidiah reached for his favorite, but Michael was already climbing to his feet, dabbing his split lip with his scarf. Rafe, swiping the snow from his eyes, was more glad to see the tears on Michael's cheeks than the blood.

"Michael Elijah, what has he done to you?" Jedidiah cried, reaching out again.

"Nothing," Michael muttered and shrugged his father off.

Jedidiah's chest heaved. In his stark black frock coat, which hid the levity of his white collar, Jedidiah looked more intimidating than usual. He'd always been physically powerful, his size better suited for smithing. Rafe had heard the whispers that Jedidiah was the antithesis of his real father, a reportedly slender, jovial man who'd humbugged entire towns as part of a traveling salvation show. Supposedly, Rafe looked and acted just like him. Maybe that's why it was so hard to understand why his papa abandoned him. Rafe had always secretly wondered: was he that despicable?

"A brawl. A brawl in my churchyard!" Jedidiah rounded on Rafe, and the children slinked out of his way. "How dare you raise a fist in anger here. Have you forgotten what day this is?"

Mama's burial day. Rafe winced as shame lashed through him. *Mama, I'm sorry. I'm so sorry! Please don't hate me for fighting on your—*

"Christmas," Jedidiah sputtered, while Rafe remained too upset to speak. "It's Christmas Day!"

Bile burned its way to Rafe's throat. Why should

it stun him that Jedidiah Jones hadn't thought first of his dead wife?

"Wherever I find the devil's work, Raphael, I seem to find you," the preacher railed. "In my charity, I took you in. I gave you my name. I sought to save you from your sins, and what gratitude do you show me? You strike my firstborn! You spill his blood on his mother's grave! Wicked, willful, spiteful child, what have you to say for yourself?"

Rafe climbed slowly to his feet. His shoulder throbbed. His left eye was swollen half shut, and his nose trickled blood. But with Mama gone, there was no one to notice, much less care. Certainly the preacher who'd pretended to be his father all these years didn't.

Rafe glanced longingly at Michael, standing so rigidly and glaring at him. For a moment, he remembered a lonely, desperate time when he'd wanted his brother to like him, to play with him, to give him just ten minutes of the attention Jedidiah had denied him. Gabriel had eventually come along to fill that need, and then Sera, but by that time, Rafe had grown leery of loving anyone. The children were still too young to understand why he was "unwashed and unholy," as Jedidiah had once described him. They would grow older, though, and when they did, Michael would teach them.

As Jedidiah had taught Michael.

Raising his head, Rafe met the preacher's gaze with a hard-won dignity and a smoldering stare. "I say nothing. God is my witness. Let Him be my judge."

Jedidiah purpled, as Rafe knew he would.

"Salvation is far from your grasp, young man, as your impudence attests!" He pointed what Rafe secretly called The Forefinger of Doom. "Heed me well, Raphael. The wages of sin are death and eternal damnation! As long as you fall short of the glory of God, it is up to me to see you repent.

"Therefore, you will take yonder shovel and repair the damage to your mother's grave. You will walk home to cool your temper. And when you arrive, you will receive twenty lashes for the injuries you inflicted upon your brother."

Rafe's jaw dropped. "What about *my* injuries?"

"Aunt Claudia can see to them once you've been disciplined."

Rafe clamped his mouth closed on the futility of argument. Once again, Michael was presumed innocent, while he suffered the responsibility and the punishment. It was unjust. It was unkind. More than that, it was unbearable.

"Seraphina," Jedidiah barked, "Gabriel, go to the wagon."

The children tensed like fiddle strings as they became the focus of their father's attention. Taking a nervous step toward the gate, Sera hesitated, then raised worried eyes to her father.

"Papa," she asked timidly, "what's a whore?"

"To the wagon," he ordered ominously. *"Now."*

She gasped, scampering for the gate. Rafe's scarf slid off her shoulders. Gabriel, too intimidated to pick it up, ran with his dog after his sister. His coughs echoed in the brittle air.

Jedidiah retrieved the shovel. Thrusting it into the snow, he left the handle quivering by Mama's marker before he turned his back on Rafe and strode away.

Michael was the last to go. For a moment, he stood, broad and foreboding, a hulking shadow that all but obliterated the setting sun. With his breaths curling before him, he reminded Rafe of an angry bull.

Suddenly, Michael stooped. Pulling the scarf from the snow, he shook it off and tossed it at Rafe.

"Here," he said grudgingly. "You'll need this."

Then he was gone.

Rafe's fists tightened over the scarf. He stood that way for many minutes, his heart pounding into his ribs, his throat nearly too tight to breathe. A dusting of flurries tumbled from the sky.

At last he spied the buckboard. It bounced over the frozen ruts and headed down the hill. Seated in the back, the children turned toward him, their little bodies jolting beneath their brazier-warmed blankets. Sera raised her mitten to wave good-bye. After a moment, Gabriel did too.

A tear spilled down Rafe's cheek. Angrily, he dashed it away. Tossing the scarf around his neck, he grabbed the shovel and plunged it into the snow. Dirt was hopelessly scattered throughout the drifts; still, he did his best to dig it up, to pack it down and make amends.

"I know you're in heaven, Mama," he muttered. "Good people go there."

That's why I won't.

He bowed his head and rattled off his prayers. Mama had taught him the words. To hear him pray had made her happy, so for her sake, he recited every one he could think of. He knew he wouldn't be saying them again, not after this day.

Shoving his hands in his pockets, he cleared his throat, searching for something real and meaningful to say. He told his mama he loved her. He told her he was glad she was in a happy place at last. He asked her not to worry about him anymore.

Then he said good-bye.

Turning from his mother's grave, Rafe forged a

path through the snow away from Jedidiah's house. He didn't have a plan in mind; he just walked down, down, down the hill, too stubborn to let the bitter blasts of night knock him off his feet.

At least if I reach hell, I'll stay warm.

A livery stable huddled at the foot of the hill. He'd helped paint the building, and he knew the animals well. He figured the owner would be drunk and snoring somewhere as usual, so Rafe decided to steal a horse. It would serve the old man right for beating his animals. Besides, what difference would it make? Stealing a horse, saving a horse—it was all the same when your soul was damned.

"You're mine now, Belle," he told the filly after he'd saddled her and led her out into the moonlight. She didn't seem opposed to the idea, which made him feel better. Damned or not, he still had a conscience. He supposed he'd have to work a little harder not to care.

Reining in at the city limits sign, he pulled up his collar and tightened his scarf. His teeth were chattering, and his hands were nearly numb. It occurred to him he should have stolen food and some blankets, not to mention extra gloves and a box of matches. The problem was, he'd never stolen anything, excluding Belle. He'd never run away before either. Now what should he do?

He squinted into the frosty luminescence of the wilderness. A tendril of smoke curled against the moon. He could just make out a caravan of wagons in the silvery drifts in the distance. His heart thumped faster with hope. He suspected he'd found the theatrical troupe Jedidiah had helped chase out of town two days ago. They must have been caught in the ensuing storm. *"Thespians are harlots, liars, thieves, and drunkards,''* Jedidiah had thundered, no doubt still fuming over the actor who had played him for a cuckold nearly fifteen years earlier. *''Let Satan's disciples peddle sin elsewhere.''*

Blinking the flurries off his lashes, Rafe gave his horse a mirthless smile. "It seems kind of fitting, eh, Belle, that I join those lost souls now?"

A good three miles later, he was shivering uncontrollably and beating his fist against the door of a painted wagon. Scantily clad cupids and sighing ladies adorned the mural, the focal point of which was the dimpled and derbyed man who flexed exaggerated arm muscles on either side of the door. The portrait's face split open as the door swung wide, and Rafe blinked, dazzled by the starburst of light that silhouetted the behemoth looming over him. The man's head was hairless save for the drooping moustaches that covered his mouth.

"Bloody hell, it's a beggar. Be gone, brat. You won't find any handouts here."

Rafe raised his chin. A tantalizing blast of heat wafted out from behind the Brit—that and the mingled smells of mincemeat and rum. He had to get inside. It was inside or freeze, because he was not going back to the town of Blue Thunder.

"I'm no beggar. I'm here about the job."

The behemoth snorted. "We aren't any Punch-and-Judy show. Get on with you, now."

A painted female face, afloat in a stiff cloud of blonde hair, appeared beside the door. The matron looked Rafe up and down, paying particular attention to the body parts below his waist. Her cagey green eyes lit appreciatively.

"Aw, the tyke looks cold, Freddie luv. Let 'im in. It's Christmas Day."

"We aren't a bloody orphanage, Fiona."

"He said he's here about the job," she cooed.

"That's right," Rafe said quickly, pointing to the wind-ripped billboard that flapped beside the door. "It says here you're looking for a Falstaff. I'm your man."

The two thespians seemed to find this uproariously funny, and Rafe fidgeted beneath their guffaws. He had to admit, he didn't know what a Falstaff did, but he was good with a hammer and a paintbrush. Anything else he could learn.

"Know a lot about Shakespeare, do you?" Fred asked.

"Oh yes," Rafe lied, and quite well too, he thought, considering how little practice he'd had. "He wrote some very fine plays."

Fiona snickered. "He's got nerve enough for the footlights."

"Hmm. Maybe you're right." Fred was smirking as he rubbed his chin. " 'Fraid that's an old billboard, lad. That job's already been taken. By me." When Rafe's face fell, Fred added smoothly, "But you just might fit the bill for another show we're putting on in Louisville." He winked at Fiona.

She grinned. "Why, sure. He'd be perfect—once the swelling in his eye goes down."

Fred stepped aside, motioning Rafe up the step into the wagon. "What's your name, lad?"

Rafe loosed a ragged breath. The coals on their brazier had made the interior so toasty that he could feel a thaw moving through his limbs. "Rafe. But I can't leave my horse—"

"I'll see to your horse," Fred drawled, closing the door behind him. He laid a beefy arm across Rafe's shoulders. "So tell me. What do you know about *Romeo and Juliet*?"

Chapter 1

Summer, 1886

At last!
Silver Nichols eagerly reread the letter in her hand. For what seemed like an eternity, she'd been waiting for this kind of response to the inquiries she'd mailed across the nation. She'd hired bank examiners, Pinkerton agents, lawyers, even a retired Civil War spy. She'd turned them out in droves to help her build a case against Celestia Cooper, a modern-day witch who anyone with a lick of common sense could see lusted after her papa's fortune, not his love.

But not one of Silver's informants had uncovered anything quite like this. She hugged the parchment to her chest, half-tempted to kiss it. *At last!* Here was the proof she needed—proof of a deed so dastardly, so despicable, that the mere mention of it would make the angels weep. It had taken a church organist, writing in a fit of evangelical outrage, to finally bring to light this Celestia Cooper atrocity. The skeleton this letter had exhumed would put to an end that wretched woman's social climbing in Aspen. Now Silver could prove to her father beyond a shadow of a doubt that he was planning to marry a monster.

15

She grinned at her reflection in the polished mahogany of her prized box piano. *Good things* do *come to those who wait!*

Feeling a lightness she hadn't known for years—at least not since the night she'd fled her maternal aunt's boardinghouse—Silver hummed a Stephen Foster ditty and struck a match, watching the stack of her more benign letters ignite in the urn on her piano. The vessel was fashioned of sterling silver, a king's treasure dug from the richest of her father's four mines. So were the bookends, wall frames, doorknobs, and a variety of other bric-a-brac that adorned her lavish sitting room. She'd taken pains to convert the downstairs parlor into a sort of entrepreneurial trophy chamber, mainly to impress investors and potential clients. Although she entertained often in her father's Hallam Street mansion, she hosted business functions far more than social ones. Papa owned the most prosperous silver mining company in Colorado, and helping him maintain his social status required the ability to decorate and entertain with extravagance.

However, keeping Papa from frittering his fortune away required skills of a different nature.

Silver sighed as her soaring spirits were checked by the thought. Unbridled generosity might earn her father a place in heaven, but it wasn't going to feed him or keep a roof over his head. The man had never tempered his goodwill with practicality. Before she had arrived five years ago from Philadelphia, he'd already let himself get hoodwinked into portioning off one of his most promising claims. Fortunately, his partners couldn't raise the capital to develop it, and she'd persuaded them through some savvy negotiation to sell back their shares. That mine, Silver's Mine, as

Papa had called it, had turned out to hold his wealthiest vein, a bonanza that had brought him worldwide acclaim—and the attention of a fortune-teller-turned-hunter who billed herself as "Madam" Celestia.

Silver wrinkled her nose, waving away smoke. Thank God for conscientious, letter-writing citizens like that church organist from Kentucky. Otherwise, in six weeks' time, she might have been forced to call a circus sideshow act Mother.

The bell jangled over the front door. Silver started as her butler's staccato footsteps echoed in the foyer. Who on earth could be calling at this early hour? Perhaps it was her driver. She *had* been a bit distracted last night as she'd instructed him regarding the Leadville journey. Papa had disappeared as usual after dinner, and she'd been forced to see to his traveling bags as well as her own. She'd so wanted this journey to go without a hitch; indeed, nervous anticipation hadn't let her sleep past the first rays of dawn. For the first time ever, a woman had been invited to speak before the board of directors of the Leadville Mining Exchange. She, who had once been so penniless that she'd been reduced to cooking meals at the boardinghouse, would address some of the wealthiest brokers and stockholders in the mining industry.

But even more importantly, Silver thought with a bubbling sense of excitement, she'd have Papa all to herself for two days. It was a dream-come-true for the girl who'd been forced to grow up nearly a continent away from the daddy she adored.

Dumping the ashes into the unlit hearth, Silver hastily replaced the urn and stepped into the foyer. She left the parlor in time to see the front door bang open and her chubby father stand huffing on the threshold. Oddly enough, he was dressed in last night's dinner suit.

"Let me help you with that, sir," the butler said as Papa struggled over the threshold, his arms and back weighted down by bulging satchels.

"No thanks, Benny," Papa called jovially, listing to the left as he kicked the door closed. Oblivious to the heel mark he'd left behind, he grinned up at the solemn Englishman. "I've gotta get used to toting loads again so I can hoist my bride over the threshold."

Benson had the good grace not to smirk. Silver pressed her lips together. Celestia Cooper was one load Papa would *never* carry, if she had anything to say about it.

"Papa, for heaven's sake, you'll hurt yourself," she chided, hurrying to lend a hand. "Those knapsacks look much too heavy—"

"Now daughter, I'm a miner. And miners don't let a couple of rocks get the better of them." He doubled over, his ruddy face turning a shade redder as he hauled his bags toward the parlor. " 'Sides, this here's a special lode. And you know what that means, don't ya?"

"A special lode needs special care," she chimed in dutifully.

He chuckled, and her heart warmed. She loved Papa's laugh. The sound always reminded her of sleighing and Christmas and chestnuts roasting over the fire. Maybe those images came to mind because for most of her lonely childhood, Papa had only come home to Philadelphia when the snows had made it too hard to prospect.

She trailed behind him. When Papa swung the knapsack from his back, she tried not to mind that

Benson had to grab a priceless Oriental vase out of the way. And when Papa banged his satchels onto her table, she did her best not to worry whether the cloud of rock dust could be brushed out of her prized Persian carpet.

"Let's see what we've got," Papa said, rubbing his hands together.

Benson stood gravely at attention, but she moved closer, her heart quickening. Papa's enthusiasm had always been infectious. Even in the days when she'd preferred rag dolls to nuggets of ore, she would run to sit by his knee and help him paw through bag after bag of quartz for the glimmer of gold he'd sworn he'd found.

She held her breath. But when he unbuckled the fastenings and dumped out the satchels, she could tell in an instant he'd been prospecting a dream lode. She supposed some things never changed. "Papa," she said gently, "these are nothing but country rocks."

He squinted, holding a particularly plain piece of granite to the window. " 'Course they are, daughter. They're spiritkeepers."

"Spiritkeepers?" she repeated dubiously.

He nodded, his blue eyes twinkling above his salt-and-pepper beard. "Yep. Cellie says we need a whole barrel full so we can choose the best ones for the séance."

"Séance!" Silver nearly choked biting back her oath. *Ooh, that woman and her cockamamie schemes.* "Papa, why on earth would you want to hold a séance?"

" 'Cause I want to talk to that dead Injun and make him quit spooking our miners." Chucking the first rock back on the table, Papa reached for a second and shook it, hopefully, next to his ear. "Hmm. Nothing," he muttered. "I wonder how you're supposed to tell which ones the spirits live in?"

Silver almost groaned aloud. When she glanced at her butler, his stony, straight-ahead gaze was belied by his dry smile.

"Uh, Benson, would you be kind enough to close the parlor doors when you leave?"

"Of course, madam." Once again the model of imperturbability, Benson bowed and backed into the hall.

The cherrywood panels closed with a *snick*, and Silver turned to her father. He was fishing inside his coat pockets for something, most likely his ever-present magnifying glass. As she watched his crumpled vest strain across his well-fed belly, a feeling of such profound tenderness washed over her that for an instant, she was moved to tears. Just five short years ago, when he'd finally made good on a lifetime of promises and sent for her to come live with him beside his "mother lode," he'd been bonier than a half-starved sparrow. Maximillian Nichols had sustained himself on dreams for forty-four years, sacrificing his own needs to send her and Aunt Agatha what little money he could scrape together to help keep them off the streets.

Now, hale and hearty and wealthier than even he had ever imagined, Maximillian Nichols was still living on dreams. She understood that it wasn't the pot of gold but rather the rainbow chasing that made him happy. And she wanted him to be happy. Her papa was her whole world. If he needed to believe in some silly ghost and the mythical treasure he'd hired Celestia to help him find, then Silver was willing to pretend she believed in them, too.

However, she was not willing to stand by and

watch her papa be made a public laughingstock because he was too kindhearted to conceive that Celestia
Cooper might prey upon his fantasies by turning an
old Indian legend to her advantage.

"Papa," Silver said, "I'm sure we can find a way
to avert a miner's strike without holding a séance. We
don't want to fuel the men's fear of Dancing Moon,
after all."

"Not to worry, daughter." He opened the eye he'd
squeezed closed to peer at his rocks. "We'll keep it
small. You, me, the Union leaders, and maybe Brady
from the *Times*. 'Course, there's no telling how many
spirits'll show up around here, if you know what I
mean."

She smiled weakly. To her discomfort, she knew exactly what he meant. That's why she'd never told him
about her nightmares. The last thing she wanted was
for Papa to decide Dancing Moon was haunting her
boudoir and then enlist Celestia to perform some sort
of exorcism rite on her bed. Silver could just imagine
the snide editorial Brady Buckholtz would pen then
about "the Sterling Spinster," as he'd dubbed her.

Shrugging out of his coat, Papa rolled up his shirt-
sleeves and rummaged once more through his rocks.
"It turned out to be a fine day, eh, daughter? A fine
day for hunting treasure. Cellie says I'm on the right
trail now. That cache ol' Dancing Moon extorted
from the citizens of Cibola ain't but another blast or
two away. Say, you want to ride to the mine? I'll
show you where Cellie and me are gonna dig next."

Silver's heart cringed. She didn't know what was
worse, watching her father's face light up when he
mentioned that dreadful woman's name, or imagining
what else might "light up" if Celestia got her hands

on a stick of dynamite. "Uh, thanks, Papa. But there really isn't enough time."

"Hmm." He squinted at his pocket watch. "I reckon you're right. Dang, I gotta get me into some dungarees. Can't very well go digging in broadcloth, eh?" He winked cheerfully. "Leastways, that's what you always tell me."

For a moment, Silver was too stunned to do anything but blink. Did Papa mean to imply he wasn't going to Leadville?

"Well, gotta hurry," he said, sweeping his rocks back inside the satchels and slinging the packs over his back. "Burning daylight and all that. Cellie's waiting for me to come back to her hotel room."

"Wait a minute!" Silver grabbed his arm, indignation overcoming her shock. "What do you mean, Cellie's waiting for you to come back?"

He gazed at her as if she'd gone daft. "Didn't you hear me? Cellie says I'm on the right trail. Shoot, if our luck holds out, we might even find a clue that'll lead us to Cibola!"

Silver gaped. She didn't know whether to be outraged by his change of plans or scandalized by the notion that her sainted Papa was wearing last night's suit because that horrible woman had *seduced* him in a hotel!

"Papa," she sputtered, "surely Cibola can wait. We're scheduled to leave for Leadville in twenty minutes."

His brow furrowed. When he continued to look baffled, she added, "The directors' meeting. At the Mining Exchange, remember?"

"Oh." His ruddy face fell. "That was today?"

"It's tonight. But you know we'll need most of the afternoon just to ride across the pass and get dressed for dinner. It's going to be quite a formal affair.''

His good humor returned. "Well, you go ahead then, daughter. I never did care for formal affairs. You know more about stocks and dividends anyway, and you've always been better at hobnobbing with investors. That's why I made you my partner.''

"But Papa," she protested, unable to take pleasure in what she would normally have considered high praise, "I was going to give the speech tonight.''

"And a splendid speech it will be. I have every confidence in you, daughter.''

Wounded to her core, Silver could only stare at the man she'd worshipped for twenty-three years. Her papa had been her knight in shining armor, the only bright spot in a childhood made dreary by "Aunt Hagatha," as Papa was fond of calling her, and a maternal grandfather who didn't know the meaning of affection. Only after Maximillian Nichols had struck the mother lode he'd named in her honor had Silver been permanently reunited with her papa. She'd vowed then they would make up for all the time they'd lost. Didn't he understand how much their weekend meant to her?

"But I had other plans for us too," she said, petulance creeping into her voice. "I bought tickets for the new Shakespearean production at that fabulous Tabor Opera House. And I was hoping we could eat dinner at Charley's Restaurant and then take a stroll afterward to look at the constellations just like we used to do before—" her chin jutted, quivering the tiniest bit "—before *she* came along.''

"Now, daughter." Papa's face was growing redder the longer his packs weighed him down. "You know I'm a 'Grand Anvil Chorus' kind of a fella. Give me a mug of beer and a cheek to pinch, and I couldn't be happier. 'Sides,'' he patted her arm consolingly, ''you don't need me in Leadville like Cellie needs me here. You know all the things that can go wrong when you're digging underground. Cellie says Dancing Moon won't give up his treasure without a fight. That's why the men keep hearing moaning.''

So that's what Cellie says, eh? Well, what would Cellie know? Silver blew out her breath. Anyone with a modicum of scientific knowledge would understand that settling timbers groan. The miners were hearing the shifting beams above their heads, not the moaning of ghosts. How dare that pestilential nuisance spread rumors that Silver's Mine was haunted?

Obviously Celestia didn't have the slightest concept of what a strike would do to production—not to mention the fortune she was plotting to marry. The hardrock stiffs were already grumbling about their three-dollar wage, saying the miners at the Comstock Lode were getting paid four dollars a day. Of course, the miners in Nevada were also working under unbearable conditions, Silver thought a tad righteously. She, on the other hand, had done her very best to protect her men from the gruesome accidents and tragic deaths that had made the Comstock infamous.

But that was another matter entirely. Damn Celestia Cooper. The woman knew very well how much this day—this outing—meant to Silver. The quack also knew how hard Silver was trying to get rid of her. Celestia had concocted the whole ghost melodrama, of course, so Silver couldn't get Papa alone long enough to bend his ear with the mounting evidence against her.

And in the polite vernacular, Silver thought grimly, that meant war.

''Papa, I am deeply concerned about this dig you're undertaking.'' *No doubt Celestia is using it as an ex-*

cuse to poke around our richest vein. However, Silver knew better than to point this fact out. Papa would get that glazed look in his eye, nod politely, and not hear a blessed word she said. Over the last six months, he'd resisted every reasonable entreaty to unburden himself of his fiancée. Maximillian Nichols was the kind of man who saw a rose long after the bloom had withered. His refusal to recognize failings in any person, place, or thing was one of his most endearing—and most vexing—characteristics.

And right now, Silver was vexed.

"In light of recent information I've received," she continued briskly, "I'm not sure you would be safe underground."

Already looking longingly toward the door, Papa swiveled his head back toward her. She was gratified to know she could still capture enough of his attention to keep him from walking out of her life.

"Safe?" he echoed, the miner in him no doubt pricking up his ears.

"Yes, Papa. Whether or not there really is a king's ransom worth of buried treasure—"

"Oh, but there is, daughter. Cellie stakes her reputation on it."

Silver swallowed a less than gracious retort. Papa was obsessed with Dancing Moon's treasure because he hoped it would lead to the so-called City of Gold. Recently, treasure seemed to be the only thing he cared about. That and Celestia, of course.

"Yes, well—" Silver cleared her throat "—I must strongly advise you to rethink your plan to dynamite anything."

"What do you mean?"

Silver squared her shoulders, ignoring a momentary pang of remorse. What she knew about Celestia's past was going to hurt him. "Papa," she began again, choosing her words as judiciously as her own hurt would allow, "Celestia is not the best companion you could have on a mining expedition. The danger to yourself and to others would be prohibitive."

"Well . . ." His brows knitted. "It's true she isn't as knowledgeable about mining safety as you are, but—"

"Papa—" Silver struggled with her impatience. *Would he never open his eyes?* "Celestia is an arsonist."

He blinked owl-like at her.

In the eternity of silence that dragged by, guilt had plenty of time to needle her. She blushed. She fidgeted. She decided she should never have been so blunt. *God forgive me, why did I have to bludgeon him with the news? Now look at him. My dearest papa, and I've broken his heart—*

"Arsonist?" he interrupted her thoughts, still looking bemused.

"Er, yes." She cleared her throat. "There was a church. In Kentucky. The preacher raised a public outcry about Celestia's fortune-telling. He called her a witch, and when the marshal tried to run her out of town—"

Papa began laughing so hard that his mound of a belly actually jiggled.

Silver's ears burned. "What's so funny?"

"You, thinking Cellie would set fire to a church."

"You mean you *knew*?"

"Sure. Cellie told me weeks ago. She was all torn up about it, too. That church burning down was a terrible thing, but it wasn't Cellie's fault."

"Papa! You can't possibly know that—"

"Sure I can. I know Cellie." He grinned, a flash

of pure impishness in his beard. "Well, gotta go, love.
These packs aren't getting any lighter, if you know
what I mean. Have a safe trip to Leadville. And hurry
home so you can tell me all about it."

"Papa, wait—"

"Now, don't you worry, daughter. I won't let Cellie play with any dynamite." His chuckle floated back
to her from the hall. "At least, not the kind of dynamite you're thinking of."

The parlor doors slid closed behind him.

"Ooh!" Silver stomped her foot. She wasn't sure
which upset her more, the fact that her bomb had exploded and still missed its mark, or that her father had
chosen Celestia's company over hers. Angry, humiliated, and close to tears, she thought about canceling
her speech to spite Celestia. After all, the woman had
torched a church. Maybe she was dangerous, *really*
dangerous, not just eccentric and conniving.

Silver, don't be a goose, Common Sense counseled
sternly. *Go to Leadville. The better you get at managing your father's affairs, the more he'll value you over
someone as useless to him as Celestia. Besides, Papa's
safe. Even with all those lanterns, fuses, and sticks of
dynamite gathered outside the shaft, Celestia won't
harm him. He wouldn't be any good to her if he's dead.*

No, of course he wouldn't be, Silver thought
grimly. First, he'd have to marry her. Then he'd have
to add her name to his will. . . .

She caught her breath. Fear slammed into her gut
so hard and fast that she felt nauseous. Gripping the
table edge, she tried desperately to ward off dread.
But it wasn't any use. The seed of suspicion had already been sown.

*Dear God, I have to stop that wedding. More than
ever, I have to find a way.*

Chapter 2

⟨∼∽⌒∩∩⌒∽∼⟩

Rafe wanted to leave this high-society shindig.
In fact, he thought, gazing irritably around
him at the Grand Hotel's assemblage of tuxedoed ten-
derfoots, he wanted to leave Leadville. Only three
summers had passed since his last visit here, and already "Cloud City" had lost all resemblance to its
wilderness heritage. The lawless mining town he'd
watched spring up beside his beloved Mt. Massive
was now a provincial little city. Civilization had taken
such firm root here that a huckster could hardly ply
his trade anymore without some damned policeman
blowing the whistle. Temperance was even becoming
fashionable, thanks to the hoity-toity petticoats they'd
imported from back east. Rafe couldn't remember being stuck in a more demoralizing place—except, perhaps, for Blue Thunder.

He grimaced into his fake gray mustache and
beard.

Now where had that ugly memory come from?
Blue Thunder, more than any other Christian paradise, was the embodiment of hell to him. Only an
imbecile would have wasted enough brain space to
hold on to the memory. He couldn't imagine why he
had, much less why he'd let it surface to plague him

now, when he needed all his mental faculties to pull off this con—unless, of course, the reason had something to do with Fred and Fiona.

He made another face. Unfortunately, the bloated windbag who'd been bending his ear didn't take the cue to scurry off.

After ten blissful years of calling the shots in his cons, Rafe had had the misfortune of crossing paths last night with Fred and Fiona. Much to his dismay, his train had been re-routed to Leadville due to a spring snowfall-turned-avalanche, and he'd been forced to disembark. Fred had been standing on the platform, hawking handbills for his theater troupe's latest comedy of errors. With nothing else to do but stand on the depot's porch, Rafe had made the mistake of inquiring after Fiona; Fred had started blubbering like a baby; and Rafe had apparently been robbed of his last shred of common sense. Why else would he risk recognition by his old nemesis, Sheriff "Rooster" Crow, by helping Fred swindle the members of the Leadville Mining Exchange?

Rafe tossed a dour look at the Windbag, who seemed to think stories about hydraulic mining, in which whole hillsides washed away, made riveting conversation. *Pompous ass.* Clearly he'd been too busy raking in gold dust to worry about the waterways he was making unfit for travel or drink. Robber barons like the Windbag were marks Rafe delighted in fleecing, when Sheriff Crow wasn't stalking the premises. On occasion, as the inspiration presented itself, Rafe became rather like a nineteenth-century Robin Hood, stealing from the rich to save Mother Nature—a hobby Fred deplored, since it smacked of sentimentality.

Rafe scowled as his thoughts drifted back to his

former employer, a man he'd once naively hoped might become his second father. Playing on that youthful aspiration, Fred had begged him to visit Fiona at the wagon. And Rafe had gone, dragging his feet all the way. The old reprobate had duped him one too many times into performing with the troupe after Rafe had gotten the itch to strike out on his own.

But Fiona was sick. Really sick. If Rafe hadn't seen her with his own eyes, he might not have believed it. And Fred . . . well, never had he seen Fred so convincingly lost. The Brit had filled Fiona's wagon with bouquets of wildflowers, a tender gesture completely alien to the man, and then, confiding in broken whispers that Fiona only had six months to live, he had vowed before Rafe and God Himself that he would find a way to make his "Fee" well again.

Unfortunately for their sakes, Rafe thought gloomily, consumption didn't have a cure. He'd watched his mother succumb to the lung plague, and six years later, Sera's letter had found him in Texas, bringing news of Gabriel's decline. The boy had battled bravely, postponing his rendezvous with Saint Peter until Rafe could say a personal good-bye.

Of course, on the afternoon Rafe had dared show his face at the house, Michael and Jedidiah had barred the door so Gabriel's soul wouldn't be contaminated. Rafe had threatened to beat them both senseless until ten-year-old Sera had sneaked Gabriel out the window and around to the front porch. Weak but exuberant, the boy had fallen into Rafe's arms, begging to be taken back to Texas so he could live out his days as a cowboy. Content with Rafe's promise, Gabriel had died that night in his sleep.

Rafe's throat constricted at the memory.

Needless to say, Rafe was all for finding a cure for

consumption. But cheating death of Fiona's soul would take doctors, medicine, an extended vacation in a hot, dry climate, and money. *Lots* of money. Fred, as usual, had none.

That's why Rafe, against his better judgment, was risking Sheriff Crow's recognition to help Fred humbug the silver barons of Leadville. The rest of his reasoning, Rafe supposed, he owed to his own embarrassingly low finances. Keeping Octavia housed and fed was costing him a damned sight more than any female had a right to cost. If Tavy hadn't practically become his whole world, he would have dumped her back in the mountains where he'd found her.

Twitching his nose in a futile attempt to stop his mustache from itching, Rafe finally yielded to the need to scratch, swallowed an oath to find the glue still wet, and prayed he hadn't shifted the irritant off-center.

Damn Fred anyway. He should have burst through the ballroom doors fifteen minutes ago. His penchant for missed cues was going to jinx this hoax, because Fiona or no Fiona, Rafe had an eight o'clock stage to catch. Three summers ago, a bit too drunk to think straight, he'd blustered his way into this very hotel— and the bed of Sheriff Crow's wife. At the time, he'd believed the woman's claim she was a widow; the good sheriff, of course, had been unsympathetic to his alibi. Needless to say, Rafe would have been breaking rocks at the state penitentiary if it hadn't been for Mrs. Crow's finesse with a lock pick. And since he wasn't particularly interested in mounting another escape from the Leadville Jail, he preferred not to attract attention now.

That's why he was feeling a bit uncomfortable after

his encounter with the resident robber ''baroness.''
He might have been flattered by the woman's ap-
praisal if her smile hadn't frozen the moment they'd
been introduced and she'd arched a brow over eyes
as startlingly blue as sapphires.

Something about him, Rafe mused, had caused unmistakable disapproval in Miss Silver Nichols. At the
time, he'd been relatively certain he hadn't knocked
his theatrical whiskers askew, so he couldn't help but
wonder what had put her off. Surely it hadn't been
anything he'd said, unless, of course, she was the
overly virtuous kind who took offense to a man's simple hello. Or maybe she didn't favor East Coast
dudes. He prided himself as a mimic, and he knew
he'd gotten the Philadelphia accent down pat.

Half-intrigued, half-irritated, he glanced around the
richly paneled, plushly carpeted room until he spied
its lone female occupant. She stood beneath the center
chandelier, holding court. Three plump stockbrokers
gathered around her, each of them a good thirty years
older, and three inches shorter, than Silver. In fact,
they looked rather like lapdogs panting in the presence of royalty, despite her conservative dress: a high-
necked gown of lilac silk.

Every now and then, Her Royal Highness would
incline her perfectly chignoned head, which was a
fascination in itself, since her otherwise coal black
hair bore a streak of silver. Surely her twenty-odd
years didn't make her old enough for the distinguish-
ing mark at her left temple. On the other hand, her
youth lent her none of the giggling silliness he'd
come to associate with females under twenty-five.
There was a sophistication about Silver Nichols that
most overindulged women didn't exude until their
fortieth year. It was her sophistication, Rafe decided,

coupled with those eyes and that hair, that made Silver striking. Her nose was too long, her forehead too high, and her chin too angular for him to classify her as beautiful.

Still, beautiful or not, he was puzzled to see Silver at an all-male business function. He was even more puzzled to see no obviously preferred beau staking out his territory by her side. Her daddy reputedly had more money than the Rockies had snow, so it seemed to Rafe that eligible bachelors should be standing in line, begging for her company.

As if to comment on his notions of propriety, she laughed. The low, vibrant peal was as mellifluous as a golden bell, making it hard to mistake in the din of rough male voices. He wondered what the lapdogs had told her, and if, by chance, her gesture toward his side of the room had anything to do with him. Then the flash of red fire caught his eye. The ring on her left hand must be worth a king's ransom, but it hinted of rubies, not diamonds. How strange that an heiress her age wasn't even betrothed. Was she risking spinsterhood because she liked playing queen without a king? Or did she have some hideously huge but well-hidden flaw that no fortune could compensate for?

Rafe's curiosity climbed another notch. He was just trying to imagine what feminine flaw could possibly keep *him* from courting an heiress, when suddenly the double doors banged open. Fred, puffing madly on a cigar, swept across the threshold in a top hat, tuxedo, and spats. No wonder the old humbugger was late. He'd probably spent all afternoon rummaging through the prop wagon to dig up his evening wear.

"Gentlemen," the master conniver crowed. He thumped his cane to command the crowd's attention. A hush fell over the room, and all eyes turned to

Fred. He plucked off his gloves with a grandiose gesture that was impeccable in its timing.

"Is there a man among you who has an interest in diamonds?"

A ripple of gasps swept through the men. Rafe groaned aloud. Damn Fred and his improvisations. They'd agreed to bait the brokers with gold, not diamonds.

"I have here in my coat pocket," Fred continued in his resonant bass, sounding more like a medicine show pitchman than a western financier, "one thousand shares of my client's diamond mine, secreted away in the Gore Mountains by Rabbit Ears Pass. Not since the legendary strike of Central City has Colorado seen a mother lode of such overwhelming proportions."

Only through sheer force of habit was Rafe able to keep his expression from betraying his feelings. A diamond mine, for God's sake! How the hell was he supposed to pretend expertise on something he knew so precious little about? He had half a mind to lead the rush when Fred's change of plan would backfire and twenty outraged stockbrokers would beat the tar out of him.

At that inopportune moment, Rafe made the mistake of looking at Silver. Her gemstone gaze cut straight through the tobacco smoke to drill a hole to his soul's rotten core. The sensation wasn't reassuring to an imposter who risked exposure with each passing heartbeat. Biting off an oath, he dragged his gaze back to Fred and racked his brain for facts about diamonds.

"Step forward, gentlemen, don't be shy," Fred meanwhile boomed like the mining promoter he was purporting to be. "You'll want to take a gander at these little beauties. They came straight from the heart of Mr. Elliott Beachum's mine.''

With theatrical flare, Fred raised a satin pouch and spilled into his hand what would most likely prove to be a lump of coal and three glittering chips of quartz. Rafe could almost feel the avarice escalate in the room. As one man, the board members surged forward. The wave of greed swept up the Windbag, too, and Rafe prayed silently for both his and Fred's sake that the ''diamonds'' didn't crumble, crack, or shatter under Sheriff Crow's inspection.

A gentle ''Eh-hem'' and the captivating whiff of lavender distracted Rafe from his worries. To his surprise, he found Silver Nichols standing companionably by his side. With her hands clasped behind her back and her gaze focused on the milling men, she appeared to be unaware of him. In fact, as her silence dragged on for another minute, Rafe began to think she'd stopped beside him by accident, that she was merely waiting for her opportunity to jockey closer to Fred.

Then the corner of her mouth curved in a half-smile.

''I suppose,'' she murmured, ''the gentleman with the, er, *diamonds* is a friend of yours?''

The velvety timbre of her voice reclaimed his attention more thoroughly than a clap of thunder. He hadn't expected her to sound like she looked: rich. Sinfully rich. He was entertaining a delicious vision of hot fudge and cherries, when the full implication of her words slammed into his brain.

''I beg your pardon?''

''The man in the top hat. I daresay he's your accomplice?''

Somehow, Rafe managed not to choke on his

tongue. A dozen questions went shrieking through his brain at once, not the least of which was how the hell had she linked him with Fred.

"My dear young woman, I fail to understand—"

"I rather doubt that," she cut in smoothly. "You look much too intelligent. Canny, in fact. However, I am willing to believe that you are somewhat naive when it comes to miners' juries and the swift justice they dole out." She turned her face to him at last, that same amused smile flirting with the corner of her mouth. "I take it you and your friend weren't aware that to salt a mine is a hanging crime around these parts?"

Rafe steeled himself against any reaction other than an arched eyebrow. He figured she'd believe a show of hauteur more readily than a denial. Besides, no one had salted any mines. Fred's whole acting troupe wouldn't have had the resources for that. No, the Brit had simply made up the diamond mine story, counting on human greed and the Gore Range's scarcity of rail, stage, and telegraph lines to persuade these high-dollar speculators to invest in his hoax. He'd figured by the time they confirmed whether or not diamonds really could be unearthed near Rabbit Ears Pass, he and Fiona would be at least fifty thousand dollars richer and living in Mexico.

However, Rafe hadn't spent the last fifteen years as a professional flimflam artist to let some cheeky millionaire's daughter get the upper hand now. He eyed Silver with a nerve he'd honed at fourteen, bluffing his way through the role of Juliet while the all-male audiences pelted him with tomatoes.

"My dear Miss Nichols. With all due respect, you are suffering under some misconception. I do not know the gentleman with the diamonds, and I certainly am not affiliated with any mine salting. Why you should think such a thing is beyond my comprehension.''

She turned once more to watch Fred's con, playing out so flawlessly before them. Any minute now, Fred would expect him to step forward, to "inspect" the bait and declare it valid, then fan the fires of avarice by staking his own money to purchase a hundred shares of bogus stock. Fred had even stationed his nephew on a telegraph pole outside the city limits to intercept all dispatches coming and going to Steamboat Springs, the only town within a hundred-mile radius of Rabbit Ears Pass. Frankly, the con should have gone without a hitch. So what had tipped off Silver?

"Before you make an utter fool of yourself," she said softly, as if in answer to his thoughts, "I think you should know I've dined with the geologist you're impersonating. Mr. Bartholomew Markham is about two-thirds your height, twice your weight, and his pate is just shy of bald.''

His neck heating, Rafe entertained a vision of throttling Fred, who had assured him the renowned Pennsylvania geologist had been so busy running his coal-processing company that he hadn't set foot in a western mining town for the last twenty years.

Too much was riding on this con, however, for Rafe to give up the ghost now, especially on account of some know-it-all petticoat who'd had more money, privilege, and opportunity than he'd ever glimpsed, much less known, in his twenty-nine years.

"Good heavens," he said, warming his words with a low chuckle. "Uncle Bartie and I look nothing alike. Now I'm beginning to understand your confusion, Miss Nichols.''

"Uncle Bartie, eh?"

He inclined his head. "Yes indeed."

He could feel her appraising gaze again, poring over him with the same attention to detail that a book-keeper might use on accounts. He couldn't help but lament the irony. Here he was, standing practically thigh to thigh with an unmarried heiress, and they were talking about some old man she'd once dined with. What was worse, instead of being able to woo her with all the flash of his practiced roguery, he was insisting he was a middle-aged greenhorn, who, in her eyes, probably held as much sexual appeal as an apple barrel. He wondered how she might look at him if he wasn't sporting these asinine whiskers and a pillow for a paunch.

"So you claim to be Mr. Markham's nephew," she said slowly, an unmistakable lilt in her voice. "You must be from Philadelphia, then?"

"The Cradle of Liberty itself."

"How delightful," she drawled. "I'm from Philadelphia, too."

"Yes, well, I, er, was merely born there," he recovered as gracefully as he could. Damn her anyway. Was she really from Philadelphia? Unable to take that chance, he hastened to add, "I spent most of my youth in . . ." Hesitating, he cast her a sideways glance. Where would a lawless sport be safe from female busybodies? ". . . Dodge City. And later, in Abilene."

"Abilene? Oh my." Her eyes twinkled like twin stars as they laughed up at him. "A geologist in a cowtown. I can just imagine what you must have dug up."

He glowered at her.

"So tell me Mr. Kansas geologist," she purred,

tilting her head slightly, so that the captivating streak in her hair gleamed like liquid silver beneath the chandelier. "In what sort of rock formation might one find bituminous coal?"

Their eyes locked, and Rafe's heart sank. He didn't have the vaguest idea.

"I believe, sir," she said quietly, having the poor grace to smirk, "this is where you might say 'The jig is up.' Would you like to call off your hoax, or shall I?"

A muscle twitched along Rafe's jaw. She'd backed him into a corner, and she knew it. He glanced at Fred. The wily old cheat was still talking a mile a minute and casting impatient, but furtive, looks his way. Two things occurred to Rafe then. The first was that Miss High Society hadn't denounced him immediately. The second was that she'd given him a way out. He had to ask himself why on both accounts.

"Before I answer your question, madam, might I ask one of my own?" he murmured, deliberately shifting closer so that the heat of his breath blew in tantalizing gusts against her ear. He was gratified to glimpse the flutter of her pulse. "If you're so sure I'm a footpad, then why didn't you alert Sheriff Crow the moment we were introduced? One cannot help but wonder why an upstanding young woman would risk being charged as an accessory to a crime."

It was her turn to redden. "I . . . wished to be certain of your character, of course."

"You mean the character you think I'm role-playing?"

He straightened, returning her stare boldly, hoping his audacity would rattle her nerve. As far as he was concerned, she'd already tipped her hand. She was playing some game of her own. He didn't know what it might be, but chances were, she wasn't a strait-laced daughter of virtue as he'd first thought. She'd come here unescorted, hadn't she?

Darkening to a pretty shade of rose, she looked away. "That you are not Bartholomew Markham, nor even a geologist, goes without saying, sir. No, I dare-say you are more of an actor—a quite passable one, really—which, I think, might be useful if you were looking for . . . legitimate employment."

Passable, was he? Rafe was hard-pressed not to snort. He was a hell of a lot better than passable, if his recent successes at impersonating a French am-bassador and a California bank president were any indication. Then again, one could not publicly boast of these performances unless, of course, one wished to conduct all future performances from jail.

"Are you offering me a job, Miss Nichols?"

Her bodice rose, fluttered, and held. She seemed uncertain how to respond, which cued him further that her motives were shady.

Before she could answer, though, the Windbag chose that inopportune moment to hail him from across the room.

"What say you, Markham?" the nuisance boomed, weighing Fred's coal in his pudgy hand. "Could there be diamonds in those hills?"

Twenty pairs of money-glazed eyes bored into Rafe, and he marshaled the discipline not to flinch. This was the part of the con where he was supposed to wax poetic about quartz veins and Markham's ex-pertise as a rock hound. The problem was, gold was no longer Fred's bait of choice, and the geology of diamonds was about as familiar to Rafe as the moon's landscape.

"I wouldn't presume to speculate," he told the

Windbag. He watched Fred's jaw drop before he turned once more to Silver. "How about you, Miss Nichols?"

She seemed surprised that he'd drawn her into the debate. It was a gamble, of course, but since she'd taken his side thus far, he was hoping whatever use she secretly had for him would keep her from throwing him to the wolves. Besides, his perverse side wanted to see if she had the moxy to handle a hostile audience, which is surely what these men would become if she dared to throw in her feminine two cents worth about their greed.

To Rafe's relief, and his amusement, his gamble paid off.

"A wise course, Mr. Markham," she countered coolly. "I daresay further study *is* in order."

A rumble of disappointment circled the investors. Fred looked like he wanted to bash some wealthy heads.

"Now see here, gents," the huckster cried, stabbing his cigar toward Silver, "are you going to let some slip of a female tell you how to run your business?"

"Perhaps you and I should converse," Rafe interjected quickly, hoping to stave off one of Fred's "meddling doxy" tirades, which, he was certain, wouldn't leave Silver inclined to help them. "You might even wish to join me on the next eastbound train, so we can, er, confer with a lapidary. Analyzing gemstones such as yours is a delicate matter better left to eyes more highly trained than mine."

Fred turned florid. However, the man was nothing if not cagey. He knew when the deck was stacked against him, and, thankfully, he took his cue to fold. "Then lead the way, my boy. I have no doubt my ore will stand the test of a hundred such examinations. If it's proof you want, then proof you'll get. After all, we want to keep the little lady satisfied."

Rafe suspected this last dig was meant for him, not Silver.

Meanwhile, the speculators were all grumbling, squinting at Fred's chips and trying to decide whether to risk investing now, or to let "Markham get first crack at those diamonds." Fortunately for the suckers, dinner was announced, and the president of the Mining Exchange suggested their debate be tabled until after the meal.

"It seems you'll be able to make your getaway after all," Silver said, her expression turning wry as a half dozen arguing gentlemen jostled past them, intent on roast beef, port, and diamond mines. "Congratulations."

She offered Rafe her hand as if to take her leave. He found her calling card tucked artfully into her palm.

"If you wish to discuss an arrangement, I'll be at this address until tomorrow noon. Come alone," she added with a pointed glance at Fred. Then she inclined her head and joined the men converging on the chairs.

A heartbeat later, both Fred and his smelly cigar stood smoking at Rafe's side. "What the bloody hell were you about, making time with that petticoat when Fiona's lying abed, wasting her life away?"

Rafe grimaced, waving away the tobacco fumes, and fixed his partner with a withering glare. "Trying to keep your ungrateful hide out of jail. You want to tell me why you improvised with diamonds?"

"Fiona figured diamonds were a safer bet," Fred growled back, matching his low tone. "Even the brats around these parts can tell pyrite from gold." He scowled after Silver. "Damned bluestocking. She was on to you, eh? What do you think she'll do now?"

"I don't know."

Rafe watched narrowly as one of the lapdogs seated her near the head of the long banquet table. Then he ran his thumb over the engraving on Silver's card. So she'd be at that address until noon, eh? Perhaps one nonrefundable stage ticket would be well worth a visit to the First Lady of Sterling's abode—and an extra night in Leadville.

"Don't worry, Fred." Tucking the card beneath the flap of his coat pocket, Rafe gave his fuming partner a wink. "The lady may have won the battle, but she hasn't won the war. She's about to meet sweet conquest at the hands of Raphael Jones."

Every gaslight was ablaze as Silver paced the Aubusson carpet in her Grand Hotel suite. She was far too restless to consider disrobing and falling onto the feather mattress. Her day had been one disaster right after another, and as if that weren't enough reason to lie awake all night, she now had a decision to make. And she had to make it before the departure of the eight o'clock stage.

With an impatient glance at her bureau's porcelain timepiece, ticking off the last fifteen minutes of the day, Silver picked up her pace, as if the muffled tattoo of her heels could somehow speed up her resolution.

Guilt was such a trial. Here in her grasp—she waved a rolled-up edition of the *Rocky Mountain Sun*—she held the ideal plan to ruin Celestia, and yet she was having second thoughts. Doubts, for heaven's sake! How many times had she told herself she couldn't afford to have scruples when the opposition had none?

She blew out her breath. Maybe she'd be less squeamish if Papa's love weren't at stake.

Her bottom lip quivering at the thought, she swept past the moonlit balcony and the French doors she'd opened to counteract the blast of piped-in heat from the hotel furnace.

Damn Celestia Cooper's greedy soul. Papa should have been at the meeting tonight. Silver had *needed* Papa at the meeting, if not for protection, then at least for moral support. When she'd accepted her speaking engagement two months ago, her business mind hadn't allowed her to consider the fact that she might be ogled like a common tart. But that's exactly what had happened, triggering the insidious old fears. Why couldn't she seem to escape them after all these years? No one had wanted to listen to her discourse on mineral high-grading, thanks to the diamond mine furor, and the few members of her audience who had paid her any attention had stared glassily at her breasts. She'd battled a queasy feeling the entire time she'd been on stage. Looking back on those nerve-rattling twenty minutes, she liked to think she'd handled the front-row lechers with aplomb; even so, she couldn't quite shake the sensation that she was still being . . . well, watched.

Shivering, she gripped her newspaper tighter and did her best to put such nonsense from her mind.

Needless to say, the only saving grace of the Mining Exchange fiasco had been the plot she'd concocted against Celestia. That fraudulent Mr. Markham had given her the idea—an unscrupulous idea, to be certain, but one that was no less ripe with potential. Celestia had proven she lacked conscience. She'd made a lifelong career out of duping hardworking, God-fearing people. To Silver's way of thinking, it was time to fight fire with fire.

She winced. *Now that was an abominable pun.*

Still, there was no denying Celestia could use a taste of her own medicine. The woman probably deserved a whole lot worse—a jail term, for starters—but she'd been too clever for the prosecutors. With the law predisposed to be lenient to females, Silver knew the only way she'd be able to protect her father was to stoop to Celestia's level.

Well, not exactly to Celestia's level, Silver corrected herself, taking another brisk turn around the room. She could never physically hurt someone or damage their property. She wasn't above teaching Celestia Cooper a lesson, though. In fact, she felt morally obligated to. Hadn't God shown her the way by crossing her path with that Markham imposter? If meeting a scoundrel-for-hire wasn't the result of divine providence, Silver didn't know what was.

Sighing, she halted beside the bed.

Even so, her plan was not without its risks. A hundred or more things could go wrong, all of them at a moment's notice. With her father's fortune, his happiness, even his safety at stake, dare she take a professional swindler into her confidence?

This was the question that plagued her more than any other as she stood by her bedside, worrying her bottom lip. Every now and then her gaze strayed indecisively to the contents of her carpetbags, strewn across her quilt in preparation for packing. She still had time to abandon her scheme for a less imaginative one, she reluctantly reminded herself. She doubted a man of her would-be conspirator's character would rise with the sun, so she could slip out of the hotel, avoid the office address she'd so impetuously given him, and book herself a seat on the morning stage. No one would be the wiser. No harm would be done.

Except, of course, that Celestia would have used the day to her advantage, worming her way further into Papa's affections, while Silver had wasted her time conversing with morally deficient men.

Exasperated by the sheer unfairness of it all, she stalked out onto the balcony for relief from the furnace's carbony smell. A chilly breeze riffled a rowan, whose weighty branches bowed low over the railing as if to invite her to sample the fragrance of its blossoms. She shivered irritably instead. Aside from the occasional wildflower bouquet, which she allowed her servants to decorate the parlor with, she'd always found nature to be a nuisance, something to overcome in the struggle to unearth ore or to freight modern conveniences across the mountains to her father's mansion. Frowning up at the sky, she recalled how little she liked the moon. Out here, it made the dance of light and shadow enigmatic, a lover's shroud for stolen intimacies.

The notion conjured more uncomfortable memories. Trying to shake them off, she focused on the clouds instead. There'd been a time when she'd waxed romantic about the allure of celestial bodies, but she was older now and sadly wiser. She'd learned not to succumb to the enchantment of the moon after it had tricked her into trusting Aaron.

Satisfied that the sky wasn't going to unleash itself and keep her from a mud-free getaway at dawn, she started to turn, intent on packing her bags and abandoning her scheme, when something glinted, catching her eye. It had come from the rowan's quivering maze of leaves and flowers. Curious, she stepped nearer. A pair of silvery eyes stared back at her from the canopy's shifting, velvet shadows.

"But soft," her voyeur purred in a liquid southern drawl, "What light through yonder window breaks? It is the east, and Juliet is the sun."

Dumbstruck, Silver blinked for a full heartbeat before she could rally her wits enough to confirm that a man, not an angel, was perched in her tree quoting Shakespeare. His hair, she decided, was what had made her doubt her senses. Ivory-gold, perhaps amber, it gleamed with a pale luminescence above a high, intelligent brow. As much as she liked to think herself unmoved by masculine beauty, she couldn't help but gawk at his chiseled cheekbones, clefted chin, and lips so sinfully sensual that she didn't know whether to be alarmed or mesmerized when they smiled. Surely a face such as his had inspired the masterworks of Michelangelo.

Nonsense, Silver. You've been associating with grizzled, unkempt miners for too long.

With supreme effort, she recovered the use of her wit and her tongue. "You've mistaken your balcony, Romeo. No ladylove waits for you here. Perhaps you should try the plum tree next door."

He chuckled, a sensual melody that played over her senses with all the golden resonance of a cello. "Fair Juliet mistakes me, I fear. Did you not ask me to meet you alone? To discuss an arrangement?"

Silver started. This time his swallowtail coat, white bow tie, and watchfob registered on her brain. Then came his cologne, a tantalizing whiff of sandalwood and pine. An electrifying jolt smoked down her nerves. It was the imposter!

"B-but how is that possible?" she stammered. "I mean, your hair. And your whiskers!"

"Stage makeup, my dear Miss Nichols. Theatrical whiskers and a wig. You're not disappointed that I'm not an overfed graybeard, are you?"

She swallowed. Good heavens, no. Or rather, yes! Lord, what was the matter with her? The man was a liar and a thief. Judging by his mouthwatering good looks, he was probably a rake as well. She'd become far too acquainted with the dangers of rakes to linger in the moonlight with one.

"I must ask you to leave my tree at once," she said firmly.

"Forgive me." He looked far more contrite than he sounded. "I've shocked you. But I assure you, Miss Nichols, you have nothing to fear from me. After all, you were kind enough not to sic the marshal on me. I owe you a debt of gratitude."

She moistened her lips. She had everything to fear from him, she realized uneasily, and precisely for the reason he'd mentioned. "Y-you followed me here?"

"At your invitation."

"I invited you to my office, not my boudoir!"

"Ah, my mistake." He smirked. "Perhaps I should indeed leave your tree."

To her consternation, he swung down beside her, his broad shoulders all but blotting out her view of the French doors. Escape through the bedroom was impossible now.

"Do you know what time it is?" she hissed, backing as far from him as the railing would allow.

"Yes, before noon. That was a condition of your summons, was it not?"

"You know very well I was asking you to make a proper morning call."

"Do I?"

A tiny tremor, half thrill, half fear, tiptoed down

her spine. The balcony hadn't been designed to accommodate petticoats, tree limbs, and a six-foot-tall rogue. One sweeping gesture from his arms, and she'd be pushed over the edge . . . or pulled hard against him in a steamy embrace. Her stomach somersaulted at the thought.

"I am quite certain I never conveyed more than an intent to do business with you, sir."

"There are all manner of businesses, Miss Nichols. But very few are done alone between a woman and a man."

She flushed, realizing the error she'd made in being so vague. Still, only a cad would dare to suggest her motives had been anything other than ladylike.

And just what did you expect, Silver, given what you already knew about the man?

She winced inwardly.

No wonder she'd felt like she was being watched. The rounder had apparently stalked her, having the absolute gall to crouch in her tree for a good half hour or more. Undoubtedly he'd been using the time to confirm she was alone and unprotected.

She waited for the old apprehension to seize her at this thought. Strangely, it didn't. The knowledge that he'd been watching her for as long as he had actually helped calm her. That, and his passive demeanor. If harming her had been his intent, he could easily have carried out any number of dastardly deeds. Besides, he'd said so himself: he owed her a debt.

Straightening her spine, she tried to make her stare more withering than wary. "My dear Mister . . ." She blew out her breath. How did one upbraid a man whose identity one didn't know? "Might I have the courtesy of your name?"

Something like cynicism marred the refined roguery of his smile.

"By a name, I know not how to tell thee who I am," he taunted softly. "My name, dear saint, is hateful to myself."

How odd. She knitted her brows. She could almost have sworn he'd been mocking himself, rather than her, with that piece of Shakespeare.

"Romeo would, were he not Romeo call'd, retain that dear perfection which he owes without that title," she quoted.

Appreciation flickered over his features. "You know your Shakespeare, Miss Nichols."

"A bit. So, as I suspected, you are an actor."

"At the moment." His irony wasn't lost on her. "Raphael Jones is my name."

She caught her breath. A scoundrel with an angel's name? Should she consider his arrival another stroke of divine providence?

"I'm . . . not so sure this is an opportune time for us to talk, Mr. Jones. I was preparing to pack my bags."

"I see," he said gravely. "Then I shall be happy to await your convenience."

She felt the heat slowly build in her cheeks. The reprobate! He'd quite literally meant he'd wait for her to clear the bed.

"How very considerate you are," she said dryly, glad she'd had the presence of mind to litter her quilt with shoes and toiletries.

Despite his scandalous lack of decorum, she couldn't quite dismiss the notion that Raphael Jones might be a gift from heaven. He'd appeared in the nick of time, saving her from abandoning what was, admittedly, a desperate scheme. Everyone always said

God moved in mysterious ways. Maybe He was giving her a sign.

"What do you want here, Mr. Jones?"

"Why, to be of service to you, of course."

"Then you should be aware that you and I have very different ideas of what your, er, service should be."

"Perhaps."

He eased his exquisitely sleek length backwards, putting more space between them. She breathed a sigh of relief—until Jones propped his derriere on the railing and carelessly spread his thighs. She gaped to see how precious little the gaslights left to her imagination.

"So tell me, Miss Nichols. What's on your mind?"

Mortified, she yanked her gaze back up to his eyes. They were pearly gray, mocking, and far more perceptive than any man's had a right to be.

"I, uh, was going to, uh, make you a proposi—" *Oh!* She bit off an oath. "I mean a deal," she amended hastily. When he hiked a brow, she balled her fists. "I meant a business deal."

"Do tell."

"I am sorely tempted not to. Would it be too much to ask you to behave like a decent gentleman?"

"Certainly you may ask."

Odious man. She added impertinence to his growing list of sins.

Still, if anyone could star in the script she'd been writing in her head, Raphael Jones could. His audacity was one of his greatest—albeit vexing—qualifications. His lack of whiskers made him look younger than she'd first thought, but he'd proven his ability to pass for an older man of means. Besides, there was no denying that what he lacked in maturity he made up for in a scintillating sexuality . . .

He cleared his throat. She squirmed to be caught red-handed. *Silver, for heaven's sake, keep your eyes above his belt! Remember what happened the last time you were so bold?*

Repressing a tremor, she squared her shoulders and folded her arms. She wouldn't make that mistake again. Not ever.

"Mr. Jones," she began again in her most businesslike voice, "let us understand one another. On no account do I condone your behavior at the Mining Exchange. But I find myself in the indelicate position of needing to hire someone with your, er, particular dramatic flair. In order to determine your appropriateness for the role, therefore, I must ask you certain questions."

"Questions about acting, Miss Nichols?"

"Questions about your background, sir."

"Ah." He flashed a smile so unrepentant that it would have made the angels sigh. "You mean my past. I give you fair warning, it is not the sort of fare I usually inflict upon a lady's ears."

"And yet if I am to hire you, Mr. Jones, I am entitled to know all—within the realm of good breeding, of course."

A long, well-manicured finger tapped his lips, as if to hide another smile. "Please. Call me Rafe."

She raised her chin. She wasn't about to encourage his familiarity. Moonlight, balconies, and bedrooms to the contrary, she was suffering the ne'er-do-well's company only because she couldn't hope to hire a man of integrity for the plot she'd devised. It was high time he understood that, too.

Thinking to put him in his place, she fixed him with

the stare she usually reserved for insubordinates and Celestia.

"Let us proceed with our business, shall we? Have you ever visited Aspen?"

"Regretfully, no. I've limited my, er, pleasure trips to Leadville and Denver."

She pressed her lips together. She should have guessed he couldn't answer a perfectly proper question without a ribald afterthought.

"Do you recall ever meeting my father, Maximillian Nichols?"

"No."

"Are you sure? This is most important."

He regarded her for a long moment. She sensed he was weighing his response, trying to determine what advantage he'd gain by changing his answer. Any prior association he'd had with her father would prove disastrous to her scheme, of course, so she did her very best to keep her expression more bland than creamed corn.

"I'm sure."

The air fled her lungs in a rush. Only then did she realize she'd been holding it, and she cursed herself for telegraphing her feelings. Raphael Jones was a professional prevaricator. She could see the keen mind at work behind his lazy fringe of lashes, and while his quick wit was certainly attractive, not to mention necessary, it presented a problem, too. Would she be able to stay one step ahead of him? Could she keep him under rein? Unlike Jones, she didn't make her living by swindling people.

Calling upon a finesse she'd honed while haggling over wages with the miner's union, Silver shuttered her expression once more.

"I could not fail to notice you played a geologist

this evening, not an investor. We're both acquainted with the abysmal results of that choice. Am I to assume you're unfamiliar with the sort of financial speculation that's discussed in mining circles?"

The amusement was back, flickering over his mobile mouth and high cheekbones before taking up residence again in his gaze. "I read the stock pages."

"Yes, but if you were in the company of my father, could you discuss stocks and dividends and grades of ore with assurance?"

"Most certainly."

Her heart quickened. Even if he was lying, he was doing a bang-up job. Mastery in the art of deception was no doubt essential if a man was to survive in his world.

"Very well." She chose her next words carefully. "Mr. Jones, the sort of work you'll be doing for me will require that you . . . uh, not have a wife or fiancée waiting in the wings. At least, I would not feel comfortable employing you if you were so committed."

"Indeed?" The lilt in his bourbon-smooth drawl was unmistakable.

"I assure you, Mr. Jones, you'll be playing a part, nothing more."

"I see."

He didn't see anything yet, damn him, but she clamped her mouth shut anyway. She couldn't keep letting his mockery goad her.

"Mr. Jones, I am considering you for the role of a lifetime. A performance requiring such talent, such daring, such supreme mastery of the dramatic arts, that thespians across this continent would weep to learn they'd missed this opportunity."

She paused expectantly, waiting for some reaction—*any* reaction—other than the smirk that was beginning to make her wish she dared reach out and shake him.

"Do go on, Miss Nichols. I love performances."

She gave him a sharp look. Just what did he mean by that?

"Your exposure to Shakespeare should be most helpful in this role. However, a certain savoir faire will be required if you are to play the part convincingly. Tell me. Have you ever been cast as a nobleman?"

"Hmm." He began to swing his leg, making his knee skim her skirts in the most provocative, nerve-jangling way. "In addition to Prince Hal from *Henry IV*, I've played Don Pedro in *Much Ado About Nothing* and Antonio in *The Merchant of Venice*."

She frowned at the mention of Prince Hal, a carousing reprobate whom Shakespeare never redeemed until *Henry V*. The role suited her impression of Jones far too well.

"Don Pedro and Antonio are both noble characters," she said pointedly, "with the kind of refinement you'll require."

He said nothing. He just continued swinging, gazing into her eyes with that enticingly wicked, charmingly masculine smile. Her stomach fluttered.

This was it. Her last chance to change her mind. Once she told Jones her plan, she'd be stuck with him. There'd be no turning back.

Courage, Silver. This is for Papa.

"I suppose all that remains, Mr. Jones, is to tell you what I would be hiring you for."

She waited for her resolve to resurrect itself. Since moving to Colorado, she'd often had to be strong, even harsh, to protect her happy-go-lucky papa and see that his business stayed afloat. Now, once again,

Papa needed to be saved from himself. His time was running out. No matter what she might personally think of Jones, the man was quite clearly a godsend in her time of need.

Jones raised an inquisitive eyebrow. She drew a bolstering breath.

"Mr. Jones," she said crisply, "I would like you to pose as a British aristocrat in order to seduce my father's fiancée."

Chapter 3

~~~~

Rafe's jaw dropped. Then he laughed out loud. The way Silver had been trying to reel him in, he'd figured she must be plotting a fraud. Still, he hadn't given her enough credit. He'd never dreamed she was capable of such guile.

"You want me to do *what*?" he gasped, clutching the tree limb to keep from tipping over the railing.

Her face grew as red as the ruby on her hand. "I daresay you heard me correctly the first time, Mr. Jones."

"But I assure you, the novelty hasn't worn thin."

"And I assure you, this is not a laughing matter! I am not in the habit of . . . of consorting with confidence men, but my father's utter disregard for his safety, his reputation, and his business has forced me to this lamentable end!"

"And here I thought you saved my neck because you like me."

She shot him a quelling glare. "Might I continue?"

He swallowed another chuckle. "Yes, yes, by all means. So this conniving gold digger got her hooks in Midas Max, eh?"

"You said you didn't know my father," she countered suspiciously.

"I know his reputation. His magic pickax is legendary around these parts."

"Yes, well . . ."

She cleared her throat, and he suspected she was thinking what he was: Maximillian Nichols was a horny old devil with more luck than brains. Of course, she was probably thinking it in more ladylike language. Nichols was renowned for blundering into his fortune. His first strike was the indirect result of his charity to a hard-luck stiff who'd had every intention of swindling him with a worthless claim. However, that "worthless" claim yielded pay dirt almost immediately when Nichols started puttering around its shaft. After buying three more "bust" claims and striking bonanzas in every one, speculators had dubbed him "Midas Max."

She raised her chin. "You haven't met 'conniving' until you've crossed paths with Celestia Cooper, I assure you. *Madam* Celestia, as she calls herself, parades around town purporting to be a necromancer. She prescribes talismans for good fortune, potions for love, and amulets for physical complaints. She even professes to speak with spirits. Dead men's ghosts, for heaven's sake! I mean, really. Have you ever heard anything so preposterous?"

Actually, Rafe's idea of preposterous was Silver on the rampage against some harmless crackpot. Whatever did a millionaire like Max see in Celestia Cooper, anyway? She must be breathtakingly beautiful.

"But the truly worst part," Silver confided, gripping her newspaper in a stranglehold now, "is that this . . . this *witch* torched a church and burned it to the ground."

A lopsided grin tugged at his lips. "To the ground, you say?"

Silver nodded.

Well now. I'll have to shake the crackpot's hand.

"If I wasn't so certain Celestia was just a show-boater, I might be swayed to believe her love spells and potions really do work. Papa insists on marrying her, even after that church-burning incident."

Sounds like I'll have to shake Max's hand too.

"I've warned Papa time and again," Silver raved on, oblivious to his efforts to keep a straight face, "but Celestia has so thoroughly pulled the wool over his eyes, I fear he can't see how she'll fleece him in the end. He's a trusting soul. As such, he has no concept of the numbers of barracudas that swim in the backwaters of our society."

"And you do?"

She blew out her breath. "That is not the point. The point is, Celestia Cooper must be stopped from marrying my papa and breaking his heart!"

Rafe gazed into her luminous, worry-filled eyes and was sorely tempted to applaud. *Brava.* He couldn't remember a more convincing performance. Silver was turning out to be quite the little flimflammer, wasn't she? First, she'd lied to the good citizens of Leadville for him. Next, she'd tried to dazzle him with that "role of a lifetime" pitch. Now she was claiming she didn't want her daddy to marry because his happiness was her priority.

Hell, do I have sucker written all over my face?

Silver's only priority, Rafe decided, was her daddy's fortune, those very same millions she stood to inherit by her lonesome if she kept him from marrying the competition.

"So you figure you'll bait one mountebank with another, eh?" He gave her a mocking smile. "When it comes to defrauding frauds, you think I'm a sure bet?''

"Well . . . yes. Don't you?''

"Certainly. But then, I couldn't be successful if I didn't share your confidence in me.''

Her brow furrowed at his irony. "In truth, Mr. Jones, I daresay you have enough confidence for both of us.''

"You flatter me, Silver.''

She gave him another withering look. "Perhaps it will also flatter you to know you inspired my idea, *Mr. Jones*.'' She stressed the formality, much to his amusement. "Earlier tonight, when I watched you pretending to be Bartholomew Markham, I thought there might be some sort of dinner show planned. But no one seemed to know of any entertainment, except, of course, for my speech. When your friend arrived, I deduced a hoax was in progress.

"At first, I was indignant on behalf of my colleagues.'' A hint of eagerness crept into her voice. "Then I was struck by divine inspiration. According to the *Rocky Mountain Sun*, a British earl, Lord Wilber Stokes of Chumley, has been traveling through the gold-mining west.'' She paused, unrolling her newspaper and handing it to him. "You'll find the article there, on page one. The *Sun* is crying foul, because Chumley isn't likely to bring his august presence—or his British sterling—to Aspen. Apparently Chumley considers hard-rock mining far too expensive, not to mention risky, for speculation. He's been quoted in the San Francisco and Denver newspapers as saying he won't fritter his fortune away.''

Rafe raised an eyebrow. Come to think of it, he had heard the gossip surrounding Chumley's travels. Last night, in the gambling hall below his lodging,

he'd overheard a one-eyed Texican and his incredibly
dumb crony blathering about the earl's "crown jewels" and how they would have lived like kings on
such "loot."

With a wry smile, Rafe stepped closer to the gaslights and skimmed Silver's newspaper article. If the
Sun could be believed, Chumley was the typical British blue blood with all the personality of a tree stump.
As far as investing went, though, Rafe couldn't blame
the Brit. Most silver speculation was perpetuated by
confidence men. Mining companies hired these so-
called promoters to seek out widows, war veterans,
salesclerks, farmers—in short, anyone whose gullibility or greed made them easy marks. One out of
every ten of these mining companies actually paid
dividends to their investors, and the dividends never
came close to the shareholders' full investment. Even
legitimate mines, like the ones owned by Silver's father, sometimes had trouble paying off their capital
investors. Mother Earth didn't let anyone gut her innards without putting up a good fight.

"With careful hinting," Silver continued, her enthusiasm sparking a charming blush, "I can see that
rumors of Chumley's arrival reach the appropriate ed-
itors. They will spread the news Chumley has had a
change of heart, that he has, indeed, decided to investigate the financial opportunities in hard-rock mining. You, of course, will pose as Chumley when you
reach Aspen. I am certain a handsome young man
such as yourself, perpetuating the illusion of an English title *and* more wealth than he knows how to
spend, will be just the sort of temptation to make
Celestia show her true colors."

"And your father?" Rafe asked dryly. "How do
you think he'll react if his fiancée proves fickle?"

''He's not likely to shoot you, if that's what you mean.''

Rafe started. Actually, the risk of a showdown hadn't entered his mind. ''That's certainly comforting.''

''My father is a gentle man, Mr. Jones. He's incapable of the violent acts perpetrated by vigilante Miner's Juries that hold sway in the more lawless camps of this region. I daresay the news of Celestia's perfidy will give Papa a dreadful case of the blue devils, so much so, he will retire to the mountains for a sulk.

''But it cannot be helped,'' she added briskly, as if to strengthen her own resolve, ''not if I am to save him from a much greater heartache later on. My papa is endowed with a cheerful constitution, and I have every confidence it will be restored to him in time.''

Rafe shook his head, bemused again by the lengths to which Silver was going to humbug her father. Her *father*, for Christ's sake. If Rafe's soul hadn't already been blacker than a stormy night, he would have soiled it gladly to have a father, a *real* father, not a Scripture-quoting Simon Legree.

''So,'' he said. ''When would you like Lord Chumley to make his *grande entrance*?''

''As soon as possible. I myself shall return to Aspen tomorrow to make arrangements for your arrival. You will have a room at the Windsor Hotel, and a package of information will await you so you can research your role. If questioned beforehand, you can always plead ignorance about silver mining, since Lord Chumley is universally considered to be unaware of its advantages.

''I'm sure I do not need to tell you, Mr. Jones,'' she added, ''your discretion in this affair is crucial to our success. I am prepared to draft a bank statement that will allow you to obtain suitable clothing and transportation befitting an English lord, as well as two weeks of food and lodging. I should think fourteen days would be sufficient time for a man of your, uh, accomplishments to complete this mission.''

Rafe smiled to himself. So she wanted to get rid of him in a hurry, did she?

"I'm humbled by your confidence in me, Miss Nichols," he said, sliding oh-so-casually closer. "But seduction does involve a certain degree of delicacy. And, of course, time."

She stiffened.

"If the lady in question is even the least bit unwilling, a great deal of expense must be incurred to woo her," he continued silkily. "She must have love trinkets and flowers, hats, jewels and gloves, lavish meals and entertainments, and, of course, one cannot overlook the importance of outfitting the assignation bower itself."

Silver cleared her throat. "Yes, well, I'm sure in Celestia's case, a bower won't be—"

"One should never underestimate the power of ambience in achieving the desired effect," Rafe chided, letting his left hand drop between them. "Your father is successful, well-respected, and pleasantly aged. That makes him a worthy opponent, wouldn't you agree?"

Silver glanced warily at his fingers, hovering so innocently beside her thigh. "Yes, but—"

"And he'll be a persistent rival too, I daresay, particularly since his heart is engaged. We can't be at all certain he will quit the war in a mere two weeks' time. No, I should think he will lay siege to love's door, employing every weapon at his disposal. This battle of suitors could rage a good six months or more.''

''Six months!''

''Or more,'' he drawled, relishing the utter outrage on her face. Moments like these made all the tedious plotting and practicing for cons worthwhile.

Of course, Octavia was going to be a problem if he had to live in a hotel room for six months. Even when Fiona wasn't sick, she didn't like to share the limelight, and over the last twenty hours, Tavy had begun to claim the lion's share of Fred's attention. Why, the old scapegrace had even talked about adding Tavy to the act, as if Rafe would ever hear of such a thing. No, Tavy was going to Aspen with him.

As for Fred and Fiona . . . well, guilt held only so much sway over him. He might be able to milk a few extra thousand dollars out of this con for Fiona's sake, but he'd be damned if he'd cut her or Fred in any further. The less they knew about the pot of gold he'd stumbled into, the better.

''Six months is out of the question, Mr. Jones,'' Silver said, interrupting his scheming thoughts. ''You have exactly one.''

Damn.

''My dear Miss Nichols,'' he protested, positioning himself close enough to belie his next words, ''one month is hardly enough time for a gentleman to steal a kiss, much less—''

''In one month's time, my father will be marrying that witch and accompanying her on a wedding tour to Niagara Falls!''

Silver escaped to the center of the balcony. Rafe hid his disappointment. Only one month to milk the golden cow, eh? He'd been hoping to stretch it to nine. He supposed he'd have to find some other scam to keep him and Tavy fed through the winter, especially if he couldn't teach her how to survive without him. She was so ridiculously trusting that in April, when he'd been caught in a mountain snowstorm and had had to trade whiskey to the Utes for a blanket, she'd wandered into some squaw's tent and had nearly lost her hide.

Tavy, little darling that she was, could be a liability at times.

He supposed until he decided what to do with her, he'd have to build himself a nice fat bank account at Silver's expense. Either that, or marry the girl.

He smiled at the notion. Now *there* was an amusing proposition: a wife with even fewer scruples than he had. He could just imagine the wedding party Satan would throw on their behalf.

"I'm afraid your situation is more dire than I thought," he told her gravely. "We shall have to march into the fray with all our guns blazing, so to speak. Of course you will be paying for my meals, clothes, and lodging, but in order to turn Celestia's head, I shall also need an allowance. Given our shortage of time, I'm afraid the amount will have to be significant. But your devotion to your father has touched me deeply. In consideration of your plight, I shall see how far I can stretch five hundred dollars per week."

"Per week?"

"Yes, of course. You, yourself, have cast me in the role of aristocrat. One cannot play the part on a shovel stiff's wage."

Her hands flew to her hips. "Now see here, Jones, I'll allow you two hundred dollars, and you'll be happy to have it."

"Four hundred."

Their eyes locked.

"Two-fifty," she countered.

"Three-fifty plus a horse and buggy."

She looked like she'd relish the act of barbecuing him. "Three hundred and the promise not to sic the sheriff on your sorry hide."

"Five hundred and the promise not to mail your father a most eye-opening letter." He smiled pleasantly.

"Y-you wouldn't dare!"

"Not for five hundred dollars," he lied soothingly. "After all, you did spare me from spending the night in jail."

"Your gratitude overwhelms me, Mr. Jones."

He inclined his head to hide his smirk.

"If I agree to your terms," she said in grudging tones, "what guarantee do I have that you'll perform the job to satisfaction?"

"Well . . ." *Really, Silver. You should know better than to lead with a line like that.* He rose leisurely. "I could give you my references."

"If you think I'd take the word of your scalawag of a partner—"

"Oh, no." He strolled to where she was so charmingly silhouetted by the flicker of gaslights. "Not Fred. Fred would be entirely unsuitable. He doesn't have firsthand knowledge of my performance in these . . . affairs."

She straightened her spine. "I'm sure I would think twice before believing the word of any acquaintance of yours, Mr. Jones."

"Why, then our relationship already shows great promise. I suspected you'd say that very thing. Knowing how one's partner thinks is important in a close-call scenario."

Silver's mouth grew uncomfortably dry as his voice dropped to a throbbing murmur. She would have liked to say their "scenario" was close enough, but she didn't want to give him that satisfaction. His bawdy innuendos had triggered too many of her old fears. She'd as good as hired the rounder now, so she'd have to get a grip on herself if she was to show him who was boss.

She fixed him with her best keep-your-distance glare. "None of which answers my original question."

"You speak truly."

He halted less than an arm's length away. She could actually feel his heat, smell his mountain-fresh cologne. A tendril of uneasiness coiled in her belly.

"Perhaps you would prefer a demonstration," he said.

"A-a demonstration?"

His hand reached out to catch a strand of hair, one of the prematurely gray ones that had always made her look so old and ugly. When he tucked it behind her ear, she felt the whisper of his knuckles against her cheek. She wanted to die of mortification. Surprisingly, however, the feeling came less from his touch than from her vision of herself as a frightful, windblown mess.

"Mr. Jones, I don't think . . ."

His eyelids drooped in the most hypnotic, pulse-stirring way.

Run! her head shrieked to her feet. Instead, she stood rooted and breathless, wrapped in the silken bonds of girlhood fantasies and dreams of romantic love. They'd only led to moonlight madness, foolish choices that had caused her indescribable pain, and

yet still she stood before him, like a rabbit charmed
by the fox who'd invited her to dinner.

"What would satisfy you, Miss Nichols?" he whispered, his thumb skimming her jawline until it dipped
lower, pressing against the hammering vein in her
throat. "Words of poetry? A bouquet of roses?" His
lips inched nearer. "A kiss?"

That was it. The instinct for self-preservation took
over where common sense had failed.

"I must ask you not to do that," she said, snatching
his fingers from her cheek.

"But your guarantee. I couldn't have you thinking
me unequal to my role."

She swallowed. Somehow, he'd managed to wrap
his hand around hers. Now it was his prisoner, her
palm embarrassingly moist beneath his thumb. "I . . .
daresay I shall have to take your word in the matter."

"Are you quite certain, Silver? I would be only too
happy to shoulder the burden of proof."

She tried not to notice how rapidly her insides were
warming to his game. "That you thoroughly enjoy
seduction, I have no doubt," she retorted, wishing the
butterflies in her stomach would alight. "Save your
bag of tricks for Celestia."

He chuckled, a rich rumble of sound that vibrated
into her fingertips and danced down every nerve. "As
you wish. But if you should ever change your
mind . . ." He raised the back of her hand, and the
moist touch of his lips sent goose bumps scuttling to
her toes. ". . . I am, of course, at your command."

She rather doubted that, but when he released her,
she was too relieved to debate him. God forbid her
tongue should stumble over the words, somehow turning them into another proposition.

She ran her damp palms down her skirts in an effort

to rally her composure. "Since we are agreed, Mr.
Jones, you'll find your first payment and your instructions waiting for you at Aspen's Windsor Hotel. I'll
send for you there."

"So thrive my soul."

She suspected he was quoting Romeo again. Apparently the man had a one-track mind. For the future,
when they'd have to rendezvous secretly to discuss
their conspiracy, she made a mental note never again
to meet him on a balcony—or worse, in the moonlight.

"And now, if it's not too much to ask, sir, I'd like
for you to leave."

"Ah, me. The lady grows weary of my company."
The corner of his mouth quirked. "Very well."
Sweeping low, he performed a flawless bow. "Sleep
dwell upon thine eyes, peace in thy breast . . ." He
straightened, his hand pressed forlornly to his heart.
"Ah, would I were sleep, and peace so sweet to rest."

She blushed in spite of her strong counsel against
it, and he gave her a naughty wink.

"I shall count the hours, Miss Nichols. Until
then . . ." He reached for the tree. "Good-night."

As agile as any swashbuckler on a ship's rigging,
he swung onto the limb. Pausing, he saluted her. Then
he pivoted, swung to a lower branch, and plunged into
the huddled shadows of the night.

Silver gulped a ragged breath.

She listened for his landing, her ears straining
above the thunder of her pulse. When she heard nothing, not even his retreating footsteps, she crept closer
to the railing and peered over the edge. A glint of
gold caught her eye. It had been her first glimpse of
him; now it was her last, before he vanished so completely into the darkness that she wondered if he

hadn't hung a dark curtain below to make his exit more dramatic.

Her other thought, that he was an angel with a slipping halo, was too preposterous to believe—at least, in the literal sense.

She gazed down at her tingling fingertips, still warm and slightly tremulous from his touch. A dreamy smile curved her lips.

Celestia Cooper didn't stand a chance against that man.

Then a more disturbing notion struck.

Did any woman?

Chapter 4

Rafe was pleased with his night's work.

He'd avoided arrest, put off Fred, and won an audience in an heiress's boudoir. True, Silver had surprised him when she'd rejected his advances and hired him to warm another woman's bed, but he was confident they'd be sharing the same pillow by month's end. If she had been a sweet young thing, with high ideals and a heart as pure as gold, one of his few remaining scruples might have balked at her seduction.

But Silver was the female equivalent of his own rotten core, so he didn't see any reason to deny himself the pleasure of wooing her. It wasn't as if she were headed for heaven, and his tainted soul stood in her way. No, when God had passed out the road maps to hell, Silver had been allowed to plot her own course. He was the one who'd been denied a choice in the matter.

He grimaced, the old bitterness lancing his chest.

Once upon a time, he'd been so desperate for love that he'd let hope worm its way back into his heart. He thought back to his first romantic role, young Claudio in *Much Ado About Nothing*. Although he'd only been sixteen, he'd been stunned by the number

71

of sighing, swooning females who'd crowded back-stage. Regardless of his bastardy, they'd offered him their favors, and in his naivete, he'd thought they loved *him.*

Only after they'd grown bored with Raphael Jones had he come to understand that women were infatuated with *romance*—the heroism of Hotspur, the poetry of Lysander, the tragedy of Romeo. Thus, he'd learned to answer late-night invitations with a bouquet of roses and Shakespeare's best love sonnets.

Such would be his approach with Silver. She was no angel, and he was no saint. But Silver, being female, would want to believe she was virtuous. She'd want to feel desirable and experience the grand romantic gesture: to be swept off her feet. Rafe wasn't opposed to the idea; after all, he was a dramatist. Pirate, poet, prophet, prince—whatever she wanted, he could play the part. And if Silver preferred to pretend her lover was a real-life nobleman rather than some fictional character, then so be it. Imposters were his specialty.

He hadn't played himself in years.

The thought made him wince. Shaking himself, he chose to forget it. He saw no sense in dwelling on the injustices of his life. Long, hard experience had taught him to concentrate on the present. The past was too painful, and the future—an eternal captaincy in Satan's army—was too bleak. Only in the moment could he ever hope to find relief. And if Rafe didn't use that precious moment to examine his feelings too closely, he could convince himself he was happy. After all, the moon was full, the wind was alpine fresh, and the mountain laurels smelled like summer wine. He had an heiress in his back pocket, and the promise of wealth to sweeten his dreams. For now, these were enough.

Whistling as he strolled, Rafe passed through Leadville's business district, with its respectable, cobbled streets and glowing gaslights. He set his sights on the dusty, moonlit alley where his own lodgings lay. Unlike the opulence of Silver's Grand Hotel suite, his room was cramped and shabby, a virtual closet above a noisy gambling hall. He hadn't had much choice in accommodations, though, not with threadbare pockets and a traveling companion like Tavy—

Damn. Tavy. He'd left her with Fiona.

Sighing, he turned in midstride only to collide with an elegantly dressed man who was hurrying—slinking, actually—out of the alley leading to the Tabor Opera House.

"Damnation," the man muttered as his top hat tumbled into the gutter.

"My middle name," Rafe countered dryly, thinking to make amends by retrieving the hat.

But the man shoved him aside. "Clod," he snapped, wading through the refuse himself. His accent was unmistakably eastern.

"As you say," Rafe murmured, noting the scar that arched above the tenderfoot's left temple.

Brushing off the brim, the easterner tossed him a malevolent look, jammed on his hat, and hurried in the direction of the Grand Hotel. Rafe shook his head. With that scarlet-lined cape flapping out behind him, the easterner could have been Tabor's own phantom of the opera—except, of course, his leading-man good looks hadn't been marred badly enough for *that* role. Too bad about the scar, Rafe mused. Fiona's stage makeup could have fixed him up in a heartbeat . . .

Damn. He made a face, thoughts of Fiona reminding him of his mission. The last thing he wanted to do was face his foster parents again. Fiona was bound to wheedle, and Fred would undoubtedly ask questions. The less those two old hucksters knew about Silver's scheme, the better. Rafe couldn't very well extort a lifetime worth of savings from the Nicholses if he had to split his take with Fred and Fiona.

No, he'd have to come up with some kind of reasonable explanation to throw them off his trail. The question was, what?

Rafe was still searching for an answer when he rounded the corner of the magnificent brick edifice that shopkeeper Horace Tabor had built after he'd grubstaked enough miners to earn his fortune. Rafe hardly glanced twice at the opera house, though. Instead, he wound his way through the debris of its rear alley until he came to what was left of a fire-ravaged livery. Fred's Piccadilly Players had parked their wagons here in a semicircle, Injun-fighting style, around the wreckage.

An inexplicable pang of homesickness seized him when he glimpsed the same lantern that had drawn him out of the snow, fifteen years earlier, to Fred's door. He didn't want to be bound to his former employers, yet he didn't know how not to be. Despite all of Fred's bullying and Fiona's manipulation, the Brits had been better parents to him than Jedidiah Jones.

Scheduled for a six-week engagement, the theater troupe had turned the blackened lot into a miniature neighborhood. Rafe ducked a clothesline, smiled crookedly at a pair of patched bloomers, skirted a water barrel, and paused wistfully before a rocking horse before he finally climbed the wagon's step and beat his fist on the foot-long likeness of Fred's nose.

The door cracked, and the master prevaricator himself appeared.

"Well, ho! If it isn't the conquering hero," the Brit boomed in a voice that, Rafe was certain, rattled the windows in each of the six other wagons. "Fee, my sweet, you'll never guess who's come to call." He tossed this sally over his shoulder, even louder this time, before turning to squint once more at Rafe through his ever-present fog of smoke. "What a rare treat, to see you after midnight—and after Miss Silver's gone abed too. You must have missed the company of us regular folk. Either that, or your high-falutin' heiress threw you out on your ear."

Rafe endeavored not to glare.

"You're awake late," he parried in his best offhand manner. "I didn't interrupt anything between you and Fiona, did I?"

"Bloody hell. I can't remember the last time me and Fee were doing something we could get interrupted at. She's a sick woman, lad. A bloke can't go around demanding conjugal rights from a sick woman—unless, of course, he doesn't mind losing a favorite piece of his anatomy."

Rafe winced inwardly. Only sixty seconds after he'd arrived, and Fred was already heaping the guilt on uncomfortably thick. "Words to live by I'm sure. And how is Fiona?" he asked dutifully.

"Hacking her lungs out." Fred seemed to remember his cigar and abruptly extinguished it against the door. " 'Course," he added sheepishly, "I'm sure she feels a whole lot better knowing you've come to keep her company."

As if to corroborate this statement, a shriek ripped from the rear of the wagon, followed closely by a noise that sounded like a shoe striking the wall. Fred started, turning, and Rafe could see beyond his bulk. An enormous cloud of facial powder was rising behind the red-and-white checkered curtain that dissected the cluttered wagon and hid Fiona from his view.

"Fred!" she shouted ominously.

He cleared his throat. "Fee, honey, good news," he called in placating tones. "You've got a visitor. It's Rafe."

"Rafe?" Her angry vibrato immediately steadied, lowering in pitch to a martyr-like groan. "God has answered a dying woman's prayers. Come in, my boy, come in."

Rafe bolstered himself against another breaker of guilt and, pushing past Fred, parted the curtain. Through the settling dust, he spied Fiona on a narrow cot, her nightcap askew and her cheeks pasty white against the backdrop of yellowed linens. She managed to look weak and pitiful, despite the fact that only moments earlier she'd been yelling at the top of her lungs and hurling shoes.

Then he noticed many of her vases were overturned on the floor. Spilled water and petals mixed with clumps of red, green, and blue stage makeup, toppled containers, and the broken pieces of glass from the hapless powder jar. Beneath her window, an auburn braid had been happily chewed, while on top of Fred's trunk, a second, straw-colored hairpiece had been tramped by tiny, rouge-stained paws.

Tavy had been busy.

Narrowing his focus, Rafe tracked his pet's webbed prints—in all their various colors—around her circular path of destruction. After a moment, he spied a trail that cut straight across the wagon, making a beeline for Fiona's bed. He knelt and raised the quilt.

There, trembling in the back of her cage, was his four-month-old otter pup.

With her tail tucked between her legs, her ears squeezed shut, and her snout pressed contritely to her forepaws, Tavy looked the very picture of misery. Rafe suspected things had been pretty bad between Fiona and Tavy if his pet had voluntarily placed herself behind bars.

"Come here, Tavy," he crooned, stretching out his hand.

The otter baby gave a chirp of relief. Scrambling past her prison's open door, she threw herself at his feet and wrapped her length around his ankle. He could feel her body quivering through his boot leather.

Fred chuckled. "Well now, you see? Fee and Tavy are getting along much better than they were this morning, aren't you, Fee?"

Fiona muttered something about "stinkin' rodents." Tavy blinked big wounded eyes at Rafe as if to say, "Grandma's being mean to me."

"I'm sorry she was such a bother," Rafe said, prying his pet's paws free so he could lift her into his arms. "Otters are supposed to be tidy, like cats."

"Well, they're *not*," Fiona grumbled, giving Tavy a look that, if she'd had nine lives, would instantly have snuffed out five or six.

"Aw, the little tyke's just curious," Fred said magnanimously, patting Tavy's head. "Once she starts learning tricks, she'll be too busy keeping the kiddies entertained to ransack any wagons. Why, I figure she could work for peanuts, kind of like one of those circus monkeys—"

"Otters don't eat peanuts," Rafe said pleasantly,

disguising his irritation, "and the only trick Tavy is going to learn is how to swim. We've got a one-way ticket to the high country, where there'll be plenty of otters to help me teach her how. In fact, we're leaving Leadville in the morning. Say good-night, Tavy."

Fred snorted. "You expect me to believe you'd rather teach some orphaned otter how to survive in the wild than hump the richest, unattached female in the state? Hell, lad, what's the matter with you? You can lie better than that. I taught you how."

Rafe flashed a well-rehearsed grin. "Who says I didn't already satisfy Miss Nichols?"

Fred eyed him speculatively.

"So that's it with the heiress?" Fiona demanded. "No fancy dispensation? No souvenir for your poor, sick Fee?"

"I didn't steal her hairbrush, if that's what you mean."

"Here now," Fred growled, "you watch that tongue of yours. You're talking to a dying woman."

Fiona wheezed.

Rafe fidgeted, averting his eyes to Tavy. She gazed adoringly back at him. She was always glad to see him, whether he brought her trinkets or not. She never made him feel like his only real worth was the money he brought in.

"Sorry to disappoint you, Fiona," he said dryly. "My pockets are as empty now as the day you took me in."

Fred snorted. "They would've been a whole lot fuller if you hadn't let a blooming bluestocking sniff out our con. Hell, lad, you've gone rusty. And then to let the chit slip through your fingers without pinching as much as a silver dollar off her—"

"Freddie, luv, the boy can't very well go and force

himself on the woman if she doesn't have any use for him.''

Rafe smiled blandly at Fiona's dig. "My sentiments exactly.''

He took a step toward the door, but Fred folded his arms, barring his way.

"And you're not going to do a bloody thing about the way she made a jackass out of you tonight?''

"Which time?'' Rafe asked evenly.

For a moment, Fred's brows lowered in a thunderous expression. Silence fell so fast and thick that Rafe couldn't even hear Fiona's breathing.

Then the old huckster laughed, a loud and hearty sound. "I've got to hand it to you, lad. You had me going there. 'Which time,' indeed. So what's the plan? Are you going to break her heart? Or are you just going to rob her blind?''

"That'll all depend on my mood, I suppose,'' Rafe said, playing along. To pretend his business with Silver was that of a spurned suitor bent on revenge was, ironically, one of the few businesses in which Fred wasn't likely to interfere. At least, that was Rafe's gamble. If Fred caught the scent of profit wafting out of Aspen, there'd be no keeping him in Leadville. Fred might have a certain fondness for him, but that fondness wouldn't keep him from employing every wile—including extortion—to get his hands on Nichols silver.

Fiona, meanwhile, was shooting furtive, daggerlike glares at her husband. Pasting on a motherly frown, she turned back to Rafe. "And how do you think you're going to keep yourself in champagne and caviar long enough to get this heiress to notice you? You don't have a blooming dollar to your name, lad. Forget the bluestocking. Like as not, she'll be as lively as a wet dishrag in bed anyway.

" 'Sides,'' Fiona continued, wheezing faintly, "my physic says I'll be pushing up daisies by year's end. This may be the last chance my fading old eyes get to watch you tame the shrew. You were the best Petruchio we ever had, Rafe. And we've always been guaranteed a full house when you bare your soul as Romeo. Then there's your Benedick—you know Fred's too old to play the role—and your Hotspur always makes the ladies swoon—''

"No deal, Fiona. I've had enough. After Fred's little improvisation tonight, the prospect of hanging around Leadville has taken on a whole new meaning for me."

Fred scowled, his bottom lip jutting. "I already told you how it was. Baiting those suckers with pyrite would have gotten us both lynched."

"Face it, Fred," he retorted. You can't help yourself. You'll be a showboater 'til the day you die. I need a stage of my own."

Fred's chest swelled up with wounded pride. "So that's the way of it, eh?"

"That's right," Rafe said more quietly, cursing himself for feeling the old twinge of guilt. If Fred and Fiona had cared about him rather than the money they thought he'd bring in, he would have been tempted— sorely tempted—to bail out on Silver and forfeit her fortune. But when one faced an eternity in Hell, he reminded himself bitterly, one had to take what little comfort one could get. His foster parents should be pleased to know they'd tutored him so well. Money was all he cared about.

He glanced down at the baby dozing so trustingly in his arms.

Well ... money and Tavy.

Fiona was making distressed rasping sounds. "What's the matter with you two, bickering over a dying woman's bed? I won't stand for it, you hear me? I want my last days to be happy ones, with my family gathered 'round me. Fred, you tell Rafe you're sorry. Rafe, you apologize to Fred."

The two men glared at each other.

Fiona made a hiccuping noise. When the threat of her sobs didn't work, she promptly burst into tears. Fred blew out his breath.

"Now Fee, honey," he murmured gruffly, groping for his wife's hand, "don't work yourself up. It can't be healthy in the delicate state you're in. Besides, the boy and I aren't feuding." Fred shot Rafe a warning glance. "Isn't that right, Rafe?"

He sighed. "We're not feuding, Fiona. It was a difference of opinion, that's all."

"So ... ?" She sniffled, peering up at him with watery eyes. "So you'll make an old woman's last days happy? You'll join our theater family again?"

Rafe gritted his teeth. "I told you how it was, Fiona. I'll be hanged if I'm recognized here."

"God have mercy, God have mercy," she wailed, throwing herself into Fred's arms and rocking back and forth. "How will we survive? The creditors, they're camped out at our door, and we can't afford my medicine ..."

"I'll send you some of Silver's money," Rafe ground out.

"You will?" she whimpered. "When?"

"Just as soon as I get my hands on it, okay?"

She sniffed again. Fred solemnly handed her a handkerchief, and she blew her nose loud and long.

"You were always a good boy, Rafe," she said

wistfully, dabbing her eyes with the corner of her sleeve, "a better son than our own turned out to be. I knew you wouldn't let us down."

"There now, Fee," Fred soothed. "You lie back and rest yourself. No more worrying about money, you hear?"

She nodded contritely, settling into her pillows once more. Rafe looked away, swallowing bile. He didn't know whether to be outraged or heartsick. That she would use her illness as a weapon against him was perfectly in character for Fiona. That she would rank him in favor higher than her own son was not. *Christ.* Rafe didn't think he could bear it if he had to watch her waste away the way his mother had.

"I should be going," he said gruffly.

"What about Tavy?" Fred demanded.

Wariness quickly bolstered his defenses. "What about her?"

Fred shrugged, giving Fiona's hand a last squeeze before rising from the bed. "I wouldn't think otters and bluestockings mix well socially. 'Course, I don't mean anything personal by that, Miss Tavy," he added gallantly, winking at the pup. He reached out to stroke her silken fur, and she gave a sleepy chirp. "As far as I'm concerned, the world could use a lot more otters and a lot less bluestockings." He gave Rafe a sideways glance. "As hoity-toity as that Nichols chit is, I suspect you're going to need a couple of weeks at least to bring her down a peg and woo some money out of her. Tavy's welcome to stay here until you do."

Rafe's chin hardened, and he eased Tavy away from Fred's petting. He remembered only too well how Fred had sneaked off a mere two weeks after they'd left Blue Thunder and had sold Belle to pay off creditors. The next day, Belle's well-whipped, well-lathered carcass had been found in a roadside ditch with a broken leg and a bullet through her brain. Rafe might have killed Belle's new bastard of an owner if he'd had the vaguest inkling how. At the time, Fred had acted just as furious as Rafe had felt, but he'd never apologized for stealing the filly. And he'd never given Rafe one penny from her sale.

"Thanks, but I think Tavy'll be just the thing to break the ice with Silver Nichols."

"You do? Really?"

Not at all, Rafe thought. But he'd be damned if he'd let Fred get his hands on Tavy. The man might start out with good intentions, but greed and debt invariably whittled them away.

"Fiona needs her rest," Rafe hedged, "and Tavy's been enough excitement for one day. I'll wire you in a week or so, once I get settled. I trust your show will run at least that long," he added dryly.

He raised Tavy to his shoulder. She draped herself around the back of his neck with a contented little sigh. Inclining his head, Rafe took his leave.

Fred frowned thoughtfully after him.

"Is he gone?" Fiona whispered irritably.

The self-professed master of dramatic timing, Fred didn't answer immediately. Instead, he fished in his vest pocket and pulled out another cigar.

"For now," he answered, striking a match.

"Then get rid of these bloody weeds so I can start breathing again," Fiona grumbled, tossing aside her blankets and shimmying out of her sweat-soaked nightdress.

Fred eyed his wife's matronly chest and plump thighs in a mixture of affection and resignation. She'd been a looker in her day. But then, so had he.

His lips curved faintly at the pun. If his old lady hadn't been so damned sharp-witted, he might have gotten away with more mischief over the years. But it was that mind of hers that kept luring him back to her bed. That mind and her incomparable skill as a shyster.

"We can't toss out the flowers yet, luv. The boy might still decide to bid you a proper adieu in the morning."

Fiona muttered an oath. Throwing open the window, she fanned herself vigorously, noisily dragging in the cool alpine air through her mouth. Good old Fee. She was even willing to suffer hayfever to pull off a scam. Too bad the otter had spilled all her facial powder. If Rafe returned, they'd have the devil of a time re-creating that red nose of hers. Hmm. Maybe it would be enough to keep the wagon in shadows . . .

"I felt like a blooming Christmas goose, sitting on that bed warmer," Fiona groused, interrupting his thoughts.

"As accomplished as you are, even you can't sweat on cue, Fee, although I must say—" he blew a stream of smoke into the air and gave her a cheeky grin "—you certainly warmed up to your role."

She tossed him a withering glare. "I should never have let you talk me into this. Consumption, for God's sake! And when columbines are out of season, and I've stopped wheezing like a bellows, how am I supposed to explain myself to the boy?"

Fred waved her concern away, leaving a swath of cigar smoke in his wake. "Mexico dries out the lungs, I hear tell."

"The boy's not green anymore."

"He fell for your act hook, line, and sinker."

"That's because I'm the best. And the poor sot

thinks of us as family." She shivered, slamming the window shut again, and hugged her arms to her breasts. "I hope you're happy now. I'm likely to catch pneumonia, and he's still not coming back to the troupe."

"Sure he will. Right after that heiress kicks him out on his ass."

Fiona shook her head. "You're underestimating him. You always have. Just because he doesn't swing his fists and call you a bastard to your face doesn't mean he's a Milquetoast. He's got his own ways. And he's damned cagey about them. What woman can resist a man who spouts poetry and woos like a cavalier? What's more likely is he'll marry that Nichols woman and win himself a fortune. Then we'll lose him for good."

Fred cocked an eyebrow. "You're underestimating Miss Silver, luv."

Fiona snorted.

Retrieving a clean nightdress from her trunk, she tugged it over her head. "In any event," she said, moving back to the bed and yanking the warmer out from under the sheet, "he's never going to forgive you, Fred. Not this time," she added, a hint of regret tinging her voice. "I hope you've got the stomach for that."

His chin rose with a trace of its old, youthful belligerence. "He knows the way it is with creditors."

"That may be. But that doesn't mean he'll excuse you for turning him into a sap."

Fred shrugged, telling himself he didn't care. He was the boss, and business was business. Besides, if it hadn't been for him and Fiona, that wide-eyed preacher's boy would have wound up six feet under. Never in all his fifty-three years had Fred met an urchin so unschooled in the ways of the street. He'd taken advantage of the kid a couple of times just to toughen him up. Rafe hadn't been too appreciative of his education, but the way Fred saw it, he'd been doing Rafe a favor.

His gaze turned wistfully toward the wagon door and the flickering gaslights beyond.

Still, it was a bloody damned shame Rafe was harboring so many bad feelings about those years. The resentment had been unmistakable in the boy's eyes whenever Fred had gotten too close to his precious Tavy.

"It's not too late, Freddie," Fiona said more quietly. "I say we come clean. Tell him the truth before he leaves on the morning stage."

Fred got a hold of himself. Sentiment—especially maudlin sentiment—he reserved for the limelight. As far as he was concerned, Rafe owed them, and lately, the lad hadn't been paying his dues.

"Hell, no. Don't let all that boyish charm make a sucker out of you, Fee. Our young Romeo's pulling a scam of his own and cheating us out of the take."

Fiona blinked, her jaw dropping.

"How do you know that?"

Fred gave her a crooked little smile.

"I followed him to Miss Silver's balcony."

Chapter 5

Four days later, Silver was a nervous wreck—and not just because "the Earl of Chumley" had yet to check into the Windsor Hotel.

No, she'd had to save her worry that Rafe had scammed her for some other afternoon, because Papa, who couldn't keep a secret to save his life, had flapped his jaw. His séance idea had become the front-page headline in the *Aspen Times*, and pernicious Brady had penned something inflammatory on the editorial page, too. Now her miners were convinced they worked in untenable conditions, and the Union was clamoring for a wage increase.

Silver had tried to table negotiations for two more days so she wouldn't be up to her eyeballs in lawyers while she was averting last-minute calamities for her father's engagement party. Unfortunately, this tactic had only led Union leaders to growl ultimatums. Needless to say, a strike was every mine owner's nightmare. Purported ghost sightings in Silver's Mine had already cut production quotas by half, and she just knew the whole operation would shut down if she didn't stop Papa's séance.

So here she was, forty-eight hours before her father's engagement party, trying to prevent public humiliation *and* financial crisis by sneaking his stupid spiritkeepers out of the office in a picnic basket festooned with pink and yellow ribbons.

Thanks to Celestia Cooper, she was now a petty thief.

Silver glanced around the corner, her heart hammering against her ribs. The building that housed the mining offices was almost deserted, thanks to the ghost sighting nearly twenty minutes ago. After a score of white-faced shovel stiffs had poured out of the mine, vowing never again to go back, Papa had dragged the superintendent and a reluctant engineer below to prove the subterranean chambers were safe for human habitation. While they'd been occupied, she'd slunk back to Papa's desk, unloaded the dinner Celestia had packed him, and dumped his worthless rocks inside the basket. The way her conscience was crying foul, one would have thought she'd robbed the safe.

Silver scowled, wishing she'd come up with some better idea to prevent Celestia's séance. Unfortunately, she'd been a bit pressed for time, what with her miners on the rampage, her father planning marital suicide, and her French chef—the one she'd so triumphantly lured away from the Chloride Restaurant for the party—threatening to quit after Papa put pigs-in-a-poke on the menu.

Yes, her life was just a bowl of cherries, she thought irritably, watching as a stout, thick-muscled charcoal burner chose that inopportune moment to leave the smelting house. Forget for a moment that she didn't consider Papa's entrapment by a booby worthy of celebration. Forget, too, that the only reason anyone was *coming* to the party was to get a good belly laugh at his expense. She'd finally agreed to host the farce because she so dearly loved the man whose hand-tooled gifts had been her only source of comfort after Mama's carriage accident.

But that didn't mean she was even *remotely* resigned to entertaining the harpy who'd seduced her precious daddy!

Silver's jaw jutted, and she blew a lock of hair out of her eyes.

One of these days, Raphael Jones or no Raphael Jones, she'd get even with that portly floozie. Celestia Cooper had *no right* to take her sainted mama's place. The very idea of Papa kissing that Jezebel was enough to make Silver's gut roil. She wasn't immune to the pitying glances and murmurs of ridicule she had to ignore every day in the street. How in heaven's name could Papa be?

Trying to ignore her sweaty palms, Silver watched the charcoal burner, who had taken his time approaching, stroll past her, and finally enter the privy. She loosed a ragged breath. *Hallelujah.* The coast was clear.

Struggling to hoist her now back-breaking load, she made a break for it, hobbling at tortoise speed toward the pack mules.

Well, one thing was in her favor, she thought, huffing as she strapped the basket to a burro. Aside from the charcoal burner, the mining compound was practically deserted. The sun wasn't yet low enough in the sky for the few remaining stalwarts who manned the stamp mill to begin the evening candle parade down the mountain to their homes. In fact, the machinery still boomed in the building behind the mule corral, making the earth tremble. She hardly noticed, though. She was used to industrial activity. When her teeth buzzed in the vicinity of her sawmill, or the china in her kitchen cabinets rattled from the dynamite blasts at her mine nearly five miles away, she figured it was a small price to pay for turning Aspen into a bona fide town. In 1883, before she'd raised the money to process silver ore locally, Aspen had been little better than a clapboard village, shipping its ore over the mountains to Leadville.

Of course, since Brady Buckholtz couldn't abide the words "woman" and "proprietor" in the same sentence, the *Aspen Times* had hailed Papa as the hero who'd brought the first smelter to the city. Silver had been irritated, but she'd let Papa take the credit. She'd been the first female to manage a prosperous *and* legitimate business in this town, and she'd had to cope with many a belligerent male. In the face of such anger, she'd learned to pick her battles. And thanks to Aaron Townsend, she'd learned the hard way.

Shaking herself free of such hair-raising memories, Silver hurried the burro to her horse. *So far so good*, she thought in true criminal fashion, squinting at the sky as she mounted her mare. The sun hadn't sunk below the treetops yet, and that meant she had plenty of time to dump the rocks and ride home before dark. Unfortunately, she couldn't take the usual route. Papa would follow her and rediscover his wretched stones. Heaven forbid she should have to go through all this slinking and skulking *again*.

She brightened as an idea dawned. *The Roaring Fork.* The river was so thick with sawdust that Papa would never find his rocks. She could dump the whole basket in the current and rest assured she'd never see the wretched thing again.

Murmuring "gee" to the mule, she spurred her mare past the pine stumps that littered the once-forested compound. The dead wood jutting up from the earth made the yard look junky. What was worse, big pink weeds, like pussy paws and dogbane, had seeded themselves between stumps. She wrinkled her nose at the hearty wildflowers. She'd heard the Utes actually had a use for such eyesores, but she couldn't imagine what that might be. One of these days, she thought idly as she reached the end of the pine graveyard, she'd have to order this land cleared. Dogbane was poisonous to pack mules, and surfaced roots made treacherous footing.

A sudden, sticky chill accompanied this thought. She shuddered, her goose bumps unexpectedly visceral. Considering the fact that spring was in full flower in the Roaring Fork Valley, she couldn't help but mark the odd sensation especially after her mule, for no apparent reason, loosed an ear-splitting bray and reared. She fought to hold on to its tether, muttering oaths between her croons of comfort. Usually, burros were docile creatures unless they smelled a coyote.

"Come on, Jenny," she soothed. "It's all right. See? Liberty's not worried."

That wasn't entirely true, since her mare's eyes were now rolling. But Silver was less worried about surprising a coyote than losing a valuable pack animal. Coyotes had nowhere to hide in a stump forest. Horses and mules, on the other hand, could hurdle themselves through the debris and break a leg.

For the rest of that journey, Silver battled her uneasiness. Her animals weren't much consolation, since they spooked each time a bee buzzed or a magpie shrilled. It was downright eerie. She tried to tell herself she was being silly, that no predator large enough to hurt her could hide behind a tree stump, and that included outlaws. Nevertheless, her shivers continued. Instinct told her something she couldn't quite see or hear was following her—just as she'd dreamed in her nightmares about Dancing Moon.

The realization was far from comforting.

Uncertain whether to be agitated or relieved when the landscape changed and the gray-green aspen trunks closed around her, she hurried her animals to the riverbank. City-born and bred, she'd never much cared for forests. Now that her nerves were stretched to their limits, she couldn't even enjoy the beauty of the columbines, stretching like an azure field of stars across the valley. Her slick fingers fumbled with Jenny's buckles. When the basket slid free of its straps, crashing bottom-side-up under Jenny's belly, she scowled, envisioning a hoofprint in her forehead as she stooped to retrieve the nuisance.

"Come on, Jenny," she muttered, leading the animal a safe twenty feet away. "I sure wish I knew what had you so jittery."

The twig that snapped behind her was nearly her undoing.

"Maybe the ol' girl's in heat," drawled a familiar Kentucky accent.

"*Jones!*" She practically shrieked his name. She didn't know whether to be relieved or outraged to see him. "How dare you sneak up on me like that! Were you following me all this time?"

" 'All this time'?" He flashed a lopsided grin, leaning his flannel-clad shoulder against a tree. "That all depends. How long do you think someone was following you?"

Ooh, wretched man. She would have loved to wring his neck. "Never mind," she snapped, hiding the tremor in her hands beneath the folds of her tweed riding skirt. "Just where the devil have you been?

You were supposed to register at the Windsor Hotel two days ago.''

"Why, Silver, I'm touched," he purred. "That you would miss me—"

"Oh, stop it."

He chuckled, his pewter eyes like polished mirrors in the slanting shafts of light. "Very well. But might I remind you of your instructions? I was supposed to purchase a conveyance suitable for a British lord. I couldn't very well do that in Aspen, now, could I? All the social-climbing busybodies would have been appalled to know that our noble Lord Chumley haggles over pennies like a horse trader."

She narrowed her eyes at him. He had a point. Still, she knew better than to drop her guard. He was as lean and lithe as a puma, and probably twice as dangerous—at least to her peace of mind. She tried not to notice how his blue jeans strained across his thighs or how the red-checkered plaid of his shirt accentuated the width of his chest. The wind-teased curl that spilled so boyishly across his forehead couldn't quell her misgivings. Raphael Jones smiled like a fallen angel. And *fallen* was the operative word here.

"I left you more than enough money to rent a coach," she rallied briskly. "And if you would have gone to the Windsor Hotel, as we'd *agreed*, you would have found the bank draft waiting for you. Not to mention," she muttered with a twinge of remorse, "a score or more sycophants all eager to meet 'a real live aristo.' "

Honestly, the stir she'd caused was disgraceful. After one bald lie to the greenhorn who operated Buckholtz's printing press, the whole town was rolling out the red carpet for her hornswoggler. The *Aspen Times* and the *Rocky Mountain Sun* were vying to run the biggest banner headline in history to commemorate Rafe's—or rather, Chumley's—arrival. Shopkeepers, restauranteurs, and whores were all hanging signs of welcome, most of which were abysmally spelled.

Even Benson seemed to be getting into the spirit. He'd starting sporting a gold watchfob and cuff links, extravagances she'd once thought alien to his nature. In fact, when she'd surprised her butler on Galena Street yesterday, emerging from First National Bank with a wad of greenbacks in his hand, he'd seemed immensely embarrassed and had hastened to divert her from his windfall.

Come to think of it, she thought fleetingly, he'd diverted her from entering the bank, too. That meant she'd have to get rid of Rafe, dump these rocks, and ride to the vault before it closed.

Silver pressed her lips together. Why was nothing simple?

"Well," she said in her best businesslike voice, "you're burning daylight, as Papa would say. The commercial district closes in about an hour, so I suggest you hurry back to town for a discreet chat with Signor Marzetti. He's Aspen's most distinguished tailor, and he can help fit you for Papa's engagement party, which, by the way, I expect you to attend Saturday evening. For dinner tonight, you'll no doubt want to put in an appearance at the Chloride Restaurant. Celestia will be most impressed. Everyone who's *anyone* eats there. It's rather like the 'Delmonico of the West.'"

Rafe looked amused by her haste to dismiss him. "My dear Silver, you wouldn't be trying to get rid of me, would you?"

"Certainly not," she lied, and none too elegantly.

"I just assumed you'd want a hot meal after tramping through the mountains."

"Why, how very thoughtful, considering you'll be paying the tab. But in truth, I'm a bit of a sucker for home-cooked meals," he drawled. "So tell me. What's on today's menu? Goose liver pâté? Salmon roe with sweet, creamed butter, lemon crackers, and champagne?"

She blinked, momentarily speechless. He wanted her to open the basket? To her consternation, she felt the blood creeping up her neck. "Uh . . . no. Not exactly. There's nothing edible in this picnic chest."

"There's not?"

Her cheeks were growing warmer by the second. She figured she'd now thoroughly telegraphed her guilt. "No, there's not," she retorted, striving for firmness. "This basket's full of rocks."

"Rocks, huh?"

She fidgeted beneath his mocking gaze. Well, they *were* rocks. Of the most common variety. He didn't have to know the importance Papa attached to them. "That's right." She raised her chin. "I put rocks in this basket to . . . uh, train Jenny. Yes, that's it. She's still learning to be a pack mule. Aren't you, Jen?" Silver patted the burro's nose. Actually, she had no idea what the mule was called. She'd never seen this animal until she'd forced the poor thing to become a four-footed felon. But since female donkeys were called jennies, she'd figured the name was close enough . . .

She blew out her breath. Why was Rafe *smirking* at her that way?

"You know, Silver." His voice lilted, actually *lilted*, damn him. "I've heard a thousand lies, and I've made up at least as many. But yours is truly inspired. So tell me. Where is Romeo? Running late for your romantic tryst, is he?''

Her jaw dropped. "T-tryst?" *Really*. Leave it to Raphael Jones to leap to the most sordid conclusion. "I'll have you know there *is* no tryst, romantic or otherwise."

"Is that so?" he taunted softly.

Her face felt hotter than a four-bell fire now. For heaven's sake, what was the matter with her? She should have just confirmed she had a lover. The threat of his arrival would have been the fastest way to get rid of Raphael Jones.

"Must you read artifice and scandal into *everything* I do? There's nothing but rocks in that stupid basket."

When he arched a tawny brow, she blew out her breath.

"Oh, for heaven's sake. Here, see for yourself."

She marched over to the basket, intent on turning it over, but when she shoved, the straining wicker split open. A mini avalanche tumbled onto her skirt, pinning her where she knelt. It also made her prey to the ugliest, *hungriest* arachnid she'd ever seen. She took one look at all those bristling black legs, racing toward her over the rubble, and she lost what was left of her reason.

"*Spider!*" she shrieked, making Jenny bray, the aspens quake, and Rafe come running to her side.

"Kill it. *Kill it!*" she squealed, struggling frantically to free herself.

He swept up the spider and knocked the rocks to the ground. She scrambled to her feet, clapping a hand to her mouth.

"Is . . . is it dead?"

He had the good grace not to laugh. Still, the mirth in his eyes was hard to mistake. "Perhaps the more pressing question,'' he countered, his gaze caressing the bodice of her silk vest, ''is are you hurt?''

''N-no,'' she croaked, her knees knocking uncontrollably. That deathlike chill was all around her again, and for the life of her, she couldn't shake it off.

''Good. Then I want you to see something.''

He stepped closer. She gulped. She would have run for her horse if her legs had thawed. Instead, she could do nothing more than watch, speechless with horror, as he opened his fist. The night crawler had hunkered down in his palm, not squashed and harmless, as she'd hoped, but rather fat and hairy, and as ominous as a ticking bomb.

''See? It's quite tame.''

''It is *not*. It *bites*! I had one crawl into my bed once and . . . and my ankle swelled up for a month!''

''That must have been painful,'' he murmured.

''It *was*.'' Reason was starting to burn its way back into her brain. For God's sake, why was she so cold? She felt like the very arms of death were wrapped around her, even though the sun was shining full on her back.

Rafe cocked his head. ''Are you going to faint?''

''*No*.'' The humiliation of such a notion had the force to heat her toes. Still, the uneasiness lingered— the same uneasiness that had plagued her ever since she'd decided to raze the dogbane. Inexplicably, she remembered her nightmares, in which Dancing Moon always seemed to be stalking her with a dead plant or animal. She shuddered. *It's a damned good thing I don't believe in ghosts.*

''Well, since you're not going to faint . . .'' His lips quirked. ''Can I tell you a secret?''

She swallowed, nodding.

"You're not ever going to get over your fear of spiders if you don't learn to understand them."

She grimaced, tossing him a daggerlike glare. "Don't you even *think* of putting that creepy-crawly thing on me."

"I wouldn't dream of it." His eyes captured hers. "But you live in the wild and woolly west now. And you've got to learn to live peacefully with bugs and varmints. The good news is," he continued, an uncharacteristic edge creeping into his voice, "most things don't deserve their bad reputations. Take spiders, for instance. They eat pests, like mosquitoes. And they feed a lot of birds. Most of them are completely harmless to humans. In fact, on the average, I daresay spiders are more afraid of you than you are of them. I know *I* would be"—his dimples peeked as his playful demeanor returned—"if I were the size of this wolf spider, and something your size tried to stomp on me."

Silver's lip jutted as she hugged her arms to her chest. Maybe he was right. Then again, maybe he wasn't. The point was, no matter what their reputation, she had good reason to dislike spiders. Just as she had good reason to distrust handsome, smooth-talking men.

She watched narrowly as he guided the spider to an aspen and let it crawl safely up the trunk. It occurred to her then that she might have made a fatal mistake, hiring a scoundrel who had a soft spot for things most people considered despicable.

"Do you intend to seduce Celestia?" she blurted out.

He started, turning toward her again. "Why? Are you having second thoughts?"

"No," she lied again, wanting to kick herself for

being so transparent. "But it's clear to me you've been stalling."

"Is it indeed?" A smile teased the corner of his lips.

"Well, sure. Rather than hastening to make her acquaintance, you've spent the better part of—what, three days?—prowling around this godforsaken valley. Just what are you doing out here, when you could be dining on caviar and sleeping on eiderdown at the Windsor Hotel?"

He arched a brow. "You think the Roaring Fork Valley forsaken?" He glanced incredulously toward deforested Aspen Mountain, toward the cattle now grazing on ancestral buffalo ground, and the wheat struggling where prairie grass once had grown. "You should have seen this valley eight years ago," he murmured, "when *Aspen* was nothing more than the name of a tree."

She shifted uncomfortably. His wistfulness had been hard to mistake. "You . . . prefer the wilderness?"

His jaw hardened. "To razed forests and poisoned rivers? Indeed I do."

A glimmer of accusation harshened his stare.

"Oh, for heaven's sake." She marched past him, intent on disposing of the spiritkeepers, *in the river*, as planned. "You act as if we're standing in a desert instead of a veritable forest of aspens." She squatted, starting to chuck rocks into the current. "And obviously, you've never taken a drive down Main or Center Streets. Unlike other clapboard towns across the west, you'll find we actually have shaded sidewalks. The Ladies' Aid Society organized a tree-planting campaign four years ago. As for waterways, you'll find Crystal Creek as pure as its name."

"But for how long?" His gaze was dire as he focused on the pasty yellow crud that clung to the reeds and muddied the shallows. "Isn't your sawmill near Crystal Creek?"

So what if it is? She pressed her lips together, refusing to shoulder one more ounce of guilt for the day. He had some nerve, bilking her out of five hundred dollars per week and then criticizing the way she earned the money to pay him!

"Perhaps it will come as some consolation," she said tartly, "that your wage is dependent upon dirty little nuisances like my sawmill. And my sawmill, of course, is necessary to my mines, *which*, by the way, also help to pay your inflated fee.

"Then again," she said dryly, pushing closed the flaps of the basket, "I could cut production entirely, save a couple of trees, make you and a herd of elk happy, and watch the four hundred and fifty people I employ lose their homes and all their possessions—assuming, of course, they don't starve to death before the bank forecloses on them."

Rafe winced, averting his gaze. She had a point. He had to admit, he liked civilized conveniences as much as any man. God knew, he hadn't come to the Roaring Fork Valley to condemn free enterprise—not that his opinion would have mattered to anyone here if he had. Wherever he looked, he saw what the wealth seekers touted as "progress." And maybe it was. All he knew was he'd come to this river to teach Tavy to swim. And she'd been less eager than he to wade into the cheesy, yellow filth that choked the water.

"I stand corrected," he conceded with a touch of

irony. "Heaven forbid I should stand in the way of progress."

"Or your bank account."

"Just so." This time, his mockery was directed solely at himself.

She rose, cool and dignified once more despite the incongruity of the basket, which dangled in strawlike tatters from her elbow. As her gemstone gaze clashed with his, he had to admit that he preferred this callous Silver to the one who'd nearly swooned at his feet. Silver the Ice Princess was easier to dislike than Silver the Damsel in Distress. And the Ice Princess would be easier to jilt, too, when the timing was right.

"What a relief to know we can actually agree on something," she said, her sarcasm thinly veiled. "I trust I'll see you—or rather, Lord Chumley—at my father's party promptly at eight o'clock?"

"I shall count the hours."

"Good."

Inclining her head in dismissal, she strode to the mule and strapped the basket in place. Courtesy winning out over his irritation, he offered her a hand, but she refused it, just as she refused his offer to boost her into the saddle. If she hadn't grown so stiff as he'd moved closer, he might have been annoyed by her snub. But her pinched cheeks and white lips struck him oddly. To watch her shy out of his reach, he wouldn't have described her so much as haughty as . . . well, unnerved.

His eyes narrowed speculatively as he watched her ride off. Silver Nichols was proving more human than he'd expected. For one thing, she'd grown endearingly flustered after he'd accused her of entertaining a lover. For another, she'd turned appealingly vulnerable as she'd recounted the spider bite story. He was almost tempted to believe there was another, *warmer* Silver lurking beneath all her frost.

A wicked smile quirked his lips.

Just what would happen, he wondered, if the Ice Princess met the heat of his kiss?

Chapter 6

Peering out his coach window, Rafe gazed in awe at the Nicholses' massive, Romanesque mansion. Its unflappable stone face and metal roof were practical in design, no doubt to prevent one of the fires that had helped to wipe out other mining towns. Of course, since Midas Max hadn't built his legend on practicality, the Peachblow sandstone had probably been chosen by Silver, Rafe mused. No doubt hers had been the sparing hand that had decorated it, too. Frilly curtains, flowerpots, and gingerbread trims were nonexistent in the ponderously squat, solid shape. In fact, the only frivolous element of the mansion's design, if one could call it frivolous, was the upper story's stained glass windows. Glittering blue, green, and red jewels seemed to wink from every casement, and a rainbow of fire spilled out upon the immaculately manicured lawn.

Rafe cocked his head and smirked. Judging by the lights, music, and laughter, the party was well underway. He'd taken great care to arrive last.

Timing was everything in the theater.

Giving the coach roof a whack with his walking stick, a shiny new acquisition that amused him to no end, he displayed the bored manner of a British blue

blood. His demeanor was no small feat, considering
the result of his whack. The vehicle lurched; the
wheels bounced; and he was nearly flung from his
seat as the coach listed, jolting to a shuddering halt
in a rut.

Jimmy, God love him, had finally located the
coach's brakes.

Rafe heard a thump and the eager pounding of
boots. A heartbeat later, his driver, an impossibly gullible youth whose vocabulary was roughly limited to
exclamations, flung open the door.

"Man alive, your worship sir," Jimmy panted, his
ruddy cheeks bulging above the collar that he, in his
less auspicious job as a cantaloupe picker, was un-
accustomed to wearing. "That house sure is some
pumpkins!"

Rafe gazed fondly at the youth. Jimmy was decked
out in a red livery that had cost Rafe—or rather, Silver—at least twice as much as every item of clothing
Jimmy had ever owned. Jimmy was another new "acquisition" that amused Rafe to no end, and he
couldn't wait to spring the lad on Little Miss High
Society.

"That house?" Rafe gestured toward the grand edifice with a limp hand. " 'Some pumpkins,' you
say?" He sniffed disdainfully. "Lud, my boy. You
have yet to see my kennels."

Jimmy's eyes bugged out, making him look like a
guppy with spikey blonde hair. "Golly!"

Rafe hid his smile. Tossing his cape back with a
flourish, he stepped briskly up the cobbled walk that
wound toward the door. He'd been waiting two excruciatingly long days for this moment. For the last
forty-eight hours, he'd been holed up in a hotel
bathtub, surrounded by kettles of fish. Somehow, it

seemed inanely appropriate that of all the motherless otters in the world, he had adopted a defective one. The minute Tavy hit the water, she sank like a cannonball. She was quite possibly the only webbed-footed creature on earth who didn't have a clue what to do with her paws.

He'd had some fancy explaining to do each time the hotel clerk knocked on his door, sheepishly mentioning the complaints of his neighbors, who swore they heard some kind of "dog" yapping in his quarters. He couldn't very well admit he'd smuggled an otter inside, much less that he was teaching it to swim. As eccentric as he'd been painting Lord Chumley, he suspected there was a limit even to his retinue's gullibility.

He groaned to himself. How was he supposed to return Tavy to the wild if she couldn't even paddle her way across a bathtub?

But that was the least of his troubles.

When he'd agreed to seduce Celestia Cooper, he'd assumed Silver was matching him up with a modern-day Jezebel. He'd conjured in his mind a woman so sinful, so voluptuous, that no mortal man could possibly have resisted her. Silver had never bothered to correct his misconception.

Well, yesterday morning, while he'd been sneaking fresh fish up the back stairs for Tavy, he'd glimpsed the inimitable siren herself. In fact, he'd nearly collided with Midas Max as he was boyishly stealing a kiss from his lover in her doorway. Rafe was sure his jaw had dropped to the carpet when a short woman with plump arms, a double chin, and wild blonde corkscrews hastily gathered her sheet and ducked out of sight. Max's *affaire d' amour* was no smoldering, pert-breasted fantasy. What was worse, Celestia Cooper was old enough to be Rafe's mother.

Rafe halted before Silver's door, scowling at the memory.

He'd been so furious—disappointed, too—to learn his conquest was no tempestuous beauty that he'd had half a mind to vanish into the wilderness and let Silver sweat out her father's engagement.

Unfortunately, his finances wouldn't permit such rash behavior.

Even if he could have mustered the lust to woo a woman who reminded him so forcefully of Fiona, he'd be loathe to try. He had one or two scruples left, despite his every effort to purge them, and they were both adamantly against tricking old women and breaking their hearts.

Of course, he wasn't about to let Silver know that. No, his cohort-in-crime had a little lesson to learn about bamboozling Raphael Jones. He'd thought long and hard about his options, and he'd finally decided on the only sensible alternative: revenge. That's why he'd scoured the valley for a suitable retainer. Hiring Jimmy had been integral to Rafe's plan. Spending a king's fortune on Silver's credit had also been part of his mischief. But best of all . . .

Rafe snickered to himself.

Best of all were the character improvements he'd made in the role Silver had scripted for him.

Rapping his cane on the Nicholses' glass-and-mahogany door, Rafe envisioned the look on his co-conspirator's face when he unveiled the new Lord Chumley. To his surprise, though, Silver didn't greet him on the threshold. Instead, a pine tree of a man-servant, in impeccable swallowtails, appeared at the entrance. The man barred his way, looking down his hooked nose.

"Hullo, my good man," Rafe said in his best British fop's voice. "Do step aside and tell Miss Nichols the Duke of Chumley has arrived."

The manservant arched an eyebrow. One sweeping, flesh-scoring glance later, he'd masterfully conveyed what he thought of Rafe, Rafe's attire, and all of Rafe's ancestry.

"The *Duke* of Chumley, you say?" the servant repeated in an unmistakably British accent.

Rafe started, and the back of his neck turned blistering hot. Damn Silver anyway. She'd also neglected to tell him she had an English butler!

"That's correct." Rafe fixed the servant with his haughtiest stare and vowed to make Silver the Shyster pay double—no, triple—for this second breach of contract. "Run along and fetch your mistress."

"And I suggest, sir, that *you* run along before I have you thrown into the gutter."

A heartbeat later, the wooden portal slammed, and Rafe was left staring at his reflection in the quivering opaque glass.

Silver, my love, that's another one I owe you.

For her part, Silver nearly dropped an entire tray of champagne glasses when she heard Rafe's voice— and her butler's threat. Hurrying into the entrance hall, she rounded the corner just in time to see Benson slamming the door on her long-awaited guest.

"Benson!" she choked, certain she'd blanched. For once heedless of the proprieties, she made a beeline through the couple who was signing her guest register and tried to console herself that this night couldn't possibly get worse. First, her illustrious chef had arrived tipsy, an empty bottle of cooking sherry jutting from his coat pocket. Next, her pricy Denver orchestra had turned out to be little more than a tone-deaf

oompah band. Then, her father's bride-to-be had
grabbed the mayor's hand and started predicting his
reelection returns.

But these had only been the preamble to disaster.
Five minutes after her guests had started arriving,
members of the Miners Union had staged a rally on
her lawn. With a scribbling reporter in tow from the
Rocky Mountain Sun, they'd announced to anyone
who would listen that they had never agreed to work
in a haunted mine and that the only fair alternative
was to double their wages. Thanks to the timely arrival of Marshal Hawthorne, Silver had postponed all
further blackmail attempts by agreeing to a morning
mediation, although she'd been sorely tempted to fire
every one of the blackguards right on the spot.

But the final horror on this night of horrors, Silver
groaned silently, would be to watch her nobleman-
for-hire be unmasked by her very own butler.

It was moments like these when Silver wondered
if Celestia had fashioned a rag poppet in her likeness
and was gleefully jabbing pins into its head.

Racing to the door, Silver thrust her tray of glasses
into her bemused butler's hands. "For heaven's sake,
Benson, what's the matter with you?" she whispered,
throwing open the door. She almost sobbed with relief
to see Rafe still standing on the stoop. He managed
to look unperturbed, as if nearly getting his nose
smashed against a windowpane was an everyday occurrence.

"My Lord Chumley, I am so sorry!" she greeted
him, genuinely mortified. "Please do come in. I don't
know what has gotten into my butler. Obviously,
there's been a misunderstanding." She shot an ominous glance at her manservant. "Benson, apologize
at once to his lordship."

Benson drew himself up to his full six feet, seven inches. "With all due respect, Miss Nichols, this man is an impos—"

"Benson!" Silver choked as Mr. and Mrs. Trevelyan, the couple by the register, turned curiously toward the commotion. "Lord Chumley is my guest. Kindly do as you're told."

The butler's face mottled at her lady-of-the-house voice. However, years of serving, not to mention the tidy stipend she paid him, must have won out over his pride. With a coldness that would have endeared him only to penguins, he inclined his head. "My apologies to . . . Your *Grace*," he added disdainfully.

Silver started. Your Grace? Wasn't that a duke's address?

Rafe's smile was bland as he craned his head back to peer at her butler. "Odd's fish, m'dear," he said, fluttering a handkerchief beneath the servant's nose. "Wherever did you recruit your man? From one of your colonial lumber camps?"

Benson's jaw grew rigid at the insult.

"Of course not," Silver interceded, wishing Rafe was close enough for a good elbow jab. "Benson comes from a long and distinguished line of menservants. Why, his grandfather served in Lord Wellington's household."

Rafe didn't look the least bit impressed. Silver suspected he didn't have a clue who Lord Wellington was. So much for her pipe dream that he would actually rehearse his role. As relieved as she was that he'd finally arrived as promised, the impression he was making was far from the desired effect. For some unfathomable reason, he'd selected a gold velvet coat, a chartreuse waistcoat, and matching green spats for his shoes. His cravat was a frilly, overly elaborate affair that no doubt would have smothered a shorter man, and the tawny, muttonchop whiskers he'd pasted to his jaws gave him a comical, rather than sophisticated, air.

"Benson, kindly take that tray to the parlor," she said, deciding she would be wise to debrief her imposter once more.

Benson nodded stiffly, giving Rafe one last, skin-flaying glance before turning with the champagne. Unfortunately, that gave Rafe enough space to step inside.

"I say," he drawled, affecting a faint lisp, "what a smashing little cottage you have. All these colored windows and glittery . . . thingamabobs." He waved his handkerchief at the two thousand dollar crystal-and-sterling chandelier tinkling in the breeze from the open transom. "I wager that keeps your lumberjack of a manservant busy come polishing time, what? Oh, and dear me, look." Before Silver could block the smart aleck's escape, he'd ambled over to the priceless Chinese vase and the stunning arrangement of mountain laurels that dominated the register's table. "Posies!" he exclaimed, inhaling noisily.

Pasting on a smile for the Trevelyans, Silver caught the troublemaker's arm. "Come along, my lord. I'll see to your cape."

"Jolly good." He started to hum, waving his handkerchief in time to the off-key ditty, and Silver gritted her teeth, dragging him under the circular staircase.

"Must you be such a trial?" she whispered, snatching that ridiculous linen from his hand. "You're late. Don't tell me you spent all this time at Signor Marzetti's, because clearly you did not. Where on earth did you get that waistcoat?"

Rafe's lips twitched as he lovingly smoothed the

brocade. "Rather festive, don't you think?"

"You don't want to know what I think." She had the sneaking suspicion he'd been striving for the reaction she'd just given him. Mentally cursing herself, she stuffed his handkerchief and gloves into his top hat and tossed his cape over a hook. The last thing she wanted was to encourage his buffoonery.

Drawing a calming breath, Silver opted for reason over ire. "Well, you're here now, and nothing can be done about that waistcoat. You should have told me you couldn't get an appointment with Signor Marzetti. I would have arranged for—"

She realized Rafe wasn't listening. He was too busy gawking through his quizzing glass at the statue her love-struck father had commissioned for the alcove. The sterling maiden was supposed to represent Aphrodite, but Silver had never ventured close enough to admire its artistry. All its shameless, bare-chested glory made her blush.

Rafe, on the other hand, was fairly smirking at the sculpture's pronounced places.

"Oh, for heaven's sake," she muttered, grabbing his sleeve and yanking him toward less scandalous vistas. "Will you please pay attention?"

His lazy golden lashes swept lower, lingering on her own modest décolletage. "I should be delighted."

Her insides shriveled with embarrassment. Despite the caress in his gaze, it was hard to feel adequate compared with the Greek goddess of love. "We have little time to talk." She did her best to assume a businesslike whisper, despite the distraction of his nearness. His heat gusted over her bared shoulders like a sultry summer night, and his scent, an enticing aroma, filled her head like a sensual fog. "Sandalwood," she murmured.

"I beg your pardon?"

She started, realizing she'd spoken aloud. She'd been trying to guess the essence of his cologne. *Good Lord.* Thirty seconds alone with the man, and already she was babbling like a mooncalf!

"Never mind. Because you're so late, I've had the devil of a time inventing reasons to keep Brady Buckholtz away from Celestia. He's the editor of the *Times.* He's no fool, so I suggest you get your story straight. I trust you have some plan in mind?"

"Seduction does require forethought."

Her toes curled. She couldn't immediately say why. Perhaps it was due to the smoky timbre of his voice. "Good. Then I shall distract Papa. Only—" Her stomach flipped at the prospect of her treachery. Honestly, she thought she'd overcome these annoying pangs of guilt. "Be discreet. Papa does have feelings, after all."

"Oh, your papa won't feel a thing."

She eyed him sharply. Was he being ironic? Or was he up to no good again? It was hard to believe he'd suddenly developed compassion for her papa. "I shall expect significant progress from you tonight," she reminded him.

"My progress, dear Silver, is the one thing on which you can depend."

He smiled, smiled in such a way that her entire body tingled, as if those full, firm lips had sipped the taste of hers. She heated from head to toe.

"Kindly focus, sir." Folding her arms, she retreated a step, hoping to appear more miffed than ruffled. Her Aunt-Agatha glare, the one that used to make her shriek and dive under the quilts as a child, wasn't intimidating him in the least. But maybe she just wasn't doing it right. Or maybe, she admitted reluctantly, she liked his wicked innuendoes. Their verbal parries made her feel feminine, earthy, and . . . well, alive. How long had it been since she'd actually felt desire rather than revulsion for a man?

Not since that awful night in the garden with Aaron.

Still, she couldn't let Rafe know she was attracted to him. Theirs would be a disastrous affair, considering the reason she'd hired him.

"I know this is just a lark to you," she whispered fervently, "just another performance. But my whole world will come crumbling down if you don't pull off this role."

Those pewter eyes held her spellbound. For a moment, she forgot that she'd sold her soul to this tawny-haired devil. She forgot that one poorly-timed lie, one spiteful wisecrack, and he could destroy every happiness she'd ever known. Instead, she let her trust be wooed by the reluctant nobility stirring in his gaze.

"This *is* the point of no return," he said softly.

His words sizzled along every repentant nerve. He was right, of course. She had an entire ballroom full of guests, all of whom had come to laugh at her father's choice in brides. *Desperate times call for desperate measures*, she reminded herself staunchly. Papa's life might be in danger from his arson-minded floozie. Still, to hire a specimen like Rafe for seduction, then surrender him to Celestia without first putting up the slightest fight . . .

Silver's bottom lip jutted. Well, that pretty much said it all, didn't it? She was an idiot for letting her moral self get huffy. In the final analysis, Celestia was getting the better part of this bargain!

"Don't tell me you've suddenly developed a conscience," she chided tartly.

"Nothing so drastic." A smile teased the corner of his mouth. He'd become Rogue Romeo again, and no amount of whiskers, sashes, lace flounces, or other fripperies could detract from his sensuality. "But I trust I'll be a busy man in the nights to come. And I was noticing how much you seem to . . . admire me."

"*Admire* you?" *Good Lord.* She wanted to crawl under a potted fern. Was she that transparent, or was he only fishing?

"The very thought of Celestia in my arms makes you jealous," he drawled. "Admit it."

Her cheeks were growing hotter by the second. "You, sir, suffer from delusions."

"Come now, Silver." His voice lowered to a throbbing murmur. "I can see how your pulse speeds whenever I draw near. Your eyes dilate, your skin flushes . . ." He shifted, his lips parting above hers in the most hypnotic way. "You would much rather I lavished my kisses on you."

She felt the truth of his words in a flash of moist heat, one that pooled in her private places and left them strangely yearning. To her mortification, she realized her pulse *was* racing faster than a thoroughbred stallion's. What was worse, her knees were trembling. But he couldn't know that, too, could he? Not beneath her gown?

Swallowing, she stood her ground—albeit shakily. Raphael Jones was a practiced roué, she reminded herself. Men like him toyed with women the way cats toyed with mice. The realization was somewhat deflating.

"You are, without a doubt, the most insufferable man I ever had the displeasure of knowing. Only in my worst nightmares would I succumb to a rake like you."

"So you dream about me, too?"

"*Oh!*" She wished she had some recourse other than glaring to put him in his place. "You know very well what I meant."

"Indeed I do."

The amusement in his eyes left little doubt he knew that *she* knew she was lying. *Odious man.* Raphael Jones and Celestia Cooper deserved one another.

"Quit stalling," she said testily. "It's time you proved your worth. I've invested quite a bit in this evening's outcome, not the least of which, apparently, went to that waistcoat. After using my money to indulge yourself in such whims, I'll thank you to get on with the job—unless, of course, you're feeling unequal to your role?"

He grinned. Actually grinned, damn him.

A heartbeat later, she understood why.

"And what role might that be, daughter?" her father called jovially from behind.

Silver whirled, nearly strangling on her gulp of air. Through the blue haze that spewed through their cigars, she spied her father and Brady Buckholtz strolling out of the ballroom. The slender newsman, dressed in his habitual black, towered over her squat, ruddy-cheeked papa like a Puritan scarecrow. The description wasn't that far off the mark, either, Silver thought in gnawing dread. The man was so morally uptight that he supported the Temperance movement, a rare sentiment for a male in a mining town. His righteous intolerance was almost as off-putting as his refusal to advocate votes for women. Silver had never liked Buckholtz. What was more, they'd clashed publicly on more than one occasion, since she'd had the so-called temerity to make business decisions for her father's mines.

Why, oh why, she groaned silently, had she let Papa talk her into inviting every member of his precious Roaring Fork Club?

Hastily, she recounted her last few seconds of conversation. How much had Papa and Buckholtz heard? And why hadn't Rafe warned her they were approaching?

She shot a dark look at her coconspirator. His insipid expression nearly made her groan again.

"Papa!" she cried, hoping she sounded more enthusiastic than blameworthy as she ran out from under the staircase. "Goodness, you gave me such a start. Look who just arrived. It's Lord Chumley! My lord," she continued, breezing through the introductions in an attempt to change the subject, "I would like you to meet Brady Buckholtz, the editor of our very own *Aspen Times*. He has written quite extensively about your arrival and, I'm sure, hopes to learn more about your intentions—particularly when it comes to investing in the S&M Nichols Mining and Smelting Company."

"I can speak for myself, my dear," Buckholtz said, barely glancing her way.

Silver heated, clamping her mouth closed. She should have known better than to think Buckholtz had paid enough attention to her to notice her culpability.

Rafe darted her a discerning look.

"So, Chumley," Buckholtz continued, tapping his ash over her mountain laurels, "I take it you've finally come to your senses by visiting Aspen. Denver's a waste of time, unless, of course, a man prefers to be a pauper. There's a fortune to be made right here in Aspen."

Rafe arched a brow at the leaf that now had a smoldering hole in its center. "Sink me, my dear fellow.

I already have a fortune. Five or six, to be precise.''

"To be precise?" Buckholtz repeated, his dry little smile conveying just how peerless he considered his grammatical expertise.

"Just so," Rafe answered, assuming a mincing pose. "What the devil would I do with another one?"

Papa chuckled. "He does have a point, Buckholtz."

"As you would know, old chap," Rafe said with a bow.

"Come now, Chumley." Buckholtz had all but snorted his disbelief. "You mean you can't think of a single blessed use for, say, another million pounds?"

"Not a one."

"Uh, Mr. Buckholtz," Silver interceded, worried that Rafe was digging his grave with his tongue. The newsman was constantly lording his moral and intellectual superiority over everyone else. If he hadn't been so quick with a .45, he would have been gunned down long before this. "Has Papa told you that Lord Chumley acquired his last million pounds through investments in Cornwall's copper mines? He is quite a savvy speculator."

Buckholtz wouldn't be put off that easily. "I am much more interested in how his lordship lost his first million pounds. There was rumor of a young woman's involvement, was there not, Chumley? An Irish singer, to be exact?"

"Come now, Brady." Papa was frowning, his worried glance shifting from the newsman to Rafe. "This here's a party, not an inquisition."

"It is my rare privilege to be a newsman, sir," Buckholtz said haughtily. "My job does not end because the champagne begins to flow." He folded his arms across his chest. "Well, Chumley? What do you have to say for yourself?"

"Odds fish." Rafe began swinging his quizzing glass around his jutting middle finger, a gesture that somehow didn't appear to be coincidental. "What a droll sense of humor you colonial newsies have."

Buckholtz arched a bristling black brow. "Then you categorically deny you were bamboozled out of a million pounds by an Irish tramp?"

Rafe chuckled. "My dear Mr. Buckshot—"

"It's Buckholtz," the man corrected him tartly.

"Er. Right. Buckhorn, then—"

"I said *Buckholtz*," the newsman ground out.

"Isn't that what I said?" Rafe blinked innocently. Raising his glass, he stared with one grossly magnified eyeball at Buckholtz. "As I was saying, my dear fellow, I quite understand your position. And I applaud you for speaking so boldly. Sink me if it isn't the only way a country yokel like yourself can come to understand the trials of class and wealth."

Buckholtz stiffened. Silver ducked her head, stifling laughter. Here she'd been worried Rafe would be called to some alley and pumped full of bullets for the lies she'd paid him to speak. She should have known the wiseacre could fend for himself.

"The trials of wealth?" Buckholtz bit out.

Rafe gestured with a limp hand. "Money is monstrous tedious, old chap. It's always attracting tax collectors, solicitors, and long-lost kin of some sort or another. Why, just last month," he continued in that same lethargic drawl, "some dying old fellow named me his heir. Turned me into a duke. Bloody inconsiderate of him, if you ask me. Did I ask to be a duke? No, not once. The very idea." He gave a theatrical shudder. "Now everywhere I travel in your American

West, lumberjacks and cowboys are calling me 'Gracie.' ''

Papa's lips quirked, and his eyes twinkled above his lopsided grin.

"You're a *duke*?" Buckholtz's brow creased in a mixture of confusion and suspicion. "That's not what the Denver newspapers reported."

"That's because they got it wrong." Rafe tapped his glass on Buckholtz's shoulder. "That just goes to show, you can't believe everything you read in your provincial American papers, what?"

Papa chuckled. It was a warm and hearty sound that sparked a flush in Buckholtz's darkening countenance. "Not to worry, Chumley," Papa interceded. "You won't find that kind of inattention to detail in the *Aspen Times*—will you, Brady?" Papa winked at Rafe.

"So tell me, Your Grace," he continued, waving with his cigar for Rafe to accompany him to the ballroom, "if it's not another fortune you're after, why did you come to Aspen? It's a bit too early for sleighing and such."

"I daresay you're right. Sleighing would be devilish slow without a good snow." He laughed gaily. "Why, lookie there. I'm a poet!"

"Byron is no doubt rolling in his grave," Buckholtz said.

Unlike the newsman, Papa appeared charmed. "Say, Chumley, have you read Lewis Carroll?" he asked eagerly. "The Walrus and the Carpenter is a real ripsnorter." Screwing up his features like a scholar, he tucked his thumbs under his arms. "The time has come, the Walrus said, to talk of many things, like shoes and ships and sealing wax, and cabbages and kings."

"And why the sea is boiling hot," Rafe chimed in grandly, "and whether pigs have wings!"

The two guffawed. Silver rolled her eyes.

"Why, you're just like a regular old Yankee," Papa said. "Hardly snooty at all, which is more than I can say for that British butler my daughter hired."

Buckholtz cleared his throat as he and Silver trailed behind Rafe. "Might I inquire, Your Grace, when you'll be divesting our fair city of your presence?" His irony was hard to mistake.

Rafe shrugged. "Hard to say, old chap. I rather fancy what your clean mountain air does for a body."

"You're not here for your health, then, are you, son?" Papa asked in concern. "I'd thought the journey from Denver a bit too rugged for a lunger."

"Dear me, no." Rafe smirked over his shoulder at Silver. "I'm here to take a wife."

She wheezed, nearly tripping over her skirts.

"A wife, you say?" Papa sounded pleased. "So you're not married?"

"Alas, there is no Duchess of Chumley to soothe my lonely heart."

"One can't help but wonder why," Buckholtz interjected.

Papa and Rafe ignored him. They'd skirted the dance floor and were now headed directly for Celestia's retinue of gawkers. The Queen of Con was comfortably plumped up on the cushions of a wicker chair so she might squint at the sweaty palms—or was that the gold rings?—of the hopelessly naive.

"If it's a bride you're after," Papa told Rafe, "you've come to the right place. America *is* the land of milk and honey. Why, I found my own true love right here in Aspen."

Silver choked, stumbling to a halt. *How could*

Papa? she thought, her chest constricting. How could he call *anyone* other than Mama his true love?

Only Rafe seemed to notice her upset. His steps slowed, and he glanced over his shoulder at her. She was certain his keen pewter eyes saw right through the smile she tried to resurrect. She was forced to look away.

" 'Course," Papa continued heartily, nudging Rafe to direct his gaze back to Celestia, "that little beauty in the turquoise turban is already spoken for. But Aspen is a booming town, son. I think you'll find we've got a couple more gems to unearth round here."

Oblivious to the knife that was twisting in Silver's chest, Papa blew his fiancée a kiss. Celestia pinkened like a bonbon. Clasping her well-corseted bosom, she made a great show of blowing back her answer, and Papa chortled, reaching up to catch it. It was more than Silver could bear.

"Papa," she said tersely, "perhaps it's time you introduced Lord Chumley to your fiancée. I'm sure Celestia might be persuaded to tear herself away from her palm-reading long enough to ... uh ..." She tossed Rafe a withering glance. "Meet a *duke*."

"Odds fish," he drawled, squinting through his quizzing glass at Celestia's outlandish attire. "A palm reader, is she?"

"She sure is." Papa nodded proudly. "She talks to spirits, too. Why, we're planning on having a séance to talk to that pesky ghost," he continued over Silver's sputtered objections. "You know, the one that's been haunting our mine and driving all the shovel stiffs away."

"A ghost, you say?" Rafe said, looking like he might laugh. "Lud, what rotten luck. Can't be good for business, what? My great grandmummy's castle was haunted once,'' he continued brightly. ''The bugger kept driving her sheep away. It was deuced inconvenient; they kept drowning in the moat. Turns out, Sir Harry—that was our ghost—had it in for the critters. Choked to death on a leg o' lamb, you see. So he'd ring a cowbell to lure them over the drawbridge.''

Silver narrowed her eyes at her smart aleck. ''Fortunately, there are no sheep in Silver's Mine.''

''But there is a bell,'' Papa added thoughtfully. '' 'Course, it's supposed to be a warning bell, but it's got all the men spooked 'cause it rings for no danged reason. Or at least, that's what we used to think. But maybe Dancing Moon's been trying to warn us away. Do you suppose that's why he's resorting to more drastic measures, like snuffing out lanterns and dumping lunch pails into the abyss?''

''Papa,'' Silver ground out, ''Dancing Moon is *not* roaming around our tunnels, upsetting lunch buckets. The very idea is preposterous.''

''Now, daughter, you can't be so sure. No one knows for certain what happens to the spirit after it leaves its fleshy abode. Cellie says we can ask Dancing Moon anything we like during the séance, and I mean to ask him to stop harassing our stiffs. Besides,'' Papa added more ominously, ''who knows what Dancing Moon might do next if we keep ignoring him?''

''A séance *is* a rather novel approach to avoiding a miners' strike,'' Buckholtz noted dryly.

Silver scowled. So much for trying to keep *that* headline out of the paper. ''Our miners are reasonable men,'' she told the newsman with long-suffering dignity. ''I'm sure their, er, peculiar set of grievances can be logically explained. If the gentlemen are hearing strange noises, there could very well be a problem with the overhead timbers. With safety, of course, being our primary concern, I shall direct our mining engineer to reinspect the timbering for buckling and cracking. I'm sure this will allay the Union's fears once and for all.''

''Dash it all.'' Rafe wore a hangdog expression. ''Does that mean there won't be a séance? I was so looking forward to chatting with a real, live ghostie—''

Silver furtively stomped on his foot.

''And so you shall, my boy,'' Papa boomed, slapping Rafe on the shoulder. ''Cellie will be delighted to have you there. I'll go tell her right away. In the meantime, daughter, why don't you show Chumley how we westerners hoof it? A polka is next on the program.''

He winked, then trundled off through the crowd, leaving Silver to curse him heartily under her breath.

''Oh, jolly good,'' Rafe said gaily as a wheezing trombone bore out Papa's prediction. ''I do so love a polka. Shall we dance, Miss Pennies?''

She glowered at him, hoping to hide her momentary panic. The thought of Rafe, his hand spanning her waist, his thighs pumping rhythmically against hers, reminded her all too forcibly of that night in the garden. She hadn't danced with a man ever since. She wasn't sure she could ever bring herself to do so again, knowing, as she did now, that some men considered dancing an improper invitation—no matter how many times their partners said no.

Fortunately, Buckholtz, of all people, came to her rescue.

''Miss Pennies, indeed,'' he mocked Rafe. ''How on earth could the lady refuse?'' Curling his lip, he turned a chilly shoulder on him. "I believe I've seen and heard enough for my story, Miss Nichols. If you'll excuse me, I can show myself to your door."

"Oh. Uh . . . yes. If you must," Silver stammered, unsure whether to be worried or relieved. "Good night then, Mr. Buckholtz."

Rafe screwed up his features in mock dismay. "Dear me, such a fussbudget. Pray don't go running off yet," he boomed, grabbing two champagne glasses from a passing waiter. "We shall drink to your health, sir. I daresay, it would be the kindest thing we could do," he added as Buckholtz stalked away. "Any man that full of himself has got to be constipated."

A smattering of giggles rippled through the couples eavesdropping around them. Silver hardly heard them above her heart. It was still hammering due to her near escape from the dance floor.

"Really, Your *Grace*," she said quickly, grabbing one of Rafe's glasses as her next line of defense. Although he maintained a respectable distance, she was aware of his heat, as if it were magnetic, luring her nearer. "You mustn't provoke Buckholtz. He's a crack shot."

His eyes laughed at her above the rim of his glass. "Why, Miss Pennies, I'm touched by your concern."

She scowled, but she refused to dignify his taunt by correcting him. "Yes, well, I wouldn't want Celestia to be deprived of the *pleasure* of your acquaintance. Perhaps it's time we joined her by the—"

"I have a better idea," he whispered wickedly. He ran the tip of his tongue over his bottom lip, presumably to catch a drop of champagne. "Would you like to hear it?"

"Not particularly."

His smirk only broadened. "Ah. Then you'd rather I *showed* you, hmm?"

"Stop it," she hissed nervously, glancing around her for the dozen or more sycophants who, only an hour earlier, had been chomping at the bit to meet a "real live Aristo." Surely, at the very least, Mrs. Trevelyan should be bursting through the crowd, now that Brady Buckholtz wasn't standing here to bully her. "Your behavior is off-putting. Why didn't you stick to our original plan?"

He hiked a brow. "Why didn't you tell me you had a British butler?"

She winced to recall the disaster at the door. Earlier that day, she'd tried to give Benson the night off, but he'd purpled like an eggplant. Why he'd acted so insulted when he could have enjoyed an afternoon of boxing, like he usually did each Saturday behind the Pioneer Saloon, was a mystery.

Then again, Benson had been acting oddly ever since word of Chumley's arrival had "leaked" into the papers. Why, just yesterday morning, while he'd supposedly been fetching the week's mail, she'd instead spied him conferring rather heatedly outside the bank with a man. The stranger had reminded her, of all people, of Aaron—but then, that would have been impossible, since Aaron was back in Pennsylvania. Still, the encounter had struck her oddly. She'd been a half block away when she'd hailed them, and the stranger, turning up his coat collar over his heavily bruised jaw, had hurried away.

Honestly, Benson's fondness for pugilism was earning him the most unsavory-looking friends.

And speaking of unsavory . . .

She glared at Rafe. "Benson would not have been

a problem," she whispered fiercely, "if *you* hadn't claimed to be a duke."

"Never fear, darling. I have matters well in hand."

"I am *not* your darling. Save the sugar-coated lines for Celestia. And speaking of Celestia," she added anxiously, "she is not the fool her costume would have you believe. Our agreement was for you to woo her, but even an *addlepated* gold digger wouldn't prefer your Chumley to my papa! You said you knew how to seduce a woman, but I've only seen evidence to the contrary."

She realized too late that goading him hadn't been her wisest recourse. His eyes glinting with a predatory gleam, he prowled a step closer, lowering his head slowly, deliberately, until his breath teased her pearl earbobs.

"If you truly believe my expertise lacking, Silver, then you'll have no qualms about walking with me in the garden."

Garden was the operative word. It spawned goose bumps all the way from her pearl-trimmed bodice to the fingertips encased in her white evening gloves.

"Out of the question. I won't have you weaseling out of the next waltz—with Celestia," she hastened to add.

"Very well. I'll meet you in your boudoir in half an hour."

Her hand shook, nearly spilling champagne down her indigo satin skirts and all over the ridiculous but sinfully tight gold velvet of his breeches. He wouldn't dare . . . would he? Surely not with Papa's bedroom down the hall!

Still, she wished she'd been less fastidious about keeping dogs, especially great big menaces with thumb-long fangs.

"I'll scream this house down around your ears if you *ever* set foot outside my bedroom door."

"East wing or west wing?" he purred.

"Ooh!"

Rafe laughed inwardly to see how he was stretching his coconspirator's tether. It amazed him that she'd suffered his jibes this long. Either he was losing his touch, or she was more desperate than he'd imagined.

The notion that her desperation might stem from an honest love of her father discomfitted him. Certainly she'd worn her feelings for her mother on her sleeve. Rafe had been surprised—downright moved, in fact—to see how hurt she'd been when Max had proclaimed Celestia his true love. Even if the sentiment were true, announcing it in front of Silver had been inexcusable.

As if it were yesterday, Rafe could recall how Jedidiah used to vilify his mother and how it would enrage him. He'd been too young, too weak, too responsible for her fall from grace to champion her effectively, and he'd never forgiven himself for those failings. Thus, when Max had implied his first wife was nothing more than a passing fancy, Rafe had known the pain Silver was feeling. She'd tried valiantly to hide it, of course, but he'd known. And he'd understood.

It had been a disturbing lapse into sentiment.

That's why Rafe was so determined to put himself at odds with Silver. He couldn't afford to start thinking of her as someone with hurts, fears, and insecurities—in short, someone who needed a champion. He wasn't any good at playing the knight in shining armor. Not in real life, anyway. Heroes didn't have unredeemable souls.

Besides, he thought a tad righteously, he mustn't forget how Little Miss High Society had set him up. If it was a fool Silver wanted, it was a fool she was going to get. After all, he wasn't wearing chartreuse because he was fond of it.

Unfortunately, Benson chose that moment to reappear and spoil Rafe's fun. Wearing a dire expression and splatters of chocolate sauce, the butler leaned toward his mistress's ear. Silver grew paler than the ocean gems that winked so enticingly from her bodice. Making her excuses, she hurried toward the kitchen.

Too bad, Rafe mused, watching the blue-black sheen of her satin snake around her arresting, gloriously long legs. The first strains of the "Blue Danube" were just being struck.

Left to his own devices, Rafe saw no sense in forcing himself to make Celestia's acquaintance. Too many other, wealthier marks were eager to make his. So, taking center stage opposite the musicians' gallery, he shamelessly held court, spinning ever more outlandish yarns about Chumley's western travels. He told himself he did all this showboating to annoy Silver.

But the simple truth was, Rafe loved attention. He'd been starved for it as a child, and he'd never quite been able to appease that hunger. His father had hated him; Michael had resented him; his mother had been torn between her shame and her pity for him. He'd been so used to recriminations and ridicule that during his stage debut, when Fred had forced him to play Juliet in the balcony scene and thus spare Fiona her fear of heights, Rafe had accepted the ensuing barrage of vegetables as his just deserts.

But then something miraculous had happened.

Something that had dazzled his mind and enchanted his soul. His wig and veil had toppled over the railing, and the boos had turned to laughter. Fred, not realizing the sudden cause of mirth, had shaken his fist at the audience, shouting for "the blighters to respect the bard." But Rafe, caring little for Shakespeare, had flung off the rest of his costume and, in self-defense, had started batting cabbage heads back into the audience with a handy length of wood. The audience had roared; Fred had been upstaged; and Rafe had found his calling. That night, he'd fallen asleep during the chill of a Louisville winter dreaming of the warm, heady sensation of applause.

So, buoyed by the adulation of Silver's guests, Rafe vamped. He charmed. He improvised outrageous stories. And the richest, most powerful families in Colorado lavished praise upon him—*him*, a bastard by every definition of the term.

Of course, Silver's snooty friends all thought he was the Duke of Chumley. But that realization did little to sour the sweetness of his glory. He'd long ago grown used to the idea that he would never be admired, much less loved, for playing the part of Raphael Jones.

It was during the height of his self-aggrandizement that the musicians wheezed the final strains of the "Virginia Reel." When they struck up another polka, Rafe groaned to himself. Silver's moonstruck papa was clearing a path for Celestia all the way through Rafe's human wall of defense.

Halting at Rafe's boot toes, Max beamed up at him, boyish and flushed from his most recent dance. "Cellie's ready for another jig," he announced, squeezing his bride-to-be's hand. "You up to it, Chumley?"

Rafe glanced furtively around the room, saw that

Silver was smirking at him, and mentally cursed. Apparently Max's jig idea had been hers. Dredging up a sappy smile, he turned once more to face Max. "My dear fellow." He bowed in his best imitation of a complete idiot. "I wouldn't dream of depriving you of a jig with Madam Celery."

Cellie tipped her pudgy chin to regard him. Despite her abundance of blue eye shadow, lip ointment, and rouge, she wasn't quite as garish as he'd first imagined. In fact, she was passably pleasant-looking—for a squat woman who sported peacock feathers, harem pants, and slippers whose toes curled up like a genie's. On her arms, she wore more silver bangles than he could count. He wondered fleetingly if each one was made of sterling. He wondered, too, if Max had gifted her with the obscenely large amethyst that nestled in the folds of her turban. The headdress listed slightly aft, and he couldn't help but be amused to glimpse the incorrigible blonde corkscrews that had slipped out, tangling in the silver hoops that dangled from her ears.

Max was chuckling. "*Madam Celery!* Ain't that a hoot, Cellie? I told you this Chumley fella was a real ripsnorter."

Cellie flashed an enigmatic smile. "The spirits said you would come, my dear." Her voice was a bit raspy, reminding Rafe of unbuttered toast. "We are so very pleased you're here."

Rafe arched an eyebrow. So he'd pleased the spirits, eh? That must've been a first. "Wouldn't have missed it for the world, madam," he drawled. "Can't say I've met many necromancers."

"Chumley talks to a ghost too," Max eagerly told his fiancée. "Says he goes by the name of Sir Harry. Ain't that right, Chumley?"

"Alas, dear chap, I never did learn to talk to spirits. But I sure do like to drink 'em!" He gave a loud guffaw, and all his fawning new friends joined in. He grinned to see Silver's face darken. She was glaring daggers at him from Celestia's wicker lair.

Then he found himself meeting Cellie's eyes, two gray orbs of startling clarity. They caught him by surprise. He hadn't expected them to be quite so . . . discerning.

"We have more in common than you might think," she said with another one of her mysterious little smiles.

Now *that* was a disturbing notion, Rafe mused dryly. Poor Cellie was going to hell, too.

As if guessing his thoughts, she reached up and patted his cheek. "You're a dear boy," she crooned. Then she ran a critical eye over his sideburns. "I'll have Max send you to his barber. Mr. Perry knows just what Silver likes."

Once more, Rafe was taken aback. Before he could make sense of this peculiar comment, though, he heard a rather testy throat-clearing going on behind him.

Speak of the devil, he thought in growing amusement.

"Papa," Silver said crisply, "you mustn't hoard Celestia all night long. Not after your guests came all this way to meet her."

" 'Tis true," Rafe said jovially. "You two lovebirds need to run along and share your joy with the Trevelyans. And the Underhills. Or were they the Overhills? Dash it all, I can't recall. Say, Miss Pennies"—he gave her a lascivious wink—"are you ready to show me how to hoof it?"

She stiffened, her eyes flashing in that fiery way he

was coming to relish. "I don't 'hoof it,' " she bit out.

"Why the devil not?"

"Silver's not much good at having fun, are you, my dear?" Cellie asked kindly.

Max nodded, rolling his eyes for Rafe's benefit.

Silver tossed Celestia a withering glance. "I assure you, Celestia, under the appropriate circumstances I am quite capable of having *fun*—which polkas are definitely not. But perhaps *you* would care to dance with His Grace. I understand a minuet is next on the program."

Cellie laughed. It was a warm, breezy sound with none of the rancor Rafe had assumed she must reciprocate toward Silver. "What would I know about the minuet, my dear? I've never set foot in a finishing school."

Silver made a disgruntled noise. Intrigued by this byplay, Rafe glanced at Max. His eyes were wistful, even sad, until Silver caught him watching her. Then he donned a cheerful smile.

"Hey, Chumley," Max said. "You know where we might find some spiritkeepers? Cellie and me collected a whole slew out by the mine, but it's the damnedest thing. The whole lot of them upped and disappeared."

"Spiritkeepers?" Rafe asked politely, noticing that Silver had turned a charming shade of pink, much the same way she always did when Max mentioned something occult.

"Yep. Can't have a séance without at least twelve good ones—"

"Papa," Silver interrupted hastily, "I really don't think the *Duke* of *Chumley* is interested in rummaging through a sack of ordinary rocks—"

"Now, daughter, those rocks aren't ordinary, as I

keep trying to tell you. Fact is, I got a slew of their cousins in my study. Not to mention a box of superior cheroots imported out of Turkey.''

''You don't say?'' Rafe quipped, suspecting he now knew what Silver had really been doing with that picnic basket.

''They're damned fine with cognac,'' Max added like a man who knew of what he spoke. ''What say you, Chumley? Are you game?''

Rafe grinned to see Silver fume. ''By all means, old chap, lead the way.''

Max's study proved to be a departure from the austere elegance of the rest of the mansion. The room looked less like a millionaire's sanctum sanctorum than a mining camp's general store. Rolls of maps, geological studies, and engineering reports littered Max's desk so thoroughly that Rafe was unable to guess what wood lay underneath. Picks, shovels, and a whipsaw ornamented the walls; earth-stained satchels spilled nuggets of galena onto the winged chairs, which looked comfortably shabby. Rafe's lips quirked as Max cleared a seat, only to cough, waving away a cloud of dust, after he'd plumped a tasseled cushion.

''There,'' he announced with a sheepish grin. ''Right enough even for a duke, I imagine.''

Rafe nodded absently. His attention had already wandered past the rickety, sawbuck table with its collection of butterfly wings to alight on Max's bookshelves. In addition to the requisite *Gold Seeker's Manual* and the inevitable *Alice's Adventures in Wonderland*, Max owned five other titles: *Don Quixote*, *Ragged Dick*, and three adventure novels by Jules Verne. Judging by their tattered corners, the novels were well loved.

''I say,'' Rafe drawled, flipping through *Journey to*

the Center of the Earth and wrinkling his nose to keep from sneezing on the dust, "you've read quite a bit of Verne."

"The man's a damned visionary." Uncorking a decanter, Max jerked his head over his shoulder as he poured. "*Journey* there is my favorite, although I sure do like *From the Earth to the Moon.* Silver thinks space travel is all poppycock, but I think Verne's onto something with his rocketship idea. You ever think about flying to the moon, Chumley?"

Rafe considered, replacing the volume on its shelf. If God had made the sun, moon, and stars like the Bible claimed, then he figured it wouldn't be worth his trouble to fly anywhere. God had a long arm, and the way Rafe understood it, Hell was waiting for him no matter where he wound up dying.

"Odds fish." Careful not to let his cynicism undermine his foppery, Rafe sauntered toward the battered humidor Max was holding open for him. "You can't mine silver out of celestial Swiss cheese, old chap. Only that bloody earl of Sandwich would relish a vacation to the moon."

Max pinkened at Rafe's pun, but he laughed good-naturedly and selected a cigar for himself. "Well, I reckon it'll be another hundred years before anyone gets to taste moon cheese, anyway. At least, that's what Cellie says."

Rafe cocked a brow, puffing his cigar against the match Max had struck for him. "Your lady sees folks dining on the moon, does she?"

Max waved noncommittally, a swath of smoke unraveling in his wake. "Oh, she sees all kinds of things. You know what this is?" Rounding his desk, he swept aside a jumble of documents and stabbed a finger at an X on a hand-scrawled map.

Rafe had to admit, he didn't have a clue.

"Why, that's where Dancing Moon cached his treasure. Right smack dab at the center of the earth. Well, almost at the center," Max added exuberantly. "It's at the bottom of Silver's Mine. Legend says Dancing Moon lived deep in the earth, in a crystal cave. The prettiest thing you've ever seen, with an underground river that leads straight to the surface. Shoot, that's why I started digging down there in the first place. Never reckoned I'd strike the mother lode. And now, I got more sterling than I got uses for, at least in this lifetime."

Rafe smiled to himself. Apparently the discovery of Max's richest vein was yet another example of the man's uncanny luck. It boggled the mind to think Max didn't give one whit for anything his miners unearthed except for a few baubles some Indian had stashed in a mythical cave.

"I say, this Dancing Moon fellow sounds like a queer fish," Rare drawled. "I didn't think Indians had much use for treasure, being the migratory sort."

Max shrugged, continuing to squint at the X. He looked like a chubby chimney, the way he was puffing on his cigar. "I reckon he wasn't one of them honest Injuns. The legend says Dancing Moon was an outcast from his tribe, a shaman who spent all his time working magic. He could talk to plants and animals—mountains, too. And one day the mountains told him about a City of Gold being built in the foothills.

"So Dancing Moon journeyed to Cibola," Max continued solemnly, "and didn't like what he saw: great gaudy spires blocking the sun from the sky, withered trees, and empty creek beds. Dancing Moon told Cibola's king to stop building temples because the plants and animals were suffering. When the king laughed, Dancing Moon got so riled, he put a spell on the city to make it invisible. Caravans bringing diamonds and gold from the mines, or fruits and grains from the valley, couldn't find the city gates. And Dancing Moon would only tell the poor caravan drivers how to get home to their valley if they left their treasures in his cave.''

Rafe thought Dancing Moon was a bit of an opportunist.

''A lot of folks in Cibola starved,'' Max continued gravely. ''Others who left the city to seek help never found their way back. In the end, nobody knew where Cibola was but Dancing Moon. And he took the secret to his grave.''

Rafe was hard-pressed not to snort at this last piece of melodrama.

''I say, old chap, where do *you* suppose this Cibola is?''

Max darted him a cagey look. ''Now there's a question for the sages. Dancing Moon must have worked one helluva spell, eh? 'Course, as you and I both know, Chumley, no wrong deed goes unpunished. Cellie calls it The Law of Threes.'' Max puffed out his chest, intoning grandly, '' 'That which you do, be it good or evil, comes back to you three times.' At least, that's what Cellie says happens in the realms of magic. Dancing Moon might have walked away with a king's ransom, but he didn't get to enjoy it. He spent all his time worrying, jealously guarding it from other thieves. Finally, he was buried alive with it in an avalanche. I reckon that's the moral to the story.''

Rafe shot Max a keen glance.

The millionaire's only reaction was a sip on his cognac.

Deciding Max couldn't possibly suspect him, after all, he'd been playing the role of ducal idiot to perfection, Rafe reached for his snifter of cognac. "From what you've told me, my dear fellow, Dancing Moon has good reason to haunt your mine."

Max nodded. "I'm glad you can see the sense in all this, Chumley."

Rafe wasn't sure he'd go *that* far. He did believe that Max believed he had a ghost problem and that Cellie could fix it for him. The poor sot had fallen hook, line, and sinker for the lady's con.

Knowing Max was so easily duped made Rafe uncomfortable. He hadn't set out to like Silver's father. Hell, he knew better than to feel anything but contempt for suckers. But Max was a loveable old fool, and Rafe was beginning to see Silver's dilemma.

Cursing himself for a sap, he flashed his most inane smile and racked his brain for a subtle way to discredit Celestia. "Between the moors and the castles, ghosts are a dime a dozen in Britain, old chap. Cranky, noisy, dispirited buggers, if you ask me. Not a one of them is fond of mortals. They're more likely to wreak havoc than lend a hand. No, I wouldn't put much faith in what this Indian spirit tells you. Dancing Moon sounds like the *last* ghost on earth who'd tell Cellie where to find his treasure."

Max chuckled, giving Rafe a wink. "Not to worry, Chumley. Cellie knows *lots* of spirits. I'm sure she can find one who'd love to spill the beans on Dancing Moon's big secret. There's really not much honor among thieves, 'specially the dead ones."

"Oh, jolly good. Or perhaps I should say Jolly Roger. Dead men *do* tell tales, what?"

Max joined him in a hearty guffaw, which was more than Rafe's abysmal pun deserved. He felt the flush of elation from being so appreciated by his audience. At this rate, he'd be juggling for Max by midnight.

"I like you, Chumley." Still grinning, Max dropped into a leather captain's chair and propped his feet on the map-littered desk. "You're funny. And laughter's in short supply around this house. You have any children?"

Caught off guard, Rafe felt the momentary constriction in his chest. Hell, *children*. He tried not to think about them. After Gabriel's death eight years ago, Sera had insisted that Rafe keep a secret correspondence with her. He'd agreed because he loved her; even so, he couldn't help but worry about his influence over an impressionable kid sister, or any child, for that matter. His was a doomed soul. What kind of legacy could he leave a child—other than shame?

"No," he admitted, his tone betraying more longing than he'd intended. "No children."

Max sighed heavily, twirling his glass stem and watching the flash of amber highlights. Rafe had never seen the man so pensive; indeed, moments earlier, he would have sworn Max didn't have a melancholy bone in his body. Intrigued, he lowered himself onto the lumpy, green-and-blue plaid of a wing chair. Not until the rock dust finally settled did Max rouse himself to speak.

"Silver's . . . well, she's changed. She's not as happy as she used to be. Back in Philly, I mean. Out east, she'd caught the eye of a bright young man, he'd come from good stock . . ." Max's voice trailed off, and he shook his head. "Everything seemed to be going well, judging by her letters. But then, like a bolt out of the blue, she wanted to move west. I never could understand why. She wouldn't talk about it much."

Max waved toward the inky, star-speckled night beyond the window. "I mean, look around you, Chumley. I'm a grizzled old miner, and Aspen's not exactly high society. There's not much here to offer a well-bred city girl like Silver. Hell, five years ago when she came here, the best lodging I could offer was a tent. Meanwhile, Townsend— that was her sweetheart's name, Aaron Townsend— he was building on his daddy's ironworks fortune. Folks said he had a knack for politicking. He's already snared a congressional seat in the Pennsylvania legislature."

Rafe arched a brow. So Silver had left her hoity-toity beau to live with her papa? In a tent? *Interesting*. Rafe couldn't help but wonder why. He had a hard time picturing a mining-camp Silver, hammering stakes into the earth, scrubbing clothes on a boulder, pouring flapjacks on a flame-licked griddle . . .

"Silver must be devilishly fond of you," Rafe murmured as these visions began to fade. The genuine warmth in his voice surprised him.

Max's eyes twinkled, hinting at their old mischief. "That's just it, Chumley. My daughter's *too* fond of me." He rubbed out his cigar on his boot heel. "I reckon Silver means well, but we don't see eye to eye. Especially about Cellie. Silver wants me to be respectable in this pissant town. Hell, I just want to hunt treasure and love my woman. A son would understand a man's needs, but a daughter . . ." He grimaced. "It's gotten so that I have to sneak out the back door of my own house!"

Rafe nodded sympathetically, somehow managing not to laugh. That sounded like Silver, all right.

"It's a sad state of affairs," Max grumbled, "when a man can't even, uh, *entertain* his fiancée in the privacy of his quarters. Here I am, walking around as guilty as a schoolboy, and I'm the parent in this house!" He reddened, smiling sheepishly at his outburst. "What it all comes down to, I reckon, is that Silver needs a distraction."

"A distraction?" Rafe asked mildly.

"Sure. Something to take her mind off fornicating—well, off mine, anyway. Don't get me wrong, Chumley. I love my daughter. Think the world of her, in fact. She's sharp as a tack. Knows her way around a dig. Good company in a rainstorm, too. It's just that . . . well, these days, she's a bit of a nuisance."

Rafe did a masterful job of keeping the grin off his face. "I daresay a grown daughter *would* be a tad inconvenient," he commiserated. "Females can get persnickety when it comes to a gentleman's romance."

"You catch my meaning?"

"Oh, quite."

"Good." Setting down his cognac, Max leaned across his desk. In an uncharacteristically bold manner, he raised his eyes and drilled Rafe with a stare of sapphire steel. "Chumley," he said bluntly, "how'd you like to marry my daughter?"

Chapter 7

~~~~~~~~◯◯◯~~~~~~~~

Rafe nearly choked on his cognac. "Marry her, you say?" How he kept from laughing at this latest proposition from a humbugging Nichols, he'd never know.

"Silver's a helluva gal," Max insisted. "You won't find any better. And I saw the way you eyeballed her. You're not opposed to her looks."

Rafe's jaw nearly hit the carpet. Max had watched him leer at Silver? And Max hadn't run for the nearest shotgun in paternal outrage?

"Why, this . . . this is all very sudden," Rafe managed to gasp.

"You saw the kind of shindig she throws," Max countered hastily. "I hear shindigs are popular among you blue bloods back in London. And Silver's real refined. She's got class. You won't have to worry about her dancing a reel when she should be dancing a jig, or some such thing. Why, she graduated with honors from Miss Trudy Pureheart's Finishing School in Philadelphia. She can play the piano, and bake tea cakes, and embroider like a dream. She's even got a knack for arranging flowers. You can't hardly go wrong with references like that."

"I daresay you're right," Rafe agreed, dangerously

141

close to guffawing. Imagine Silver's father handing her over to him on, well, a *silver platter*!

"What's more, my Silver's got a heart of gold. Loyal to a fault, she is," Max boasted, his swelling chest straining the buttons of his waistcoat. "And she's strong. Healthy, too. You won't find her swooning at the drop of a hat or boo-hooing when the going gets tough, like some of those whey-faced, East Coast debutantes. Criminy, I don't know how that fool Townsend let her slip through his fingers. But Townsend's loss'll be your gain, my boy. That girl of mine'll be richer than King Midas after I pass on.

"Not that I plan on kicking the bucket any time soon," Max amended hastily. "But she'll have a sizeable dowry, one big enough even for a duke, I reckon. Shoot, I'll even throw in one of my mines. You've been wanting to learn the business, right, Chumley? Well, I can teach you. We'll be partners. You, me, and Silver. God knows, that girl knows more about smelting and assaying than I do. Whaddaya say, Chumley? You game?"

Rafe struggled to keep a straight face. He thanked God Max could only read his expressions, not his mind. Poor Papa hadn't yet realized he was offering his lamb to the proverbial wolf in sheep's clothing!

If he had one whit of conscience left, Rafe chided himself, he would confess immediately that he was a cad and a playactor.

Fortunately, he was clean out of whits.

"Sink me." Rafe dabbed at his eyes. They were trickling with mirth. "I'm moved, old chap. Genuinely touched. That you would consider me a candidate for your son-in-law is . . . well, more than I deserve."

"Like I said, Chumley, I like you. You're the best

thing that's happened to Silver in a long time.''

''I am?''

''Sure. I saw how she looks at you.''

Rafe's brow arched at that. He was almost tempted to ask when. Fortunately, even his vanity had its limits. A fortune was at stake. He had to play his cards carefully. Staying on Max's good side might be the only thing that saved him from the penitentiary when Silver tipped his hand. *If* Silver tipped his hand, he mused, his ready humor rising to the fore. After all, he wasn't the only one with everything to lose in this game.

''There's just one other thing, Chumley,'' Max said so solemnly that Rafe's survival instincts snapped to attention. ''We ain't got any kind of deal unless you make my little girl happy.''

The older man fixed him with a dire stare, and Rafe flinched, feeling acutely base once more.

''Shower her with roses and fofarrow, fine wines, and love poetry,'' Max said, his underlying warning hard to mistake. ''I expect you to woo her in style. Hell, I don't have to tell you what a woman like my Silver likes.''

''No indeed,'' Rafe murmured.

''And just so there can't be any misunderstanding between us, Chumley, I expect you to keep your mouth shut. About our deal, I mean. Silver will never marry you if she thinks the whole thing was my idea. She's stubborn that way.''

Rafe averted his eyes. For the first time since he'd started this con, the magnitude of his deception sank in. If he married Silver, would he have to play this asinine duke for the rest of his life? In private, as himself, he had no doubt of his ability to seduce Silver. He hadn't yet met a woman who could remain impervious to his charm. But *marriage* to her, for God's sake. He'd only toyed with the idea until now, and he certainly hadn't toyed with it in any context other than his *own* wretched identity. As little as he liked Raphael Jones, was he ready to sacrifice the bastard entirely?

"As a gentleman, I'm sure I shall do everything in my power to satisfy your daughter," Rafe said, careful not to let too much irony drip from his words. "But what if she doesn't take to the idea, old chap? I'm amenable to trying. Silver is, as you say, a rare gem, but a woman's heart is a fickle thing. She might not have the least interest in marrying me."

Max waved a dismissive hand. "You'll just have to get more chummy with her, Chumley. Tell you what. Why don't you move into the guest wing to make it more convenient-like? I'm sure, with the right kind of encouragement, my daughter will like you just fine. You're a pleasant-looking man. You've got good breeding, a sense of humor, a keen wit . . . Silver's not any kind of fool, you know."

That was the one thing Rafe *was* worried about.

"Just you be sure she falls head-over-heels in love with you, son. That's the important part. Even after the nuptials, I want my baby girl singing your praises. I won't stand for anything less. And if I hear one little peep out of her about you not treating her like the thoroughbred filly she is, well . . ." Max's round face actually grew ominous. "I'll thrash you within an inch of your life. And don't think I can't do it, Chumley."

Rafe glanced at the chapped and calloused hands resting on the desktop and recalled that Max still swung a pickax. He suspected the stocky millionaire could indeed beat the tar out of him, if given a

chance. But Rafe had no intention of giving Max a
chance, much less a reason. Why would he? The man
had just offered him a multi-million-dollar silver
mine, a partnership in his family business and, most
mind-boggling of all, his paternal blessings if Rafe
were to seduce his daughter into matrimony. For the
first time in his life, Rafe thought he might die and
go to heaven.

Unfortunately, his practical side reminded him that
he couldn't play Chumley forever. One way or another, he'd be found out. Then Max would never
stand for the wedding. And Silver . . . well, she'd be
happy to wash her hands of him. Inevitably, he'd be
forced to disappear like he always did to avoid sher-
iffs, marshals, and those pesky Pinkertons.

In the meantime, Rafe thought, brightening at the
prospect, he could have a lot of fun at the Nicholses'
expense. He wondered how much money he could
scam out of Max and Silver. Seeing how they were
both using him to scam each other, it only seemed
fair that he earned a tidy sum for his cooperation.

"Pish posh," Rafe said in jovial tones. "There's
no need for thrashing, old boy. Devilish messy. Billiards are so much tidier between gentlemen, don't
you agree?"

Max's eyes twinkled, belying his attempt to appear
foreboding. "Poker's tidier still."

"Ah, poker," Rafe drawled with a lopsided grin.
"The sport of the self-made Colonial. What a smashing idea. When in Rome, do as the Romans . . ."

Max chuckled, a warm and amicable sound.
"You're all right, Chumley." Opening a desk drawer,
he pulled out a box of black and scarlet markers.
"There're a couple fellows in the back room you

might like to meet. Especially if you're set on making a fortune in this town.''

"You don't say?"

"Not in front of Silver, I don't."

It was Rafe's turn to chuckle. "I take it she frowns upon gaming?"

"You've gotta spend money to make money, Chumley. That's my motto."

"And the opening ante?"

"A thousand bucks."

Rafe smiled like the Cheshire cat. Just imagine the profit he could fleece from Aspen's millionaire tin-horns. "I'll consider it an investment."

"You do that, my boy," Max said heartily, winking as he rose. "All's fair in love and poker."

Clutching his box of chips under one arm, Max linked his other with Rafe's and guided him toward the rear of the study. Rafe was at first surprised, then amused, to spy a narrow door in the maple-wood paneling. It had been effectively camouflaged, thanks to the shadow of an enormous elkhorn trophy. He suspected that Silver wasn't supposed to be privy to her papa's high-stakes amusements. Bless his rascally soul, Midas Max was nothing more than an ordinary mountebank.

This realization warmed Rafe's heart, making him like the mining baron even more. Poor Silver. She was so smitten by her papa that she didn't know he was bamboozling her.

Max threw open the door, and a cloud of cigar smoke rolled into the study. The clink of crystal and the gruff rumble of male voices could be heard somewhere beyond the eye-stinging assault of tobacco. Rafe cast a sideways glance at his host. God was clearly falling down on the job, letting Rafe have so much fun. Who would have thought he'd find a kindred spirit in a millionaire? Why, the man was willing to board a beau to keep his daughter distracted from his amorous mischief.

And speaking of mischief...

"I say, old fellow," Rafe drawled as they stepped into the antechamber, "are you fond of baby otters?"

Somehow, Silver survived her night of living horror—no thanks to Rafe. From the moment he'd arrived, he'd sabotaged her plans. As if his ridiculous whiskers and that odious quizzing glass hadn't been bad enough, he'd invented the story about his grandmummy's haunted castle. Between his tales of Sir Harry, the Pied Piper of hapless sheep, and Papa's stories of an Indian spirit wreaking havoc in her mine, was it any wonder she'd dreamed again of Dancing Moon?

Glaring at her sleep-starved eyes in the looking glass, Silver carefully disregarded the thought that maybe she really *was* being haunted. Even if she had believed in ghosts, she couldn't imagine why one would waste its time trying to frighten her with feathers and acorns. If she were a ghost, and inspiring terror was her mission, she would get right to business, moaning and rattling chains.

Of course, she was a practical woman, and that would have made her a practical ghost. Maybe Dancing Moon was a bit addlepated.

She scowled once more at her reflection.

That was just the point, she reminded herself tartly, dabbing a touch of rose water behind each ear. She was a *practical* woman. Although the mysterious appearance of last week's eagle feather was easier to reason away than last night's acorns, she had no doubt

there was a logical explanation. After all, hadn't Rafe
tried to finagle an invitation to her bedroom?

Silver nodded emphatically at this memory, because it was so much more plausible than the delusions she'd suffered at two o'clock that morning,
when she'd imagined herself watching an outraged
Indian warrior break an oak limb over his knee and
scatter acorns all over her window seat.

Yes. Rafe was to blame for her misery *and* those
blasted acorns. She'd concluded that while she'd been
busy in the kitchen last night, he'd sneaked upstairs
and left his strange little calling card. No doubt he'd
thought himself too clever for words, and he'd be
right. What on earth were the acorns supposed to sig-
nify? His virility?

She blushed at the thought. *His virility indeed.* If
she weren't so mad at him, she might have been . . .
well, unnerved. The thought of him prowling around
her bedroom in the moonlight, leaving tokens remi-
niscent of some pagan fertility rite, was enough to
make her knees go weak.

Unfortunately, that weakness wasn't due entirely to
uneasiness.

Silver shook off that traitorous notion. The last
thing she needed was the distraction of Raphael Jones
when she had a miners' strike to avert. Her accomplice was in need of a comeuppance, and she had
every intention of giving it to him—right after she
dealt with the blackguards who were trying to extort
her.

Silver grimaced as she coiled her heavy mass of
hair into a knot at the nape of her neck. Her head was
splitting, and she was running behind schedule. She
abhorred being late, not that she had any great desire
to rush off to a meeting with the Miners Union, but

she did pride herself on setting a good example for her employees.

Besides, those pesky reporters, who had nothing better to do than invent half-truths, would tout her tardiness as proof of supernatural troubles in her mine. She could just throttle Rafe for encouraging Papa to prattle on about Dancing Moon and toppled lunch pails in front of Brady Buckholtz. Union leaders would pounce on such rubbish as proof that their members were being abused.

Jabbing a pin into her jaunty black beaver hat, Silver arranged its blue veil over her chignon and grabbed a parasol before hurrying for the door. She was so preoccupied with thoughts of her impending negotiation that she didn't notice the ruddy-faced youth in the scarlet livery racing toward her from behind. In fact, she didn't hear his thundering footsteps until they jolted the stairs beneath her feet.

"Make way, miss," the youth panted, his cheeks nearly as red as his jacket. "Gotta draw a bath for Miss Tavy."

Jostled against the stairwell's banister, Silver barely had time to gasp "Miss who?" before the youth shouldered past her and galloped like a runaway bull down the hall toward the kitchen.

"How rude." She narrowed her eyes after the young man who'd flattened her to near pancake width in his zeal to serve his mistress. "And just who, might I add, are—"

"Miss Silver."

She winced, recognizing the testy tones of her butler. Benson stood stiffer than petrified wood at the foot of the stairs, glaring up at her as if *she* were the one who'd just committed some heinous breach of etiquette.

"Uh, good morning, Benson."

"Good morning, miss. May I have a word with you?"

Stepping down to ground level, Silver glanced impatiently at the hall's grandfather clock. It read ten minutes after eight. "Can't it wait, Benson? I'm rather pressed for time right—"

"It's about your father."

Silver groaned inwardly. *Of course it was.* Benson always wore that dire expression when he was miffed at Papa. No doubt Papa's attempts to get Benson to dance a waltz last night—with her, no less—had been the final straw.

Silver cleared her throat, remembering the servant's mortified expression when Papa had shoved them toward the dance floor. Humiliated and secretly hurt, she'd interpreted Benson's reaction as a slur upon her breeding. Thanks in part to Papa, she supposed her butler would never consider her *haut monde.*

She did her best not to care.

"Benson, please be patient with Papa. He was in unusually high spirits last night, celebrating his"— she tried not to choke on the word—"engagement."

"Last night is another matter, miss, which I had hoped to address with you," Benson said with cool diplomacy. "As for *this morning*, however, I must protest on behalf of the staff. Cook cannot hope to find enough frogs' legs to fill such an impossible breakfast order, and we do not have enough water on hand to refresh a copper bathtub every two hours—"

"Papa wants to bathe every two hours?"

"Not exactly, miss."

"Comin' through, folks!" bellowed the red-faced servant as he kicked open the dining room doors and hurried back through the foyer, a sloshing pail of water gripped in either fist.

"Benson," Silver murmured, watching in alarm as the youth splashed puddles onto the beeswaxed cherrywood of her floor, "would you mind telling me just exactly who—"

"Hullo, miss." Skirting Benson's formidable spine, the youth gave her a toothy grin. "Jeepers, you sure are ragged out today."

Arching a brow at this awkward compliment, Silver watched the ruddy anomaly with the golden epaulets climb her stairs and disappear into the guest wing of her home.

"*That*, miss," Benson said in arid tones, "is Mr. Jimmy Bob Roy, Miss Octavia's . . . er, groomsman."

Silver's brows knitted. "Miss Octavia?"

"The duke of Chumley's ward."

Silver choked, suspecting she'd turned beet red as her gaze flew back to Benson's. "The duke has a . . . a *ward*?"

"Alas yes," Benson said dryly. "Perhaps you should speak to your father about the sort of, er, *gentleman* he is entertaining for the summer."

"*For the summer?*" Belatedly, Silver realized she was gaping at this latest example of Rafe's audacity. "Now Benson," she forced herself to say more mildly, her hands itching to box the ears of a certain playactor she knew, "I'm sure you and the duke just got off on the wrong foot last night."

"Your pardon, madam." Benson's spine never broke its rigid line as he bowed. "But that is precisely the point. There is no duke of Chumley. And even if there were, I assure you, no duke would hire a . . . a *pumpkin* picker as his manservant."

"You mean melon picker," came Rafe's impossibly cheerful voice from the open front door. "Jimmy picks cantaloupes, Bennie, old boy. Pumpkins are gourds."

Silver frowned, spying the rogue himself in a lavender waistcoat and pink vest as he leaned against the jamb. Somehow, he looked more dapper than clownish as he braced a strong, arrestingly masculine hand against the doorframe. Of course, the wind-tumbled curl across his intelligent brow did give him an advantage compared with last night's slickened hair style. So did the wolfish gleam in his pewter eyes.

She tried to concentrate on his insolence, not the kindling admiration in his gaze as it swept intimately over her traveling suit. The man had some kind of gall, tricking Papa into housing a floozie for him, then devouring *her* with his eyes, as if she were the proverbial icing on his cake! Hiking her chin, she carefully ignored the spike of jealousy that pricked her heart. She had just enough time to wonder how long Rafe had been eavesdropping on her and Benson before Papa's head bobbed under the open window.

"That's right, Bennie," Papa called, leaning beneath the sash. "Last night, Chumley explained all about getting his dukedom. Reckon you'll feel more at home now, having a real live royal to serve for meals. How're you coming with those frog legs?"

Benson looked like he might spout steam from his ears.

"Uh, Papa," Silver interceded, "to what do we owe the honor of His Grace—" she tossed Rafe a withering look "—and His Grace's *ward* as guests in our home?"

"I couldn't have one of our biggest investors wasting all his money on a hotel room, now could I?"

Papa winked at Rafe, and Rafe winked back, much to Silver's irritation. It was bad enough that she'd found the two of them in cahoots last night, running a high-stakes poker game. They were obviously conspiring again. She didn't know which was worse: that her papa could be so easily bamboozled by a tale as transparent as a ward named Octavia, or that Rafe had somehow charmed her papa into letting him move in. But more to the point, just how did Rafe think he was going to seduce Celestia if they weren't rubbing shoulders in the same hotel?

The clock chimed a quarter after the hour, and Silver muttered an oath. As much as she wanted to scold the living daylights out of Rafe, she didn't have time now.

"Thank you, Benson, for your, uh, attention to these matters," she said crisply. "I'm afraid I'll have to leave the frog-legs matter in your capable hands." She gathered her nerve and swept toward the door—and right into the devil's own playground.

"I say," Rafe drawled, raising his quizzing glass and refusing to move out of her way. "What a smashing chapeau. I do believe you and Madam Cellie could be setting the millinery fashion for ghost-chasing all over the Colonies."

Despite his affected manner, Silver heard the rumble of sensuality in his voice, felt the provocative throb of his heat. They stood boot toe to boot toe, and only she could see the wicked invitation behind the lashes veiling his gaze. She hated that her heart quickened in response . . . and that her palms grew moist.

"Ghost-chasing?" she repeated sharply. She hoped to appear more stern than flustered, despite the quickened flutter of lace at her throat.

He smiled his rogue's smile, letting only one dimple crease the corner of his mouth. "Why, yes. Tally-ho, and all that. We've been chomping at the bit, waiting for you to rise and shine and finish your beauty ministrations, my dear. But the devil take me if it wasn't worth the wait. Don't you agree, Max?"

"Sure do!"

"Cellie even packed a picnic lunch," Rafe crooned.

Silver started. The indignation she'd been feeling because he'd left acorns in her room, then had ensconced his mistress in her guest wing, had come back full force, only to be melted away in an even hotter blast of ire when she heard him speak the name of her nemesis.

"Cellie?" she bit out, too upset for the moment to consider that she was actually jealous, not angry.

"Over here, dear," Cellie called absently.

It was then that Silver looked beyond Rafe and spied Celestia, dressed in full mining gear and a peach turban, sitting on the porch steps and staring into a teacup. Celestia waved a distracted hand, all the while mumbling to a young man who listened eagerly to her predictions about the sweetheart he would someday marry. A camera and tripod were balanced across his lap.

"Papa," Silver asked suspiciously, watching him cross the porch to kiss his fiancée's cheek, "you *are* accompanying me to the Union meeting this morning, aren't you?"

He started guiltily, and she bit her tongue on an oath.

"Papa! We're supposed to meet with the Union in half an hour."

"Uh, right. The Union. I was sort of hoping you could stall them, daughter."

"*Stall* them?" She gritted her teeth. "Papa, please don't tell me you forgot about the negotiations."

" 'Course I didn't forget, daughter. But I figured it would be best if you held down the fort while Cellie and me met with the engineers to inspect the timbering for poltergeists. Brady sent his photographer along to help."

Silver felt the blood drain from her face. "You invited the *Times* photographer to . . . to document poltergeists?"

Papa beamed. "Actually, it was Chumley's idea. And a damned fine one too, if you ask me."

"Indeed?" She glared at Rafe.

He winked back. "Not to worry," he said in a rascally undertone. "No matter how fast Brady's boy is with his shutter, he isn't likely to catch a ghost. Seems like we can use his photographs to our advantage."

Silver choked back her protest, especially about the "we" and "us" Rafe had so casually used, as if counting himself among those who had a vested interest in her mine. As much as she hated to admit it, Rafe's strategy had merit. If the publicity stunt went according to plan, she would have a newspaper photographer and his pictures to refute the miners' claims.

Still, Rafe didn't have to look so smug. It made her think he had more up his sleeve than the salvation of her mine, which was probably a safe bet, she mused, wrinkling her nose. She stepped aside, letting a pair of hired hands huff across her threshold with a battered traveling trunk and a sealed barrel smelling unmistakably of fish.

Rafe accompanied her onto the porch. "I say,

Max," he called in boisterous good spirits, "now that we have these two lovelies together in such fine ghost-chasing chapeaus, why don't we have their photographs made?"

Papa's blue eyes sparked eagerly. Silver cringed. She could almost read his mind: his daughter and his fiancée at long last calling a truce over hats.

"You mean a 'Before They Ventured into the Haunted Pit' sort of photo?"

"Papa." For the photographer's benefit, Silver forced a smile. "I am not at liberty to dally this morning. If you insist on going to the mine, then I am needed posthaste at our lawyer's office."

"Oh." Papa's face fell. "Well, I suppose that's true."

Silver hated to see his hopes dashed; she hated even more to see Celestia, all a-flurry and disturbingly convincing, wrap her arms around his waist.

"We'll get a photograph of me and Silver at the wedding," Celestia crooned, resting her cheek on Papa's shoulder. She darted a sidelong glance at Rafe. "We haven't so very long to wait now."

Rafe smirked. For once, Silver was relieved to see him do so. Maybe all wasn't lost yet, she thought grudgingly. Celestia appeared to be casting sheep's eyes at him, despite his abysmal fashion sense. Perhaps his dressing like an Easter egg had actually endeared him to the woman, whose own peculiar wardrobe seemed to be borrowed from *The Arabian Nights' Entertainments.* Silver gave her coconspirator a brief, albeit reluctant, smile. After all, he *was* planning on having a picnic that afternoon with Celestia. Acorns and wards notwithstanding, Silver reminded herself sternly, she was paying him to woo Celestia.

"A pity you have to rush off, Miss Pennies," he

purred as she sought to breeze past him. ''I do so look forward to our getting better acquainted. Perhaps later this evening, now that a mere stone's throw keeps us apart?''

Unable to ignore the glint in his gaze, her stride faltered and her pulse leaped. She suspected he was thinking more of acorns than stones.

''Yes, well . . .'' She did her best to sound prim, hoping he wouldn't notice the flush stealing up her cheeks. ''I'm sure we have a great deal to discuss, Your Grace, not the least of which are your living arrangements.''

Swishing past him, she nodded to Papa, then snapped open her parasol. She huddled under its tasseled shade less as a defense against the sun than as protection from Rafe's sultry stare. She could feel the heat of his gaze through every flounce of satin, every scrap of muslin lace, as she hurried along the path to the carriage house. The sensation drove her feet faster.

Somehow, before this day was over, she promised herself, she would hire a locksmith to install a bolt on her bedroom door.

Unfortunately, Silver had little time to think about locksmiths and bolts until well after sunset, when every merchant had closed shop for the day. The meeting with the Miners Union had been unbearably long, and little progress had been made toward a resolution. Mr. Kilkarney, the head of the Union's Irish faction, had demanded to know how she could deny the existence of ghosts when the *Aspen Times* had reported that her father was holding a séance. By the time Papa and Celestia had arrived with the engineer, Union leaders were in such an uproar that the survey results couldn't appease them. One thing had led to another, and Papa, who'd never been good at prevaricating, had blurted an invitation to Kilkarney and the others to attend the spook powwow—not his words precisely, but close enough, Silver mused darkly.

No sooner had she left the Union meeting than the manager of her sawmill had demanded an audience. He'd had dire news about production shortages, and he hadn't been encouraging when she'd announced that she needed additional timber to brace the innards of Silver's Mine. The oak forest she'd purchased in the valley was growing sparse. At this rate, her sawmill would be idle by Christmas, and that wouldn't bode well for the families who relied on her lumberworks for jobs.

Silver sighed, wearily climbing the steps to her porch. If only the earth wasn't so blasted heavy! Solid rock took its toll on wood no matter how well-braced a cavern was. She'd have to speak with Papa about purchasing additional woodlands.

Pausing in the foyer, Silver was relieved when Benson appeared, stepping out of the parlor to greet her. At least fate had deigned to be kind once today: her butler hadn't walked off the job—yet.

"Good evening, Benson. I trust the frog-legs matter has been settled?"

"For the present, miss. Your father has gone to speak with a mountainman."

"A . . . er, mountainman?" she repeated dubiously.

"Yes. To set traps. Apparently when frog legs aren't in season, *Tavy*, as I believe they call her, makes due with crayfish."

"Oh." Silver's brows knitted. *An odd woman, this Tavy.* "Perhaps I should see her. Is the, uh, duke in?"

Benson's nose flared in disdain. "Not to my knowledge."

Silver blew out her breath. Well, so much for calling Rafe to task before dinner.

In his absence, she supposed she could confront this troublesome Octavia. She'd like nothing more than to order the creature to pack her bags, but then Silver had no way of knowing how much Rafe had told her. What if Octavia knew about the plot to seduce Celestia? *Damn Rafe anyway.*

Silver tried to tell herself her outrage had everything to do with Rafe's audacity and nothing to do with the twinge of disappointment she'd felt upon learning he'd attracted a mistress. Just how did he think he could seduce Celestia and entertain a lover all at the same time? Truly, the man's opinion of his virility was a bit . . . intriguing.

Her face flamed at the thought.

Intriguing? Honestly, Silver, what is the matter with you? Raphael Jones is a rogue and a rake, and God knows, you've suffered from that *particular combination before. Get your mind off that track before the train runs you down.*

"Thank you, Benson." Nodding in dismissal, she headed for the stairs. Obviously, the Octavia matter would have to be handled with delicacy. As appealing as the prospect was, barging into the guest suite and tossing the woman out probably wouldn't be her wisest course.

Pausing on the landing, Silver clutched her parasol to her chest, telling herself the brisk climb, not the prospect of confronting Rafe alone again, at night, was the cause of her hammering heart. A hot bath would relax her, she decided, and help her strategize. Besides, as long as Rafe was out of the house, she'd be safe in the indulgence.

She glanced toward the guest wing, and her bottom lip jutted.

She just wished she didn't feel so deflated, knowing he planned to rendezvous with some other woman later that night.

Rafe whistled as he approached the long walkway leading to Silver's porch. Twirling his walking stick, he allowed himself a smug smile as he caught his reflection in the polished brass of the knob. Yes, he was quite the devil, wasn't he? Jedidiah Jones was probably rolling in his grave, a fact that only heightened Rafe's pleasure as he recalled his last twenty-four hours. He'd earned nearly twenty-five thousand dollars after only two hours of poker, all of which he'd come by legitimately, thanks to Max's generosity with his whiskey. Liquor made bettors reckless, especially *wealthy* bettors. Of course, pretending to be drunk, and stupid, had gone a long way toward earning the trust of Max's millionaire cronies. They'd been planning on fleecing him, and he'd turned the tables with a sharp wit and a modicum of patience. In one sitting, Rafe had stuffed more money in his pockets than he'd ever laid claim to in his life. Feeling that wad of banknotes in his trousers had been the closest he'd ever come to a spiritual experience. Hell, he could quit this scam now and live comfortably for the next five years. Of course, he couldn't live in *luxury* for more than two. And he did have a score to settle with Miss Silver Nichols.

Rafe sighed lustily. He supposed he could suffer himself to stay a while longer in Aspen—as long as he kept his wits about him. According to the Windsor Hotel's desk clerk, he'd received several visitors since he'd acquired new lodgings: Mrs. Trevelyan, a *Sun* reporter, Signor Marzetti, and a one-eyed Texican. Apparently they'd all asked questions about him. The reporter had even stooped to poking around Rafe's former suite before the chambermaid could tidy it. If he hadn't been so amused, he might have been annoyed. Apparently all of Aspen was starved for gossip about the duke.

He rapped his walking stick on Silver's door.

"Howdy do, Bennie," he greeted jovially after the butler came to scowl at him. Max had confided that Benson abhorred being called "Bennie." Benson also abhorred disorder, creepy-crawly things, and anything that shed its skin or fur. If Rafe didn't have so much respect for snakes and spiders, he would have ordered up a whole barrel of them to be dumped on the butler's hoity-toity shoes.

"You've returned," the Brit observed distastefully.

"Quite so," Rafe taunted, sweeping past the servant. "I say, is that a wrinkle on your sleeve?"

Benson's gaze snapped to his arm.

"Dear me, and look. A piece of fluff." Rafe knocked an imaginary speck from the man's shoulder. "Don't tell me you've been frolicking with the scullery maids, old boy."

Blazing brown eyes locked with Rafe's. He laughed guilelessly.

"Well, we'll just keep it our little secret, eh, Bennie? How's Miss Tavy? Did she eat all her frogs?"

A muscle twitched along Benson's jawline. "Your *otter*, sir, has *feasted* on her frogs, leaving a barbarous mess to be cleaned."

"Jolly good." Rafe paused with his foot on the stairwell's bottom step. "I say, Bennie," he called over his shoulder, "don't forget to put fresh sand in

Tavy's scat box. I daresay she'll be making rollicking good use of it, if she hasn't already.''

Snickering at his vision of Benson crouching on his hands and knees to scoop up misfired otter droppings, Rafe began his climb to the second story.

Yes, he was quite pleased with himself today. He'd arranged for fifteen thousand dollars to be transferred to Leadville and deposited in a bank account in Fiona's name—not Fred's. Fred would only do something selfish or stupid with it, like trying to salt a diamond mine. Fifteen grand should be enough to buy Fiona her medicine *and* let her and Fred retire in style. If it wasn't, then the old scam artist was herself being scammed.

For the first time in ages, Rafe felt a lightness. He recognized it as relief. Ten years ago, he'd walked out on his foster parents' show, and they'd forever held his feet to the fire, claiming he'd cost them untold ticket sales over the years. Frankly, he couldn't imagine being worth more than ten grand, no matter how riveting his Romeo was, but in any event, he'd settled the debt, throwing in another five grand because . . . well, because he loved the old rascals.

His throat constricted at the thought.

Today was indeed the day to repay old debts. Eleven years ago, on this very day, Gabriel had died. Sera had taken it badly, being only ten. She'd wanted Rafe to stay in Blue Thunder, to fill the shoes of the brother she'd lost. Rafe couldn't do that, of course. Even if he'd been ready to forgive Michael and Jedidiah for every cruelty they'd ever inflicted, their hatred of him still poisoned any hope of a truce. Jedidiah had gone as far as raging to his congregation that Rafe should have been the one in that grave, not Gabriel. And in spite of every wisecrack to the contrary, Rafe had secretly agreed.

So under a midsummer moon, in the freshly turned earth beside Gabriel's grave, he'd had to tell Sera he was leaving again. She'd thrown herself at him, little fists flailing, until he'd been able to wrap his arms around her and let her sob out her heart. He'd felt so useless, so he'd promised to take care of her. He'd vowed on Gabriel's grave that she would always be able to find him, no matter where he traveled.

Michael and Jedidiah, of course, would have forbidden her to receive his letters, so Rafe had made a secret pact with their lifelong neighbor, "Aunt" Claudia Collier, to sneak his correspondence to Sera. Claudia loved mischief, and she'd never made any bones about disliking Jedidiah, so she'd been eager to help. Thus, Rafe had been faithfully writing to Sera, by way of Aunt Claudia, once a month ever since.

If Aspen's 'Express Mail' lived up to its name, Rafe mused, Sera would learn about his latest adventures, slightly censored, of course, by the end of next week. He just knew she'd love the part about him smuggling an orphaned baby otter into the mansion of an heiress. Rafe grinned to himself, but he couldn't quite ignore the catch in his chest. He missed Sera. He regretted not being able to watch her grow up. Judging by her letters, he suspected he and she were a lot alike, a fact that probably didn't endear her to Michael, who'd become her guardian upon Jedidiah's death two years ago.

Damn that holier-than-thou bastard. Jedidiah Jones was finally rotting in his grave, but nothing had changed. He'd passed the torch to Michael.

Rafe scowled as he reached the top of the stairs.

The only things he had to tie him to his sister were a couple dozen letters, and they weren't enough. But until Sera married, or turned twenty-one, Rafe knew he'd be facing Michael's shotgun if he ever dared return to Blue Thunder to see her.

His lips twisted bitterly. He wondered what Michael would say if he knew Rafe had just deposited twenty-five thousand dollars in legitimate earnings in a bank. By Sera's accounts, Michael's medical practice was barely keeping a roof over their heads. If not for Aunt Claudia—she'd paid off Jedidiah's debts, including his mortgage—Michael and Sera would be walking the streets. Michael certainly deserved such a comeuppance, but not Sera.

Rafe sighed. Maybe he should go back to the bank tomorrow and arrange for another ten thousand dollars to be sent to Michael for their kid sister's sake . . .

The sight of his open bedroom door interrupted Rafe's reverie. He frowned. He specifically remembered closing it that morning before walking down the stairs. He'd learned this habit the hard way. Tavy was a master of unlatching her cage, and besides, he didn't have the heart to keep her cooped up like some circus sideshow. Had Jimmy gone to play with her, then forgotten to lock the door?

In ten brisk strides, Rafe traveled the length of the hall and pushed inside his ornately furnished room. The usual otter chaos greeted him: the toppled washstand, a gnawed shaving brush, scattered cigars, a broken vase. Yellow pollen had been tracked in ambling circles to the next mischief site: the white dinner shirt that Silver's housekeeper had pressed for him. It had been liberally trampled beneath the rainbowed glass of the room's vaulted, southern window. The goose-down pillows from his four-poster bed had been scattered across the burgundy and green weave of his Turkish carpet, and a couple of feather tufts stuck out of the carpet's fibers. In the next glance, he ascertained that Tavy wasn't huddled in her cage or crouched in her scat box.

"Damn," he muttered. Closing the door behind him, he hoped against hope that she was still hiding somewhere in the room. "Tavy?" he called, hurrying to the bed. He flipped up the quilt and peered under the mattress. No bright, adoring eyes blinked back at him.

He looked under the maple armoire, beneath the brimming copper bathtub, even inside his well-battered traveling trunk. No Tavy. How the hell was he supposed to find her in a house this size? He cursed again, more vehemently this time. He thought he'd put the fear of God in Jimmy about doors, locks, and otters.

Then a more sobering thought struck him. One that made his gut clench. Had that sonuvabitch Benson sneaked in here out of spite? Had he turned her loose in the streets to be struck by some runaway wagon . . . or mauled by some stray dog?

Rafe's heart crawled into his throat as the gory images flashed through his mind.

"So help me God, Benson," he growled, forgetting his accent as he ran down the hall, "if I find out it was *you* who set Tavy free, there'll be hell to—"

A muffled shriek cut him off. Sliding to a halt by the main stairwell, he gazed toward the bedroom door at the far end of the family's wing. He knew the room was Silver's. He'd taken special pains to learn this information, in fact. He planned on using it to his advantage one night very soon.

Silver screamed again—or was that an oath this time? He strained his ears and heard the muted sound of otter chirping, followed by a rather lusty splash. His lips quirked, and he raced to the rescue.

Tavy, apparently, had been found.

Chapter 8

$\sim\!\sim\!\!\!\!\!\!\!\!\!\!\!\!\!\sim\!\!\!\!\!\!\!\!\sim$

Silver heard the pounding of boots in the hall-way; she heard the rattling of peg lamps and the trembling of brass hinges before the door crashed open, and a very heroic Rafe burst across her threshold.

"Silver!"

She had a breathlessly long heartbeat to stare. For a moment, she forgot her dishabille, her consternation, the *thing* that had fled the bloomers she'd tossed across her bed and that was now rollicking in her bath.

It was as if time started crawling the instant Rafe charged through her door. His sun-gilded features were flushed and anxious; his gray eyes were black with concern. From beneath rakish curls, he gazed wildly about him, as if seeking the cause of her shriek. Despite his lavender waistcoat, he looked every inch the champion, looming larger than life against the backdrop of rose-patterned wallpaper and rainbowed window sashes. His clenched fists and pugnacious pose told her things she hadn't guessed about Raphael Jones: that he was a scrapper, certainly. That he'd survived the ugly side of life, more than likely.

166

But most eye-opening of all was his readiness to defend her, *her*, the woman he took such delight in tormenting. It was a mind-boggling revelation. *Never* had she had a man on whom she could rely. During his precious visits to Philadelphia, Papa had always been more playmate than father, and she'd become resigned at an early age to the fact that she must fend for herself. She'd had to do precisely that against Aaron Townsend.

And yet, here stood Rafe, her scoundrel-for-hire. An unlikely knight in the least daunting armor she'd ever seen, he'd nevertheless raced to her rescue. The knowledge touched her in a dangerously romantic way. For a moment, she was confronted by Raphael Jones the Hero, not the Rogue, and she thought him the most wonderful man in the world.

Unfortunately, the moment passed quickly.

"Silver!" he exclaimed again, striding valiantly to the tub. "Put down the fire poker. You'll hurt her!"

She blinked, somewhat dazed by his command. It wasn't exactly what she'd imagined a champion might say, especially her champion, who'd come to rescue her from the *thing*.

Her senses affected once more by the passage of time, Silver became aware of the bite of iron in the palm of her hand and the tickle of woolen fibers beneath her toes. Her pulse hammered against the fist that clutched the neckline of her dressing gown; her hair spilled across the forearm that had been bared by her voluminous jade sleeve. The caress of cool hall air against her thigh warned her that the paisley fabric was revealing more scandalous vistas of flesh, and she straightened, hoping the shimmering folds would conceal everything north of her ankles and praying the satin was opaque enough to withstand the backlighting of her hearth.

She needn't have worried, though. Rafe wasn't even looking at her.

"Tavy?" he breathed. His face transfused with wonder as the creature chirped and dived, chasing a cake of lavender soap. "You're swimming!"

Silver narrowed her eyes first at Rafe, who, contrary to all his wicked propositions, appeared too enamored of the bewhiskered creature sullying her bath to make good on his threats. She next glared at the animal itself, which was happily sloshing water all over the tarpaulin that, thankfully, she'd spread to protect her Persian rug.

"Tavy?" she choked out. "You mean this . . . this . . ." She hesitated, momentarily bemused. What the devil was the creature, anyway? A rat?

She quailed and retreated a step, tightening her grip on the fire iron. Other than its sleek little body and a disturbingly long tail, the thing was hard to see clearly. It kept splashing and submerging, lobbing bubbles into the air as if it were having the grandest of times wasting her imported French soap. Personally, she'd never laid eyes on a rat, having always prided herself on keeping an impeccable larder, but she wouldn't have put it past Rafe to own a pet rodent. Or better yet, a pet weasel!

"Do you mean to tell me this . . . this water-logged *weasel* is Octavia? Your *ward*?"

He was too busy grinning at the creature to do more than dart her the barest of glances. "Tavy's an otter, not a weasel. And look, she's swimming!"

Silver gritted her teeth. An otter. The rounder had smuggled an *otter* into her house! And Papa had clearly been in cahoots.

She was just about to explode into a denunciation of pests, prevaricators, and papas when Tavy's impish paw slapped the water, showering soap over Rafe. He laughed. The sound was a rumble of pure, unaffected delight. It was her first hint that his roguery sheltered a more innocent nature, and Silver, her breath catching, once again stood transfixed.

Before her eyes, her scoundrel-for-hire had turned sweetly boyish. Gone was the feral cast to his features and the haunted shadow she sometimes glimpsed in his eyes. In that moment, Silver came to understand that her playactor performed a multitude of roles. Beneath the guise of rascal and thief lurked the real Raphael Jones. She couldn't help but wonder if now she was seeing the authentic man for the first time.

She cleared her throat. It was hard not to be smitten by a man who cared not one whit for the soapsuds running down his cheek and into his collar. He simply splashed his otter back.

"Well, of course Tavy's swimming," Silver acknowledged grudgingly. "Otters *do* that, you know."

"Not this otter." Kneeling, Rafe beamed like a proud father as Tavy paddled after a sponge. "Tavy was orphaned. Couldn't have been more than four weeks old when I found her. Otters need their mamas to teach them how to swim. It's not an instinctual part of their nature."

"How . . . do you know that?"

He cast her a sidelong glance. "I've spent a lot of time in the mountains."

"Hiding out from bounty hunters, no doubt."

His dimples flashed at her lofty tone. Still, he didn't deny her charge. "I think a coyote must have killed Tavy's mother," he said, watching the baby pounce. "The rest of the litter starved. I found Tavy huddled beneath the others, trying to keep warm. There was a late snowfall, you see.''

Silver frowned, edging closer to peer over the tub's rim. The baby was now squeaking ferociously, rolling end over end, causing miniature tidal waves to lap onto the tarp as she battled the recalcitrant sponge. ''So . . . you took it upon yourself to be Tavy's mother?''

''Someone had to.'' His jaw hardened. ''All young ones need their mothers,'' he added in a fierce undertone.

Silver frowned. Was she imagining things, or had she heard sorrow beneath that gruff declaration? Until this moment, she'd never thought of Rafe as anything but a bad seed. But even bad seeds had to have mothers—and a mother's love, she realized fleetingly. Had something happened to Rafe's mother? Had he lost her at an early age, like she had lost hers?

Silver's heart twisted. She wondered with uncharacteristic shyness if she should broach the matter, assuring him she'd felt a similar pain following Maria Nichols's carriage accident.

Rafe masked his grief quickly, though, and Silver thought better of her confession, especially when she sensed the return of his mischievous streak. He sneaked a hand behind Tavy and dunked her. The baby sputtered, splashing to the surface. When she gave him an indignant whack with her tail, a lopsided grin quirked Rafe's lips.

''I'll be damned. She's not a cannonball after all. How'd you do it, Silver? How'd you get Tavy to swim?''

He looked up eagerly, giving her his full attention for the first time since bursting through the door. She felt her throat constrict. With the fire shining in his pewter eyes, striking bronze highlights from the sopping, golden strands of his hair, she could imagine the child he must have been, chasing bullfrogs off their lily pads or hollering at the top of his lungs while he'd jumped into a swimming hole. Somehow, in spite of everything he had seen and done to become what he was, Raphael Jones hadn't lost his innocence. And she envied him that. She envied him the youthful pleasure he could take in watching an otter pup chase soap bubbles.

"I didn't do anything," she answered, her voice sounding unnaturally husky. "I was delayed, wiping up the soot your otter tracked out of my hearth, if you must know, and the water got so cool, I had to build a fire to . . ."

Her voice trailed off. She realized, with a nervous thrill, that Rafe's eyes were no longer trained on her face. In fact, he had begun a leisurely inspection of her mussed hair, clinging gown, and bare toes. She could feel the warmth of his stare like a naughty caress, smoothing over her skin, chasing tingles over her breasts and belly. To her embarrassment, her nipples actually puckered, and she hurriedly crossed her arms, making the tender rosettes chafe. *So much for his innocence*, she thought as his appreciative gaze returned to her own. She hiked her chin, thanking God she still gripped the fire poker and praying he couldn't sense her uneasiness.

"Now that the soot has been thoroughly cleaned from Tavy's paws," she said, forcing tartness into her tone, "I'll thank you to remove your otter from my bath."

The corners of his eyes crinkled. He had the most endearing way—no, *annoying* way, she corrected herself quickly—of displaying all those perfect teeth and pulse-stirring dimples when she was doing her best to admonish him.

"I never thought to fill Tavy's tub with lady things to get her to swim," he purred. "Must have been the soap bubbles that did the trick. Lilac-scented, are they?"

She narrowed her eyes at him. "The soap is lavender, if you must know."

"Hmm." He cocked his head, making a great show of mulling over this information. "So you and Tavy both like lavender in your bath. What a quaint coincidence."

Her heart picked up speed as he continued to assess her. Self-consciously, she hugged herself tighter. She couldn't help but think back to that night at the Grand Hotel, when he'd taunted her much more intimately, his lips hovering only inches from hers. His heat had been so intense that her breasts had grown flushed and damp, and the only thing that had kept him from pressing his advantage had been, ironically, his honor.

Or perhaps it hadn't been honor at all, she reflected nervously, but a perverse sense of play. If she were again the mouse to his cat, what was to keep him from pouncing this time?

She grew a little queasy at the thought.

"Are you aware that I forbid pets in this house?" she demanded, desperate to feel in control of a situation that had gone hopelessly awry the moment she'd spied a soot-covered snout poking out of her unmentionables. Now that she stood practically naked before a man who, in spite of his soap-sudded costume, was too self-assured for my peace of mind, the fire poker wasn't bolstering her confidence. What if Rafe were able to wrestle the weapon from her? What if he actually *tried*?

His eyelashes swept lower, veiling the intensity of his gaze, but she instinctively knew he was watching her, perhaps even more closely than before.

"I believe Max did mention your distaste for fleas—something about your bedroll and a mule, as I recall?" Rafe flashed his fallen-angel's smile. "But you see, Tavy's my ward, not my pet."

Silver's face heated as he mentioned her bedroll. She couldn't miss the sultry innuendo in his tone. She wished Papa hadn't told Rafe about the blanket she'd sacrificed to keep the sun off their pack mule's blistered back. In those days, she hadn't had two dollars to buy lye soap, much less a salve to treat mule sores. She'd been clueless how to mix an ointment herself, so she and Papa had tramped nearly a hundred miles, carrying the better part of Billy's load until he healed.

But Rafe didn't need to know that. And he certainly didn't need to know about her sleeping arrangements in the mining camp!

"Ward, pet—I fail to see the difference," she retorted, hoping she sounded less flustered than her flaming cheeks implied.

"I plan on returning Tavy to the wild, once I teach her to fend for herself. So you see, she's hardly a pet." He nodded encouragingly at the baby, which, in a parody of otter fierceness, was crouched on the far rim of the tub, preparing to pounce on the sponge. "It just never occurred to me that Tavy might need a more . . . female influence. How would you like to visit a swimming hole with us tomorrow on Smuggler Mountain?"

"Out of the question!"

Tavy missed her mark. Water sprayed, and the sponge hit the tarp with a soggy *smack*. Rafe chuckled. "Really, Silver, for a woman who once camped out with shovel stiffs, you sure can be persnickety. Max tells me you weren't always that way. He said you used to be fun, that you liked dancing. He said you even used to be good company in a rainstorm. He made that sound like it was a rare talent in a woman." Rafe tilted his head. "Sounds to me like something must have happened," he murmured more gently. "What changed you?"

She stiffened, blinking back tears. She'd been prepared for all kinds of assaults by Raphael Jones, but never once had she thought she'd have to rally a defense against compassion.

"Papa had no right to gossip about me," she said hoarsely, tightening her grip on the fire poker.

"He thinks you hung the moon, Silver."

She raised her chin. The traitorous thing quivered anyway. "What Papa thinks is none of your concern. Nor is it any of your concern how I used to spend my time in Philadelphia. Now kindly remove your otter from my bathwater and your presence from my bedroom!"

The impish glint crept back into his eyes. "You sure you wouldn't like some help, say . . . in scrubbing your back?"

"*Get out!*"

He smirked, pushing up his sleeve. "All right. All right. Tavy and I know when we're not wanted. Don't we, Tavy?"

The baby's ears pricked up at his croon, and she paddled closer, wrapping herself around the bared forearm he'd dunked into the water. He cuddled her close for a moment, then draped her, sopping fur, suds, and all, across the back of his neck. Rivulets of water rolled into his collar, soaking the lace at his throat and the velvet sateen of his waistcoat. Nevertheless, he rose with great aplomb, as if it were an everyday occurrence to have a wet otter nuzzling his cheek. "I fear you've made a poor impression on our hostess," he whispered *sotto voce*.

Tavy sighed happily. When he kissed her snout, with its abundance of catlike whiskers, Silver suffered the most ridiculous pang of jealousy she'd ever known.

Turning once more toward Silver, he pressed his hand to his heart. "Hereafter, in a better world than this, I shall desire more love and knowledge of you," he quoted in the melodious murmur she'd come to associate with his Shakespeare. "*As You Like It*, act one, scene two." He inclined his head. Then he gave her a crooked grin. "A pleasant bath to you, mistress. I'm sure *I* shall never look upon lavender soap, paisley satin, and fire pokers in quite the same way."

With that wicked sally, he sauntered from the room, dripping suds in his wake. Enormous brown otter eyes blinked back at her, and Silver, watching Tavy bob out of sight atop his expansive, paternal shoulders, privately admitted that she would never view Raphael Jones in quite the same way, either.

Rafe reclined in the shadows of Silver's parlor. Despite the care he'd taken to melt into obscurity, a beam of moonlight sliced across his untied cravat and the gaping placards of his shirt. He supposed he could have drawn the hunter green bombazine across the glass, but then, he would have had to unfold his limbs and hoist himself off the velveteen comfort of Silver's settee. He was enjoying Max's imported brandy too much to go to the trouble.

Besides, he rather fancied the glitter of real Austrian crystal in his hand and the gleam of sterling

sconces, knickknacks, and frames on every wall. Like
the thief he was, he preferred darkness to moonlight;
still, he had to admit, Diana's stark, pale beauty
brought a certain fairy-tale charm to a millionaire's
parlor.

He closed his eyes, savoring the brandy and the
perfect stillness of the house. No Benson. No Max.
No sycophants. Only silence, absorbed into his bones
like a balm. He'd forgotten how exhausting it could
be to playact twenty-four hours a day. Ever since he'd
learned he'd been hired to woo a woman old enough
to be his mother, he'd wanted to teach Silver a lesson.
But his impetuous plan to make a fool out of her had
backfired. Max loved the blithering Chumley Rafe
had created, and that meant Rafe was stuck with the
game. At least, he was stuck with it as long as he
wanted to woo Silver without Max's interference and,
in the bargain, earn himself a business partnership
with a millionaire.

Always on guard, always on his toes, he'd had no
choice but to continue his farce over the last ten days.
His asinine "Sink me's" had become the new slang,
and chartreuse, much to Signor Marzetti's horror, had
become the rage. Not a day passed when Rafe
couldn't find at least one report about him in the Society Pages, a phenomenon that had wreaked havoc
on his privacy. Merchants trotted after him like lapdogs; hostesses hounded him with invitations. He
couldn't seem to walk down the street without that
one-eyed Texican and his idiotic sidekick grinning
lecherously at him. Rafe might have reported the nuisances to Marshal Hawthorne if he hadn't been worried the lawman might recognize him from some
dated wanted poster. Now his nerves were on a ra-

zor's edge. The only person whose company he still welcomed was, ironically, Silver.

He sighed, resting his head against the settee's burgundy backrest. While it was true he liked not having to play Chumley for her, he wasn't sure exactly how he'd let her get under his skin. Max's tales of her grit in the face of hardship had both moved and mystified him; perhaps they were to blame.

Or perhaps, he conceded with a trace of self-ridicule, his pride just couldn't abide rejection. It was a sticky game, gambling on his ability to spark her jealousy, to make her want him in her bed before she forced him beyond a mere flirtation with Cellie. In spite of Silver's business approach to their rendezvous, his provocative whispers and wicked innuendoes tempted her. He was certain of it. Her blushes gave her away every time.

Still, seducing Silver hadn't been nearly the child's play he'd anticipated. In fact, she was the first woman who'd ever flat out refused him. He was too accomplished at the game to think the problem might lay with him, although he could kick himself every time he considered that the Chumley he'd created was hindering his progress. Even so, he'd finagled a great many private moments with Silver. Charming, witty, seductive, he'd plied every trick he'd learned from the heroes in Shakespeare's repertoire. He'd given her plenty of opportunities to come to her senses.

So why was little Miss Millions resisting him?

Rafe's lips curved with a touch of cynicism. He'd just have to try harder, he supposed.

Max had confided the other night that his daughter was gun-shy when it came to romance. Well, that had been an understatement. One moment, Rafe would catch her furtively staring at him, her eyes misty with yearning; the next moment, she'd turn stiffer than a railroad spike, her demeanor just about as cuddly. Sometimes he thought her behavior went beyond the bounds of maidenly honor or virginal uncertainty. Sometimes, he thought she was . . . afraid.

Take that night in her bedroom, for instance, when she'd been so appealingly attired in a robe of slinky jade satin. He hadn't subjected himself to Tavy's soapy showers for his health. If Silver had given him the slightest encouragement—say, by discarding that fire poker—he would have had her naked beneath him and moaning his name. But his every instinct had warned him against it. Etched in firelight, her bodice heaving beneath the scalloped edges of her gown, her every muscle quivering like a doe poised for flight, there'd been an unmistakable alarm about her, an alarm that simply couldn't be justified by the presence of an otter in her bath.

Rafe frowned.

Was Silver afraid of *him*?

He wracked his brain, trying to recall something he'd inadvertently said or done to frighten her, because never once had he *intended* to scare her. God knew, scaring her off was the last thing he wanted. He hated to admit it, but on those rare occasions when he glimpsed the authentic woman beneath the hoity-toity facade, he liked what he saw. Hell, if Max's stories could be believed, Rafe even admired her. She'd carried a thirty-pound pack and suffered flea bites to help an ailing mule, for God's sake. Maybe they had more in common than he'd thought, he mused, his memory flitting to Belle.

He grimaced and quickly shoved the hurtful recollection aside. Was it the brandy, or was he getting maudlin?

Still, he had to admit, he'd softened a bit toward
Silver. Because she'd duped him, failing to mention
Cellie's age, he'd wanted to teach her that Raphael
Jones was nobody's fool. But for some reason, he'd
started to waver. He liked to think it was lust, and
nothing more, that made him too fascinated with the
wench to make good on his vow of revenge. Silver
was a rare beauty, after all. Why hadn't he seen it
before he'd burst into her bedroom, he mused. Hair
like sable satin, thighs like ivory silk. He nearly
groaned aloud just imagining them wrapped around
his hips.

Rafe slid lower onto the cushions, closing his eyes
and giving his imagination free rein. He could almost
smell the lavender as he removed her hairpins, one at
a time, to loose that streak of silver across her pouty
breasts. He imagined the taste of dew on her rosy,
bath-puckered nipples, the moist shyness of virginity
as her thighs trembled open, coaxed by his patient
caress. He would love her long and achingly slow,
watching every crest of feeling in the sapphire pools
that were her eyes.

He loosed a shuddering sigh.

What did a woman like Silver dream of when she
fantasized about lovers? Could he play the part?
Would she let him?

From somewhere beyond the inky blackness of the
French doors, a clock chimed two. The utter stillness
of the house made it possible to detect faint sounds
in the bedrooms above him. He heard the groan of a
mattress, then the *snick* of an opening door. He
cracked open an eye.

Silver.

He knew it had to be her. Max had sneaked off to
Cellie's hotel room around midnight.

For a moment, he listened, wondering with a perverse sense of irony if she'd chosen to come to his bed on the one night that he'd vacated it. His mind's eye could see her tiptoeing down the hall, her hair glinting softly in the glow of a taper, that slinky dressing gown sliding over her naked skin like a jade waterfall.

He was seriously considering bolting back up the stairs, two at a time, when he heard the furtive creak of the first step. Then the second. His pulse quickened in understanding. Silver was coming downstairs. But why?

His brow furrowed. He'd like to think she was searching for him, but the chances of that were slim. Perhaps she was searching for Max. Since Max had timed his rendezvous well after his daughter retired, Silver was probably unaware of her father's escape.

Rafe strained his ears, but it was the faint whiff of lavender, not the rustling of satin, that heralded her arrival at the parlor doors. She glided past him, her hair spilling over her modest décolletage like a perfumed veil, the white muslin of her night wrapper billowing like angel wings in her wake. He thought how incongruous his carnal urges were in the face of this apparition of purity. But then, he was a product of lust, eternally damned for the sins of his parents. Old habits died hard.

More silent than the shadows that camouflaged him, he watched her intently, a predator hungry for the feast that paced just an arm's length away. He had imagined many methods of seduction; he had plotted many scenarios in which to woo her. His fondest fantasy had always been unconditional surrender, in which she'd come to him, aching, unable to resist her own need for pleasure. Was this the signal he'd been waiting for? Was this the night he would finally taste her?

She seemed agitated. He wondered if she sensed him there. She made a brisk circle around the room before pausing before the piano. Her chest heaved, and she quivered. She appeared reluctant to linger, and yet her fingers slowly, grudgingly reached, as if drawn by some magnetic force. For a moment she did nothing more than touch the keys. Just touched them. The upset on her features dissolved into something wistful, perhaps melancholy. Intrigued, Rafe stilled even his breathing.

She traced a tentative finger along the ivory. Not a single note was struck, and yet the longing in that feather-light caress tugged at Rafe's dormant conscience. He thought he should announce himself, but she suddenly sat, turning her back toward him. Her fingers spread in earnest. Low, mournful, and haunting, the first few notes she played made him think better of intruding. The melody was unmistakable to his ears.

"Softly goes my song's entreaty, through the night to thee . . ." Rafe could almost hear the lyrics in every plaintive stroke of the keys. His mother had also been fond of the bittersweet *Serenade* by Franz Schubert. His throat constricted, and he closed his eyes, lost for a moment in the chords that plucked at his own heart. *"Ah, I know a lover's longing, know the pain of love . . ."* Mama would sing the song over and over, consumed by her own misery. Was that how Silver felt? Was she still in love with this Aaron Townsend? Or was the melody she played for some beau closer to home? Rafe's jaw jutted the tiniest bit. Was that why she barely gave him a second glance?

Let thy heart as well grow tender,
Sweetheart, why so coy?
Anxious, fevered, I await thee.
Come and bring me joy.
And bring me joy.

The repeat of the final plea reverberated in his mind as the last chord sighed into the darkness. Slowly, inevitably, the music faded into silence. Silver sat as still as a bust of her namesake, and he drew a long, winding ribbon of breath. For once, no witticism came to mind to leaven the spell.

"Forgive me," he murmured, "for intruding."

She started. "Wh-where are you?" she demanded, rising quickly, her anxious eyes raking the shadows.

He sat up, and moonbeams splayed across his brandy, shirt, and hair.

"You should have announced yourself," she accused shakily.

He inclined his head. "I know. But I couldn't. You play so . . . beautifully."

He heard her swallow. He wondered fleetingly if it was his presence or merely his compliment that had her so unsettled.

"I often play when I can't sleep."

"*Ständchen* is hardly a lullaby."

She raised her chin, but its quiver betrayed she was not her confident self. "You are familiar with Schubert, then?"

"That particular piece, yes. But for pianos, I prefer the *Moonlight Sonata*."

"Beethoven?" She sounded incredulous.

He smiled to himself. No doubt she thought his musical tastes ran toward "Jeannie with the Light Brown Hair." "Do you know it?"

"Not well enough to play for an audience."

"Would you allow me, then?"

"Y-you play?"

"Of course."

Crossing the room, he set his brandy snifter on top of her box piano. She moved quickly out of his way, as if she were frightened of him again, and he frowned, wondering if his nearness or his half-buttoned shirt were to blame. He couldn't think what else might alarm her.

"Where . . . did you learn Beethoven?" she asked tentatively.

Her curiosity appeared stronger than her wariness. He was glad for that. Perhaps he could lure her closer.

"My mother," he answered truthfully. "She preferred the classics to church music. It was the one other thing Jedidiah couldn't break her of."

"Jedidiah?"

Rafe's smile was mirthless and fleeting. He hadn't meant to crack open that powder keg, especially not tonight. "My siblings' father."

"But not yours?" she murmured.

He steeled himself against a sharp retort. He should have known better than to think she would leave that keg firmly sealed. Glancing over his shoulder, he cast her a veiled look. "You sound surprised. Don't tell me you didn't once suspect that I sprang from the bowels of Satan."

Her brow furrowed. "Why would I think something so horrible?"

"Jedidiah did."

He lowered onto the bench, placing his feet on the pedals. She shifted the tiniest bit closer. He could feel her warmth, like springtime, hovering just beyond his range of vision. He willed her closer, but kept his back turned, rolling the overly long lace at his cuffs. As much as he wanted her sitting beside him, her muslin-swathed thigh pressed to his, he wasn't willing to open the Pandora's box of his childhood to achieve her seduction.

"You sound angry when you speak of him."

Sympathy throbbed beneath the unspoken question in her voice. He grimaced, then hastily smoothed the telltale irritation from his face.

"Do I?"

He heard the rustle of fabric. He suspected she'd fidgeted, dissatisfied by his response.

"You're so good at hiding your feelings. I . . . don't think I've ever seen you angry before."

"Ah. Well, it's terrible to behold, isn't it?" He stretched his fingers over the keys.

"Rafe?"

He hesitated, reluctant to yield even that small concession.

"What happened to your mother?"

He tensed. He hadn't expected that question. For a moment, a flood of feelings welled inside him, feelings that he managed to lodge somewhere between his throat and his tongue. He couldn't be funny or witty about Mama. He couldn't spin heroic yarns to absolve himself of his bastardy or make light of the shame that he'd caused her. He couldn't ever avenge the degradation she'd suffered at the hands of Jedidiah Jones. And for those reasons, he couldn't bear to speak of her.

"She's dead," he said flatly.

Then he struck the first note of the last piece Mama had ever taught him. Beethoven's *Moonlight Sonata*. He played it for her.

Silver listened in perfect stillness, barely daring to

breathe. The nightmare she'd suffered was temporarily forgotten, and her growing fear of ghosts—at least, the ghosts that haunted her sleep—faded from her mind. At last, Raphael Jones's playactor's mask had slipped to reveal his own, private haunting.

Silver's stomach churned in a mixture of guilt, empathy, and relief. When Rafe first surprised her here, she feared that he would try to press his advantage, that he would capitalize on her vulnerability, the moonlight, and her utter aloneness the same way Aaron once had.

But the man sitting at the piano wasn't even thinking of her. His eyelashes fanned lower, as if his hands would feel their way across the ivory, and to her bemusement, they did—passionately, poignantly, and without error. He was lost in the music, in the memories that flitted like specters across his chiseled features. His throat worked; his chest rose and fell to the melodic lament. Watching the tumult he struggled to keep corked inside him, she felt like a voyeur.

But more than that, she felt foolish to have presumed he would pounce on her like some savage jungle cat. By the river, in her bedroom, and during the few times when their conspiracy had necessitated a secret rendezvous, he'd had plenty of opportunity to force his attentions upon her. But that wasn't Rafe's way, she realized in growing wonder. He might be wild and wicked in ways she couldn't comprehend, but he wasn't heartless. He wasn't cruel. In spite of the untold hurts he must have suffered, perhaps at the hands of this Jedidiah, he wasn't violent. And he didn't take what he wanted by force. No, she realized with a tiny, shivery thrill, he waited with canny patience for the thing to come to him.

The last strains of Beethoven's masterwork shivered into silence. Silver could almost feel the perfect stillness of the mansion crowding her throat and weighting her shoulders. She knew that Rafe felt it, too. His fingers moved, impossibly slow, lifting from the now soundless keys. An aching sympathy speared her chest. She told herself that was the only reason she allowed herself to perch beside him on the bench.

"I miss my mother too," she murmured.

His head turned slowly, and his eyes, more haunting than the ghost that had robbed her of sleep, glistened when they touched hers. He said nothing, but she sensed that, too, was his way.

She fidgeted on her seat. Call her a fool, but as difficult as it was for her to trust him, she couldn't bring herself to believe he was pretending grief just to woo her. Not after his chest had shuddered when he'd played. Not after the mirrors of his eyes had gone nearly black with hurting.

"How old were you?" she whispered.

His jaw tensed, and she instantly regretted her question.

"I didn't mean to pry, Rafe, I just—"

"Fourteen."

She swallowed. She hadn't expected him to answer.

"I was eight," she offered tentatively.

"Your father told me."

"He . . . did?"

He nodded, and she bit her lip. Had Papa left *any-thing* about her to Rafe's imagination?

"What else did he tell you? About Mama, I mean?" she added hastily, afraid that Aaron's name would somehow roll off Rafe's tongue. She reminded herself for at least the thousandth time that fear was groundless. After all, the truth of that matter would

never reach Papa's ears. Not unless Aaron himself
had an attack of conscience.

She prayed to God he never would.

"Max doesn't talk about her much," Rafe said, his
tone tender with sympathy.

"Oh." She wondered if she sounded as deflated as
she felt. She hated to think Papa never grieved for
Mama. She hated to think . . . well, that anything her
maternal grandfather had ever said about Papa's fickle
heart was true.

"Why don't you tell me about her?" Rafe murmured.

She blushed. He hadn't moved a muscle, and yet
she felt closer to him than ever before. She wondered
if it was the heat of him, so subtly alluring, so se-
ductively tangible. Or was it the comfort their newfound comradery gave her? She really wanted to
believe he cared about her hurt, the way she cared
about his.

She raised her uncertain gaze to his. "I don't remember much. She was . . . Mama. And I loved her."

His thoughts were unreadable in those moon-
silvered eyes, but she sensed poignancy in his silence.

"I never understood why God took her away." She
felt compelled to keep speaking, to touch him with
words in a way she dared not touch him with her
hand. "I tried to convince myself she was needed in
heaven. I liked to think she was an angel, because she
was so beautiful. And because she laughed a lot. Not
like Aunt Agatha."

He nodded. She wondered if he was thinking of his
own mother or if Papa had told him some harrowing
tale of Aunt "Hagatha."

"Papa wasn't home when the accident happened,"
Silver continued, the creep of grief turning her hoarse.

"But Grandfather blamed him. I remember how he came to take me away. Papa was so much like a child himself, you see . . ."

She averted her eyes, recalling the bitter accusations her mother's wealthy father had made, claiming that Papa was irresponsible, that he was unfit to raise a child. Even though Mama had been wholly responsible for hitching the gig and driving out in icy weather, Grandfather had reasoned she would never have been tempted to such foolishness if Papa hadn't won the conveyance through poker. On that horrible day, as Grandfather had dragged her out the door, screaming for Papa, he had vowed Papa would never ruin Silver the way he'd ruined her mama.

"Grandfather never approved of Papa," Silver said thickly. "He didn't like the fact that Papa's parents had been German immigrants. Grandfather convinced himself Papa was worthless, that he'd never amount to anything, and that he'd seduced Mama for her dowry."

Silver caught her breath, groaning inwardly as the truth slipped out. She hadn't meant to unlock *that* particular skeleton from the family closet! *She* wasn't even supposed to know she'd been conceived out of wedlock. She'd stumbled across the truth when she'd learned how to add.

She hastened to defend her parents' marriage. "I don't think Mama could have been very happy under Grandfather's roof. I think she fell in love with Papa because he was spontaneous and carefree, a far cry from her overbearing father." It had taken Silver years to understand why her mother's family had hated Papa. In retrospect, she was amazed Grandfather had allowed Papa to visit her on holidays. But until she had understood Grandfather's prejudice, she had blamed herself for Papa's absence. At the age of eight, she hadn't known that a wealthy grandfather could influence a judge and prevent an impoverished father from living with his child. For the longest time, she had believed Papa had left her behind with her authoritarian grandfather and her dour, spinster aunt not because Papa had been determined to strike it rich and fight fire with fire but because she'd displeased him in some way.

Not until her fourteenth year, when Grandfather had died and Aunt Agatha had become her sole guardian, had Papa confessed he'd been afraid to cross his powerful father-in-law. That had been the summer of 1876, and shortly afterward, Grandfather's ill-advised attorney had invested Aunt Agatha's inheritance, costing her everything but the boarding-house. With Papa's savings consumed by the search for gold, even he had understood that his was no life for a fourteen-year-old daughter. He had told her she'd be better off cooking three meals a day to help care for her aunt's boarders than rubbing elbows with the hustlers, hookers, and thieves that preyed on mining camps. So, once again, she and Papa had been separated.

"Aunt Agatha used to tell me my mother, her younger sister, had been an incorrigible and wayward child." Silver plucked at her gown as the hurtful memories once again threatened her composure. "I think Aunt Agatha hated Papa even more than Grandfather did, that she was jealous of Mama and Papa, because she'd never had many beaux. She told me once she thought it was her God-given duty to cure me of my parents' legacy."

"And did she?" Rafe asked softly.

Silver's cheeks warmed. She recalled a time, a time

so long ago that now it felt like another life, when she had been lonely and rebellious, when she had thought to defy her well-meaning but annoyingly prudish aunt by sneaking out of windows and meeting sweet-talking beaux in the moonlight. She'd met Aaron numerous times that way, and he'd stolen a kiss or two. It had seemed so romantic. She had thought herself hopelessly in love with the young ironworks heir, and she'd believed he loved her, too— until the night he'd pinned her against the garden wall. Until the night he'd said it was time to call her bluff, that he was tired of all her cockteasing . . .

"Silver?"

Rafe's gentle touch on her arm startled her, and she leaped to her feet, pressing her palms to her flaming face.

"Y-yes," she gasped, doing her best to fight off the frisson of panic that galloped up her spine. "I was cured."

She spun hastily away, and when she crossed to the window, Rafe frowned. What had he done this time to spook her?

For a long moment he studied her, assessing every word, every gesture she'd made since sailing through the parlor doors. When she'd sat beside him on the bench, he'd thought he had finally moved her. He'd thought he was making progress, that she was beginning to trust him, and all because his damned feelings had been genuine. More genuine than he cared to feel. Who would have thought he and Silver had so much in common: a mother who'd risked scandal for love, a legacy that was . . . well, less than favorable. The only difference, he supposed, was that Max had done right by Silver's mother. His father, on the other hand, had disappeared like a thief in the night.

Rafe grimaced to recall something so useless and hurtful.

Was that his problem, then? That he couldn't stop himself from empathizing with Silver because he, too, had suffered the disapproval of the dictator who'd raised him? Rafe hoped so, because sentiment he could ignore. His pesky conscience was another matter. Why the hell had he sat there, a mere hair's breadth from her lips, and made not a single, solitary attempt to kiss her? Wasn't seduction his game? Wasn't he playing to win?

He scowled. *Jones, you're getting soft. What are you doing here, if it isn't to woo the girl's trust, take her money, and get out before she gets wise to your lack of progress with Cellie?*

His gut roiled as he posed the question, but he pretended not to notice. Despite the uncanny way Silver had of helping his conscience rear its ugly head, she was a mark, like any other—only richer. He'd be a fool to waste this chance.

Fortunately, all wasn't lost. She still stood by the window, worrying her full, moist lip and gazing up at the moon as if she thought she might decipher some mystical knowledge from the clouds wreathing its face.

And as any professional rake knew, the moon was a handy tool for seduction.

He moved toward her, but her voice, so full of trepidation, made his feet falter beside the settee.

"Do you . . . believe in ghosts?"

"Ghosts?" His brow furrowed. He liked to think he understood women, but that question had come like a bolt out of the blue. He'd been hoping to capitalize on their newfound bond of childhood despair. What had happened to all her angst about Mama?

He chose his answer carefully. "I've never had occasion to."

She fingered a hunter green tassel hanging from the draperies. Was it his imagination, or did her hand tremble as it wrapped around the knot?

"I have to ask you something, and . . . I need to know you'll answer truthfully."

Truthfully? He'd never wooed a woman with the truth before. He'd never found the unvarnished facts about himself terribly appealing. Why should a woman?

More curious than cautious, however, he decided to see where this train of thought derailed. "All right," he purred in his most melodic baritone. "What do you want to know?"

If she noticed the sultry transformation in his voice, she didn't mark it.

"The night of the engagement party, did you, uh, carry out your threat to . . . um, visit my bedroom?"

He hid a smug smile. Had she wanted him to?

"No."

She looked truly agitated now. "Are you sure?"

He arched a brow. "I think I'd remember," he murmured.

She swallowed audibly. He had stopped a foot or two away; still, when she turned to face him, he swore he could hear her heartbeat. Certainly, he could see its wild cadence in the fluttering of her gown. He battled a rising sense of guilt. As much as he'd like to believe he saw longing in her eyes, he had to concede that fear, not lust, stared back at him.

"Rafe, please," she choked, "please tell me you've been sneaking into my bedroom at night and leaving acorns. And broken bird eggs. And . . . and some sort of shriveled seed pod."

He frowned, genuinely concerned by her upset—another lamentable lapse into sentiment. Even if he took into consideration the ghostly wash of the moon, she looked much too pale. Yet when he reached to comfort her, she backed into the draperies as if his arm were a striking snake. He froze in midgesture, his skin crawling to think he could inspire such terror in anything, much less a woman.

"Silver." Somehow he managed to force gentleness out of the vise that squeezed his throat. "Honey, I swear, I have never meant to frighten you. And I've never been inside your bedroom, except that one time when I heard you scream. Because of Tavy. Remember?"

She closed her eyes and nodded. Her haggard features couldn't quite conceal her struggle for composure, and he watched the rare show uncomfortably, wondering at the clash of raw emotions.

"I-I'm sorry." She pasted on a weak smile. "It's this nightmare I keep having. It has me a bit jumpy, I suppose."

He frowned. Nightmare be damned. This was Silver Nichols, his cool-as-ice princess, the same woman who negotiated their business deal the way a barracuda negotiated a coral reef. "What's this really about, Silver?"

She tore her gaze away. For a long moment, she faced the window, staring glassily toward the fountain and hedgerows in the sculpted garden beyond. The muffled *tick, tick, ticking* of the hall clock knelled in the silence between them.

Finally, she moistened her lips.

"I think . . . I'm being haunted."

"Haunted," he repeated dubiously. He supposed he didn't have to tell her how ridiculous that sounded.

However, he knew better than to try dragging the truth from her. If she were anything like him, and she was proving to be very much so, she'd fight like a badger to keep her secrets hidden. "And why would you think that?"

"If I tell you, you'll think I'm hysterical."

"I'm more likely to think you're your father's daughter."

She blew out her breath, as if to imply that notion was even more disturbing. But when she folded her arms across her breasts, uneasiness, not exasperation, creased her profile.

"Swear you won't laugh."

"I swear."

She didn't look convinced. In fact, she looked like she regretted telling him what she had. Finally, she dropped her arms and sighed.

"I suppose I can't expect you not to laugh. If you'd told *me* you were being haunted, I would have laughed. Uproariously. But you see, it's not funny when it's happening before your very eyes and . . . and there's no logical explanation."

He watched the old, businesslike Silver trying to break through the fear. He was glad. The shrinking inconsolable Silver threw him off his game, making him feel . . . well, inadequate.

"Go on."

She fidgeted, avoiding his eyes. "I started having the nightmares about three months ago, shortly after Papa ordered the new tunnel blasted in Silver's Mine. Shortly after he told me he was marrying Celestia." Her face twisted in a faint grimace. "I used to think Papa's incessant talk about ghosts was influencing my dreams. But then, *things* started appearing on my windowsill. Things like . . . feathers. And pebbles. Of course," she added quickly, "those were easy to explain away, because the sash had been open on those nights, and I figured a bird or a squirrel had left them inside. I didn't immediately link them with my dreams of him."

"Him?"

"Dancing Moon." She darted Rafe an anxious, mildly embarrassed look. "I know it sounds absurd. But I've exhausted all reasonable explanations for the acorns and the eggshells."

"So." Rafe carefully modulated his response. "You think some two-hundred-year-old dead Indian left them behind?"

Her cheeks reddened. "What else am I to think?" she asked plaintively. "I've questioned all the staff, as circumspectly as I was able, of course; I've nailed my windows shut; I've even taken to locking my door at night."

"Have you told Max any of this?"

"Papa?" She looked aghast. "Absolutely not. He'd have me drinking protection potions and stringing garlic around my neck. Besides, Papa's not very good with confidences. He'd blurt my tale to Benson, or Celestia or, God forbid, to Brady Buckholtz, and I'd have an army of gawkers and newspapermen camped out beneath my window. I was hoping . . ." She fidgeted, shifting from foot to foot. "I was hoping you'd come clean and tell me your otter had sneaked in and had left the acorns and eggshells behind."

She gazed at him so beseechingly that he was indeed tempted to concoct a tale about a secret passageway that only wily, bubble-stalking otters could navigate. Then whose story would be more absurd?

"Do you want to know what I think?" he asked after a judicious moment of silence.

She nodded, her eyes so wide and misty again that he forgot himself. He reached to cup her cheek. She trembled, but she didn't bolt. This time, like a ghost of the old Silver, she stood her ground. Glad to see it, he traced the pad of his thumb along the damp hollow that cradled her lashes. Beneath her tears, her skin felt like velvet.

"Silver." He didn't have to pretend; the huskiness in his voice came naturally now. "Sweetheart, I don't think you're being haunted."

"Y-you don't?"

"No," he said softly. Damn, why wasn't he agreeing with her? Why wasn't he blowing her fears out of proportion like any self-respecting ne'er-do-well would do? Then he wouldn't have had any trouble convincing her not to sleep alone.

But some dormant nobility possessed him, and he couldn't whisper the lie. He knew he'd be sorry. He knew he was a fool. Nevertheless, he told her exactly what she didn't want to hear.

"I think you're feeling guilty. I think you know Max loves Cellie, and she loves him. You hired me to break up their romance not because Cellie's a gold digger but because you can't bear to see Max married to anyone but your mother."

She winced, wrenching free of his hand. "That's not true!"

Rafe sighed. He hadn't really expected her to agree. Still, after spending ten minutes alone with the giggling, kiss-throwing couple, a person would have to be deaf, dumb, and blind—or bitterly resentful—not to realize that Max and his fiancée were genuinely besotted with each other. Hell, Rafe hadn't even believed love was a real, viable reason for marriage until he'd listened to Max prattle so eagerly about his wedding plans. Or until he'd watched the old man's chubby face turn dark with menace as he'd vowed to thrash any husband who wasn't head over heels in love with his daughter.

Call him a sucker, Rafe reasoned, but he liked Max. And damn him if he didn't like Cellie too. No one was more uncomfortable than he when he watched Silver snub her. And whenever he saw Max observe the same thing, and the old man's face puckered with secret hurt, he wanted to grab Silver by the shoulders and shake her. Cellie was the kind of woman Rafe might actually have prayed for in a mother—except, of course, that she could be eerily accurate at exposing truths.

A particularly hair-raising incident flitted through his memory, a carriage ride he'd shared with Cellie two days after the engagement party. At that time, he'd been concerned for gullible old Max, and he'd been prepared to expose Cellie as a fraud. But when he'd even thought about sliding across the seat and putting his arm around her shoulders, she'd given his knee a motherly pat and fixed him with those discerning gray eyes.

"There's a ghost that haunts you, dear boy. A ghost named Jedidiah," she had said with such earnestness that his toes had curled, his heart had raced, and his eyes had grown a good deal wider. *"Love never talked to a child the way he talked to you. Jedidiah might have preached the gospel, but he forgot that God forgives. You mustn't blame yourself for your parents' sins. You're a good boy. And Silver needs you. She just doesn't know how much yet."*

Looking back on that carriage ride, Rafe still wasn't sure how Cellie knew about Jedidiah. But there had to be a logical explanation. Just like there had to be a logical explanation for Silver's ghost.

"That's preposterous," Silver meanwhile insisted, her eyes briny with accusation. "Celestia has nothing to do with my nightmares. There are *bird eggs* materializing in my locked and bolted bedroom. And they appear only when I dream about *him*."

Rafe arched a brow. "So you've convinced yourself you're not really dreaming, is that it?"

"Y-yes." Her bravado blew out like a candle the moment her anxiety crept back in. "He frightens me. I mean, I know he's only leaving acorns and seed pods and such, but . . ." She clasped her hands so hard that her knuckles actually whitened. "He's so threatening."

Rafe's brow furrowed. Nightmare or not, he didn't like the sound of that. "Threatening? In what way?" he asked more gently.

"He's always beside himself, yelling, and gnashing his teeth. He stomps his feet and thrusts dead animals and . . . and uprooted plants at me."

"Does he say anything you can understand?"

She began to quake, and her hand flew to her mouth. "He yells. He yells something about . . . raping the Mother."

Jesus. Rafe's gut clenched so hard that he felt like a fist had plowed through it. "Silver, don't." Her tears were spilling uncontrollably now, and he pulled her into his arms. "It's all right, honey. It was just a nightmare."

She whimpered. He could feel her softness shrinking from his embrace, as if she feared his comfort, so he hushed her and stroked her back, cupping her head against the steady cadence of his heart. It was an unfamiliar chivalry that seized him. Tenderness, protectiveness, and strength all melted through him in one

golden, satisfying glow. For once, he behaved by instinct rather than design, and the realization shook
him. He wasn't a selfless man. He wasn't any hero.
And yet, for perhaps the first time in his life, he
wasn't playacting for a woman, either.

Silver shivered against the warmth of Rafe's
length, letting the sweet solace of his thrumming heart
soothe the ragged endings of her nerves. She hadn't
meant to let him hold her; she hadn't meant to rest
her cheek against the crisp, tawny hairs that blanketed
his chest, or let her fingers slide beneath sagging linen
placards to touch firm, vital flesh. Never in a million
lifetimes would she have thought she could feel safe
with Raphael Jones. Never would she have dreamed
she might trust him to cradle her waist, or comb his
fingers through her hair . . . or kiss her temple.

Her pulse did a dizzying little dance as his lips,
petal-soft with persuasion, drifted lower. Warm, moist
breaths skimmed her cheek and tickled her earlobe
before she felt the nuzzling caress of mouth and
tongue in the tender hollow of her throat. Her heart
leaped hard enough to burst the fortress of her ribs,
and when she moaned a weak protest, he kneaded the
base of her skull, coaxing her head higher.

"Silver." His voice was velvet, shimmering over
her senses, a golden thread of reason in the dazed,
white numbness of her brain. "Let me kiss you."

She couldn't think how to stop him, much less why
she should. Her arms, more rubber than sinew, bowed
as he pulled her closer, and when she might have
protested the intimacy of her breasts, pressed so deliciously flat against the hardness of his chest, his
tongue tasted hers. It was a heady sensation. If she'd
had one shred of common sense left, she would have
backed from his arms. But his palm spanned her but-

tocks, tucking her hips against his, and she was imprisoned in a wondrous cage of seductive pressures and shivery pleasures.

His lips coaxed and teased. The sweetness of brandy slid over her tongue. She wasn't sure where the taste of him ended and the scent of him began; he was citrus and pine, sandalwood and leather, and the faint, alluring pungence of tobacco. Her vague uneasiness splintered, scattering like smoke on the wind. When his thumb stroked her throat, when his feathery kisses rained down on her eyes, nose, and jaw, she felt the restless rise of longing. It seemed right and natural somehow for her hand to creep to his hair, to revel in the thick, burnished waves that slid through her fingers before she pulled his head lower, guiding his mouth back to hers.

"Silver."

His kiss was hungrier this time. Entranced, she sank deeper into the web of sensation that he spun. His lips slanted across hers; his tongue pushed and plundered. She trembled as moist heat pooled in the pit of her belly. She gasped as his fingers slyly brushed her nipple and his maleness grew more prominent against her femininity.

"Rafe," she warned uneasily.

His head rose, and his hands stilled instantly. She could hear the ragged sawing of his breaths, the fevered tempo of his heart. She didn't know what she regretted more, the cool gust of reason that shivered up her spine, or the glittering disappointment that blazed through her limbs.

"I . . . we . . . please." She knew she wasn't making sense. She wanted more, so much more, and when she gathered the courage to meet his heavy-lidded stare, she knew she could have it. All of it. But she was afraid.

"I have to go," she whispered lamely.

"Silver."

She trembled, faltering in midturn. Nothing held her but the smoky softness of his voice. She liked to think she heard concern in its timbre. But she didn't dare trust her senses. Not after the way he'd made them betray her.

"Since you're afraid of intruders, I could accompany you to your bedroom and—"

"No!"

He grew very still.

"I was merely going to suggest," he continued with resolute calmness, "that I would inspect your door and windows to make sure they're secure."

Tears threatened to rob her vision. "That won't be necessary."

"Silver."

The gentleness of his voice stopped her again in midflight.

"You have nothing to fear from me."

She ventured a glance over her shoulder. He hadn't moved. He hadn't even pushed back the hair her questing fingers had spilled across his brow.

"Can I really believe that?"

"Yes."

She fought down a sob. She wanted to trust him. She wanted nothing more than to lull herself into that warm sense of security she'd felt so strongly in his arms.

"Th-thank you. Good night."

She hurried for the stairs, half afraid he'd lied, half afraid he'd follow. When he didn't, she was mortified to feel more deflated than relieved. God help her. She was falling under the spell of the very same Romeo whom she'd hired, with open eyes, yet, to woo Celestia!

Pausing before her yawning, dimly lit chamber, she touched shaking fingers to her lips. She was almost tempted to call Rafe, to beg him to hold her safely through the night and trust him to keep his word.

Instead, she forced her feet across the threshold and closed the door behind her. Ghosts she could handle, she told herself weakly. They melted into the bright, sunny dawn of a Colorado morn. But Raphael Jones?

Her heart somersaulted, and her skin tingled in a frightfully exquisite shiver.

She worried his kisses would haunt her night and day.

Chapter 9

After her humiliation in the parlor, Silver spent the next few days avoiding Rafe. She couldn't bear the notion that she'd be fair game for his wit. After all, it was bad enough she *thought* she was being haunted. Why had she admitted it to a wiseacre like Rafe?

Of course, her confession hadn't been her sole lapse into lunacy. Never mind how sweetly concerned Rafe had seemed. She knew full well the consequences of kissing a man. She was lucky he hadn't ripped open her bodice and forced her to the floor. She'd paid so dearly for cockteasing Aaron—although, in truth, she hadn't known the meaning of that word until much later. Five harrowing years ago, in that moonlit, Philadelphia garden, the man she thought she loved had taught her a shameful lesson about irresponsibility.

That's why she couldn't bring herself to face Rafe. As horrible as Aaron had been, she couldn't forget that she'd *wanted* him to kiss her . . . at least, at first. And she'd wanted Rafe to kiss her, too. Considering what she'd hired him for, she held herself fully accountable for her stupidity. Unfortunately, she wasn't sure she'd be any wiser the next time she was alone with him. She wasn't sure her fingers could resist the temptation of the incorrigible, sun-gilded curl that always spilled across his brow. She even doubted whether she'd have the strength to ignore his fallen-angel smile or a whiff of his mouth-watering cologne. The man was too handsome, too virile, too heart-stoppingly charming for her peace of mind. And she wanted him out of her house.

The trouble was Papa. He'd come to dote on Rafe and his annoyingly disarming otter.

"Now, daughter," Papa had told her the morning after the bathtub incident, "you can't throw a cute little bugger like Tavy to the wolves. They'd munch her up and spit her out faster than you can say hors d'oeuvres."

And Tavy had blinked up at her with those incredibly huge otter eyes, making Silver feel like the first cousin to Genghis Khan until the little sneak had web-footed it back to her bedroom and trampled lip paint into her carpet.

Each time something similar happened (and the incidents numbered at least one per day), Rafe would arrive to scold Tavy, grinning all the while. Silver wouldn't have been surprised if, the moment they were out of her sight, he'd rewarded the creature with fish treats. Why his otter couldn't stay locked in its cage was something Rafe still hadn't explained to her full satisfaction. Silver had the sneaking suspicion Tavy's freedom was another of Rafe's ploys to cross her path.

Yes, as astonishing as it might seem in a house with as many rooms as hers, avoiding Rafe had become nigh impossible, Silver mused wryly. If Tavy didn't sniff out her whereabouts, Rafe did. Not by coincidence, Silver was certain, had their chance encounters grown more frequent after she'd kissed him. He was too wily, too persistent, too exasperatingly creative, to let a whole day go by without engaging her.

And to her secret amusement, each of his excuses was more outlandish than the last.

For instance, after a very red-faced Jimmy had spilled chocolate sauce down the front of his coat, Rafe had insisted on a late-night consultation to discuss the youth's new livery.

"Can't have my retainer looking like he bathed in whipped cream and cherries, now, can I?" Rafe had drawled in that seductive purr of his. "Not when I've got *Cellie* to impress."

Then there had been the oh-so-necessary tête-à-tête to discuss his sideburns crisis. Apparently Tavy had helped him misplace the paste he'd been using to attach the whiskers to his jaw.

"Maybe it's just as well," he'd lamented with a gusty sigh. "*Cellie* says she just doesn't like whiskers on a man. Too bushy for kissing."

But his most blatant attempt to goad her, Silver recalled with a reluctant thrill, had come one evening after she'd ordered her bathwater removed. The moment the servants had trooped out of her bedroom, Rafe had materialized and propped his shoulder against the doorjamb.

"Silver, honey," he'd crooned after she'd so foolishly hesitated to slam the door in his face, "you didn't bathe in lavender water again, did you?"

"Why?" she asked suspiciously.

"Well . . ." A suggestive smile teased his mouth. "I know how much you dread nightmares. And in all good conscience, I couldn't let you go to bed without at least offering to uh, keep you distracted through the wee hours of the night.''

Her face flamed, but she did her best to ignore his proposition. ''W-what does lavender have to do with nightmares?''

''You mean you didn't know?'' He let his throaty whisper throb beside her ear. ''Cellie bathes in lavender water every night to see ghosts.''

Silver's throat constricted at the memory. She tended to believe he'd made the whole tale up. But even if he hadn't, he couldn't really expect her to believe her French soap had induced visions of Dancing Moon. In fact, she wanted to believe his soap story even less than she wanted to believe he'd finally wooed Celestia enough to witness her evening toilette.

Silver stared glumly at the accounts she was supposed to be balancing. What was the matter with her? It was bad enough she'd wasted nearly an hour, reliving again and again the few precious minutes she'd stolen with Rafe. Now she had to come to terms with the rather shameful realization she was jealous—jealous that he might actually have succeeded at the job she'd hired him for!

Silver fidgeted in her chair.

Papa's wedding was little more than a week away. She should be ecstatic that Rafe was so close to compromising Celestia. Instead, just picturing the two of them together, Rafe so sinfully charming, Celestia so pathetically smitten, made Silver's stomach hurt. She tried to convince herself her upset stemmed strictly from the pain her father would feel when Rafe proved, once and for all, Celestia's perfidy. But somehow, that rationale rang false. As much as she looked forward to Rafe's flirtations, Silver mused uneasily, she had too many reasons *not* to encourage them. Any attention he showed her now would foil their plot to ruin Celestia.

Besides, how could she let herself believe that a dyed-in-the-wool rake might ever feel genuine affection for her? As refined and well-born as Aaron had been, he'd taught her not to trust professions of love.

But more than that, he'd dashed her hopes for a doting husband, children, and a happy home.

Silver blinked back tears. She was a fool. Knowing the money she paid Rafe was his only real interest in her, how could she have grown so fond of him?

Disgusted with her folly, and her mathematical incompetence, Silver slammed the ledger closed and reached across her desk for the stack of mail Benson had left on the corner. She thumbed irritably through the envelopes, her fingers hesitating only when she came to the stilted scrawl and the Philadelphia postmark. Aunt Agatha had, undoubtedly, sent her regrets for Papa's wedding.

Silver let a mirthless smile touch her lips. The letter was sharp and uncompromising, much like her aunt. *"I see no reason,"* Agatha had written, *"to travel half a continent to encourage my poor sister's widower to legitimize his lust for a circus performer."*

Silver sighed. She could only imagine what Agatha might have written if she'd known Celestia had burned down a church. Sometimes, that knowledge was the only thing Silver, herself, had to cling to when the enormity of her crime touched her conscience. After all, Papa acted so blissfully in love with the woman . . .

Silver blew out her breath. Well, the arson question would be solved shortly. Unable to abide Rafe's accusation that her guilt was the sole reason she

dreamed of Dancing Moon, she'd decided to prove
him wrong. She'd hired yet another detective, this one
to investigate the organist's accusations. Of course,
retaining an agent had been just a formality. Silver
had every confidence the organist's charges would be
confirmed. Just as she had every confidence Dancing
Moon would leave yet another morbid calling card on
her windowsill. But at least she would be vindicated—
on both counts.

Smiling grimly, she put her aunt's letter aside and
reached reluctantly inside the envelope for the newspaper clippings Agatha always enclosed. Aaron was
usually the topic of those clippings.

"Explosion Kills Congressional Candidate and 26
Others," the first headline blared. "Townsend Denies
His Luxury Hotel Unsafe for Guests."

Silver winced, her heart lurching into a painful and
unsteady pace. The article, which had come from the
front page of the *Philadelphia Enquirer*, was dated
twelve weeks ago. She mumbled a short prayer for
the victims.

"Hotel Tragedy Yields No New Evidence," the
second headline read. "Grand Jury Dismisses Townsend Murder Charges."

Silver didn't know whether to be disturbed or relieved. This wasn't the first time a murder charge in-
volving Aaron had been dismissed. Two years ago,
Aaron's older brother had died during a hunting accident. In one of Aunt Agatha's newspaper clippings,
Aaron had claimed he'd heard a gunshot as he'd been
gathering firewood. He'd supposedly run back to the
cabin only to find that Charles's rifle had misfired
while he'd been cleaning it. That accident had made
Aaron sole heir to the family fortune. After the ensuing investigation, he'd emerged as a tragic hero in

the society pages. In her letters, Agatha had berated Silver for letting such a "promising young man" slip through her fingers.

Aunt Agatha's third and final headline read, "Iron-works Magnate Travels West to Raise Capital."

Silver's gut clenched at the news. *Oh, no. Aaron here?*

Her dread wasn't eased any when she spied Agatha's notation in the margin: *"Perhaps you'll have a second chance. They say Townsend also wants to raise an heir."*

Silver shuddered, imagining Aaron's lily white hands bruising her throat once more.

A loud rap on her office door made Silver jump in her seat. As usual, Papa didn't wait for her summons but barged in, Rafe strolling in his wake. Silver caught her breath. Dropping the clippings, she forgot about Aaron altogether as she tried to hide her silly schoolgirl delight at seeing Rafe. Then she saw Celestia trailing behind him, and her frown came more easily.

"Good morning, daughter," Papa boomed, peering under her ornately carved mahogany credenza. "Haven't seen Tavy anywhere, have you?"

"She's missing again?" Silver countered warily, her nerves starting to stretch as Papa combed through the fern fronds in the sterling planter by the book-shelves. She'd been so desperate to keep him from running off any more miners, or investors, with his séance nonsense that she'd pilfered his newest stash of spiritkeepers.

Of course, she'd had every intention of smuggling Papa's rocks to the backyard and dumping them in the pond. Unfortunately, Dancing Moon had made her leery of wandering alone beneath oak trees in the dead of night. Too, there'd been the matter of Rafe, prowling around her house like a hungry panther, and she hadn't wanted to chance any more midnight encounters with him. So Papa's spiritkeepers, much to her chagrin, were stuffed in a satchel of ore samples that she'd hidden behind her draperies.

She glanced at Rafe. She didn't suppose he would actually help her *divert* Papa from his search . . .

"Uh, Papa, I've been working here all morning," Silver said quickly. "And I'm quite sure if Tavy were in my office, she would have knocked something over or chewed on something to give herself away. Don't you agree, Your Grace?"

She gazed beseechingly at Rafe. The rogue's dimples peeked.

"Sink me," he drawled, striking one of his foppish poses. "I don't believe Octavia's much of a morning chewer. She so loves to break her fast with fish, you see. She'll gorge herself quite shamelessly, then curl up somewhere for a nap. I daresay a little tyke like Tavy needs a great deal of rest to be ready to gorge again for lunch, what?"

She wanted to smack him.

Meanwhile, Papa had dropped to his hands and knees and was poking his head under the ticking that protected Silver's wing chairs from the sun. He was only five feet from the draperies, and hence, the hidden satchel. She bit her lip.

"Honestly, Papa," she said, rising and hurrying to protect her cache, "I can't imagine why you'd think Tavy is napping in here. She doesn't like me in the least, you know."

"Pish posh, my dear." Rafe perched on a corner of her desk and began swinging his leg in a lazy rhythm. "Tavy adores you. Why, until she'd met you, she didn't have the foggiest notion what lavender soap and lip paint were for. I daresay she's developed quite a taste for them.''

Silver cleared her throat, dragging her gaze away from Rafe's arrestingly muscular thigh. ''Well, I . . . uh . . .'' She shook herself and glared into his laughing eyes. ''I can quite assure you I keep no soap or lip paint in my office. So you see, Papa,'' she continued briskly, ''there really is no reason to think Tavy sneaked in here.''

Papa straightened, red-faced and huffing. '' 'Course there is, daughter. The spirits rapped once when Cellie asked 'em.''

She tossed a withering glance at Celestia. ''They rapped once?''

''One rap means yes; two raps mean no,'' she explained in her enigmatic alto.

Silver hoped Tavy was contentedly gnawing a shoe somewhere on the other side of the house. It made her crazy when Celestia's predictions proved accurate. ''With all due respect to your spirits,'' Silver retorted coolly, ''this is not a convenient time to launch an otter search. I have our lawyer's answer to the Union's accusations sitting here, and I must edit the draft before the morning's through. I promise you, if I find Tavy, I'll call Jimmy. Now, if the three of you don't mind . . .''

''Ah-ha!'' came Papa's muffled exclamation. He emerged from behind the firescreen. ''The little rascal's got to be around here somewhere, Chumley. Look!'' The bedraggled, ash-smeared ribbon he held was staining his fingers black.

''Dash it all.'' Rafe made an exasperated sound as he lowered his quizzing glass. ''And I went to such trouble picking the precise shade of pink for her bow.

One can't wear just any shade when one is otter-brown. Cellie, my dear, do you think you might spare a bangle or two for Tavy to wear for her newspaper photograph?''

"Photograph?" Silver nearly choked on the word.

"Why, yes," Rafe crooned. "Tavy is going to pose with that delightful Mrs. Trevelyan for the society pages. Mrs. T invited Tavy, as my ward, to be the guest-of-honor at her charity ball.''

Silver groaned. It was bad enough that Rafe's preposterous quotations were appearing in one of the newspapers daily. But did his otter have to make the headlines, too?

"Uh . . . has Mrs. Trevelyan ever *met* your ward?'' she asked him.

"Odds fish, my dear. Of course she has." Swiveling, he reached for the *Aspen Times* she'd tossed into the wastepaper basket. Breezing past the stock pages, which she read more religiously than the Bible, he turned to the section of the paper she'd come to dread. "Look you here," he said, snapping the sheets open with a flourish.

Reluctantly, she edged away from her post to peer at the headline. She needn't have bothered, though. The type splashed across the society pages was a full six inches high: "Teamster Baron and His Wife Host Charity Ball for Orphans and Motherless Otters."

Silver cringed. Brady Buckholtz was having a field day at Daisy Trevelyan's expense. Even though Rafe had been careful not to let his own likeness be photographed, leery as he was of attracting bounty hunters and tinstars, not a day went by when Silver didn't worry he'd be recognized. Pernicious Brady would have a field day at *her* expense, then.

"Aren't you supposed to be looking for a suitable

stream stocked with plenty of fish and frogs," she reminded Rafe accusingly, "instead of splashing Tavy's likeness across the society pages?"

To her surprise, he grimaced, averting his gaze.

"Me and Chumley are going up to Swindler's Creek this very afternoon," Papa called, his voice echoing from one of her cabinets.

"So far?" Silver was momentarily distracted by the news. "But that's nearly a two-hour journey from Silver's Mine. Surely you can find a stream closer to home."

Papa straightened, red-faced and huffing. "That's just it, daughter. What with all the lumberyards around here, it's just not safe for otters. Why, even a living, breathing submarine like Tavy can't swim too good through sawdust. 'Sides, Cellie's spirits say there are otter lodges further up the mountain."

"Otter *dens*, dearest," Celestia corrected him gently. "Beavers live in lodges. Try looking for Tavy on the window seat."

"Whatever you say, sweet pea." Grinning, Papa threw her a kiss and moved toward the draperies.

Silver quailed.

Suddenly, the dark-gold bombazine rippled. Papa had no sooner reached for the drawstring than something svelte and brown dove past his ankles. He chuckled. "Shoot. I shoulda known Tavy would be snoozing in the sunshine."

Silver had to choke back an oath. Those galloping otter paws had dislodged the satchel strap, and it was in full view now.

Meanwhile, Tavy chirped sleepily and trotted over to Rafe. Wrapping around his ankle, she sighed and settled on his boot, as if she intended to continue her nap. His throat worked as he stooped to lift her.

"Well, that mystery's solved," Silver said with less asperity than she'd intended, for Tavy was snuffling at Rafe's cheek and he, wonder of wonders, wasn't cooing about fish kisses. She wondered at his introspection, because he'd never allowed his Chumley facade to be anything less than groanworthy.

"There, there," Celestia crooned. She crossed to Rafe's side and gave his arm an affectionate squeeze. "The spirits will find Octavia plenty of otters to play with. And you can visit her new den any time you choose."

Silver bristled at their obvious accord.

"That's right," Papa chimed in. "Why, she'll practically be our neighbor. Since me and Cellie'll have more rooms here than we can use, you and Silver won't have to go far to see her."

Silver started, eyeing her father sharply.

"That's deucedly decent of you, old fellow," Rafe said quickly. Other than the veiled look he shot Papa, his Chumley mask was firmly back in place. "But alas, I can't sell Chumley Manor. It's been our family home since the Crusades. Why, William the Conqueror dined there. And Robert of Locksley, too."

"Robert of Locksley?" Papa's eyes brightened. "You mean *Robin Hood*?"

"Quite so." Rafe cuddled Tavy, lucky Tavy, against his chest. "Why, 'tis rumored we're distant cousins."

Silver rolled her eyes. *They were distant cousins, all right.* She took refuge in exasperation, preferring to be miffed by Rafe's Robin Hood hogwash rather than jealous of his otter. Besides, Papa was just gullible enough to believe Rafe's fabrication.

She started to help Papa save face, but Tavy distracted her. Poking her head out from under Rafe's elbow, the pup twitched her whiskers at the open ink-well. Visions of paw-stained contracts flashed before Silver's eyes, especially when Tavy stretched out a tentative foot. Hastily, Silver reached around Rafe for the stopper.

To her consternation, her breast brushed his arm.

"Doesn't your otter have an appointment with a photographer?" she snapped, backing hastily away. She tried not to notice how fast her heart was speeding or how taut her nipple had grown from that innocent contact.

Rafe's smile was pure wickedness. "Why, Miss Pennies, I do believe you're flustered. Was it something I did . . . or didn't do?"

"I'll be damned!"

Silver jumped at her father's expletive. He was behind the bombazine now, and her heart sank to her toes.

"Cellie, honey, look! Spiritkeepers!" He emerged with the gaping satchel and a grin that stretched from ear to ear. " 'Course, you're the expert," he added eagerly, holding out a fist-sized rock for her inspection, "but I *think* they're spiritkeepers."

"They are nearly spherical," she conceded, turning her own sample critically in her hands.

"And they don't have any fissures," Papa added, "so the spirits can't slip out."

"Hmm." Celestia passed her chubby, bejeweled fingers over Papa's rock. Her gaze strayed to Silver, who was blushing profusely. Then she passed her palm over the rock in her other hand. Her eyelids fluttered closed. Silver watched uncomfortably as the moons and stars on Celestia's blue tunic shuddered with her breath. She filled her lungs a second time, equally as deep and dramatic.

"The spirits," she intoned finally, "say these will do."

"Hot damn!" Papa was practically dancing a jig. "We can have our séance!"

Celestia's eyes were still closed. "It is most important," she continued in portentous tones, "that the message of the spirits be heard at sunset tomorrow."

Papa pivoted, his eyes round and mystified. "Why?"

Her lashes fluttered open, and she gave him a patient smile. "It's the full moon, dearest."

"Oh." He brightened again, slinging the satchel over his shoulder. "Daughter," he said, his grin a dazzling white crescent in his beard, "we're gonna get to the bottom of those groaning timbers and those missing lunch pails. The Union's gonna settle, and the men are gonna report back to work. And it's all because of you! Who woulda thought you had a slew of spiritkeepers right here, in your ore pouch?"

Silver's throat constricted. "Yes, well . . ." She caught Rafe's eye and burned hotter with shame. "They looked like country rocks to me."

"That's only 'cause your eye's not trained," Papa consoled her. "But if you can learn to spot a hunk of ore, you can learn to spot spiritkeepers—just like I did. Right, Cellie?"

Celestia gave her a warm and motherly smile. "I'm sure Silver can learn anything, once she puts her mind to it."

Silver forced herself to meet Celestia's gaze. Try as she might, she could spy no accusation there. Nor could she detect a trace of gloating. But surely Celestia was canny enough to have guessed why the missing spiritkeepers had materialized amidst *her* ore samples?

From the depths of the house, a chime faintly echoed.

Papa's brow furrowed. "Sounds like the doorbell. You don't reckon that's that photographer fella, do you, Chumley? I thought you told him to meet you at the Trevelyans' house."

"Quite so, old chap. And now that Tavy has to be re-combed and re-fluffed, I'm afraid we're running a bit behind schedule."

"Not to worry, my boy. I'll send a message right quick to Daisy." Papa kissed the back of Celestia's hand before he began dragging her out the door. "C'mon, Cellie, honey. We've got invitations to send, and candles to arrange. . . . Hey, how do spirits feel about snacks at their séances?"

Their footsteps faded down the hall. Silver swallowed, feeling more ashamed than relieved that she'd escaped her papa's suspicion. Hiding his rocks seemed like the most heinous act in the world now that she'd seen the childlike joy their discovery had given him.

"Curses," Rafe taunted gently. "Foiled again."

Silver's chin quivered. Mortified by the threat of her tears, she ducked her head, busily straightening the sheaves of paper on her desk. "I don't have the foggiest notion what you're talking about."

"Don't you?"

Tavy scampered onto the ledger, batting the pen out from under its pages. Aggravated by this play, Silver snatched the instrument away.

"If you're referring to the séance, well then, yes. Of course, I'm dismayed. I've been trying to stop it for weeks."

"By stealing spiritkeepers?"

She hated that her hands shook. Scowling, she

slammed the papers back on the desk. "Yes. *Yes.* There, I've said it. Are you happy now?"

She flopped into her chair. If she could barely stomach herself after pilfering a few worthless rocks, how would she ever forgive herself once Rafe lured Celestia into a lovetrap?

"I thought . . . I *didn't* think," she corrected herself gloomily. "That's the real problem. I should have known Papa's séance idea was his befuddled attempt to save the mine. But honestly, Rafe, he's been so preoccupied with Cibola and Dancing Moon's treasure, and then with Celestia and his wedding plans, that I didn't think he cared about anything else."

"You mean about *anyone* else?"

She winced. Leave it to her to hire an insightful crony. "What gave me away?" she asked dryly.

"Oh, I don't know." His eyes were warm with understanding. "Maybe it's the way you dote on him."

She sighed, fingering the pen. She wondered if all playactors read *between* the lines so well.

"Contrary to what you might think, I hate lying to him."

"I know," he said softly. "But take heart. All isn't lost. For one thing, I don't think he suspects you."

"That's because he's too trusting. It will never cross his mind that I might have stolen from him. Or that I'm conspiring against Celestia." She groaned, rubbing her hands over her face. That's what made her feel worst of all: her father trusted her when she was so blameworthy. "I just wish this whole stupid séance idea had never reached the newspapers. I could just strangle Brady Buckholtz for blowing it out of proportion—"

She hesitated, instinctively uneasy. Rafe had grown

quiet, too quiet. Peering through her fingers, she caught him reading the newspaper clipping with Aunt Agatha's scrawled message. A cold splash of dread drenched her.

Oh, no.

She probably should have said something; she probably should have snatched the article away. Why it bothered her that Rafe had learned about her love affair with Aaron was more than she cared to ask in that moment. All she could do was sit frozen in distress, counting the heartbeats that lodged in her throat, until Rafe's eyes finally rose to hers.

For an eternity, she melted into the liquid pewter of his gaze. Deeper than the ocean itself, it was full of emotions she couldn't quite fathom. They flitted too quickly beneath the mirrorlike calm, betraying an intensity that stole her breath away. She had no language to describe the cryptic dance of thought and feeling, no clues to guide her to his deepest hope or fear. She ached to know more, to understand the glimpse of genuineness he'd shown her, but a fleet second later, only her reflection stared back from that placid surface.

The return of his nonchalance, so well-rehearsed yet so unreal, left her choking on frustration. Ever since that night in the parlor, she'd known there was more to Rafe than the cavalier he played. Why wouldn't he show her who he truly was? Why wouldn't he reveal the man behind the facade?

She never got the opportunity to ask. A brisk, measured stride sounded in the hall. Rafe resumed his Chumley mask, and Benson, another master of facades, halted before the open door. The butler's expression was bland as he bowed, but when he

straightened to announce his purpose, his tone was
disconcertingly smug.

"Pardon my intrusion, miss. But His Grace has a
visitor downstairs. A Mrs. Fiona Fairgate, by name.
She brought no calling card, but she claims to be his
mother.''

Chapter 10

Silver held her breath as the two men locked eyes. For a moment, no one spoke. No one moved. And no sound resonated through the room but the crumbling of her heart. Who was this Fiona Fairgate? The idea that Rafe's mother might actually be alive, and standing in her foyer, sickened Silver.

Her stomach roiling, she gazed at his frozen profile. Had Rafe lied to her that night in the parlor? Had he made up the whole poignant story of his mother's death to woo a naive woman who'd dared to sit beside him in her nightdress?

Rafe pasted on one of his inane smiles. If he hadn't turned so ashen, she might have thought the news of his caller hadn't troubled him in the least.

"My mother, you say?" His chuckle was a trifle high-pitched. "Lud, Bennie, old boy." He dismissed the butler's announcement with a limp wave of his handkerchief. "Mrs. Fairgate is lampooning you."

"Is she indeed, Your Grace?"

If Benson's sneer piqued him, Rafe did a masterful job of concealing it. "Just so. Mrs. Fairgate *helped* rear me after Mummy died. I daresay she considers me one of her own."

Benson didn't look impressed. He didn't even look convinced.

Silver wished she could be.

She cleared her throat. "Benson, show Mrs. Fairgate up here so she and the duke can enjoy a private reunion."

Benson marshaled blandness once more. "Very well, miss."

She suspected he'd left the matter unchallenged only because he relished the impending confrontation between Rafe and Fiona.

As Benson's footfalls receded in the hall, Silver rose. She couldn't fail to notice how carefully Rafe kept his back to her. His rigid pose and darkened countenance weren't reassuring. In fact, they triggered the old, dormant fears.

"You want to tell me who Mrs. Fairgate really is?" she asked quietly, somehow managing not to sound anxious or, worse, hurt.

He crossed to the window, his movements unusually stiff. "Like I told Benson," he said, his voice cool, clipped, and laced with a subtle warning, "she helped raise me."

Silver moistened her lips, his manner unnerving her more than she cared to admit. This wasn't a side of Rafe she'd ever seen. And while it was still nothing like the demon Aaron had unveiled that dreadful night five years ago, still . . . She'd been battling her fear of angry men ever since.

"So . . . Mrs. Fairgate's a relative of some kind?"

"No."

She winced. If words could lash, his would have. Still, she had every right to know. Wiping the palms of her hands on her skirts, she fought off the insidious urge to flee. "A . . . a friend of yours, then?"

He said nothing. An excruciatingly long silence passed. Silver suspected time would run out before his contrariness did.

"Rafe," she pleaded softly, "I need to know what we're up against before Benson returns."

His jaw twitched. She began to think her appeal had been wasted until finally he darted a glittering glance her way.

"She's an actress. And a professional huckster. You're already acquainted with her husband. From the Mining Exchange."

Silver frowned, momentarily baffled, until she recalled Rafe's fast-talking partner with the smelly cigar. "I . . . take it her appearance here today wasn't part of your plan?"

His chest heaved. "No."

"Rafe . . ." She bit her lip. She was beginning to suspect Mrs. Fairgate's arrival bothered him for some reason besides its sheer inconvenience. If all he was trying to do was repair the damage to some humbuggery he'd been plotting, wouldn't he have launched into a spiel of excuses by now?

"Rafe," she tried again, more gently this time, "if you didn't ask her to come here, then why would someone who presumably cares about you risk jeopardizing your—"

"I'll get rid of her. Don't worry."

Cynicism, like acid, had dripped from each word.

She glanced uncomfortably at Tavy. The pup had inched closer to Rafe, her whiskers quivering anxiously. When he paid her no mind, she scrambled up on the window seat, one tiny paw raised to his thigh. Rafe acted like stone. If he felt that sweet gesture of concern, it didn't move him. Silver felt unaccountably upset for his pet. It wasn't like Rafe to ignore his precious otter. It wasn't like him to turn so blasted cold that icicles practically hung in the air between them.

But then, what did she really know about Raphael Jones?

"I-I wasn't worried," she stammered, for some reason wanting to cry. "Not about the plan, I mean. I was just . . . uh, concerned about . . ." *you.*

God. It was true. She blinked back the traitorous sting. What if this Fairgate woman had undermined Rafe's story elsewhere in town? Silver reasoned she could protect him from Benson. She could even protect him from Papa. But what about the Trevelyans? And Marshal Hawthorne?

For the first time since hiring him to ruin Celestia, Silver shamefully faced how selfish she'd been. Rafe was taking an enormous personal risk on her behalf. And even though she was paying him quite handsomely for it, she couldn't help but feel like dung on his bootheel. He might be skilled at chicanery and frauds, but he wasn't invulnerable to a jury! Why hadn't she ever considered *his* danger? What if he were arrested for some past misdeed and . . . and she never saw him again?

Benson's return was heralded by another measured stride, one like a veritable death knell. Towering on the threshold in all his somber black, he reminded Silver of the Grim Reaper. The only difference between doom and Benson, she thought nervously, was that Benson didn't cackle.

"Mrs. Fiona Fairgate, miss," he announced triumphantly.

Silver tossed him a withering glare. But her attention was claimed almost instantly by the woman who stepped into the room. Fiona was older than Silver had anticipated, perhaps sixty, a circumstance that she attributed to the acceptable, though somewhat dated, hat upon Fiona's too yellow hair. The actress was heavily busted, if not quite as broad of hip, and Silver suspected these attributes had made her wildly popular among male audiences of her day. Any hint of the burlesque show was absent from her attire, however. Fiona's hair had been neatly rolled into a French knot, and her striped, pewter-blue traveling suit, though dusty, was not noticeably threadbare. With her cameo-studded collar, snow white gloves, gray parasol, and smartly laced boots, she made for a passable matron of society.

But the thing that indelibly marked Fiona as a woman of lower class, Silver thought despairingly, was her face paint. Fiona's powder only accentuated the crevices around her sagging features and, unfortunately, contrasted a bit too vividly with her heavily rouged cheeks, cherry lips, and the vibrant blue streaks above her eyes. Silver suspected that Benson had been quick to notice the tawdry effect and had drawn a similar conclusion.

Mustering an air of cordiality, Silver stepped briskly forward. "Mrs. Fairgate," she said with cool aplomb, acutely aware that this woman was somehow hurting Rafe—and that Benson, eager to watch, was loitering on the threshold. "I am Silver Nichols. It's a pleasure to receive you in my home."

Worried green eyes, no less canny for their upset, flickered her way. Then Fiona pasted on a tight little smile, bobbing her head in greeting. "The pleasure is mine, Miss Nichols," she said in a British, unmistakably *highbrow* British, accent.

Silver silently blessed the woman for that attempt at concession. Perhaps she hadn't come with the intention of hurting Rafe, after all. But intending to or not, her appearance had all but verified Rafe's masquerade for the ever-suspicious Benson. Now Silver had to figure out some way to convince the butler he'd reached the wrong conclusion.

And how the devil was she supposed to do *that*?

For the first time in her life, Silver thanked God her father disliked Benson. Perhaps Papa's good-natured antagonism, coupled with his growing fondness for "Chumley," would keep him from listening to accusations against Rafe.

Silver took some consolation in that thought. "That will be all, Benson."

The man tensed, his dark eyes narrowing. She might have been unsettled by the blatant hostility in his gaze if his behavior hadn't annoyed her so much. She glared imperiously at him. A tense moment passed, but he did, eventually, back down. Apparently Benson still valued his job enough, at least for this week, not to defy her openly.

However, he did neglect to close the door behind him.

Damn his arrogant hide. Silver pressed her lips together. Her esteemed British butler was getting a bit too high-handed for her peace of mind. She knew he hadn't been happy for some time in Papa's employ, but his contempt seemed to be growing, in direct correlation to the new watches and rings he'd been sporting. Why, just the other day, he'd had the nerve to pass an envelope to one of his back-alley acquaintances at the servants' entrance. Cook had complained vociferously about the incident, because the one-eyed stranger had stolen her apple pie. Silver suspected Benson was placing bets—that his gambling had given him a false sense of prosperity and he was *looking* for a reason to quit.

So help her God, if she found him eavesdropping in the hall, she'd give him one.

Meanwhile, Rafe had grown composed enough to turn and face his visitor. "Fiona," he greeted her, his voice pleasant, his eyes more turbulent than a midsummer snowstorm. "How good to see you so healthy. Why, was it only three weeks ago that you were wasting away at death's door?"

The woman visibly winced, glancing at Silver. However, whether Fiona was worried that Rafe might unleash his simmering temper on her or confused that he'd dropped his Chumley facade in front of a prime mark wasn't clear.

"I, uh, came to explain that little misunderstanding to you, luv," she wheedled in a far less cultured accent.

"You mean to confess?" His smile was as dazzling as ice in the sunlight. "Why, what a novel approach."

Silver's innards writhed at the bite of Rafe's sarcasm. Again, Fiona glanced her way, as if the woman were hesitant to discuss the matter before an audience.

Silver decided to take her cue. As much as she was dying to know what Fiona had done to make Rafe so bitter, Silver couldn't allow herself to eavesdrop any more than she had allowed Benson to. Besides, she was worried that her butler was prowling the hall, seeking information to unmask Rafe for good.

"If you and Mrs. Fairgate will excuse me, *Your Grace*—" she emphasized the bogus title —"I'll, uh, see that Tavy is made ready for her photograph."

Never having held an otter before, however, she juggled the pup none too elegantly against her chest. Tavy managed to wriggle upright, planting her front paws on Silver's shoulder, whimpering for the master she was leaving behind. Silver felt unaccountably guilty as she pulled the door closed.

At least, she thought grimly, there was no butler lurking in the shadows. But Benson was nothing if not clever, and she wondered if she might not be wise to guard the door, in case he had an attack of servile dedication and returned with a tray of refreshments.

Unfortunately, this thought was punctuated by a paw, which swiped five webbed and sharply clawed toes after her earring.

"Ouch!" She glared down into bright, inquisitive eyes and a full set of fishbone-grinding teeth. "You're going straight to your cage, fish puss. Just as soon as I find it," she added grudgingly.

Tavy stuck a wet nose in her ear. Silver nearly jumped out of her skin. *Otters,* she grumbled under her breath. *Whatever would possess a man to keep one?*

By the time she reached Rafe's bedroom, a full wing away, Tavy had apparently forgotten her master. Considering how busy the pup had been, Silver wasn't surprised. The little monster had pulled the entire left side of her coiffure down, gnawed the point of her collar, and chewed a sterling button clean off her bodice. In fact, the pup had swallowed it before Silver could pry the creature's jaws apart and fish it from her mouth.

On second thought, Silver mused queasily, recalling the heap of crayfish shells she'd once seen Jimmy toting to the kitchen, *maybe prying open otter jaws isn't such a good idea.*

"Octavia, you are a menace," she told the creature sternly, pausing outside Rafe's closed door and gathering the nerve to march in.

Tavy planted a fishy kiss on her jaw.

Silver wrinkled her nose, as much at the smell as the ticklish sensation of whiskers. She wondered if Rafe had trained his pet to kiss . . . or if otters went about kissing each other naturally. She guessed the former. *And what earthly good would* that *skill be for a defenseless baby otter in the wild?* Honestly, how did Rafe hope to send Tavy out among coyotes and wolves?

She eased the door open. Knowing that she was perfectly safe, that Rafe was probably tongue-lashing Fiona half a house away, brought a traitorous sense of disappointment rather than relief. Silver was appalled by the realization. Still, there was no use denying it. She didn't know exactly when her heart had changed, or even when the idea had taken root, but God help her, she *wanted* to feel safe in a man's arms again. And she wanted that man to be Rafe.

"He is rather charming, isn't he, Octavia?" she murmured, her heart quickening as she forced her feet across the threshold. Clutching the pup closer for moral support, she continued, "And he's dashing, handsome, and . . . well, sweet. In a wicked sort of way."

Tavy's head bobbed, as if she agreed. Silver darted her a dubious glance. *What's more likely is the little scamp just spotted the flash of an earring on the other side of my head.*

She hastily tucked that bangle, too, in a pocket concealed within the folds of her skirt.

Then, taking a steadying breath, she gazed around the guest room that, for the last three weeks, had become her scoundrel's lair. She wasn't sure what she'd expected. False whiskers, marked playing cards, carefully cross-referenced books of love poetry for dupes like her?

Instead, she was pleasantly surprised. Rafe hadn't left empty champagne bottles or the calling cards of half-naked women strewn across his bed; in fact, she could detect no visible evidence of a decadent life. His belongings were rather Spartan for a man with his flare for the dramatic. She detected only one battered trunk in the whole of the lavishly decorated room, and since it was open, she could see its contents: his flannel shirt, several pairs of woolen socks, an Indian blanket, and what appeared to be a sewing kit. Curiously, the trunk was three-quarters empty; spying Tavy's open cage on the window seat, she wondered if it fit as neatly into that void as its appearance suggested.

So that's how he smuggles his little darling into grand hotels and the homes of the well-to-do, eh?

The shaving brush and razor he'd left on her marble washstand were humble affairs, sporting wood, rather than bone or ivory, handles. His four-pronged comb still looked suspiciously like the tree limb he must have carved it from. It occurred to her then that while he played incessantly with his quizzing glass, which, he'd once confessed, he'd "borrowed" from a former employer's prop wagon, she'd never seen him wear a watchfob. Or cuff links. Or even a signet ring. Didn't he own a single manly vanity? Where the devil was he spending all the money she paid him, if he wasn't spending it on himself?

"Your master is proving to be quite an enigma," she told Tavy as the pup squirmed, barking at a monarch butterfly that had alighted on the window ledge.

Silver half smiled, lowering the pup to the floor. Tavy, rippling with excitement, waddled with surprising speed to greet the new playmate. Of course, by the time Tavy shimmied onto the seat, the butterfly had flown away.

Tavy's whiskers fell. She tried to claw her way out on the ledge, but Rafe had constructed some sort of wire mesh to keep her from taking flight herself and plummeting to the lawn below.

Silver's heart twisted to watch the pup gnaw so futilely on the cross-hatches that barred her freedom. Somehow, her original idea, to shove Tavy into a cage and bolt the door, seemed heinous now. Indeed, Silver was ashamed she'd intended it.

"I'm sorry, Tavy," she murmured, understanding now why Rafe couldn't bear to cage his pet.

But even a mansion as big as hers would eventually feel like a cage to a full-grown, twenty-pound otter. As much as Tavy had been driving her crazy with her escapades, Silver supposed it wasn't fair to expect a wild creature to sit still, nibble neatly, and otherwise behave according to human rules of decorum. Tavy needed all the outdoors in which to romp and satisfy her curiosity. In fact, Tavy needed it *soon.*

"Don't worry, sweetheart. We'll find you a home in a river far from sawmills and lumberyards, a river with lots of butterflies, and crayfish, and other otters, too."

When she realized she'd included herself in the home-finding quest, Silver shook her head in bemusement. Rafe's influence was more seductive than she'd realized. Why, three weeks ago, she'd never given a passing thought to otters, much less the rivers they inhabited.

Now she found herself wondering what happened to otters, crayfish, and frogs when the water they lived in was choked full of wood pulp. What did they eat? How did they survive?

An unsettling thought followed: *Maybe they didn't.*

A resounding slam vibrated all the way through the house.

Silver caught her breath. Even Tavy raised her head, pricking her ears at the sound.

Rafe.

Silver stood like stone, her heart thudding painfully against her ribs. She knew the culprit had to be him. None of the servants would dare slam a door in her home. And Papa's happy-go-lucky nature never allowed him to get that angry.

Anxiously, she tiptoed to the door and cracked it open. Was Rafe coming this way? Did she really want to be here, *in his bedroom*, if he was?

She'd come so far over the last five years, forcing herself not to flee from blustering Union leaders, braving the temper tantrums of teamsters, investors, and lumbermen. Nevertheless, standing in Rafe's private quarters, the old dread coiled through her gut. She hated the fact that images of Aaron kneeling over her flashed through her mind, but she couldn't stop them any more than she could keep her knees from quaking at the memory—and at what she'd had to do to break free of him. She'd been terrified; she'd been protecting herself, but who would have believed her? She'd sneaked through her window not once but several times to meet him after midnight. She was lucky Aaron hadn't sent the entire Philadelphia police force after her. She was lucky she wasn't locked in some woman's reformatory . . . or swinging from a gallows.

She shuddered, stepping into the hall. She didn't want to come that close to taking a man's life again.

Tavy yipped as Silver pulled open the door. Seeing

the rainbowed light pouring in from the hall's vaulted windows, the otter thumped eagerly down to the carpet.

"Oh, no you don't," Silver muttered as the pup, webbed paws slapping, made an awkward but no less exuberant beeline for freedom. Her hands shaking, Silver hastily shut the door. She could hear Rafe's footsteps heading her way.

"*Coward,*" she chided herself. "*He's not even angry with you.*" And he *was* Rafe, after all. Any man who raised orphaned otters and played Beethoven in memory of his mother had to be crushingly sensitive, no matter how adept he'd become at hiding wounds that festered so deeply that they never quite healed.

And if anyone understood pain of that nature, it was she.

On the other hand, his otter had practically undressed her. When Aaron had accused her of cock-teasing, she hadn't stood before him with her hair in wanton disarray. She hadn't flaunted her corset and chemise through a gaping bodice. In such a state of dishabille, could she blame Rafe if he concluded she was loitering outside his bedroom to entice him?

She winced. He'd already withstood the temptation of her bathrobe and her nightdress. She didn't want to try fate a third time.

Slinking into an adjacent bedroom, she did her best to repair herself with nervous, fumbling fingers and the broach she'd been wearing, thankfully, on the side of her gown Tavy hadn't gnawed. She needn't have gone through the trouble, though. Five minutes ticked by, and Rafe still hadn't stormed past her hideout to slam a second door. She ventured a peek into the hall. Maybe he wasn't coming this way, after all.

She was nearly as chagrined as she was relieved.

Had he left the house? His departure stood to reason, if only to keep Benson from jeering at him. Damn Fiona anyway. What if the woman had driven him away for good?

Presentable once more, Silver hurried toward the rear staircase. She was planning to go to the stables and see if a groom had seen Rafe ride away. Unfortunately, she had to pass her office on this mission. And the sobbing behind the door was unmistakable.

She scowled at the sound. Lord, what had Rafe *said* to Fiona? Or more to the point, what had she done to *him*? Recalling the hurt beneath his devil-may-care facade, Silver's fingers curled into fists. She didn't know everything there was to know about him, of course, but surely Rafe didn't deserve that kind of heartache. She had half a mind to march into the office and give that woman a verbal thrashing that would make Rafe's door-slamming seem tame.

But Fiona was in tears. And while Silver would have much preferred to comfort Rafe than Fiona, good breeding won out over personal whim. Gritting her teeth, she mustered a semblance of compassion and rapped on the door before walking in.

Fiona was huddled in the embrace of a wing chair, her eye paint muddied, her facial powder streaked red and blue. Silver sighed, fishing a handkerchief from a skirt pocket. Even without the colored rivulets that ran from Fiona's eyelashes to her chin, she would have had to be a consummate actress to fake puffy eyes and a mottled nose.

"Is there anything I can get you?" Silver asked quietly.

A rising blush helped offset the pallor beneath Fiona's rouge. "D-did Rafe leave?"

"I believe so."

"For the marshal's office?" The hope swimming in Fiona's eyes was hard to mistake.

Jesus. The woman wanted Rafe to go to the Marshal's office? Didn't she know that was the last place he should be showing his face—even in disguise?

"He didn't say," Silver replied cautiously. "Why? What happened?"

Fiona delayed her answer, dabbing at her cheeks, her nose, her eyes. Silver sensed a deception coming on.

"Let me be quite frank with you, Mrs. Fairgate. You have exactly five minutes to convince me why I shouldn't have my butler throw you out."

Her chin quivered, but a spark of ire helped to dry those moss green eyes. "Now see here, miss, I may not be as fine as you and all yer kinfolk, but in Mayfair, a lady of yer ilk would show a bit of compassion for a poor—"

"Four and a half minutes, madam."

Fiona blew out her breath. Silver arched an eyebrow.

"My Freddie's in jail."

"And Freddie would be? . . ."

"My husband."

"I see."

"You know him, miss," Fiona continued urgently. "Fact is, you two had a nice chat about business at the Leadville Mining Exchange. It would've been about three weeks ago, now. He was the big strapping bloke with the top hat and cigar," she added with a touch of feminine pride. "You remember him, don't you?"

Oh yes. Silver's lips twisted. She remembered "Freddie," all right. "So your husband's in jail," she said crisply. "An unfortunate circumstance for you both. But what does that have to do with Rafe?''

Fiona blinked at her, looking genuinely aghast. ''Why, he didn't tell you about us? How me and Freddie took him in? Straight outta the snow, we did. He'd been running away on bloody Christmas Day. The poor lad had just come from watching his Mama be buried, and that bastard brother of his started a brawl right on the poor woman's grave. 'Course Preacher Jones blamed Rafe, not his precious Michael.''

Silver frowned, uncertain how much to believe. ''*Preacher* Jones? Rafe's father was a preacher?''

''Not exactly.'' Fiona's smile was wry. ''Never told you about Jedidiah, did he? How that holier-than-thou bastard would spout scripture while he whipped the boy? Or how he'd convinced Rafe he'd been spawned from the devil's own loins?''

Silver winced. So that's what Rafe had meant that night in the parlor?

''I don't know why Rafe's Mama had the poor sense to get caught two-timing Jedidiah,'' Fiona said more softly. ''Don't know why she suffered herself and Rafe to live with an embittered old cuckold, either. But she did. And Rafe . . . well, he wouldn't leave her. Leastways, not 'til she died.''

A lump thickened Silver's throat. Rafe's mother had borne him in shame as an adulteress? If Fiona's tale was true, then . . . Silver's heart twisted. Poor Rafe.

''How old?'' she murmured. ''How old was Rafe when his mother died?''

''Fourteen.'' Fiona darted her a keen, assessing look. ''I'm telling you, miss. Rafe owes my Freddie his life. It was Freddie who taught the lad to survive. Why, at fourteen, Rafe still didn't have the blooming sense to pack food or matches when he ran away. That preacher's son wouldn't have stood a bloody chance.''

Silver did her best to swallow her outrage over Rafe's childhood. She suspected her show of sentiment had already cost her the advantage with Fiona.

''I suspect, Mrs. Fairgate, that while Rafe may indeed have you and, uh, Freddie to thank for his . . . way of life, Rafe's feelings toward you are, frankly, hostile. I also suspect that you have a fairly good idea why. A lie you told him, perhaps?''

Fiona grimaced, dropping her eyes to the linen she was twisting in her hands. ''Freddie said you were smart,'' she mumbled.

''I also suspect your husband is in jail because he got caught red-handed in one of his humbugs.''

Fiona's head jerked up at that. ''Oh, no, miss. Freddie's much too clever for some tinstar to put the finger on him. Freddie got caught . . . well, 'cause his heart's in the right place. And whenever his heart talks louder than his head, trouble's sure to follow.''

''The point in question being? . . .''

Fiona fidgeted. Either she disliked direct questions or she was wracking her imagination for a plausible lie. In either event, Silver wasn't going to let Fiona lead her down the garden path. She folded her arms across her breasts. ''You're wasting time, Mrs. Fairgate.''

''It's a delicate matter,'' she hedged.

''You will find me much more patient, not to mention understanding, if you tell the truth. What did Freddie do?''

Fiona raised her chin. Behind the mutinous glare, pride gleamed unmistakably in her eyes. ''He tried to smash the face of some rich bloke who beat the bloody hell out of one of our chorus girls.''

Silver's heart quickened as she let that information sink in. "When?"

"Two weeks ago."

An eerie shiver gusted down Silver's spine. She had no reason to doubt Fiona's tale. In fact, she had a couple of unpleasant personal reasons to believe her. "How is the girl?" she asked quietly.

Fiona shook her head, fumbling with the handkerchief again. "Not good. The doc says Amy ain't likely to dance for a long time. Maybe never."

It was Silver's turn to fidget. She had to admit, she didn't want to know that. "Is there anything I can do?"

"We take care of our own, miss. That's why I thought Rafe would want to know. And . . . well, why I need his help."

Silver frowned. "For Amy?"

"No. For Fred."

Their eyes locked. For the first time since she'd walked in the room, Silver felt an accord with the woman.

"I'll . . . speak to him for you."

"You're that close to him, are you?"

Silver felt her neck warm at the undisguised speculation in the old woman's stare.

"You are welcome to wait here, if you like," she countered primly.

Fiona rose, gathering her parasol and her dignity. "That won't be necessary, miss. If Rafe's the man I think he is, he'll come around. Just tell him not to sulk for too long. Freddie doesn't have many friends in Aspen, least of all the kind who can afford to pay his fines."

Silver started. "Fred's in Marshal Hawthorne's jail?"

"That's right. None of the tinstars in Leadville cared enough about a poor immigrant girl to risk charging a rich man with a crime. The bastard rode away as free as you please, and Freddie got so mad, he took it on himself to track the bloke down and dole out a proper punishment. 'Course, that was fourteen days ago. When I didn't hear any word from Freddie, I knew something was wrong. That's why I took the evening stage to Aspen. When I found him in jail, he told me he knocked the bloke out cold before your town marshal arrested him." Fiona's eyes narrowed. "Think my Amy got beat up by somebody you know?"

Silver's stomach roiled as a half-formed suspicion snaked through her mind. "I . . . hope not."

Fiona nodded grimly. "Well, just the same, miss, you watch your step. A wad of pocket change and a fancy address don't make a man a gentleman. You remember that. And you remember, too, that justice ain't necessarily got anything to do with the law.'Specially when you're penniless and female."

Chapter 11

⁓◦◦◦⁓

Rafe reached automatically for the chalk box. It felt good to grind that fine powder onto the tip of his stick. It felt good to smash the cue ball against the object balls, to hear the satisfying *smack, smack, smack* as the reds, blues, and yellows careened across the felt. Billiards could be a brutal game if one knew how to crack a rack just right. And Rafe had been cracking racks for years, imagining Jedidiah's or Michael's face painted across each ball he buried in a pocket. Now he was imagining smashed Fairgate likenesses. He supposed it was the cowardly way, beating the tar out of pool balls instead of his erstwhile kin.

And it was just one more reason to hate himself.

Rafe's lip curled as he let the cue ball fly again.

He'd run out of brandy more than an hour ago. If he'd had a decanter—hell, a *bottle*—of rotgut, he'd have finished that too, but unfortunately, Max only stocked aged imports that went down so smooth that a man had to be told he was drunk. Rafe craved the familiar punishments of something low class, something home-brewed and vile. He wanted his throat to smoke and his gut to burn. He wanted to ache all over so badly that the searing in his chest would feel comfortable by comparison.

240

He ground his teeth. How could Fred and Fiona lie to him? About *consumption*, goddamn them? But even worse, how could he have been such a sucker?

No doubt even Satan was ashamed of him.

"Rafe."

He stiffened, mortified to see his hand tremble at the genuine caring in Silver's voice. He hadn't heard her step on the stairs. He hadn't even heard the door creak open. But then, when one was battering oneself with recriminations, one didn't hear much of anything else.

"You've . . . been up here a long time."

His jaw jutted. So she'd known he'd been holed up in Max's attic hideaway? Then why hadn't she come sooner? Was the prospect of an unchaperoned rendezvous with him that frightening?

He bit his tongue on an uncharitable retort. It had been more than a week since he'd kissed her, but he supposed the incident still gave her nightmares. Silver wasn't quite as self-assured in intimate encounters as she'd proven to be in business, and he'd pushed her too hard too soon. He'd have no one but himself to blame if she went running back to Aaron Townsend the minute he traveled west of the Missouri River.

Then again, it was a big damned continent, right? Townsend didn't have to holiday in Colorado, much less in Aspen, and ruin everything.

Rafe groaned to himself. *Jones, you didn't seriously think Silver would lower her standards enough to marry you, did you?*

"Since you missed dinner," she murmured, striking a match to light a porcelain table lamp, "I thought you might be hungry."

He grimaced as light flared. He much preferred the cavelike atmosphere and shadow-wreathed rafters of the gaming den. Speared by shafts of illumination, he felt blind and exposed, as if he'd been shoved onto center stage to speak lines he'd never rehearsed. The analogy wasn't all that far-fetched, considering how few times he'd played the real Raphael Jones.

Something delicate and savory, like clam sauce or lobster bisque, wafted to him from the platter she carried to the sideboard. He blinked at the artfully folded napkin and its tasteful gold edging, the impeccably polished sterling condiment shakers, the appetizing and attractively arranged remains of a gourmet meal that, for his sake, should have been scraped into a bowl and rewarmed as stew. Who was he kidding to think he deserved to live this way, spearing seafood delicacies with a sterling fork, sipping imported liquors out of Austrian crystal?

He gripped the bumper tighter and punched the eight ball into a corner pocket. "You needn't have gone to the trouble."

"It wasn't any trouble," she said quietly.

His conscience balked at that sweet, female croon. Was it possible for a con to go more awry?

Three weeks ago, he'd set out to bag himself a fortune, bed an heiress, and, by exposing Celestia, generally make an ass out of anyone associated with the Nicholses' mining empire. He'd been playing a game of consequences, punishing rich people he'd wanted to believe were as contemptible as he.

But they weren't. And so the real ass was Raphael Jones. He hadn't planned on liking affable old Max. He hadn't planned on taking to heart the idea of marrying Max's daughter. He hadn't dreamed he would grow to care about Silver, much less Jimmy and Celestia.

Sentiment and cons didn't mix. He knew better, but

he'd been stupid. And his lapse into stupidity had marked him as a prime target. As he'd been hoodwinking Silver, and she'd been hoodwinking Max, and Max had been hoodwinking Silver, Rafe had come to find out Fred and Fiona had been hoodwinking *him*. He supposed he should be laughing at the irony of it all. He was a sucker, and he was getting just what he deserved—what he'd always deserved since the day of his birth.

But somehow, he found no humor in the knowledge that he'd been exploited by people he loved. Fred and Fiona hadn't deceived him as a matter of business, they'd made it personal. They knew all his weaknesses, and by claiming Fiona was dying from the illness that had killed his mother, they'd conned him in the cruelest way imaginable.

He might have been a despicable bastard, Rafe thought miserably, but he would never have gone that far to hurt anybody.

"Rafe," Silver said gently, "don't you at least want to taste the bisque?"

He was careful to keep his back turned as he racked up another set of balls. Raphael Jones, *failure extraordinaire*, wasn't a role he wanted to play before this audience, but for the life of him he couldn't recall the lines of any heroes. "Maybe later."

He heard her skirts rustle, as if she'd edged closer.

"Are you feeling all right?"

"Why?"

In the reflection of the window, he caught her sniffing the empty decanter. He cringed, bracing himself for a tirade against manly vices. Considering how careful Max always had been to hide his gambling and drinking from Silver, Rafe assumed she was the type to nag.

But Silver surprised him. Rather than browbeat him for his moral depravity, as Jedidiah Jones might have done, she quietly replaced the decanter on the liquor cabinet. Rafe released a ragged breath. He hadn't realized he'd been holding it until their eyes met in the sash.

"It isn't like you to miss an opportunity to rib Benson about his dinner service," she said with an attempt at levity.

He tossed aside the rack. "I daresay I'll have to repair that oversight tomorrow."

Her smile was fleeting. "Well, that should give Papa enough time to hone his digs. They fell rather flat this evening, I'm afraid, without you there to inspire him. And then when word got back to him that Benson snubbed you by neglecting to carry a dinner tray upstairs, Papa gave Benson a tongue-lashing like I've never heard before. Not that Benson didn't deserve it," Silver added hurriedly as Rafe hardened his jaw. "But it's not like Papa to care about such things. I've never seen him so upset at a servant. Even Celestia had trouble calming him down before they left for the Windsor Hotel. Honestly, Rafe, sometimes I think Papa considers you the son he never had."

Rafe's chest heaved, and he let the cue fly, blasting the object balls in myriad, rainbowed directions. Did Silver have any idea how much that passing comment meant to him?

"Rafe . . ." She bit her lip, waiting for the banging and thumping to end. "I think you know I didn't really come here to talk about Papa and Benson."

"No?" He reached for the chalk box.

A tense silence lengthened between them as he busied himself with his stick.

"Rafe . . ." She sounded reluctant to continue. "I

know you don't want to talk about Fiona. I know . . .
she hurt you.''

"Told you that, did she?"

"No. Not exactly. But I'm not as indifferent to . . .
to other people's feelings as you might believe.''

He groaned inwardly, circling to the far side of the
table. He'd liked their repartee much better when
she'd thought him callous and incorrigible. What had
happened to the hard-as-nails mining maven he'd met
in Leadville? Silver was supposed to be selfish and
heartless. Instead, she'd abided Jimmy's painful lack
of etiquette with martyrlike patience; she'd suffered
Tavy's rampages through her toiletries with a grudging, but no less motherly, tolerance; she'd even born
with grace the humiliation his ludicrous Chumley had
caused her.

What was more, she adored Max, and in the process of waging feminine warfare to protect him, she'd
exposed a mystifying vulnerability toward men, one
which made Rafe feel protective and . . . Christ . . .
Conscientious. How ironic that he should come to
care about a woman he'd once thought was the female
equivalent of himself.

And how disturbing that she was starting to care
about *him*, when the only thing he was good for was
a heaping dose of misery.

"If you want your sympathy appreciated, Silver,
don't waste it on bastards.''

"You're not the only bastard in this room," she
retorted quietly. "The only difference between us is
that my papa was able to do the right thing by my
mama. And he did.''

He winced at the empathy in her tone. He hadn't
meant his illegitimacy literally, but he supposed it

was too late to prevaricate. Fiona had already spilled the beans.

"You can't believe everything you hear from the Fairgates, Silver."

"I gathered that, but . . ." She cleared her throat, raising her voice above the rebounding cue. "I think, maybe, this case is an exception. I mean, Fred *is* in Marshal Hawthorne's jail. I sent Jimmy to scout for information, and he told me Fred was charged with assault and something called 'willful destruction of property.' Apparently, while Fred was brawling at the Red Lion Saloon, he threw a couple of deputies out the window and busted a half dozen chairs and tables, none of which he can pay for. So in addition to his five-hundred-dollar fine for assault, he's looking at thirty-five hundred dollars in property damage, all of which Fiona has to raise by sundown tomorrow."

"I sent Fred and Fiona fifteen thousand dollars two weeks ago," Rafe said acidly, "when I thought Fiona was dying of some lung plague. They should have more than enough money to pay for Fred's fines."

She blinked wide-eyed at him. "Y-you sent them fifteen thousand dollars?"

"That's right." He decided not to confess that fifteen thousand dollars had been part of his poker earnings from the high-stakes game Max had been running the night of his engagement party. "And if you're thinking I might have stolen a couple of your sterling what-nots to melt down, then let me ease your mind. Every penny was legitimately earned."

"I believe you."

He hardened his jaw in self-loathing. "I can't imagine why you would."

"For heaven's sake, Rafe." She made an exasperated noise. "I am not the enemy here. I had thought

we'd come to . . . well, I had hoped we'd reached a
better understanding. I know how attached you've become to Papa. And I haven't failed to notice that . . .
that you've grown fond of Celestia, too. It only stands
to reason you don't think much of me, considering
what I hired you to do. In fact, the only thing you
may like about me at all is my money, but''—her
voice caught, vibrating on a suspicious tremor—"I
can help you and Fred. I mean, I *want* to help you,"
she amended hastily.

He muttered an oath. Christ, he'd really done it,
hadn't he? He'd made her fall for him or rather, for
his playacting. If he hadn't held her one week ago as
she'd sobbed, if he hadn't realized how wrong he'd
been to think her callous and conniving, he might
have toasted his success. But tonight, seeing the glimmer of caring in her gaze . . .

He hastily averted his eyes. He had to get the hell
out of Aspen. He had to get out of Silver's life before
she threw away her second chance on a respectable
man like Aaron Townsend.

"Silver," he said more gently, "you shouldn't get
involved."

"I've been involved ever since I kept your secret
at the Mining Exchange. Fred's too." When he stiffened, she added hastily, "That's why I, uh, took the
liberty of wiring Dr. Bertram in Leadville. He's an
old friend of Papa's, and he was able to confirm that
Amy was badly beaten. She . . . she might not walk
again, Rafe."

His gut roiled at the news. Dammit. The last time
he'd seen Amy, she'd been in pigtails. *Little, laughing
Amy with the big blue eyes.* . . . At four years old,
she'd reminded him so poignantly of Sera.

His chest constricting from an all-too-familiar pain,

he sat heavily on the table, twisting the stick in his fists until they burned. He hoped the chafing would help him stave off the same overwhelming sense of loss that had left him weeping at his mother's graveside. Had Fred really been on a vigilante mission to avenge Amy? Or was Amy's tragedy a coincidence Fred had used because he'd gotten drunk and belligerent and now needed bail?

In his heart of hearts, Rafe wanted to believe some spark of altruism burned in the breast of the man who had once been like a father to him. He could still remember how Fred had saved him, and his first month's earnings, from the whore who'd tried to roll him; how Fred had interceded when his youthful wisecracks had angered the wrong gunslinger. But Rafe could also remember all the times when Fred had lied to him. And tonight, crushed by Fred's latest deception, Rafe felt as if his father were dead to him.

"Rafe." Silver moved closer, closer than she had ever willingly dared, and touched his knee. "I have a sense that . . . that you don't like to talk about things that bother you. Maybe you prefer it that way. Or maybe you've just never had anyone who'd listen. Please believe me, I haven't come here to judge you."

He drew a shuddering breath, acutely aware of the warmth of her palm against his thigh. Did she have any idea how that innocent caress affected him? Christ, it was like the promise of water to a man dying of thirst.

"Leave it alone," he rasped. "We all get what we deserve."

"According to Jedidiah?"

He flinched at her reminder. "For God's sake, Silver, can't you see what I am? A liar, a failure, a fraud."

"Is that what you believe? Is that what Jedidiah *made* you believe?"

His chest heaved. "It's true. I'll ruin you the way I ruined my mother."

"Rafe," she said more quietly, wrapping her hand around his fist. "You are not responsible for your mother's adultery. Jedidiah poisoned your mind. He made you believe in a God as petty as he was. But the God I believe in would never blame you or me for something that happened between our parents long before we took the first breath of life. Can't you see how small, cruel and *human* that kind of blame would be?"

Rafe's throat swelled. Silver's rationale held an undeniable appeal. Was it true that Jedidiah, the man whom all of Blue Thunder had relied on to interpret scripture, might have been wrong? That he'd poisoned the minds of innocents? Rafe didn't like giving the bastard that much credit. Still, recognizing Jedidiah's power over him was far less abhorrent than believing he didn't have the chance, much less the right, to redeem himself.

"You seem to have given a lot of thought to salvation," he said bitterly.

She bit her lip. "Well, I like to think mistakes are part of being human," she said, her cheeks growing steadily pinker. "Otherwise, no one would ever get to heaven. Least of all, me.

"Rafe . . ." Her voice trailed off as if she was choosing her next words. "I believe Fred's and Fiona's story."

His smile was mirthless. "Of course you do. They're unparalleled liars."

"But I have proof Amy was hurt. And Jimmy confirmed Fred was arrested for attacking some well-dressed high roller at the Red Lion."

He shook his head despairingly. "Don't try so hard to acquit them. They'll just make a sucker out of you, too."

She fidgeted. For a moment, he thought she might insist on proving her point. Instead, she frowned, staring at his boots.

"I . . . had thought you might at least want to investigate the matter. For Amy's sake."

He scowled, not liking the way she used guilt as her tool. It reminded him too much of Fiona. "Amy's got an older male cousin and Uncle Fred. She doesn't need me wading into the fray. Besides, I'm no damned hero."

"You could try to be," she whispered.

He muttered an oath. Pushing away from her, he stalked to the far side of the table. "There you go again, forgetting what I am."

"I'm not sure *what* you are, Rafe. I thought I did— once. I'm glad to say I was wrong then. I don't want to believe I'm wrong now. And I don't think Fiona wants to believe she's wrong, either. She was in tears when you left her this morning. No matter what she might have said or done, I think, deep down, she loves you, like a mother loves a son."

The old hurt burned its way up his throat. "Like a *son*?" Slamming his stick on the table, he started to pace in wild, agitated movements. "No mother," he ground out, "would lie in bed, pretending she had consumption, when she knew how devastating the news would be to her son. No mother would pretend she was dying and ask her son for money if *love* were her motivation." He spun to face her, his fists clenched, his chest searing. "Everything Fred and Fiona do is calculated to make a profit, Silver. *Ev-*

erything. That's why they took me into the troupe. That's why they tried to lure me back. Don't you see?'' he choked. ''They only care about the money I'll earn them. Money's all I've ever been to them.''

To his mortification, his voice broke. He swayed, gripping the table, fighting the grief threatening to unman him. There was nothing he could do to hide the raw emotion contorting his face; there was nothing he could do but be who and what he was. And in that moment, when he was his lowest, most pathetic self, Silver's arms wrapped around his waist.

He shuddered. Had he the strength, or perhaps the self-discipline, he would have pushed her away as he'd pushed away so many others, thinking they'd despise him for his weakness. Never had he met anyone who cared about the real Raphael Jones. Never had he dreamed he might be worth some genuine affection.

But Silver pressed nearer. She defied every moral convention to let the softness of her cheek rest against the stubble of his jaw, and the timid thumping of her heart beat against his chest. It was almost more than he could bear, the solace of her arms. Reason fled before the guttural sound that welled up in his throat. Before he could recall how undeserving he was, before he could think how crude his surge of primal longing, he pulled her mouth to his, devouring the sweetness that trembled open to appease him.

Only he wasn't appeased. Three weeks of waiting, of wanting—not to mention the last eight hours of simmering jealousy—were unleashed in that tumult of feeling. Damning Aaron Townsend, Rafe kissed her the way he'd been craving her kisses, hungrily, passionately, relentlessly. He dug his fingers into her hair; he arched her spine back; gripped her buttocks and flattened her hips against his, reveling in the heat that spread like a prairie fire between his thighs and hers. He didn't buss her cheek like a Wilbur Chumley or peck her knuckles like some Shakespearean gallant. His kiss was pure Raphael Jones, smoking, scintillating, and sinful enough to make the angels blush.

He might have lost himself completely in that sensual feast, baring her breasts, suckling her nipples, hoisting her, petticoats and all, to sit astride him on the table. But she trembled in his arms. He recognized the taste of tears on his tongue, and they weren't his. Like a splash of cold water, he remembered the fear she'd tried so valiantly to disguise in the parlor. Cursing himself, he tore his mouth free. His loins were throbbing and his breath was sawing when he dropped his forehead to her shoulder.

"Silver, I'm sorry," he gasped. "Honey, I'm sorry."

Hushing her, he held her to his heart, molding her shrinking length to his as if the very thing she most feared could somehow end her quivers. "I've stopped," he said hoarsely, cursing himself again as he tucked her head beneath his chin. "It's over now. You're safe. I swear it."

The fist gripping his sleeve slowly, shakily unfurled. He wasn't sure in that moment who shuddered with more relief, him or Silver.

Christ, I have to get away from here. I'm no good for her.

She loosed a tremulous sigh, the tension in her body ebbing. When she shyly dropped her head to his chest, he filled his senses with the springtime scent of her; he marveled at the softness of her hair and the velvety crescent of her lashes. She was a rare beauty, he reflected poignantly, his arms jealously folding her closer. How could he have thought otherwise? With her lips red and moist from his kisses, her color a rosy pink from his ardor, she looked more inviting, more alive than the porcelain princess he'd admired so cynically at the Mining Exchange . . . and taunted so mercilessly at Max's engagement party.

But for all her flesh-and-blood femininity, the Silver he held was still more fragile than resilient. He didn't know why a lover's embrace should unnerve her; he didn't know why she shrank from his caress as if his hand were a kerosine torch spitting flame. All he knew was her flawless cheek had been marred by the single, crystalline track of a tear. A tear *he* had caused.

His insides writhed with the knowledge he'd repaid her compassion with lust.

Face it, Jones, you're not Maximillian Nichols. You're not even Aaron Townsend. You'll never be worthy of the fierce, committed, all-consuming love Silver is capable of.

He burned with a soul-deep shame.

For her own good, he had to leave Silver behind. *Tonight.*

Silver squeezed her eyes closed, letting the steady thrumming of Rafe's heart mend her splintered nerves. She hadn't meant to grow skittish; she hadn't *wanted* to. She cursed the memory that, insidiously, had reared its ugly head and once again robbed her of Rafe's love.

When she'd seen his tears, when she'd heard his pain, she'd wanted nothing more than to end his torment. For the first time in years, she'd yielded to instinct rather than alarm. She'd held him, stroked him, kissed him, offering the comfort she'd so desperately longed for that awful night five years ago when she'd run panic-stricken and confused from the man she thought she'd killed. The man she thought she *loved*.

But Aaron had survived, and other than the scar he hid so artfully beneath his dashing new hair style, he'd remained unscathed, while she . . .

She gulped a shaky breath.

She relived the nightmare every time a man dared to touch her. She wanted so desperately to be held, to feel safe, to be loved. She wanted with every fiber of her being to be free of Aaron's ghost. A thousand Dancing Moons couldn't haunt her half as cruelly.

She wondered if it was possible to make Rafe understand.

She stirred, gathering her nerve. "Rafe, I . . ."

"Shh." His melodious baritone, now hoarse with feeling, crackled beneath her ear. "You have my word. It won't happen again."

Not ever?

Tongue-tied and frustrated, anxious that she might have lost her one chance with the man who had somehow come to mean more to her than any suitor she'd ever known, she withdrew, intending to explain. Somehow, she had to convince him she wasn't a tease, or a prude, or worse, disinterested in the kisses that made her head float and her senses spin with giddy longing.

But when his mist-colored eyes touched hers, the shock of his misery was visceral. It poured into her so fast and deep that her heart wrenched, overwhelmed by its sheer oppressiveness. He was drowning in a whirlpool of despair, and for the life of her, she didn't know what to say or do to pull him from the undertow.

A smile so melancholy that it made her eyes sting curved the sensuous lips that only moments ago had ignited her soul. With a whisper-soft caress, his thumb brushed the tear that dribbled past her lashes.

"I hope you can forgive me, Silver."

She nodded hurriedly, his tawny visage swimming before her. He sighed, kissing her forehead.

"I don't deserve it," he whispered, "but thank you."

He raised her hand, pressing his lips to her knuckles. Another fleeting smile, this one just as mirthless, touched his mouth. "I trust we'll both feel better after tomorrow."

She blinked, uncertain what he meant. For a precious moment longer, his fingers twined through hers. She could feel the pulse of him, the life of him that beat so forcefully beneath the onerous burden he'd shouldered since his birth. She knew he was wrong to call himself a failure. She *knew* he was more than he imagined himself to be.

But before she could say as much, his palm softly rasped from her hand.

And he walked down the stairs in the dark.

Chapter 12

If Rafe had believed in heaven as much as he did hell, he would have blamed divine intervention for keeping him in Aspen. Only minutes after he'd vowed, for Silver's own good, to flee like a cur in the night, Max burst through the front door, all but singing with excitement.

"Chumley, my boy," the millionaire boomed, stopping just short of bowling Rafe into Aphrodite, "I've found it! The perfect wedding gift for Cellie! I'm gonna build her the biggest brand-spanking new theater this state has ever seen. And I'm going to do it before that nuisance, Horace Tabor, beats me to it!" Max chuckled, rubbing his chubby hands together. "Yep, she'll be able to enjoy her circus acts, Silver can watch her operas, and I'll get to hear a rousing Anvil Chorus every now and then. It's perfect!" Beaming, he linked his arm through Rafe's. "C'mon, son. I need your help. Do you know this Shakespeare fella the Trevelyans think is such a ripsnorter?"

To his bemusement, Rafe spent the better part of four hours holed up in Max's study, smoking cigars, sketching plans, and trying not to seem *too* knowledgeable about the life he'd led since the age of fourteen.

But that had only been the beginning. At the stroke of midnight, when he'd finally earned his reprieve from the exuberant theater builder, Rafe had stumbled across Jimmy's prone form, snoring outside his bedroom door.

"Oh, yer worship sir!" Jimmy lamented, looking more distressed than rested after his snooze. "She's gone and done it again. I searched full-chisel through every inch of this house. Honest! But I couldn't find her anywhere. Miss Tavy's plumb absquatulated!"

This news was made even more aggravating for its sheer inconvenience: rather than smuggling Tavy and all his other belongings out the back door before dawn, Rafe had been forced to enlist the aid of Max, Jimmy, and, eventually, an appealingly rumpled, sleepy-eyed Silver. They'd crawled under furniture, rummaged through drawers, and pulled books off shelves until three in the morning. Empty-handed and dejected, they'd finally huddled en masse around the scarred kitchen table and a steaming pot of coffee. Silver and Jimmy had each taken turns blaming themselves for Tavy's escape while a cigar-puffing Max had griped between yawns, "If Cellie were here, her spirits would tell her where to look."

It had been clear to Rafe at that point he wasn't going anywhere. *At least, not until I find Tavy*, a petulant voice inside him whispered as he lay lonely and restless, watching dawn creep through the slats of his shutters. Christ, he hadn't thought it would be so hard, sleeping through a whole night without Tavy's wet little nose tucked under his chin.

And he hadn't thought he'd grow so glum at the prospect of leaving behind easygoing, wily old Max.

Then there was Cellie, spookily strange but kind-to-a-fault Cellie. Rafe had never dreamed he'd find a

maternal confidante in the woman he'd set out to seduce. How could he leave Cellie to fend for herself,
knowing that he was the only person who could persuade Silver to end her desperate scheme?

But most of all, how could he walk out on Silver
when she was quite possibly the woman he was falling in love with?

He squeezed his eyes closed, groaning at the insid-
ious suspicion that had been plaguing him for days.
*You're a sap, Jones. Look what love did to Romeo.
And to Juliet.*

Then again, look what it did to Max and Cellie.
What if Silver were his one chance for salvation on
his otherwise bleak road to hell?

He smiled with self-ridicule. He'd played one too
many balcony scenes. Silver had never purported to
be his divine deliverance; in fact, it had been her sheer
humanness that had drawn him to her. She'd been an
honest-to-goodness spade among all the conniving
queens of hearts. He'd been intrigued that she'd allowed him to see her flaws from the first, and that
those flaws—overprotectiveness, blind loyalty, and
single-minded determination—had proven to be some
of her most endearing characteristics. Silver put her
whole heart and soul into love; if her relationship with
her father was any indication, she would stand by her
husband even if their whole world was going up in
flames.

Still, it was scary to love, he realized uncomfortably. It was scarier than standing nauseous and
tongue-tied in the footlights, especially for a man with
his prospects. After all, he was a lawless, penniless
bastard. That was the truth, not the fantasy, of Raphael Jones. So why would he dare to believe a woman
like Silver might let her feelings for him go beyond

infatuation? Was it because he wanted her to love him? Because she'd held him when he'd cried?

Rafe didn't have the answers to his questions. But he'd spent a lifetime as a professional scam artist. He knew how to calculate odds, and he figured they weren't stacked against him as high as the night he'd met Silver.

That's why he decided to stay in Aspen. He had a séance to watch, a woman to woo, and an otter to scare up.

That night, at the appointed hour for Cellie's extravaganza, Max greeted him in the dining room amidst a throng of skeptics and crucifix-clutching believers. Robustly red in his starched linen and swallow tails, the millionaire looked like a stuffed penguin who was in serious danger of coming unstuffed.

"Evenin', Chumley," Max called jovially, his ever-present fog of smoke wreathing him from head to chest. "I hardly recognized you. No puce velvet and lace cuffs tonight, eh? Why, you're looking as drab as any regular old colonial, son. Silver must be rubbing off on you."

Rafe inclined his head, his demeanor not quite as Chumleyfied as usual. His black-and-white formal attire was all part of his new plan to develop some sophistication in Chumley. He figured in one month's time, the ducal idiot that the *Aspen Times* so loved to lampoon would be gone forever, and he could start behaving in public like the kind of man Silver might want to marry. He'd even gone as far as dreaming up a new identity—Raphael Jones, undercover detective—who'd come to Aspen to investigate allegations of claims-jumping among the miners and had decided to wed and raise a family instead.

He only hoped Silver would agree to the idea, especially the family part.

"A good woman has that effect on a man, old chap," Rafe quipped, winking at his matchmaking cohort.

Max chuckled, winking back. "Reckon you're right. Cellie badgered me for months to lose a couple pounds so she could get her arms 'round this ol' gut. Giving up Boston cream pie for four weeks liked to have killed me, but I did it. I wouldn't shave off my whiskers even for Cellie, though, son. A man's got to draw the line somewhere."

Rafe couldn't help but laugh. "Oh, quite."

Max beamed, linking his arm through Rafe's. "Say, have you met everyone here yet? This being a private séance, I only invited the bare minimum: Union leaders, our chief investors, Brady, the Trevelyans—oh. And Judge Gates. But he got detained in Leadville, so I reckon we won't see him 'til the wedding."

"The, uh, wedding?" Rafe almost choked to hear there was an officer of the court, the *federal* court yet, coming to Max's wedding. "You know the good judge well enough for him to preside at your nuptials?"

"Shoot, no," Max said, elbowing a path through the buzzing speculators. "Cellie invited him. Said they're long-lost cousins of some sort. But she invited him a week early, which befuddles the bejabbers out of me. I reckon she got her dates mixed up. Anyway, it turns out he likes spooks. Guess it runs in the family, eh?"

Rafe nodded weakly. Of all the rotten luck, he groaned. Why had he fallen in love with a woman whose in-laws would soon number a *federal judge*?

Well, there was no helping it, he told himself darkly. He'd never met Gates, and hopefully Gates had never met his wanted posters. Besides, he couldn't very well walk out of Silver's—or Cellie's—life now.

He let Max drag him around the room. Most of the men seemed to be huddled around the elegant hors d'oeuvres buffet, stuffing their mouths until their chins dripped with foie gras, caviar canapés, cucumbers polonaise, and crab puffs—to name a few. Rafe barely had enough time to squint through the tobacco cloud at the ice-sculpted goose and the basket of "golden" deviled eggs dominating the sideboard before Max whisked him into another haze, this one enveloping the potted palms that shrouded the window seat.

"There's a fellow over here I'd like you to meet," Max said exuberantly. "Hails from England, just like you. Got himself in a bit of a pickle a few days back, but he's a good enough sport. Meeting him was the damnedest thing, though. There I was, thinking to surprise Cellie by hiring a New York impresario to recruit acts for her wedding gift, a gift she doesn't even *know* about yet, mind you, when she pipes up out of the blue, 'Max, dear, the spirits tell me what you're looking for isn't in New York but in Aspen.' Then she drags me off to Marshal Hawthorne's jail, and who should be twiddling his thumbs on a bunk but—"

"Frederick Fairgate, Esquire," boomed an all-too-familiar voice. "Thespian, playwright, and impresario."

The palms parted on cue, and Rafe's hackles rose as Fred, attired in bootblacked swallow tails to hide their shabby elbows, made his grand entrance.

"Good evening, Your Grace," Fred said, never missing a beat. He swept a formal bow, one of Max's cigars spewing between his fingers. "Seems like merry old England again, what with the Cornishman and the Irish Catholic itching for a fight, eh?" He jerked his head toward the Union leaders, who stood glaring at one another from opposite ends of the hors d'oeuvres table. "Why, the Missus and me were talking only yesterday about how you used to pay us poor sots a call when you had a mind to go slumming. It's been too long, Your Grace."

Not long enough. Rafe clenched his teeth, biting back the uncharitable retort. The most civil response he could muster was a daggerlike glare.

Max, meanwhile, was heartily thumping Fred on the back. In spite of the twelve years he had over his host, Fred's tall, muscular build, honed through boxing and stage carpentry, wasn't showing the same decline that Boston cream pie had wreaked on Max's squat frame. However, Max did have the advantage in hair, since Fred was balder than a cue ball above his drooping mustache and caterpillar eyebrows.

"When Cellie and I met him," Max crowed, "Fred here had just sunk a hefty little sum, close to fifteen thousand dollars, into his own plans to build a theater. Imagine us having so much in common. Had to be divine providence. So, I bought out Fred's investment, and now he's working for me. Whaddaya think, Chumley? Could Cellie's spirits have been any righter?"

Rafe smiled grimly. He didn't put much faith in spirits. Good old-fashioned chicanery was more likely to blame for the meeting of Max and Fred. After all, like Cellie, Fiona was ensconced at the Windsor Hotel. Fiona had probably convinced Cellie that "spirits" wanted Max to pay Fred's jail fines. The rest of the con had no doubt been inspired by gullible old Max himself, who'd rambled unabashedly about Cellie's wedding gift.

"I suspect, old chap," Rafe said evenly, "that some spirits are a bit 'righter' than others."

Fred shot him a narrow glare. "As you say, Your Grace. I've heard it said that *some* spirits tell *all*, 'cause they can't abide secrets."

They locked smoldering stares. Max chuckled.

"There's not much room for secrets in a house full of spirits, that's for sure," he said amicably. "That's the first rule a man has to learn when contemplating marriage to a fortune-teller." Max winked expansively. "Good thing I can sneak my fill of pie at the Chloride Restaurant, eh?"

Rafe's smile was fleeting. He wondered how Fred thought he was going to get away with his scam once Silver walked into the dining room.

"Uh-oh." Max was gazing guiltily toward Buckholtz, who'd hustled the Union leaders into a corner and was gleefully inciting ethnic rivalries for his headlines. "Silver will have my head if she learns I let Brady out of my sight. Excuse me, gents."

Rafe didn't even bother with a facade. The moment Max had bustled out of earshot, he planted himself toe to toe with Fred. "So help me God," he growled, "if you and Fiona do anything, anything at all to hurt Max or Silver, I'll see you both pay."

Fred's jaw, with its fading row of bruises, jutted petulantly. "That's a helluva thing—a *helluva* thing— to say to me, since I'm the one who's actually playing square with the millionaire, *Your Grace*."

Rafe stiffened. "What are you doing here, Fred?"

"The same as you. Wheeling, dealing, looking out

for folks back home. Try a little forgiveness on for size. It won't kill you.''

"Go to hell."

"Still sulking, eh?"

Rafe's neck heated. "You're a sorry sonuvabitch, Fred, and I rue the day I crossed your path."

Fred rolled his eyes and stuck his cigar back in his mouth. "Are you ever gonna grow up, preacher's boy, or do I have to spend the rest of my days working you over?"

Rafe scowled. He was sorely tempted to plow his fist through Fred's gut, but he knew better. He was being baited. And he wouldn't ruin this night for Max and Cellie.

"We'll finish this later," he ground out.

"Suit yourself," Fred shrugged, rolling his cigar to the other side of his mouth. "Say, did you know Chumley's an earl, not a duke?"

Rafe bit back his retort—and none too soon. Benson halted less than five feet away, a sterling bell gripped in his spotless white glove.

"Mrs. Trevelyan and gentlemen," the butler intoned with his habitual ennui, "the spirits have arrived. Madam Celestia invites the stouthearted among you to join her in the parlor. If you would be so bold as to follow me," he added dryly.

Fred winked at Rafe. "And so the curtain rises," he murmured, trailing after a trio of speculators, who were furtively crossing themselves.

Rafe shot his old cohort a warning look as he fell into step beside Max. The millionaire was tugging a grubby, well-wrinkled parchment from his breast pocket. He practically bounced with excitement as he rubbed the ridges between his palms. "Questions," he whispered eagerly. "About Cibola. Me and Cellie worked out a code."

No doubt, Rafe thought wryly. He wondered what other shenanigans Cellie had planned for the night's entertainment, and how many of them even Max was privy to. As dear as the woman was, Rafe didn't honestly believe spirits talked to her.

Still, his skin did prickle as his eyes grew accustomed to the dim, admittedly eerie flicker of the wax-dripping tapers. Reflections of tiny flames materialized in sterling knickknacks, only to disappear when one looked too closely. They reminded Rafe of the old wives' tales Fred used to tell the troupe's children, yarns of pixies and fairies and the elf fires that used to lure unwitting mortals into the clutches of mischievous wee folk.

The entire parlor had been transformed. Most of the furniture had been removed; those pieces that remained were shrouded in ticking and had become mysterious oblong shapes against the walls. A round table dominated the space that remained. On the linen that draped it, geometric designs and arcane symbols radiated outward in twelve directions from the main triangle, which contained a spookily lifelike illustration of a human eye. To Rafe's fascination, this eye seemed to follow him as he walked around the table. He told himself the phenomenon was nothing more than a trick of two white pillar candles, which in turn framed a pedestal positioned before Cellie's vacant chair. Sitting atop the ivory pyramid was a jet black pillow, and nesting at its center was the much-anticipated crystal ball.

From Rafe's perspective, the sphere, which was a good five inches in diameter, didn't look entirely clear. In fact, it appeared cloudy, glowing a pale, iridescent blue at its center. He wondered how Cellie had achieved that feat, considering that nothing in the vicinity was that peculiar shade of aqua. Then he was struck by the unpleasant scent wafting from the censer near Cellie's place setting. He swayed, momentarily dizzy, and suspected he'd just discovered the use for the mugwort and wormwood Cellie had insisted on hunting that morning.

Grimacing, he hastened to the opposite side of the table, where he found Silver, negotiating plates of half-eaten crab puffs away from the guests who'd smuggled them past Benson. She rolled her eyes for Rafe's benefit, and he smirked, helping her stack plates on a shrouded armchair.

"Why is Fred here?" she whispered anxiously.

"Max invited him."

"*Papa*?" She quailed. "Papa knows Fred?"

Rafe was careful to keep his own concerns about the budding association to himself. "Max hired Fred. To be Cellie's impresario."

Silver muttered a decidedly unladylike oath. "Next he'll be buying circus elephants and housing them in our stables."

Rafe chuckled, and she shot him a withering glance.

"Will Fred keep your secret?"

Rafe's humor ebbed, and he glared over his shoulder at the man who had so recently made him a cat's-paw. Notorious for upstaging the principle player, Fred was already taking a strategic position beside Cellie's chair.

"I think so," Rafe answered grimly. "For now."

Max strode briskly to his own chair. "Ladies and gentlemen," he boomed in a rousing, ringmaster's voice, "the time has come to take your seats. Madam

Celestia has made contact with the spirits, and she says they are close at hand.''

Buckholtz sneered, tossing his notebook down and pulling back a chair. "So where *is* Mrs. Cooper? Is she planning on joining us, or are you going to tell us she was abducted by ghosts?''

Max blinked at the newspaperman as if he were daft. "You need some spectacles, Brady? Madam Celestia's sitting right across from you.''

Every person in the room gasped. Where there had been no sign of Cellie a moment ago, now she could be seen quite clearly, plumped up on red velvet cushions in her favorite fan-backed chair. Even Buckholtz looked unsettled to see her materialize so dramatically.

"How'd she do that?'' Edward Trevelyan demanded in a wavering voice.

"She returned from the world of spirit!'' Daisy volunteered.

"Poppycock,'' Buckholtz muttered, peering suspiciously under the tablecloth.

Fred chuckled. But Silver looked a shade paler.

"Mirrors,'' Rafe whispered in answer to her silent question. He hoped he looked more confident than he sounded. "It's an old theater trick.'' And it was. But damn. Cellie had done it unnervingly well.

Max rubbed his hands together. "That's it, that's it. Take your seats, folks,'' he boomed as Rafe seated Silver and then sat beside her. Max jerked his thumb over his shoulder. "You can see I've put a spiritkeeper behind each one of your chairs. There are twelve of us in all. One for each sign of the zodiac. That was my idea,'' he added, beaming with pride. Then he reddened, seeming to remember his role. He cleared his throat.

"Spiritkeepers are sacred to Injuns like Dancing Moon," he continued solemnly. "They're kind of an offering, 'cause we wanted him to feel at home here. Plus, the spiritkeepers will keep our circle safe. We wouldn't want any of you folks going home tonight possessed by demons or such."

"Is . . . that possible?" one green-complected investor asked.

Kilkarney, the leader of the Irish faction, winked at the nervous easterner. "Oh, not to worry, lad. Ye've got more devils here than demons."

Daisy whimpered. Silver tossed her miners a quelling look.

Meanwhile, Max had settled in his chair. "Everybody hold hands, now. You're not allowed to break the spirit circle."

"That's right," Buckholtz said cynically. "We wouldn't want to confuse Madam Celestia. Only the spirits are allowed to rap their answers on, or under, the table."

Kilkarney demonstrated with a stomping boot and a wiseacre's grin. A few nervous giggles circled the table. Cellie at last opened her eyes and stared at the man. Rafe wished he could have seen the look that slowly turned the robust Irishman white. Unfortunately, all Rafe could see was the back of Cellie's purple turban.

With Kilkarney thoroughly cowed, Cellie faced the crystal once more, her gaze focused on its blue glow. Rafe noticed her eyelids glittered with some strange, silvery powder. *The queen of flamboyance*, he thought affectionately, shaking his head at the obscenely large crescent-shaped moonstone adorning her headdress.

Cellie began rocking. Bracelets jangled as she raised her arms, spreading her hands in a caressing

motion over the ball. When she began to mumble, she
intoned syllables that, to Rafe's mind, sounded like a
bastardized version of the witches' chant from *Macbeth*. He glanced at Fred. Fred winked back in understanding. Rafe tensed. He wasn't entirely sure he
liked the Brit's assumption that they were conspirators once more.

Cellie called out in a ringing voice:

> *Oh shadows biding in the night,*
> *Sweep clear the veil that dulls my sight!*
> *Reveal the secrets yet to be,*
> *Lost wisdom, ancient mysteries!*

The mist inside the ball began to spiral, deepening
in hue, shooting flecks of pink and orange into inner
space. Impressed, Rafe shot another speculative
glance at Cellie. Just how did she do that?

> *Spirit from the tribes of man*
> *Your presence here I now demand!*
> *Dancing Moon! Come forth and speak!*

A tendril of black materialized in the center of the
ball, gobbling up the blues and pinks. Lengthening,
fanning outward, it rotated clockwise until it slowly
righted itself again in the shape of a feather—a *buzzard* feather. Rafe's heart tripped. He knew he wasn't
imagining the phenomenon because Silver sat white-
lipped and wide-eyed, her fingernails practically
drawing blood from his palm. Fred was frowning.
Buckholtz was sneering. And Max was wriggling in
his seat like an eager five-year-old.

Cellie's brow puckered. The luminescence that
crackled inside the sphere was changing color. No

longer blue, and far from pink, it swallowed the feather in a whirlpool of muddy hues. Rafe had a sense that the colors were undergoing some kind of struggle, vying for dominance.

"Something's not right here," Cellie muttered.

"Do tell," Buckholtz drawled.

But Cellie ignored him. Frowning in earnest now, she leaned toward the sphere, her features awash in a goose-pimpling crimson. The sides of the ball seemed to ooze with that crimson, and misty droplets whirled in the center. Every blue, brown, orange, pink, and black speck was sucked into that vortex until finally, only blood red remained.

"Much evil plagues a soul here," Cellie intoned, sounding more like doom than a crackpot.

"Who's evil?" Max demanded. "Dancing Moon?"

"I speak not of the Spirit Warrior, but of a flesh-and-blood mortal who would do others wrong."

Guilt burned its way up Rafe's neck.

"Is . . . is this mortal a danger?" Daisy ventured to ask.

"Only if you believe her," Buckholtz muttered, his gaze fixed accusingly on Cellie.

The newsman's cynicism helped to ease Rafe's dread. Perhaps Cellie really hadn't divined his identity—or worse, the corruption in his soul. In the rounder arena, he supposed he *did* have some competition for a change. Fred was present, after all.

Rafe gazed narrowly at his former partner-in-crime.

Meanwhile, Silver was also wrestling with issues of conscience—mostly, her appalling lack of one. Ever since she'd witnessed firsthand Rafe's devastation at Fred's and Fiona's hands, she'd been wondering how to call off her own scam. She couldn't bear to cause Papa the kind of pain Rafe had felt. And, surprisingly, she couldn't bear to hurt Celestia, either.

It was a realization she'd been fighting for days.

Ever since the night with Rafe in the parlor, she'd been haunted by his accusations. She'd worried her nightmares really did result from her guilt, that she couldn't bear to see Papa married to any woman other than her mother. And while she would rather have died than admit it, especially to Rafe, she had come to the distressing conclusion that she might very well be that despicable.

Fortunately, her Pinkerton agent had wired her today, before she could destroy her father's life:

BLUE THUNDER, KENTUCKY, 1878. CHURCH DID BURN DOWN. FAULTY LIGHTNING ROD. PREACHER INSTALLED IT. COOPER LEFT TOWN TWO DAYS EARLIER. EVIDENCE SUGGESTS COVER-UP. RECOMMEND DROPPING CHARGES.

The implications of his report were mind-boggling. Reading between the lines, Silver could only conclude that Jedidiah Jones had been a mean-spirited cuckold *and* a liar. He apparently hadn't wanted his congregation to think him incompetent, so he'd blamed witchcraft for the fire he'd caused. As a result, all of Blue Thunder, and especially the church organist, had come to hate Cellie.

Silver hoped her telegram was the proof Rafe needed to finally accept that Preacher Jones had been a hypocrite who'd abused his sacred calling. She also hoped the telegram didn't mean what she dreaded it meant: that Cellie, since day one, had known Rafe wasn't the duke of Chumley. But surely, if Cellie had

suspected Rafe's fraud, she would have told Papa . . .
Right?

And break his heart?

Silver squeezed her eyes closed, hating herself even
more.

Papa loved Rafe like a son. Just like Papa loved
her. It would kill him to know he'd been betrayed by
both of his "children." If Cellie understood that, then
it was conceivable she was keeping quiet about Rafe's
identity and the truth behind the missing spiritkeepers
to protect Papa. In fact, it was conceivable that . . .
Cellie really did love Papa.

And if that were true, Silver thought bleakly, she
would be contemptible indeed if she tried to stand in
the way of their happiness.

That's why she'd come to the parlor early tonight,
hoping to find Cellie. That's why she'd volunteered
to drape furniture and arrange candles for the séance.
She'd wanted in some small way to lend her father's
fiancée moral support, especially since she'd known
Cellie would be facing a skeptical, perhaps hostile,
audience.

Helping her mother-to-be, Silver thought glumly,
was also her small way of making amends—a very
small way indeed, considering she hadn't yet gathered
the nerve to face Celestia, woman to woman, and
apologize.

"The spirits speak of danger, yes," Celestia said
solemnly, in answer to Daisy Trevelyan's question.

"What kind of danger?" Kilkarney asked suspiciously.

Cellie closed her eyes, rocking rhythmically for a
moment.

"Retribution," she announced dramatically.

Every man who'd been holding his breath released

it on a gasping rush of air—and just as quickly gulped another.

"Hot damn," Papa muttered. "Retribution. Penhalion, you and your boys aren't planning any mischief with dynamite, are you?"

The squat, feisty Cornishman scowled. "Now see here, Nichols, we may be immigrants, but we're law-abiding. And to strike for reasonable wages is well within our—"

A nerve-jangling thump cut him short. It seemed to come from the window seat.

"Wh-what was that?" Edward Trevelyan asked, his eyes growing white around the edges.

"The spirits!" Daisy squeaked.

"I'll believe it when I see it," Buckholtz retorted.

"Then you will never believe, Mr. Buckholtz," Cellie said with great dignity, "for the spirits do not waste time trying to prove their existence. That is a human quest, undertaken by people who don't yet know who *they* are. Truth is truth, and shall always remain truth, whether you, with your closed and doubting mind, choose to believe it or not."

"How convenient."

Silver was sorely tempted to kick the newsman's shin. "Mr. Buckholtz, if you would be so kind as to save your remarks for your editorial page, I, for one, would be eternally grateful." She felt her cheeks warm as Rafe gave her hand an approving squeeze. "Now then, Cellie. I should like to know what your spirits meant by retribution."

"Me too," Papa said, his expression unusually grave. "How's it gonna go down? Knives? Bullets? Looting and mayhem?"

Silver winced. Papa always had been blessed with a vivid imagination.

"Perhaps more to the point," Penhalion growled, "who's supposed to be the target?"

"Gentlemen, gentlemen." Cellie held up her hands for silence. "One question at a time, *please*. Communication with the otherworld is a delicate matter. One cannot bully answers out of spirits. One must show gratitude. And respect." She shot a blistering look at Buckholtz.

"Now then." Cellie settled more comfortably on her pillows, threw her slipping shawl over her shoulders, and gripped her crystal ball once more. "*I* shall ask the questions. *You* will listen for answers. Spirits, is someone in this circle in danger?"

Everyone in the room jumped as an audible thud answered her query.

"Does one rap mean yes?"

A single rap answered, this time from the other side of the room.

"How will you answer no?"

Two raps sounded close to the window. So did a faint scratching noise.

"How the devil is she making those—"

"Shh!" This time, the Trevelyans and just about everybody else glared daggers at Buckholtz for interrupting.

"Is a man from this circle in danger?" Cellie continued, nonplussed.

One rap. Silver frowned, glancing uneasily at the shadow-laced walls. Had Papa helped Cellie rig the knocking noises? If so, how had he done it so . . . so *convincingly*?

"Will there be bloodshed?"

Silence rolled like a tangible fog through the semi-darkness. Silver counted five, perhaps six heartbeats before the answer finally knelled: One rap.

"For heaven's sake, who is it? *Who is it*?" Daisy wailed.

"Is it Edward Trevelyan?" Cellie intoned.

Two raps. The couple nearly sobbed with relief.

"Very well," Cellie said. "Then we shall determine who among the remaining gentlemen it is."

Forever feuding, Kilkarney and Penhalion locked eyes. So did Rafe and Fred. Silver swallowed, watching Papa watch Buckholtz. And adding to her uneasiness, she caught Cellie gazing narrowly at her.

"Spirits," Cellie called, her voice rising in volume and power, "we seek the gentleman's last name. Kindly knock when I state the first letter. A," she said slowly. "B." Each syllable resonated with dramatic authority. "C—"

"Oh for crying out loud," Buckholtz grumbled. "At this rate, we're going to be here all night."

"You have no right to be flippant," Daisy flung back, "just because you know *you're* not in danger now!"

"Not necessarily," Penhalion growled.

A horrific crash drowned out the rest of his threat. Papa leaped to his feet. So did Rafe and Daisy.

"It's the ghost!" Daisy shrieked, pointing at a renegade crab puff. It bounced from the armchair to the floor. Before everyone's astonished eyes, the remaining china inexplicably toppled, shattering into a dozen pieces. Slowly, spookily, the white ticking on the armchair began to rise.

"Jesus everloving Christ," Buckholtz choked, his eyes bugging out to twice their normal size. The ghost gave a querulous chirp, and Buckholtz, heedless of chandeliers and stained glass, not to mention human life, drew his .45.

"*No!*" Rafe shouted, lunging for the newsman's

arm. The Colt fired; plaster showered from the ceiling; Daisy wilted in a dead faint; and the ghost, barking in terror, streaked out from under the ticking and dashed beneath Silver's petticoats.

Papa roared with mirth. Fred laughed so hard that his chair toppled backwards. The other men stood blinking at one another, uncertain of the joke, while a scarlet Buckholtz shook off a snickering Rafe.

Cellie, meanwhile, stood scowling. "The spirits are *not* amused," she snapped, shooting daggerlike glares at her detractors. She tossed her pesky shawl over her shoulder, hiked her chin, then sailed from the room like a battleship in full steam.

"Uh-oh." Papa was doing his best to sober up between guffaws. "Looks like the séance is over, folks."

The gaslights flared. Benson appeared at the parlor door with a cocked .45. Several armed servants accompanied him. Without further encouragement, Buckholtz stalked from the house. Several minutes later, Benson's efficient, tight-lipped legions had reunited coats, gloves, and hats with their owners. Cellie's audience, some thoroughly spooked, some crying hoax, hastened for their modes of transportation. And Papa ran to soothe his disgruntled necromancer.

Silver sat imprisoned in her seat. Aside from the fact that unaccountable knockings, pronouncements of doom, and capricious gun-firings had left her in jitters, she now had a trembling furball wrapped around her ankle. Why Tavy had chosen her dress and her ankle for concealment when any number of nooks and crannies would have sufficed, was, quite simply, beyond Silver's comprehension. If she hadn't known better, she would have thought Rafe had trained his pet to kiss females and sneak under their skirts. In any event, Silver suspected she'd have trouble being ladylike, much less decorous, while she was yanking an otter out from under her unmentionables.

Reluctant to flaunt her petticoats before the world, she glared at her smirking male audience. Unfortunately, Rafe and Fred—*being* Rafe and Fred—refused to take the hint and leave.

"You wouldn't happen to know where Tavy ran off to, would you?" Rafe drawled, the old mischief dancing in his eyes like stars.

Despite her better sense, Silver softened beneath Rafe's grin. She hadn't realized how much she missed his smiles. Ever since Fiona's visit, he'd been battling a case of the blue devils.

She tossed an aggravated glance at Fred, who was shaking the crystal ball, pretending to be fascinated. "Rafe, you know very well where Tavy is," she whispered back.

He chuckled, dropping to one knee at her side. Her heart took a dizzying leap to see him in the traditional "marry-me" pose. It was all she could do to remember their audience.

"I was deferring to your feminine sensibilities," Rafe murmured, covering her fist with his hand.

"I . . . appreciate that." Disappointed by his response, in spite of her commonsense reminder that no man would ever propose to a woman in public, she managed to recall the problem at hand. "Rafe, what are we going to do? Tavy's terrified. She's attached herself to my . . . uh, . . . shoe like a barnacle!"

A roguish dimple flirted with the corner of his mouth. "Your shoe, eh?"

She nodded.

"Are you quite sure?"

She blushed at his innuendo, her whole body singing with warmth. "Well . . ." The smile she gave him was a bit more shy than she would have liked. "More or less."

"Then I suggest we remove her," he purred, shifting nearer. "A delicate operation, to be sure."

His forehead nearly touched hers, and she shivered with delight. She thought he would kiss her. She *hoped* he would. In that moment, as his lips hovered so provocatively above hers, she didn't care one whit who might watch them. She'd surrendered. She was lost. He'd wrapped her in a sensual cocoon of enticement, of man-scents and magnetism. It was the delicious, scandalous paradise promised by Raphael Jones. And for the first time, after all the many times he'd opened the door on this forbidden Eden, she reveled in the sheer impropriety of walking in.

Tavy, unfortunately, had other ideas. At the crisp click of servile heels on the floor, she peeked out from Silver's hem, blinked up at the butler radiating such tangible disapproval, and yipped, launching herself into Rafe's arms. Rafe chuckled and Silver sighed, watching his pet circle fretfully in the embrace she'd hoped so futilely would be hers.

Benson began clearing his throat.

"*Yes*, Benson," she interrupted irritably. It wasn't as if she couldn't feel him looming beside her like the lumberjack of doom. "What is it?"

"You have a visitor, miss."

His cheeky manner disturbed her, and she frowned, rising. "At this hour?"

Benson remembered his manners long enough to incline his head. "The gentleman apologized for the inconvenience. He said he had merely intended to leave his card, but then he heard the gunshot. And he grew most alarmed. He mentioned you were old friends.''

This last declaration raised her hackles. What on earth was the matter with Benson, believing such a preposterous tale? No gentleman called on a lady at ten o'clock at night. Weren't butlers supposed to bounce such troublemakers out the door?

Then he passed her an embossed calling card, one she recognized only too well. Her hand shook as she touched the gold leaf. She suspected her complexion had turned rather pasty, because Rafe, rising in concern, hastened to peer over her fist. The bald shock that twisted his features reverberated through every fiber of her being. In that instant, as their eyes locked, Silver didn't know whether to be distressed or elated. Although jealousy had flared in his gaze, the earlier, disconcerting dullness soon rolled in to snuff out his . . . what? Hope?

Uneasily, she turned Aaron's card in her hand. Damn him. Why had he come here? She really didn't want to deal with her own ghosts tonight. She felt disadvantaged, her nerves still frazzled from the séance.

On the other hand, if she didn't deal now in some satisfactory way with Aaron's demands, she'd have to deal with them tomorrow. Or the next day. And that would increase the risk of Papa getting involved and learning her darkest secret.

Silver gritted her teeth. She'd just known Aaron would force some confrontation with her. She'd known it ever since she'd read the news clipping about his capital-raising venture. But she could face him, she told herself staunchly. She *would* face him.

She would do it so she could finally be free.

"Very well, Benson." Silver squared her shoulders and drew a bolstering breath. "You may tell Mr. Townsend I'll meet him in the garden."

Chapter 13

Fred was practically choking on his cigar as Silver walked out the door. *"Townsend?"* he sputtered between coughs. "*Aaron* Townsend? That bastard's courting your heiress?"

Rafe scowled. Frankly, he didn't see how anything Silver or Aaron Townsend did was any of Fred's business.

"Butt out," Rafe snapped, lowering Tavy to the floor so she could feast on the crab puffs she'd been stalking before Buckholtz had turned village idiot.

The veins on Fred's neck actually bulged. "What's the matter with you, letting Townsend get his hands on your woman?"

"Silver isn't my woman."

"She bloody well could be. Hell, the way she flapped her eyelashes at you, I could feel the breeze over here."

Sure. Rafe smiled mirthlessly. *For a kiss and a tumble, Silver is going to forget her rich Philadelphian. She's going to throw away her whole future as the wife of a congressman on a penniless ne'er-do-well named Raphael Jones.*

"Leave it alone, Fred."

"For Christ's sake, lad, are you going to let some tenderfoot steal your thunder?"

"Dammit, Fred, I said—"

"The same bastard who beat up Amy?"

Rafe staggered. The blow had hit him hard. Hard enough to punch a hole through his spleen. "Jesus."

"It's about bloody damned time you heard me. Now get your arse in that garden and take care of your woman before something—"

Rafe didn't hear the rest. He was already bolting down the hall, his heart crashing in his ears. He didn't stop to question why he should believe Fred now, after vowing yesterday morning he never would again. Fear for Silver's safety coiled like a serpent around his throat. By the time he'd reached the back of the house and flung open the French doors, he could scarcely draw a breath.

Mother of God, where are they?

Twisted shadows marked the trees. Lush, summer foliage obscured his sight, shrouding each bend. Still, the night was his element. He plunged in. Letting his senses stretch, he followed the ribbon of cobblestones without really seeing. Silver was ahead somewhere; he tracked her less by scent and sound than by an elusive knowing that came from his gut.

The path abruptly ended. Before him stretched Max's fish pond, the same pond he and Tavy visited every day for hunting lessons. In the lovers' dance of moon and shadow, he could clearly see the glimmer of ivory satin. Silver chatted in cozy proximity with her suitor as they strolled along the limestone footbridge that arched so quaintly from the pond's shore to the center island. They were headed toward the pavilion Max had constructed for oompah bands and garden parties. Silver's skirt fluttered in a gust of wind, brushing Townsend's boot, and Rafe suffered a stab of jealousy. Lithe and statuesque in her Empire gown, her hair adorned simply with a green velvet ribbon, she reminded Rafe of a Grecian goddess.

Townsend, on the other hand, reminded Rafe of Dr. Jekyll.

Sudden recognition lashed Rafe like a cat-o'-nine-tails. *Jesus. That's the same easterner I collided with in Leadville!* Had Townsend been fleeing the alley that night because he'd hurt Amy?

Rafe's whole body vibrated with outrage. Never in his life had he killed a man, but in that moment, he would have done so, and gladly. The trouble was, he had Silver and her sensibilities to consider. If she were head-over-heels in love, how was he supposed to convince her Townsend was dangerous?

Grinding his teeth so hard that his jaw ached, Rafe forced himself to melt once more into shadow.

The couple halted at the top of the bridge. Only fifty yards away, their conversation carried well enough over the water to make Rafe's blood boil.

"The mountains become you, my dear," the easterner purred in a syrupy baritone. "The mountains, the moonlight . . . and white satin. I always knew you'd be a stunning bride, Silver."

He reached for the delicate, rose-embroidered shawl that was slipping from her shoulders. She retreated a full step.

"If that's your idea of a proposal, Aaron, then please don't."

His hand hovered, a classic gesture of longing and chagrin. "I can't believe you mean that."

"I'm afraid I do," she said firmly.

His hand fell, and his head tilted. The bastard's

timing was superb, Rafe mused darkly. Townsend should have been an actor.

"Your mind has changed," Townsend lamented, believably distressed, "but surely your heart has not."

Rafe rolled his eyes.

"Contrary to popular belief, absence does not make the heart grow fonder, Aaron."

Oh, brava, Silver.

Townsend's smile was fleeting—and subtle in its threat. "Your mind isn't the only thing that's changed, Silver. You've grown . . . contentious. I must say, I don't find that nearly as appealing as your gown."

"Then you'll agree that I've spared you a great deal of grief, Aaron, by declining your proposal."

His chuckle raised the hairs on Rafe's neck. "Another debt which I owe you. And I do pay off my debts, Silver. Make no mistake."

She squared her shoulders, but not before Rafe glimpsed their tremor. "So now we come to the crux of the matter. If you are seeking a loan—"

"I did not come sixteen hundred miles to seek a loan, my dear. I've come for a wife. Once we are married, we can put all the Philadelphia unpleasantness behind us."

"That 'Philadelphia unpleasantness,' " she retorted in a choked voice, "was the very thing that killed my love for you!"

He didn't bother to pretend ignorance—or even insult.

"As you say. You were naive then, Silver. Don't be stupid now. By all reports, you've become quite successful as a businesswoman, despite the liability of your father."

She bristled. "My father was the one who struck the mother lode. On four separate occasions, as your 'reports' no doubt informed you."

"*And* he thinks his richest mine is haunted. *And* he's marrying the crackpot whom he hired to exorcize the ghosts." Townsend's smile was disparaging. "I daresay he's to blame, too, for your lumber troubles. Your sawmill would produce twice as much lumber if you dynamited a trench for a flume and dammed up Crystal Creek.

"But Max isn't your biggest handicap, my dear," he continued dryly. "You seek to open another mine, do you not? To raise the capital for a second smelter? Commendable goals. But they're limited. Because you are a woman, you are doomed never to reach the pinnacle of success you deserve—much less desire. You cannot vote. You cannot hold political office. No matter how rich you become, Washington will always be barred to you.

"But it is not barred to me," he continued triumphantly, playing his ace. "I am a Townsend. I have the support of the Democratic party. And someday, when I am president, you will be First Lady. Think on that, Silver. *Think* on the possibilities for your sawmills and your mines. And then tell me if the thought of real power does not excite you."

Rafe's gut churned, stirring up feelings of inadequacy. As much as he hated to admit it, Townsend's argument was valid. Brains, grit, and wealth could only take Silver so far—assuming, of course, that she *wanted* to play in the same league as the Vanderbilts and Morgans.

He held his breath, waiting for her answer.

"You have grand dreams, Aaron," she said at last. "Mine are simpler ones: a husband who loves me, healthy children, a happy home. That is the pinnacle of success, as far as I'm concerned. And for this dream alone would I marry." She shook her head. "I could no more be your wife than you could be my husband. I'm sorry."

Rafe had to stuff his delirious heart back inside his chest.

Townsend, however, didn't take well to her refusal. He clenched his fist on the railing. "I don't believe you've fully considered the advantages to my suit."

"Aaron." Her sigh was a mixture of exasperation and compassion. "Please don't make this any harder. My heart belongs to another. Kindly drop the matter."

She turned, trying to make her escape. As swift as a snake, Townsend's hand lashed out, grabbing her forearm. It was all the provocation Rafe needed.

"I say, old chap," he called, his voice harsh with warning, "did you forget something?"

Townsend started, scanning the shadows. "Forget something?"

"Why yes, dear fellow. Your manners." Rafe swung himself over the railing. "Devilish inconvenient, you traveling all the way from Philadelphia without them."

Silver secretly thanked God when she saw Rafe swoop down out of the night. With the moon glowing behind him, striking silver-white sparks from his hair, he looked like an avenging angel.

Aaron, however, didn't share her awe. The tension eased from his shoulders, and a thin smile curved his lips.

"Ah," he greeted Rafe with deceptive pleasantness. "What a heroic entrance. I daresay we should all applaud. I take it by your accent that tonight you're roleplaying none other than His Royal Grace, the so-called *duke* of Chumley?''

To his credit, Rafe didn't bat an eye. Silver, on the other hand, nearly swallowed her tongue.

"F-for heaven's sake, Aaron," she stammered, wishing to God she had one-tenth of Rafe's aplomb. "What has gotten into you? I won't stand for such rudeness. The duke is my guest—"

"Your guest, you say?" The mockery in his stone-cold gaze pierced her like a stiletto. "Oh, my dear. I fear you and the gentleman have not been properly introduced. Pray allow me the honor. This is M'sieur Guy LeBecque, French ambassador to the fair city of St. Louis; Baxter Bancroft, president of the nonexistent First Depository Bank of San Francisco. Or perhaps, *my dear fellow*," he taunted baldly, turning to Rafe, "you prefer to be called by the less well-known but no less accurate moniker on your wanted poster: Raphael Jones."

Silver reeled. Good Lord, Aaron knew everything? *Everything* about Rafe's shady past? But surely Rafe's public performances had been too flawless for suspicion. Why, even Marshal Hawthorne had yet to put two and two together . . .

Benson. The realization hit her with the force of a cannonball. Benson had provided the clues that had tipped off Aaron! Why, that snake had been spying on her and Papa all along! That would explain Benson's sudden prosperity. *And* it would explain why Aaron was so well informed about her business plans.

She quailed as another thought occurred: Benson might also have learned she'd hired Rafe to ruin Celestia!

She bit her lip, uncertain now what role she should play. When she glanced at Rafe for guidance, though, it was clear he didn't need her help. Wisecracking scrapper that he was, he held his ground with a smile as derisive as Aaron's.

"Your reputation precedes you, too, my dear Townsend. Why, with all your threats and arm-twisting, I feared you might thrash Miss Nichols within an inch of her life, rather like you did that poor chorus girl back in Leadville. What, were you looking to add another murder to your own list of warrants?"

Silver gasped. Aaron stiffened. Carefully, deliberately, he squared off with Rafe.

"If I were you, Jones," he warned softly, "I would mind my tongue. You are upsetting my fiancée."

"Fiancée?" Rafe snorted. "If you are referring to Miss Nichols, then I would have to say she speaks quite well for herself, as I so recently had the pleasure of overhearing."

The scar marring Aaron's otherwise perfect profile stood out like lightning on his thunderous brow.

"Then you confess you're a thief *and* a spy? What stellar credentials." He turned abruptly, narrowing his gaze at Silver. "My dear, you've been rather quiet. No righteous indignation on the good duke's behalf? No pious disbelief? I find that odd."

Dread rippled down her spine. "Well, I hardly know *what* to say, Aaron. You seem to have made up your mind."

"Indeed?" The look he gave her was as sharp as splintered glass. "Pray don't tell me you turned down my suit out of some misguided affection for this fugitive?"

" 'Misguided' is no longer Silver's state of mind," Rafe interjected snidely. "Otherwise, she would still be carrying a torch for you."

"I see."

Silver squirmed, biting back her protest. She wished Rafe hadn't said that. She wished he'd had the good sense to let her soothe Aaron's pride.

The lengthening silence stretched her nerves almost beyond enduring. But Aaron wasn't beaten. She knew his look, his smile. She watched uneasily as he pulled a sterling cigarette case from his coat. With all the time, all the nonchalance in the world, he flicked a broken smoke into the pond. An inexplicable chill crept over her, seeming to rise from the water. She was reminded of her ride through the pine stumps, when she'd thought something unnatural was stalking her.

"My, this is an awkward situation," Aaron drawled, at last selecting his cigarette. He struck a match.

Despite the absence of wind, it blew out.

"I propose. The jealous lover eavesdrops . . ."

He struck a second match. It, too, blew out.

He frowned.

"You might have told me, Silver, that you'd developed your mother's taste for riffraff," he jeered, reaching for a third match. "And speaking of your father, I wonder what Max would say if he knew his daughter was fornicating—with an outlaw—under his very own roof. Or perhaps more to the point—" the match flared triumphantly between his thumb and forefinger this time "—I wonder what a federal marshal would say."

Silver's heart knelled in his maleficent silence. Rafe glowered. Before either of them could speak, though, the match exploded like a miniature firecracker. Flames engulfed Aaron's cuff, and he yelped, staggering backwards. Silver gaped. Before she could even think to help him, his forearm was ablaze, and he was frantically beating it out against the stone wall.

Smoke curled from the tatters of his sleeve. His hand was raw and blistered. Cursing vehemently, he clutched his wounds beneath his arm, his eyes wild, his chest heaving. She blinked as he rounded on her, momentarily stunned to think she'd seen the sneer of an Indian shaman in the nimbus of the fire.

Rafe, fortunately, had the presence of mind to step in front of her. "My," he told Aaron blandly, "how apropos that you should smolder like a rotted carcass. An eternity of the same no doubt waits for you in the hereafter."

"Is that a threat, Jones?"

"I don't waste time on threats, Townsend."

Aaron's healthy fist clenched, and he shook, clearly struggling for self-control. Silver could hear his teeth grinding from nearly ten feet away.

"I suggest, my dear Silver," he said in a low, dangerous voice, "that you reconsider your decision not to marry me. It might prove most detrimental to your friend."

Eyes as black as a tomb stabbed into hers. She recoiled.

"Spare us the melodrama, Townsend," Rafe bit out acidly. "No one's applauding. Simply make your exit, stage left."

Aaron's features contorted, noxious with malice. The threat that crackled between the two rivals was visceral, made even more savage by its absence of sound.

Abruptly, Aaron turned. To Silver's queasy relief, he stalked off the bridge into the garden.

Tremors wracked her whole body. Weakly, she leaned against the bridge. God help her. God help *Rafe*. Aaron made no idle threats.

She pushed herself away from the railing. Too agitated to stand still, yet too apprehensive to follow the path where Aaron might be lurking, she hurried toward the screened pavilion. She didn't see Rafe fall into step beside her.

"Silver?" His voice was a compassionate murmur as she fumbled, unseeing, with the latch. When his hand touched hers, gently opening the door, she blinked dumbly at those supple fingers, so like—and yet unlike—Aaron's. It occurred to her that if she yielded to Aaron's blackmail, she'd have to let him come to her bed. But how could she bear his touch, knowing what he'd done to Amy? How could she even pretend affection for a man who'd nearly raped her; a man who had quite possibly murdered his brother and the congressional candidate who'd been his rival?

Then again, how could she not pretend, if Rafe's freedom—or even his life—were at stake?

She raised beseeching eyes to Rafe's. Guilt crisscrossed his features. He withdrew, dropping his arm to his side, and the disappointment she felt nearly crushed her.

"Rafe, I—"

"I should go. And get Max. You're safe now, Silver."

"No!"

He hesitated, and she swallowed. How could she possibly be safe with Benson in the house? How could anyone be? As if to verify her fears, she remembered Benson's argument with his bruised acquaintance. No doubt that man *had* been Aaron. No doubt he hadn't wanted her asking questions about Fred's fistprints on his jaw, so he'd waited until he'd healed before playing the repentant suitor! God. Just how long had Benson been working for Aaron, anyway? Since he'd first arrived in Aspen three years ago, seeking her out for employment?

"Rafe please. It's not safe. Benson's been spying for Aaron, and . . . and I don't want you to go."

"I'm not afraid of Benson," he murmured.

"I know, but . . ." *Maybe you should be.* She bit her tongue on the words, though. She'd learned that challenging Rafe only made him more determined to do precisely what he shouldn't. "I . . . I don't want to be alone."

His gaze flickered behind her, and his chest rose and held. She guessed his thoughts: that the pavilion was a lovers' paradise, with its fragrant arbor of laurels and honeysuckle, its plumply cushioned chaise longue, and its breathtaking view of mountains bathed in moonglow.

"Are you sure?" he asked huskily.

She nodded, forcing her feet to move, to take the first step into Aphrodite's lair. She thought she heard him sigh. And then the door swung closed behind him with a soft click.

Goose bumps sprinkled to her toes. She was alone with him. It wasn't the first time, and yet it was different somehow beneath the enchantment of the moon and the whispery soughing of the mountain laurels. He stood etched in pewter shadow, his eyes glittering like some hungry jungle cat's behind his properly civilized mask. He kept his distance, and yet his very presence was a primal calling. It seemed to draw those subtle, screened walls closer around her. A thrill gusted through her to feel herself so caged. She wanted to forget her fears. She wanted to trust again the way she'd trusted a lifetime ago, before Aaron's harsh lesson had stripped her of every heartfelt desire to be loved.

"What are we going to do?" she said anxiously.

His smile was mirthless. "If you mean about Townsend, then I can tell you what *I'd* do. I'd lock myself in the Pitkin County Jail before I'd *ever* let you stoop to that bastard's blackmail."

"That is not an option," she countered hastily, horrified he'd even suggest such a thing.

"You're right," he said more gently. "Because it's not going to come to that."

She swayed, raised a shaking hand to her forehead. She wished she had his confidence. But then, he didn't know Aaron like she did. Had she lost her mind, strolling with him in the garden?

"Thank you," she blurted out. "For coming after me. It was stupid of me to come here alone. With Aaron, I mean," she added hastily, feeling her cheeks start to burn. Lord, did she used to stammer like this in Philadelphia? "I knew he was dangerous."

"Did you?"

She bit her lip and nodded, wishing she could read the mind behind those perfectly unreadable features. "Please don't think the worst. I was trying to put the past behind me. Coming here was a sort of . . . of test to see if I could feel safe again."

She gulped a breath, nervously twisting the edges of her shawl. Speaking the truth, the full truth, was even harder than she'd thought it would be.

"I've been afraid of Aaron a long time," she confessed, forcing the words out, syllable by reluctant syllable. "Papa doesn't know, and I'd hoped he'd never find out because . . . because of what I did. Aaron's not entirely to blame, you see. I . . . uh, encouraged him. I was in love with him then. And I thought he loved me. We used to steal away at night, to the garden. I thought I could trust him and that we would marry. But he got impatient and—'' Her voice broke.

"Silver." He moved closer, his voice throbbing with concern. "You don't have to tell me anything, if it's too painful—"

"Yes." She drew a shuddering breath. "Yes, I do. Don't you see? All these years, I've kept his secret. By keeping silent, I've given him a sort of power over me. But I'm not willing to live in fear anymore, Rafe. He's a horrible, cruel, and *dangerous* man. And the only way to stop him from hurting me—or anyone else—is to speak the truth. Even if . . . even if I have to go to jail."

"Jail?" He looked as incredulous as he sounded. "Silver, if you're trying to tell me Townsend forced himself on you—"

"No," she said weakly. "I stopped him. The garden wall had crumbled a bit, and when he threw me to the ground, there was a brick nearby. I asked him to stop. I begged him to, but he ripped open my bodice. I couldn't break free. I grabbed for the brick and . . ." She trembled, hating herself for the weakness, but unable to quash the rush of fear the memories spawned. "I hit him. It was awful. Blood was everywhere." She wiped shaking hands on her skirts. "When he fell beside me, I thought I'd killed him. Or at the very least, blinded him. That's why he has that gash above his left temple.

"I guess I was lucky," she whispered hoarsely. "He wasn't seriously hurt, but I was mortified by what I'd done. It never occurred to me I wasn't to blame. When he regained consciousness, he told the doctor he'd been attacked by ruffians. He told me privately if I ever tried to disprove his story, he'd have me locked in the state penitentiary for attempted murder.''

Rafe battled an all-consuming rage. If anyone was going to a penitentiary, it would be him—for breaking Townsend's neck with his bare hands. ''Silver, for God's sake, you were acting in self-defense.''

''I know, but who would have believed me? He was a powerful man. And Papa was poorer than dirt back then. So . . . I left town. After five years passed, I didn't think I was important enough for Aaron to come looking for me. But now he knows Papa has money, and . . .'' A sob bubbled past her lips.

''Sweetheart, don't,'' he murmured as she covered her mouth with her hand. ''Townsend's not going to hurt you or Max. I won't let him.'' He gathered her to his heart, the old futility gnawing at his innards. Silver needed protecting. Just like his mother had needed protecting. He didn't want to fail Silver the way he'd failed his mother, but what could he do? A conniving, cold-blooded bastard like Townsend wouldn't consider a penniless flimflam artist to be any more of a threat than Max would be.

''Townsend can't force you to marry him, Silver,'' he soothed, hoping the bastard's logic was as sound as his own. ''Not if your father has any say in the matter. And Townsend wouldn't dare put you through the humiliation of a trial. He doesn't want your story going public any more than you do. He has too much to lose.''

''That's not what I'm afraid of,'' she whispered raggedly, her breath warm and moist against the hollow of his throat. ''I'm . . . afraid he'll hurt you.''

He hugged her tighter. "That's not going to happen," he said firmly.

"But you don't understand! People who stand in Aaron's way seem to . . . to have fatal accidents. Like his brother!"

An icy premonition bit into Rafe's bones. Still, years of playacting enabled him to keep the uneasiness from his voice. "You needn't worry about me, darling. Townsend's not playing with a law-abiding innocent this time. If he wants an express ticket to hell, I'll be only too happy to see he gets it."

"No! Rafe, please don't challenge him to a gunfight—"

He plucked her bloodless hand from his shirt front and pressed a kiss into her palm. "High-noon showdowns aren't my style, sweetheart. No, I rather like outsmarting the Townsends of the world—and watching them hang themselves with their own greed."

She averted her eyes. "Well, I can't say he doesn't deserve it. And more. It's just that . . ." She sighed, a long, poignant spiral of sound that reverberated to the bottom of his soul. "It's just that he's so . . . violent. He scares me, Rafe. What he's capable of scares me. And I don't want to be afraid anymore: of him, of walks in the garden, of . . . of the consequences."

He rubbed her chilly fingers between his hands. "I know," he said softly.

"Do you?"

His heart tripped to hear that husky plea. The longing in her eyes nearly undid him. It sent a crackling jolt of expectancy straight to his loins.

"Rafe, I can't go on living this way, afraid of being loved, afraid of being touched. Will . . . will you help me?"

His whole damned body flushed at her meaning. *Jesus.* After her story, the last thing she needed was a confirmed rake like him. But she apparently didn't realize her danger—or the effect she was having on him. When her shaking hand raised his, pressing it to the buttons of her bodice, his fly became a risky restraint. He could feel how hard her heart was pounding against her whalebone and lace.

"Honey," he croaked, despising himself for even thinking about baring that alabaster globe to his mouth, "I don't think you're ready—"

"I am. I *am* ready."

He tried to withdraw, but she only gripped his hand more insistently against the ridge of her corset. Her eyes begged him, and God knew, he ached to oblige. There was nothing he'd like better than to act out the fantasies he'd been sweating through every night since she'd given him that sassy, all-knowing smile at the Mining Exchange. But he'd be worse than Townsend if he laid her down now to vent a selfish desire. The confrontation, the memories it had resurrected, her worry for him—all had left her vulnerable. Combine those with the spell of honeysuckles and starlight, and she couldn't possibly know her own mind.

He drew a sobering breath. "Max and Cellie will be looking for us."

"I don't care." Her chin quivered, and she pressed closer, so close that the soft, fleshy curve of her breast filled his palm. "Let them."

He licked his dry lips. "You don't mean that."

"I do! I don't care what anyone else thinks anymore, or how it's supposed to be. This may be the one chance I . . . I ever have to be with you, once the truth comes to light. Please, Rafe."

"Silver," he half pleaded, half cursed, "you'd regret this. You'd regret *us*."

"Why?" Her face crumpled. "D-don't you want me anymore?"

Oh God. He squeezed his eyes closed, struggling to quench the unholy fire that smoked through his veins. "Of course I want you. It's just that you need a decent man. An upstanding man. Someone who isn't wanted in three states. Someone with a future."

"I need *you*, Rafe. Don't you see? You're the only one who can make it right for me because . . . because I love you."

His throat tightened over the lump that had wedged there. She *loved* him, God help her. *Him*. He could see it shining in her eyes like the heaven he'd thought he'd be forever denied.

Reason failed him then. In that moment, confronted by a truth so hallowed that even his soul had to believe, he couldn't force himself to turn away. He couldn't deprive himself of the one blessing that, he realized now, he'd been searching for his whole life. Silver's love was his salvation, and salvation was within his reach. Call him callous and selfish, but he grabbed for the prize with both hands.

"Then marry me, Silver," he said fervently, cupping her face in his hands. "Marry me and be my wife and Aaron Townsend be damned."

Silver gasped as Rafe's lips swooped, possessing hers. A tender savagery had suffused him; she swayed, exhilarated and yet awed, clutching the pleats of his shirt as his mouth plundered hers. He held her enthralled, a willing captive in the wildfire of his passion. His kisses devoured her; her breath became his. Lightning danced beyond the fringe of her lashes. She was sizzling from head to toe when he clasped her buttocks, imprisoning her hips against the heat of his arousal. And just as her world was spinning deliciously, precariously out of control, he lowered her to the chaise.

The weight of him was a scandalous pleasure. She squirmed with delight, flattening her breasts against his rock-ribbed torso. She wanted more of him, all of him, and fumbled with his waistcoat and bow tie. She might have succeeded at tearing the nuisances free if she hadn't been so wickedly distracted. A sudden gust of mountain air warned her that her corset and chemise had been expertly rifled. When the sultry wetness of his mouth descended over her nipple, she gasped, blushing. She couldn't help but revel in the teasing courtship of his tongue.

"How beautiful you are," he murmured, his hands gliding lower. Stays and garters parted like smoke before his touch; she shivered, feeling the silk of her stockings cascade to her ankles. In a heartbeat, maybe two, she'd be naked beneath him. It was a heady realization, but a sobering one, too. Would the erotic fusion of flesh to flesh steal her hard-won nerve?

He was shedding his own clothes now: black worsted, linen, satin, and leather. The earthy manscents of him—sandalwood and pine—grew sharper, more seductive, as his skin was bared to her senses. He was rugged and vital, magnetic and sensual, and more heart-trippingly masculine than anything she had ever dared to admire. She let her maidenly eyes feast on his self-assured display: tight buttocks, crisp tawny hair, and the inevitable thrust of his phallus. A breathless sense of awe washed over her. She waited for the dreaded alchemy that would turn her veneration into fear. Instead, a languorous longing lapped through her. This was Rafe. The man she loved.

Shyly, she stretched her arms for him. He seemed to check himself then, drawing a ragged breath. A tender smile curved his mouth, and he caught her fingers, pressing them to his lips.

"I want this night to be special for you, Silver," he whispered, his eyes aglow with a secret promise as he pulled the ribbon from her hair. It tumbled around her in a lavender-scented mess, but he smoothed it, weaving his fingers through the curls. "I want to make your love dreams come true. Will you trust me, my darling?"

She nodded, too tongue-tied to speak. She recognized a sacredness in his manner, a reverence for the act in which she had once nearly been defiled. Rafe's very smile made her feel exalted and adored, and when he lowered himself beside her, gathering her to his chest, she wanted to cry for the sheer gentleness of his embrace.

Lips like velvet roses nuzzled hers; hands like well-worn leather massaged her buttocks and thighs. His tongue, teasing her inner ear, distracted her from her first jolt of virginal unease, but when his finger slipped inside her, she clawed his shoulders, stunned by the boldness of his exploration.

"Trust me," he crooned again, rocking her against the satiny hair of his chest. She loosed a throttled moan, and his tongue circled her navel. He feasted lower, nuzzling her groin, nipping her knees. She found herself arching helplessly, her legs jerking open as if pulled by strings, while he, the puppet master, wooed her bashful muscles to obey. Soon, the steam of his breath tantalized her most private places. A flash of insight followed, more shocking than anything she had dared to imagine, and just as she was assuring herself she was mistaken in his intent, his mouth settled and sucked.

She whimpered, nearly crawling out of her skin.

"Rafe, please—"

"Patience, love," he urged, his voice broken and breathless. "You're not ready."

Not ready? she wondered dizzily. *How could that be?* His tongue now mimicked the maddening thrust of his finger. She trembled, beginning to writhe. "Rafe," she moaned again, straining to touch him, but he twined his fingers through hers, effectively making them prisoners. Dimly, she recalled the devil in him, the wicked tormentor who could set her blood on fire with a single, bawdy grin. She wanted to make him feel the same way. She wanted to make him ache for her the way she ached for him. Twisting, she half sobbed for relief. He gentled his petting and kissed her.

"You're still too tight," he said hoarsely, his explanation distorted by the pounding in her head. "Let me pleasure you, sweetheart. Just a little longer . . ." He dipped his tongue back inside her steaming flesh, and his growl, low and guttural with satisfaction, vibrated through her on an erotic rumble of sound. "God, you taste like molten honey . . ."

It was almost more than she could bear, this insidious heat he was slowly, masterfully fanning into a bonfire. She thought she would reach the point of meltdown before she ever ignited. She thought she would lose her mind before she lost her maidenhead. Deprived of her last shred of coherent thought, she wondered if he might not be up to some nefarious purpose to tease her so unmercifully.

And then the bonfire burst fully into flame. She cried out, and he reared up, his mouth covering hers.

Before her dazzled senses could sort one sensation from the other, he'd thrust hard and clean, driving to the center of her being. She bucked uncontrollably, and he sheathed himself again, deepening the indescribable waves of pleasure that shuddered through her body.

"That's it," he groaned, his breath sawing as hard as hers in the shimmering heat. "I want all of you, Silver. All of you. Everything you are is mine now, love. Always . . ."

She couldn't respond—not in words. So she rose to meet him, again and again, pulling him deeper, clasping his hips closer. He was dynamite; she was the fuse, and when their worlds collided, ecstasy exploded, wracking body, mind, and soul with a glittering avalanche of sensation.

Rafe was still panting when he rolled to the cushions. Emotions too volatile to name ripped through him; he buried his face in her hair. Wrapping possessive arms around her, he clutched her to his crashing heart. For the first time in his life, he felt release, true release, as if the demons had at last surrendered their chains on him. And it was all because of Silver.

"Rafe?"

She tried to stir, but he hushed her with his caresses, wanting nothing more than to hold her and love her and watch the sun rise and set in her eyes.

"W-we have to tell Papa about us. About who you are before—"

"I know, sweet. Not tonight, though."

"But Benson! And Aaron—"

"You let me deal with them, all right?"

She swallowed. Reluctantly, her head fell back

against his shoulder. "I couldn't bear it if you were arrested."

He sighed. He had to admit, he wasn't fond of the idea either. But none of his offenses had been hanging ones—yet, he corrected himself darkly, envisioning Townsend's throat between his hands. Until this moment, he'd never had enough to live for to worry about the consequences of his lawless life.

Who would have thought it would come down to this? Raphael Jones falling in love—and with the woman he'd set out to fleece, yet? He'd suspected for days he'd been plugged by Cupid, but only now did he understand why. His devotion to Silver had nothing to do with face, shape, or wealth. His heart had chosen her because she'd let him strip off his mask. She'd given him back his humanity. She'd taught him wrongs could be forgiven, even repaired. But most importantly, she'd taught him he could be loved— even with imperfections. For a love as precious as Silver's, he would lay down his life.

She sighed, and he wrapped her shawl around her, watching her lashes fan lower until she drifted off to sleep. He couldn't remember a time when he'd ever faced so much happiness—and so much fear. Prayers didn't come easily to him, but as the moon began to sink, stealing behind the charcoal ridge of mountains, he finally broke his lifelong vow and talked to God.

I know I'm a sorry bastard, Lord. I know I don't deserve her. But please, don't let Townsend take her away. I'll do whatever you want, whatever it takes. I'll even serve my time, if I have to. Just please keep her safe 'til I come home. Thank you. Amen.

Chapter 14

❦

Silver dozed restlessly in Rafe's arms as dim, vaguely threatening images flitted through her dreams. She wished she could sate her mind as well as he'd slaked her body, but every bubble of bliss floating through her limbs was chased by a whitecap of worry. Before another day dragged her deeper into self-loathing and fear, she wanted to confess her crimes to Papa; she wanted to fire Benson; and she wanted to find some way to keep Rafe out of jail. Most of all, she wanted to rid her life of Aaron Townsend and start the future she'd always dreamed of—with Rafe.

But Rafe didn't seem to share her sense of urgency, at least not when it came to confessing their misdeeds to Papa. In fact, he'd seemed rather amused by her panic to dress and sneak inside the house before Benson awoke and discovered them missing.

"Darling," he'd purred, after they'd dashed hand-in-hand up the back stairwell and slumped breathlessly against her bedroom door, "we have the rest of our lives to beg Max's forgiveness and make amends. Let's just claim this morning for ourselves . . . and lovemaking."

She'd wanted to protest, but he'd already snatched

away the shawl she'd been clutching like a shield to her rumpled gown. Before she could hide her bawdy blush, he'd bowled her back onto the bed. She'd found herself distracted from her worries, laughing and scolding between pants, feeling duty-bound to at least try to instill some decorum in her scoundrel. She failed miserably in the attempt, mostly because she delighted in his hungry, prowling caress. By the time it occurred seriously to her that they should stop, that Jimmy, Papa, or, God forbid, Benson might overhear their amorous romping, Rafe had already petted her into a paroxysm of desire. She pitched helplessly beneath his mouth and hands, mortified to hear the booming creaks of the mattress, and yet too frenzied to do more than gulp a warning. He'd chuckled at her ladylike restraint, plunging deeper and snaking faster, relentless in his mission to drive her past the point of all caring. She lost her mind with her self-control, crying out his name again and again, until a throaty, desperate growl signaled the climax of his own restraint, and he drove home hard and fast, obliging her half-sobbed pleas to fill her with his passion.

She woke from their early morning loving three hours later, a sheet draping her nakedness and the aroma of sandalwood wafting faintly from the hollow in the pillow by her head. She groaned, sitting up, and scrubbed her face with her hands. Her tawny-haired debaucher was nowhere to be seen.

She sighed dreamily, touching a tentative tongue to her swollen bottom lip. Memories from the last twelve hours made her heat and ice by turn: Rafe. The séance. *Aaron.* She swallowed. Swinging her feet to the floor, she straightened, grimacing at the dull, feminine ache her first steps caused her. Still, she couldn't delay the inevitable. She had to face Papa . . . before Aaron bore out Cellie's predictions.

At nearly half past ten, Silver finally completed her toilette and eased down the steps to find Papa. She was in luck. Despite the lateness of the hour, he hadn't left the house yet for one of his Roaring Fork Club meetings or, more likely, one of his treasure hunts. She could hear his cheerful whistles and smell the pungent smoke of his cigar as she dragged her feet ever closer to his study. She peeked around the door. A bulging satchel spilled maps across his desk; in his hand was a compass, on his head sat his miner's helmet, which now sported some weird, geometric talisman for warding off ghosts. She drew a bolstering breath and rapped.

"Papa?"

He glanced up, his reading spectacles sliding to the bulb of his nose. "Daughter!" He beamed. "So there you are. And just in time, too. Cellie and me've got that wily old Injun shaman cornered."

"Y-you do?"

"Yep. Right here at the bottom of the mine," he said, pointing to a spot on one of his maps. "Time to go in and make our demands. And not a moment too soon. Tavy's stunt last night scared the bejabbers out of Kilkarney and Penhalion. They're convinced they really did see Dancing Moon. Now they've got the shovel stiffs in an uproar, and nobody reported to work today."

"Nobody?" she repeated halfheartedly.

" 'Fraid so. Even Brady has a touch of 'ghost flu,' so I hear." Papa snickered. "Or maybe it's his fear of crab-puff-chasing otters that's kept him abed."

She smiled weakly.

"Uh, Papa, I need to talk to you about something. It's . . . important."

"Important, huh?" He squinted at his compass, jotted a notation on his map, then peered up at her expectantly. "Sounds serious."

She fidgeted, not at all certain how to continue. "Yes. Yes, it is. And . . . it's going to hurt, Papa."

"Me or you?"

"You."

"Hmm." He slid her a sideways glance. "Well, I never would have guessed *that*, you being so tongue-tied."

She blushed, worrying her bottom lip. "Papa, I did something terrible to you."

"Did you, now?"

She nodded.

"Well, doing something terrible doesn't make you a terrible person, daughter."

She blinked, momentarily taken aback. To be told she *wasn't* terrible was the last thing she'd expected to hear.

"But you don't know what I did," she protested. "I hired Chumley. Only he isn't really Chumley. He's an imposter, a Shakespearean actor named Raphael Jones."

Papa started. "An actor?"

She nodded queasily.

"Well, doesn't that beat all?" He slowly grinned. "An *actor*. Imagine that. And a damned fine one, too. Shoot. I shoulda known. I reckon your average duke is too snooty for *Alice in Wonderland*—not to mention pumpkin pickers and orphaned otters. Say!" Papa added eagerly, "do you suppose Chum . . . er, I mean, this Jones fella might want to work in Cellie's opera?"

"Uh, Papa?" she interrupted, feeling unaccountably deflated by his good humor. "Don't you want to know what I hired Rafe to do?"

He gave her another sidelong look. "Is that the terrible part you warned me about?"

She nodded, fighting back tears.

"Well . . . all right, then. What'd you hire Rafe to do?"

Her throat worked around the painful lump lodged there. "I hired him to . . . to come between you and Cellie. To make her show her true colors and, um, prove she didn't love you."

Was that the light striking off his spectacles, or were his eyes actually twinkling?

"Now why would you go and do that, daughter?" he asked more gravely.

"Because I thought Cellie was an arsonist. I thought she would hurt you once you married her and . . . and named her in your will."

He folded his arms across his chest. "So what made you change your mind?"

She wanted to crawl under the rug. "I hired a detective to . . . uh, investigate the rumors about her. And he told me she wasn't responsible for the fire that burned down that church in Kentucky."

Papa nodded, the corner of his mouth twitching. "Well, I reckon you just had to convince yourself, daughter. You wouldn't listen to me."

A slow heat crawled up her face. "Y-you're not mad?" she whispered hoarsely.

His dimples peeked. "Do you want me to be?"

She half-sobbed, pressing a shaking hand to her mouth. The relief she felt at being so easily pardoned made her head spin. Giddy, free, and two tons lighter, she bubbled with laughter. The sound came out in hiccupping peals. She couldn't help herself. All these weeks of guilt, and Papa wasn't even *angry*!

"Thank you." She clasped her hands, tears trickling past her idiotic grin. "I love you, Papa. And ... and there's something else you should know. I love Rafe, too."

Papa lit up like a Christmas fir. "*Love* him? But that's fabulous, daughter!" he cried, hurrying forward to wrap her in a bear hug. "Bully for you. And bully for him, too! Raphael Jones, huh? Why, I'll be damned. Did the rascal propose yet?"

She nodded, giggling and blushing, and so overwhelmingly happy that even her fear of Aaron, for the moment, couldn't pierce the bubble of her elation. "Oh, Papa, I hope you don't mind. In light of ... of what you didn't know, he thought it best that he ask me directly."

"*Mind*? Shoot, daughter, I'm tickled by the news! Plum tickled. We can have a double wedding! Looks like I'll finally have my son-in-law, and you'll finally have ... well, *babies*!" He chuckled as she grew even hotter. "Cellie'll be thrilled. She's never had children of her own, you know. Why, I was just telling her the other day what a handsome devil Chum ... er, I mean, Rafe turned out to be, once she got him to shave off all his whiskers. I shoulda thought of it myself, since I put him up to it in the first place, but it looks like he didn't need help from me, after all. The rascal came through."

Silver blinked at him, her lightheartedness snuffed out by a slowly evolving suspicion. "What do you mean, 'put him up to it'?"

He started, flushing guiltily. "Did I say that? Er ... no. What I meant was—"

"Papa"—dread tightened its coils around Silver's

stomach—"what did you ask Rafe to do?"

He shifted uncomfortably from foot to foot. "Now, daughter, what difference does it make? You love him, don't you? And he loves you too, I reckon. Let's just go back to planning our weddings—"

"Did you ask Rafe to . . . to *marry* me?"

His chin jutted like that of a child who'd just been caught with a cookie. "I thought you were fond of him," he said defensively. "And I thought he was a *duke*. Besides, it's a father's prerogative to arrange his daughter's marriage. And I *am* your father, you know."

"You arranged my marriage?" she choked in a thin, quavering voice. "Like the rich families do back in Europe?"

"Oh, Silver, do we really have to talk about—"

"Yes! Yes, I have to know. What was my dowry? Did you make him a partner? Did you deed him a mine?"

When his eyes shifted, avoiding hers completely, she heard her heart splinter, a tinkling cacophony of falling pieces.

"I wanted you to be happy, honey," he explained, his fingers reaching beseechingly for her sleeve. "The way me and Cellie are. The way you used to be back in Philly, before that Townsend fella stopped courting you . . ."

Silver couldn't bear to hear more. Blindly, she turned for the door, her throat burning with unshed tears as she raced from the humiliation. Now she understood why Rafe hadn't been in any hurry for her to speak with Papa. Now she understood what he'd meant by his tender—or had it been triumphant?—declaration: *"Everything you are is mine now."*

Hadn't she thought he'd been up to some nefarious

purpose? The truth ripped up her insides like a thousand savage claws. She'd been naive—again. She'd fallen prey to the same vicious prank that she, God forgive her, had plotted against Celestia. She wanted to scream herself raw from the shame. But more than that, she wanted to bleed out the pain. Rafe didn't love her. He hadn't proposed marriage out of any kind of fond feeling for *her*. No, he'd seen nothing but dollar signs and stock dividends each time he'd kissed her. He was no better than Aaron!

She choked, clutching her corset as the whalebone chafed her breasts. Somehow, unerringly, her feet had planted her before Rafe's door. She could hear him humming an off-key melody above the chinking of metal against porcelain. He was shaving, she realized dimly. It was the last sane thought she entertained.

The door crashed open at her push, and Tavy, jumping a foot high, fled with her ears closed, and her tail tucked, to the bed's underbelly.

"What the dev—?" Rafe spun, his shaving brush poised in midair. He gaped when he saw her, and suds dripped unheeded onto the glistening hairs of his chest. "Silver, what is it?" he asked anxiously, taking a step closer. "Is it Townsend?"

She was shaking so hard that she didn't even have the presence of mind to fear his all-but-naked state. The only thing she could do in that moment, when confronted by the strength of those sinewy arms, shoulders, and thighs, was clench her fists in escalating rage.

"No," she bit out, her teeth chattering between words. "*It's you!* You lying bastard. After everything I told you about Aaron and me, after everything you heard him say and watched him do, *how could you?*"

Rafe blinked, dumbstruck. How could he have possibly done *anything* to evoke this much fury in the woman he loved? In the three hours since he'd tenderly kissed her and left her smiling through her dreams, he'd crawled into his own bed and slept blissfully, dreaming up ways to get even with Townsend.

"Silver." He kept his tone as steady as his startled heart, which was still ricocheting off his ribs, would allow. "Calm down. Take a deep breath. What is it you *think* I did?"

Uh-oh. Wrong approach. He could see his mistake clearly in the crimson that mottled her cheeks.

"You know very well what you did!" she flung back, her bodice heaving hard enough to strain its pearl buttons. "You used me! Just like Aaron. I was nothing more than a means to your end!"

"I'm not sure I follow—"

"You *seduced* me so you could be a partner in Papa's *business*!"

His breath rattled in his throat. *Jesus. She talked to Max.*

"Silver, I assure you, that's not true." *Dammit, Max. You* knew *she would react this way if she learned about the wedding deal.* "I don't know what Max told you, honey, but—"

"Don't you 'honey' me! I am not your 'honey.' Nor will I ever be!" A sob tore from her lips. "How could you be so cruel?"

He swallowed, not sure himself that he wasn't the biggest sonuvabitch on the planet. He *had* set out to seduce her, after all. He'd just never planned on it being the most sacred, God-affirming experience of his life.

"Silver, please. You're upset. Why don't you shut the door, and we'll—"

"No! I'm not falling for any more of your tricks,

damn you. Or any more of your lines, either! It's closing night at the Nichols Theater, although I have to
hand it to you, Rafe: Your performance was magnificent. Better than I paid for. Do take a bow.''

He flinched, and she dashed away tears with an
angry hand.

''How you must have gloated to hear me say I love
you. To hear me cry out your name again and again
as you had your way with me—ha! *Love*making, you
called it!''

''It *was* lovemaking,'' he growled, his own fists
clenching with upset now. ''What happened between
us was nothing like what happened between you and
Townsend—''

''I didn't say it was!''

Her words throbbed between them, vibrating into
a brittle, anguished silence.

Then she grew stiffer. The blast of heat from her
glare was enough to incinerate him.

''Are you proud of making me your conquest?
Does it feel good to know how much you've hurt
me?''

''My God, Silver, I never wanted to hurt you,'' he
whispered rawly. ''In the beginning, it's true, Max
approached me. But I never intended to follow
through. I never intended to stick around long enough
to *be* his business partner. I'm a renegade, a confidence man. You knew that. I never dreamed you'd
fall in love with me. And I didn't plan on falling in
love with you.''

''You fell in love with Nichols money!''

''That is not true!''

''You lied a lot better last night,'' she lashed out,
''when you said you wanted to make all my love
dreams come true.''

His breath rasped. If she had clawed open his chest with her bare hands, she couldn't have dealt him a more mortal wound.

"You know my love for you is real."

"Do I? When you make your living telling people what they want to hear?" Her lips trembled into a sneer. "About the only truth you ever did tell me was that I'd regret *us*. Congratulations: I do. And I want you out of this house by luncheon. And take your otter, too!"

She spun on her heel, storming for the hall, and Rafe reeled, his world crashing around him.

"No! Silver, stop!" Heedless of his shirtless, shoeless state, he bounded after her, panic streaking hotter than lightning through his limbs. "For God's sake, listen to me!"

But she wouldn't stop. She wouldn't listen. In his desperation, he grabbed her arm—another mistake. She shrieked, twisting frantically.

"Let me go!" Fear vied with the outrage on her features. Her petticoats tripped them both up, and when she teetered, nearly toppling down the stairs, he lunged, locking an arm around her waist. A resounding crack echoed off the walls around them. He staggered backwards, his palm to his cheek. It took a full second for the blistering heat of her slap to register on his shocked senses.

"Don't you dare touch me," she spat, retreating into the banister like a cornered animal. "Don't you *ever* touch me again!"

Then she fled, hiccupping with sobs. The broken, inconsolable sounds bludgeoned his heart. It was only when she practically bowled over Max, standing at the foot of the stairs, that Rafe realized the millionaire had overheard their entire confrontation.

Max's face, crumpled with worry, tipped up to regard Rafe. "That didn't go so well, son."

Rafe nodded weakly. He gripped the banister with a bloodless fist as he watched her run out the door to God-only-knew where. Even if he was a liar, an idiot who'd poisoned paradise with his own self-serving silence, he deserved a second chance. She'd taught him that. She'd taught him even he wasn't too heinous to be loved.

"I have to go after her," he announced grimly.

"Whoa, there." Max hastened to the center of the stairs and barred Rafe's descent. "Hold your horses, son. In the first place, you're not dressed for it. In the second . . ." He met Rafe's angry, desperate glare with an unflinching stare of his own.

"You're too riled to talk sense into anyone—much less a woman."

"That's a hell of a thing to say. Especially about your own daughter. Now get out of my way."

"How come?"

"Because I love her!"

"Yeah?" Max cocked his head and gave him a narrow, appraising look. "So you'd run naked through the streets for her, huh?"

Rafe's face burned. "Do you think I give a damn if some Hallam Street biddy sees me in shorts?"

"No. No, I reckon you don't." Max did a masterful job of wiping off his smirk and tossed Rafe his suitcoat. "But Silver might. She's, uh, kind of particular about reputations. And you wouldn't want to give her any *more* reason not to marry you, right?"

Frustrated by such a truth, Rafe dragged on the jacket—too roomy through the waist and short in the sleeves—but his attention was riveted on the sidewalk outside, where passersby strolled with fringed parasols, white mopcaps, and shaded baby carriages.

"Where do you think she went?" he asked, biting his tongue on the excruciating afterthought, *'To Marshal Hawthorne?'*

"Don't know. Can't see how it matters, though. She'll come back. And when she does, you'll be gone."

"What?" Rafe's gaze snapped back to the stoic older man's. "Now see here, Max, I'm not walking out that door until I've had the chance to redeem myself. Nothing she thinks about me is true. *Nothing.* I'd rather be drawn and quartered than make her hurt that way."

"I know, son," Max said more gently. "But she's a woman. And women like to weep and wail, and throw tantrums every now and again. I think it's in their blood. Kinda like weddings. Neither's much fun for us menfolk. But the good news is, once the lady's done, she likes to make up, if you catch my meaning. Silver loves you. She told me so herself. And that gal of mine's too full of heart to stop loving a man overnight.

" 'Course," he added ruefully, "she *does* need to blow a bit more wind out of her sails, and a squall like that could last a couple of days—at least." He grimaced, as if at some private memory. "Why don't you go on up to Swindler's Creek? Take along Tavy and see if you can't get her accustomed to being wild. In a week or so, Silver'll get to missing you, and she'll be a whole lot more reasonable. You can talk to her then."

Rafe shifted from foot to foot, seeing the wisdom in the millionaire's advice, yet reluctant to leave Silver behind. Townsend and his threats were too fresh in his mind.

"If I go, you've got to make me a promise, Max. You've got to keep her safe. And that means keeping her away from Townsend."

Max nodded, his face growing uncharacteristically grim. "Yeah. Fairgate told me. About Amy, I mean. It's a damned shame. I'd just as soon shoot Townsend as look at him. And in this state, shooting trespassers ain't that much of a crime."

Rafe smiled feebly, imagining Max, in true Western fashion, greeting the Pennsylvania congressman with a shotgun at the door. "You watch your step, Max."

The wily old miner snorted. "I ain't afraid of a man who never got dirt under his nails his whole life long. 'Sides, I got Cellie and her spooks to look after me. I can't pick up the newspaper without that woman telling me what I'm going to read on the inside—the next day. And she's always right, too. It's damned eerie." He gave a low, throaty rumble of mirth. "We're gonna have some kind of life together, huh? You and Silver, me and Cellie—and all the spooks."

Rafe avoided Max's eyes. He didn't share the man's confidence in Cellie's predictions, much less Max's belief that Silver would forgive him. But for now, with nothing else to cling to, Rafe did his best to believe.

"I hope you're right, Max."

"Well, if I'm not, we'll just get Cellie to haul out her cauldron and cook you and Silver a witchy make-up potion. You'll smell like basil for a week, but it's worth it." He winked roguishly. "You can trust me on that, son."

Silver spent the next two miserable days holed up in her mining superintendent's office. With no steam whistles to screech the changing shifts and no shovel stiffs to pound on the door with demands, she'd thought she'd found the ideal escape from her disastrous love affair.

Unfortunately, the potbelly stove, greasy window, and plain pine walls weren't much of a distraction. Nor, surprisingly, was the ten-page ultimatum Kilkarney and Penhalion had left on her foreman's desk. In all that eerie mountain quiet, Silver couldn't seem to concentrate on the Union's charges of "cruel and unusual punishment" because she "forced" her stalwart miners to descend into the "haunted abyss." In fact, the stillness of her superintendent's office seemed louder than the dynamite blasts had ever been. She couldn't help but hear Rafe's voice in that silence, wooing her with Shakespeare, taunting her with double entendres, defending her from Aaron.

Smuggler Mountain also brought memories of their riverbank encounter when Rafe had saved her from the spider. Whenever she rode through the pine tree graveyard or watered her horse at the river, she supposed she would think of him now. She couldn't help but wonder if he'd find a home at Swindler's Creek for Tavy and if, by chance, he'd ever return to visit his otter . . . or her.

Fighting back another self-pitying sob, she pressed cool fingers to her eyelids. She couldn't remember ever crying so hard, not even after Mama had died. And all this torment for what? A man who saw nothing in her but a fortune to be wooed? What was the matter with her, weeping like a brokenhearted ninny? She knew better. It wasn't as if Raphael Jones had charged out of her dreams like some knight on a white destrier. His dishonorable character had been evident at their first meeting. She'd *hired* him for it, for God's sake. Hurting over the man simply didn't make sense.

Then again, *loving* him didn't make sense, either.

She'd turned out to be quite the fool, hadn't she? She, with all her lofty education in Philadelphia's finest finishing schools, had proven to be a real addlepate when it came to choosing sweethearts. As hard as they'd tried, Grandfather and Aunt Agatha had never cured her of her mother's legacy. She heartily wished they had.

Damn you, Rafe. Did you have to make me love you? Wouldn't a simple infatuation have been victory enough?

A muffled knock rattled the door. Startled, Silver dashed away tears, reluctant to invite anyone to witness the throes of her grief. Unfortunately, her visitor didn't stand on such ceremony.

"Hello, dear," Celestia said, breezing in. She was wearing another of her bizarre overalls-cum-turban outfits, and from her neck hung an even more peculiar diaphanous blue sling. Inside it nestled her crystal ball, and she cradled the orb as lovingly as a baby against her portly middle.

"I . . . didn't know you were here, Cellie," Silver said, relief stirring feebly inside her. At least her father's fiancée was better than all this blasted silence, even if Cellie's arrival did mean she might be dragged off on a "bangle hunt." Cellie had been accessorizing for weeks, and Silver could just imagine what Buckholtz was going to write the minute he laid eyes on Cellie's wedding sari. "Um . . . were you looking for Papa?"

Apparently Cellie didn't hear her. She was too busy gazing vacuously toward the cobwebs and rafters. Suddenly her focus centered, keen and blue, on the air above Silver's head. Silver's heart gave an extra-hard thump. Cringing, she glanced up and swiped, suspicious of spiders.

"Not to worry, dear," Cellie crooned, tugging out her crystal ball. "Not spiders, spirits."

"*Spirits?*" Silver bolted out of her chair, her nerves too frazzled to rationalize such nonsense today.

Cellie nodded absently and squinted into the sphere. "Just one, actually. He was drawn by your tears. Didn't you feel him kiss your cheek?"

Silver groaned. She was already having second thoughts about Celestia versus silence . . .

Meanwhile, Cellie was nodding and mumbling. "Go home now, dear one. You're quite lost, you know. Silver will be fine. Go home and be with God."

Strangely enough, Silver felt every hair on her head stand on end. And then the chill that passed over her suddenly lifted.

Cellie beamed with satisfaction. "He's gone."

"Oh." Silver tried not to dwell on the irony of losing both Rafe *and* a ghostly suitor all in forty-eight hours. "That's good—I think. Uh . . . Cellie?"

She was holding her ball up to the window and frowning. Apparently the grease filtered out the sunlight she needed.

Silver took a deep breath and plunged in. "I owe you an apology. I've been horribly unkind to you. And . . . and you don't know the half of it. But I told Papa I'd rather you heard it from me than him." *Or Aaron*, she thought gloomily. The only bright spot of this whole shameful affair was that Aaron couldn't blackmail her anymore. She'd spilled the beans to Papa, and Rafe had safely fled Aspen. Now all she had to do was fire Benson. And she would, the minute he reappeared to claim his belongings. Strangely enough, he'd been missing ever since the night of the séance.

And speaking of strange things. . . .

Cellie was rubbing vigorously, her turban bobbing and her ear hoops swinging, as she cleaned the window with her elbow. Silver sighed, wondering how *anyone* held a serious conversation with the woman.

"I wanted to speak to you about Chumley. Or rather, Rafe. That's his real name, you see. I . . . uh, hired him to pose as Chumley."

Cellie smiled indulgently. "I know, dear. The earl of Chumley and I are old friends. Why, I read his palm in San Francisco right before I met your father."

Silver's jaw nearly hit the desk. "Y-you knew Rafe was an impostor? All this time? And you didn't say anything to Papa?"

"Of course not, dear. That would have spoiled spirit's plan."

"Spirit's plan?" Silver repeated dubiously.

Nodding, Cellie balanced her ball on the battered tin cup the superintendent had left on the window ledge. "You're supposed to marry an angel, you see. From a family of angels: Michael, Gabriel, Seraphina, and Raphael."

Somehow, Silver managed to hinge her jaw closed. "I think your spirits are talking about the wrong Raphael."

"I knew you would say that, dear. That's why I brought the crystal ball."

Silver folded her arms across her traitorously hopeful heart. Of *course* Cellie would know about the Jones family, she reminded herself. The woman had been run out of Blue Thunder by Jedidiah himself. "Are you sure Papa didn't put you up to this crystal-

ball business? He's been wanting me to marry Rafe
from the beginning, you know.''

Cellie chuckled. '' 'The Walrus and the Carpenter.'
Yes, I remember. But you see, Max wouldn't have *let*
you marry a flimflammer. Not unless he'd had some
inkling of the good waiting to be unearthed, like a
treasure, inside that dear boy. And that's why I
couldn't let Max go to the Mining Exchange with you
last month. I know how angry you were with me,
Silver, but if I hadn't found some excuse to keep Max
here, your whole future would have changed. You
would have married that murderous Aaron Townsend.
And you might not have survived the honeymoon.''

Silver felt her limbs drain of warmth. ''Y-you
know about Aaron?''

''My dear, the spirits predicted his coming quite
clearly at the séance. 'A flesh-and-blood mortal who
would do others wrong.' Weren't you listening?''

''Yes, but . . .'' Silver swallowed, not sure she
liked how neatly these coincidences were stacking up.
Cellie *could* have heard about Aaron from Fred. After
all, she'd accompanied Papa when he'd bailed Fred
out of jail. ''Well, anyway, I'm not going to marry
Aaron. Or Rafe either, for that matter.''

''You don't mean that,'' Cellie said gently.

''Yes, I do!'' To her mortification, her voice broke.
''He doesn't love me, Cellie. I was nothing more than
a mark to him. And if I never see him again, it will
be too soon.''

Cellie frowned, smoothing her hand over the ball.
''You didn't say that to *him* did you?''

''Well, not in so many words. But I did call his
bluff. I told him he made lying his business and I
wouldn't fall for any more of his tricks. Then I threw
him out of the house. Tavy too.''

"Oh dear. Tavy too?" Cellie worried her bottom lip. Squinting once more, she raised the ball to chin level. "You've set things in motion, I'm afraid. We are all connected, you see. Who we meet, and how our lives come together, are all part of a divine plan. Still, I had hoped by warning everyone at the séance, the plan could be shifted a bit . . ."

"That doesn't make sense," Silver said, knitting her brows. "If the plan's divine, how can it be shifted?"

"Our destinies may be written in the stars, Silver, but we still have free choice. That makes it hard to predict anyone's future with total accuracy. You can refuse to marry Rafe, of course, but . . ."

"But what?" Silver demanded uneasily.

"This isn't good," Cellie muttered, shaking her head. "Not good at all."

"What? What's not good?"

Cellie shook her head again.

"Cellie, please! What do you see?" She peered anxiously over the fortune-teller's shoulder, trying in vain to glimpse whatever Cellie was seeing in that perfectly clear globe.

But Cellie snatched the orb away and stuffed it back inside her sling. "I have to find Max. There's nothing we can do for Benson, but Rafe we can intercept at Swindler's Creek."

Silver nearly strangled on her breath. The truth dawned hard and fast. "Did . . . did Aaron kill Benson?"

Cellie waved fretfully. She was already on her way out the door. "There's no time to explain," she called, her words trailing after her as she dodged a barrel of dynamite and ducked into the mine.

Silver's legs were beginning to shake. She swayed against the desk.

At the séance, Cellie said blood would be shed in retribution.

She sickened, clapping a hand over her mouth.

Dear God, I have to find Rafe. I have to warn him!

Chapter 15

Camouflaged by olive green shadow, Rafe crouched downwind of the otter slide on the banks of Swindler's Creek. A trio of Tavy's cousins frolicked beneath the cottonwood trees. Forepaws pressed to their sides, round ears squeezed closed, they zipped as sleek as torpedoes down the mud-slickened grass on their bellies. A round of uproarious barking would follow each splash, and then the merrymakers would waddle as fast as their webbed paws could carry them back up the hill for another dive.

Tavy was mesmerized. As motionless as the mushrooms festooning her log, she stood on her hind paws and gawked. Indeed, the only sign of life she'd betrayed in the last half hour had been her twitching whiskers. Rafe tried to be grateful to see her so enthralled by her brethren. Otters tended to be solitary, seeking each other out only to mate and, occasionally, to play. It had been a rare coup for him to stumble across this trio of males. And he wasn't sure he was happy about it.

Christ, do I have to lose Silver and Tavy all in the same week?

Glumly, he envisioned the weather-scoured wagon, with its peeling blue paint, that creaked with each stomp of the nag somewhere behind him. He'd been forced to trade his carriage for something more practical. So much for the luxuries of dukedom. And so much for Jimmy. He couldn't afford a retainer anymore. Still, practicality hadn't been much of a consolation, not when he'd had to face Jimmy. The youth had been so crestfallen to learn he'd have to return to melon picking that he'd nearly wept. Rafe hadn't blamed him. He'd tried to gentle the blow by telling the boy to keep his livery as a souvenir of the "grand and glorious service he'd rendered a duke." Jimmy cheered somewhat at the prospect until he realized he'd have to tell Tavy good-bye.

Rafe was still commiserating.

Damn the whole lousy marriage idea, anyway. How could something so right between him and Silver go so wrong? Was God toying with his fate? Perhaps more to the point, did God even *exist*? Because if this misery was the reward sinners got for praying, Rafe thought bitterly, then God could rest assured He'd never hear "Amen" from Raphael Jones's mouth again.

A strange thumping roused him from his brooding. Frowning, he listened more intently, straining his ears for the familiar sound of creaking over the otters' barks. A shivery sense of foreboding seized him. The birds had grown quiet. Too quiet.

Unwilling to frighten off Tavy's prospective family, he eased backwards out of his nest of reeds. He intended to circle through the undergrowth, making a wide swath around the wagon, before approaching it openly. He never got the chance. Suddenly, a gun hammer clicked. Sunlight glinted off the muzzle aimed point-blank at his head. He froze, and his captor gave a raspy chuckle.

"Well, howdy Mr. Smart-ass Duke," came an unmistakable Texas drawl. "We've tracked you fer
damned near two days across this big ol' mountain,
but I reckon hide 'n seek is over now. Shit." The
expletive dragged on for three syllables. "I was ex-
pectin' you to be duded up in rubies and diamonds."

Another thump resounded through the ominously
quiet wood. Rafe suspected somebody was hammering a gun stock against the lock of his trunk. He sup-
pressed his initial inclination to go after the bastard,
and cautiously tipped his head to regard his captor.

A stream of tobacco juice nearly hit him in the eye.

Rafe did his best not to grimace. Instead, he donned
a bland smile and his smoothest Kentucky drawl.

"I apologize for the inconvenience, er . . ." *Marshal? Deputy?* He searched the foul-smelling checkered flannel of the one-eyed Texican's shirt for a
badge. None was visible, not even on the gunman's
vest, where the flies were happily swarming through
the matted, black bear fur. Rafe wasn't reassured,
though. This was the same Texican who'd been stalking him since his arrival in Aspen. And that meant he
was either a paid assassin, *bounty hunter* as the law
agencies euphemistically called them, or an outlaw.
"I'm afraid you've been tracking the wrong man. As
you can tell, I'm no more British than you are."

"Hey, Snake!" This cry, rife with disappointment,
came from the vicinity of the wagon. "The sumbitch
doesn't have any money. And no damned crown jewels, neither! Just a coupla old darned socks and this
here beat-up shaving kit."

Snake, who was no doubt aptly named, and not just
for the patch over his left eye, bared yellow teeth.
"So where'd ya hide them?" he snarled, shoving the
muzzle under Rafe's chin. "We want the jewels."

"Yeah, that's right," the second man said, thrashing into the thicket. Except for the pronounced slouch of his shoulders, someone could have run a flag up his spine; he was that lanky. "Say, Snake, the way you got that ol' John Bull on his knees, you'd think he was bowin' to royalty."

"That's 'cause Gracie here knows his place afore Texicans."

"Well, shit. The sumbitch'd have to be dumber'n I am not to be prayin' fer mercy with yer .45 shoved damned near up his nose." The second man grinned, as if he'd just made the most profound observation of his life. "Say, Snake, you gonna make him dance?"

"Later." Snake, apparently, wasn't as easily distracted. "Ye're burning daylight, Gracie." He ground the muzzle into Rafe's Adam's apple. "Start talkin'."

Rafe swallowed, cursing himself for the involuntary reaction. He was sure the outlaws would mark it as fear. "What makes you think I'd leave diamonds and rubies lying around in an unguarded wagon?" he hedged, wracking his brain for a way out of this ambush.

" 'Cause Mr. Townsend said we could have whatever jewels we found—"

"Shut up, Loon," Snake snapped, tossing his cohort a vile glare.

It didn't do the trick, though. Either Loon was too stupid to realize he'd exposed his employer and the bogus incentive that Townsend himself had probably invented, or Loon figured it didn't matter, because Snake would plug any witnesses.

"Shut up yerself, Snake," Loon groused. "I'm tired of you always being the stud buzzard. Mr. Townsend hired us both to kill Gracie, and fer the same wage. That means you ain't more important than me.''

"Whatever he's paying you, I'll triple it,'' Rafe countered quickly, deciding his ducal identity was his best chance of survival after all.

"With what?'' Snake sneered. "Patched socks?''

Rafe met the Texican's eye squarely. "I'm a duke, remember? I've got plenty of money back in England—''

"Yeah, like we're *that* stupid,'' Loon jeered. "You ain't sailing back to England to get no money.''

Actually, Rafe had been hoping for a jaunt to Aspen's busy telegraph office. Or a crowded street.

"If you don't let me wire my castle for help, how do you expect to get your ransom?'' he said evenly.

"Ransom?'' they chimed in unison.

"Sure. If you kidnap the duke of Chumley, you ought to get a couple thousand farthings, at least.''

"A couple thousand farthings? Hot damn!'' Loon cackled like his namesake, which only cast further doubt on the soundness of his mind. "Did ya hear that, Snake? We'll be rich!''

"Rafe?''

He stopped breathing. The outlaws did too. The call had been Silver's. Anxious and questing, it reverberated through the fading afternoon like a death knell—her own.

"Holy shit.'' Loon craned his long neck over his shoulder. "It's a skirt! A purty one, too. And from the looks of it, she's headed this way!''

Rafe clenched his fists, if only to keep from doing something insane: like punching one of the outlaws and getting himself killed for his chivalry. For the love of Christ, what was Silver doing *here*, on

horseback, without a single damned escort and twi-
light humming fast through the trees?

Loon and Snake locked eyes. Snake grinned. Loon
licked his lips.

"Sounds like the little filly's plumb lost her man,"
Snake jeered.

"Just like Bo Peep," Loon commiserated.

"Lucky fer her, I got me a ram."

"Hey!" Loon whispered hotly. "I saw her first!"

"Yeah? Well, bully fer you. 'Cause I'm calling
dibs."

"Gentlemen," Rafe chided, his heart doing its
bloody best to rip free of his chest, "I suggest you
both corral your mighty rams. Don't you recognize
that young woman?"

Loon glared at him suspiciously. "Why should
we?"

"Because that's your very own Mr. Townsend's
fiancé. And I daresay he wouldn't be pleased to know
that you, er, sampled her fleece before he did."

Snake snarled something unintelligible, grabbing
Rafe's collar and slamming him into a tree trunk. As
much as he itched to flatten the shorter, stockier man,
Rafe didn't struggle. The Texican had yet to lower
his gun hammer. And the only weapon Rafe carried
was the hunting knife in his boot.

"Listen here, you biggety prick," Snake growled,
"I ain't afeared of Townsend. And I ain't afeared of
humping his woman, neither."

"Yeah, but Snake," Loon whined, rubbing his
crotch longingly as he watched Silver's horse circle
the overturned trunk, "she'll go and tell."

"Not if I put a bullet through her—"

"Rafe?" More high-pitched and nervous than the
first time, Silver's call sent lightning streaks of fore-

boding through Rafe's veins. Snake jerked his head, and Loon nodded, grinning macabrely. There was only one thing left to do as Loon started stalking the woman Rafe loved. And Rafe did it.

"Silver, ride!" he called frantically. "For God's sake, it's an ambush—"

Snake's gunstock dropped like a hammer; white fire exploded in Rafe's skull. Dimly, he heard a muffled oath; even fainter came the thud of the boot that bludgeoned his ribs. Then he rolled, crunched up on the earth, gasping desperately for air.

Silver froze, her knuckles whitening on the reins. She could have sworn she'd heard Rafe. She could have sworn she'd heard his cry break through the eerie silence of these hills . . .

"Lookin' fer me, princess?" came an oily tenor not ten paces to her left.

She started, wheeling her mare, and the ill-kempt stranger lunged. The horse reared, nearly unseating her, and the stranger grabbed for the bridle. Silver cried out. It didn't take her half a second to realize this lanky blond, whoever he was, had ransacked Rafe's wagon. And it took her even less time to think, with sickening dread, that her worst nightmare had been realized.

"No! What have you done with Rafe?" she screamed, struggling against the iron arm that dragged her from the saddle.

"Ooh, ye're a feisty one," the outlaw crooned. She tried to kick him in the shin. He only chuckled. "Don't think some skirt never tried *that* on me before."

Twigs broke and bushes snapped behind them. She twisted in time to see Rafe, followed by a one-eyed desperado, stagger into the clearing. The outlaw, whom she suspected had been Cook's pie thief, shoved Rafe, and he dropped to his hands and knees, a patch of blood matting the glorious, sun-streaked hair above his ear. She sobbed, uncertain whether to be grateful or terrified.

"He's hurt!" She lunged futilely against the forearm that squeezed her ribs into her lungs. "What have you done to him?"

"Madam." Rafe spoke with obvious effort, shaking his head as if to clear it. "Do not concern yourself with me." When he raised his eyes to hers, the pewter in his gaze had turned to steel. Even she, in her panicked state, could not mistake his warning. "Your fiancé, Mr. Townsend, will no doubt rue it."

Silver frowned, momentarily baffled. Surely, after everything they'd discussed, Rafe didn't think she'd thrown him out of her house to run back to Aaron?

"Now where were we, gentlemen?"

His British accent roughened by undercurrents of pain, Rafe tried to climb to his feet. The desperado jammed a .45 under his chin. When Silver heard the hammer click, she had to bite back a cry. But Rafe only smiled. His cynicism fairly dripped.

"Ah yes. Now I remember."

"Shut your trap, Gracie, or I'll shut it fer you," the one-eyed man threatened.

"If you insist. But don't blame me if you never find those crown jewels."

Silver swallowed, fighting the panic that battered the walls of her reason. *Crown jewels?* What was Rafe talking about? And why was the one-eyed man calling him "Gracie"? Surely the outlaw wasn't stupid enough to think Rafe was a British duke? Not with those blue jeans and that eyesore of a coat!

"I thought we changed the plan to ransoming him,

"What better place to keep them safe from . . . *mortals*."

"Come now, Mr. Loon," Silver chimed in, praying that Papa actually had hired the guards he was supposed to have hired before he'd arrived at the mine early that morning, "surely you're not afraid of a little old ghost?"

Snake snorted, releasing Rafe's head with a shove. "Hell, if the woman ain't scared, why're you pissin' your pants, Loon?"

"I ain't! I'm just, uh . . . double-checking the facts."

"How very diligent of you," Rafe taunted, the gunmetal gray of his eyes fairly smoking. "If I were to venture into a haunted mine, I'm sure I'd want to know how many men had gone in before me . . . and never come back."

"Smart ass," Snake snarled, lashing out with his gun butt.

The .45 struck Rafe's temple, and Silver choked off his name, nearly strangling on her fear to see fresh blood spurt from his wound. *Oh God, oh God . . .* He crumpled like a sack of oats at the outlaw's feet. *Rafe, no. Please! Wake up! Don't be dead . . .*

"Shit, Snake," Loon grumbled as Snake kicked Rafe onto his back. "Ya think ya coulda asked him how to get to the mine, first?"

Silver had to bite back a chorus of Alleluias to see Rafe's chest still rising and falling.

"The skirt lives around these parts. She knows." Snake cast her a look that would have iced Satan's furnace. "Don't ya, sweetheart?"

Silver nodded through her tears, her tongue working frantically to carve words from the desert of her mouth. "But I don't know where the diamonds are," she croaked. "You'll need the duke to tell you—"

"Don't worry, precious. We're bringing Gracie along." Snake grunted, hoisting Rafe up under the arms and dragging him backwards over brambles and rocks toward the wagon. "Tie her up," he shouted impatiently, as Loon, pawing her hair, tried to stick his tongue down her ear. "I want to get to that mine afore sundown."

Silver shuddered, thanking God when Loon stopped groping her and started whining again.

"Ah, hell, Snake, can't we just do the skirt right—"

"No! Christ, are you deaf or somethin'? She's Townsend's woman."

"But you said—"

"I know what I said." Snake was leading two horses to the rear of the wagon. "That was fer him." He jerked his head over his shoulder at Rafe. "Use the one or two wits God gave you, Loon. You want that grand Townsend's gonna pay you, or do ya want his bullet through yer head?"

Loon grumbled something vile and not entirely coherent as he drove her before him to the horses Snake was now tying to the wagon. Silver thought better of struggling. Even if she did break free, and perhaps mounted a horse before they grabbed her and beat her senseless, she would never have left Rafe alone.

As she submitted to the rough ropes Loon was winding around her wrists, she glanced anxiously over her shoulder at Rafe. A sleek brown form distracted her. When it darted under the wagon, its whiskers twitching nervously at the outlaws' boots, Silver quailed. *Oh no, Tavy.* She watched helplessly, having visions of one very dead otter, as the pup slinked closer to Rafe and wormed her way inside his coat.

Snake hadn't noticed. He'd been too busy rummaging in his saddlebag for the rope he was now using to tie Rafe's hands behind his back. "Ya want to give me a hand here, Romeo?" he snapped at Loon. "John Bull here ain't a featherweight, ya know."

Loon muttered more expletives, shoving her into the bed of the wagon before he turned to help his crony. They heaved Rafe over the sideboard, dropping him as unceremoniously as if he were a rock. Silver winced, the resounding thud vibrating into her very bones. She ached for Rafe's bruises almost as much as she knew he would ache, assuming he ever regained consciousness.

Loon mounted Silver's horse; Snake clambered onto the driver's seat and slapped the reins across the nag's rump. The wagon jolted forward, nearly throwing Silver onto Rafe's chest. Two shiny black eyes stared out at her from his coat's inner pocket. Then Tavy ducked her head inside her cozy nest and laid her snout against Rafe's heart.

Silver prayed fervently that heart would still be beating by the time they reached the mine.

Chapter 16

Silver worried that God's failure to answer her prayers was a dire omen. Not only did Rafe fail to wake up during the ride to the mine but the help she had so desperately hoped for was nowhere to be found. By this late hour, Papa's non-Union crew should have reported for their first night shift. But the pump house, stamp mill, and offices were devoid of human life, including the armed guards that Papa must also have forgotten to hire to prevent Union marauders from sabotaging the tunnels.

The outlaws, of course, were delighted. "Hell, who needs crown jewels," Snake cackled, the setting sun turning his face a macabre shade of crimson. "We got a whole damned mine to loot!"

This reasoning did not bode well for Rafe, whom the outlaws were threatening to "plug" for being such an annoying "deadweight." Silver hastily informed them that silver didn't lie around in nuggets, like gold, but instead was found in a lead compound called galena, and required an expensive chemical process to extract.

"You might have to muck out a half ton of lead just to get a dozen pounds of sterling," she exaggerated shamelessly. "If I were you, I'd set my sights

338

on the jewels. They'll turn a pure profit, and they're a lot easier to carry.''

''Yeah?'' Snake eyed her with the same affection he might have reserved for a striking rattler. ''And what makes you think you know so much, princess?''

She drew a shaky breath. ''Because I'm Silver Nichols,'' she confessed. ''My father owns this mine.''

The outlaws' jaws both dropped. Then Snake threw back his head and howled with laughter. ''Why didn't ya say so in the first place, sweetheart? Shit, Loon, we're gonna be getting ransoms all over the place.''

Thus, after scribbling a largely misspelled ultimatum, Snake sent Loon to deliver the ransom note to Papa and then to report to Aaron. Silver tried desperately to convince Snake to leave her and Rafe trussed up in the offices, where she was certain someone would eventually find them, but Snake, reluctant to leave his hostages aboveground while the promise of wealth beckoned below, insisted on ''stashing'' her and Rafe in the farthest reaches of the mine.

''Now I'm gonna start diggin','' Snake growled, snatching up one of the two precious tapers he'd had the foresight to grab from the box at the mine's entrance. ''You stay right there by Gracie, where I can see you''—Snake patted his six-shooter menacingly—''or I'll put a couple more holes in yer head.''

She nodded hurriedly, less concerned about his shooting her than his giving her a pistol-whipping to rival Rafe's. Even in this dim light, she could see the gash that spanned the length of the nickel-sized welt on his temple. *Rafe, oh Rafe, honey, please, please, wake up.*

Desperate to touch him, to cleanse the blood that matted his hair, she waited for Snake to turn his back, then struggled frantically with her bonds. She told herself a few rope burns were inconsequential compared with the beating Rafe had suffered. Yet even though her skin rubbed off, the knots Loon had tied behind her back held fast.

She sobbed in frustration. The fear that Rafe might die and never know she forgave him was almost more than she could bear. *God please, I'll never lie again. I'll never scheme again. Just please, please don't let him die.*

Above the ringing of Snake's pickax, Silver heard Tavy, at least she prayed it was Tavy, scratching around in the dark. Visions of Dancing Moon chipped at her overwrought mind. She struggled to keep a sane thought in her head, even as the earth groaned and shifted around her, dribbling clumps of rock. The cave was far from stable.

Resting her head beside Rafe's, she fell into an uneasy doze. At least she thought she did, because one moment she'd been counting the rhythmic clash of steel against lead; the next moment, she could hear only its dull echo in the adjacent cave. Snake had wandered into the half-formed tunnel, leaving her and Rafe with their own guttering candle. It appeared at least four inches shorter now, and she guessed several hours had slipped by. Anxiously, she turned her head to check on Rafe. The pale gleam of silver eyes stared straight into her own.

"Softly," he whispered, no doubt anticipating her cry of jubilation.

She blinked, his beloved face swimming before her in the towering shadows. "H-how long have you been awake?"

"A half hour or so."

He rolled his head, grimaced, and listened. Satisfied

that Snake was still engrossed in his treasure hunt, he
met her eyes once more. She felt the heat of him
steaming through his clothes, but he looked pale. So
pale. Her throat ached as he tried to smile.

"Yeah," he said, when her gaze shifted uneasily
to his bruised temple. "It hurts like hell. You?"

She shook her head. "I-I'm fine."

His eyes roamed over her possessively, critically,
as if he didn't quite believe her and was searching for
proof of abuse. She was glad he couldn't see her
wrists.

"Where the hell are we?" he asked after a moment.

"Level Three."

His eyebrows rose. "The haunted level?"

"Papa's been blasting here, and I thought ... I
thought he'd come back and find us. So I convinced
Snake to look for the treasure here."

"Where's Loon?"

"Gone to get Aaron."

Rafe's eyes narrowed. "How long?"

She glanced uncertainly at the candle. More than
half had burned. "Four hours ago? Maybe five?"

"We don't have much time, then." He strained,
muttered an oath, then smiled mirthlessly. "I've been
tongue-tied before, but I'm afraid this is worse.
Makes me feel like one of those preposterous dime
novel heroes, who's been lashed to a dynamite keg.
It looks like you'll have to save the day this time,
darling. Feeling up to it?"

She nodded anxiously.

"Good." His tone was cheerful. Too cheerful. "I
assure you, I'm quite clear on your feelings about my
touching you. But might I persuade *you* to touch
me?"

She winced. "Rafe—"

"My boot, to be precise," he continued over her protest. "I believe you'll find a hunting knife in the left one—unless, of course, Snake beat you to it."

She averted her eyes, tears stinging them almost blind. "H-he didn't."

"Good," he said more gently. "See if you can slip it free."

She shimmied closer, but it wasn't an easy task, not with her back turned. And not with her hands bound. The combination of nerves and sweltering, un-ventilated air made her hands slip on the handle. Even with his soft encouragements to guide her, she sliced his shin before she pulled the weapon completely free of his pants leg.

"I'm sor—"

"Forget it," he whispered, motioning her closer with his head. "Give it to me. I'll take it from here."

She felt like a failure, and not just because she'd made his leg bleed. "Rafe," she ventured to say, watching his shoulders bunch while his fingers worked in exacting movements to saw through the hemp. "I'm sorry I got you into this."

"You?" He glanced her way, and a lock of hair fell across his damp brow.

She nodded, ashamed. "If I hadn't convinced you to be Chumley, you might never have been am-bushed, at least not by idiots who thought you carried the crown jewels—"

"My dear—" he gave her a lopsided grin to go with his forced cheerfulness"—I wouldn't have missed it for the world." His lips abruptly curved into a cunning, well-satisfied smile. *"Voila."*

Hope flurried in her chest as she watched his arms emerge from their prison.

"Your turn," he whispered.

"Hot damn!"

They both jumped to hear Snake's whoop, followed by the thumping of his boots as he ran across the tunnel.

Rafe muttered an oath. "Hold still," he hissed in Silver's ear.

Three slashes later, her ropes fell free, but it was already too late. Snake and his six-shooter were rounding the corner.

"Sit back," Rafe whispered, doing the same. "Pretend you're still tied."

She obeyed, frustration coiling in her gut. *Damn, damn, damn!* They'd come so close to being free. So close . . .

"I found them!" Snake cackled. A dirt-encrusted chest thudded at their feet. "I found yer crown jewels, Gracie!"

Rafe and Silver both gaped. The chest, which was small enough to carry under one arm, glimmered dully in the glow of Snake's candle as if it had been wrought from bronze. Beneath the scratches and the dust, there appeared to be intricate markings—*hieroglyphics*, Silver corrected herself. The strange, bird-like figure on her side of the chest looked half-human. She was stunned. Could this be the fabled treasure of Dancing Moon?

"Give me the key." Snake held out his hand like a petulant child.

"The key?" Rafe asked slowly.

"Yes, the key, goddammit! It's locked. Or maybe it's stuck. 'Cause I don't see no keyholes on it." He cocked his head to the side and crouched down, banging the chest with his gunbutt. "You reckon it's stuck?" he muttered, as if to himself.

Silver drew a sharp, hissing breath. She wasn't able to stop herself. There, in the tunnel behind Snake, a circle of light bobbed along the moist, oozing walls. The outlaw narrowed his eye at her warning and jumped up, his .45 glinting in his hand.

"Loon?" he bellowed, as the nimbus grew brighter.

Stones scrabbled, dislodged by a boot. Silver felt, rather than saw, Rafe tense, drawing his feet beneath him. A ghoulish shadow rippled over the uneven blackness of the walls, bending itself around the corner. And then she smelled the faint odor of cigarette smoke.

"Loon is . . . indisposed at the moment," a rich, mocking baritone drawled. Aaron himself appeared then, lean and impeccably attired in black worsted, as if he were going to the opera rather than an execution.

"Oh, it's you." Snake's chest heaved as he jammed his Colt back in its holster. "Damn. I thought you was a ghost."

"Not yet." His lips curved in a haunting smile as he watched Rafe rise to his feet. "Although I daresay by night's end there will be several more ghosts to add to this mine's legend."

Silver swallowed, easing closer to Rafe. His muscles were wound so tight that they fairly hummed.

"And what have we here?" Aaron asked, gesturing with his cigarette toward Snake's box.

The outlaw's craggy face split in a grin. "It's the crown jewels. Jest like you said, Mr. Townsend!"

"Indeed?" Aaron exhaled a long tendril of smoke. "I take it I've interrupted the opening ceremony?"

Snake chuckled, rubbing his hands together. "Ye're just in time, if that's what you mean. I was about to blast the lid off this hunk of junk. But, uh, you can do the honors if you like, Mr. Townsend.''

Aaron's smile was dry as he lowered his lantern to the floor. Tucking his unbandaged hand in his coat pocket, he puffed once more on his cigarette. ''I wouldn't dream of it, my dear Snake. Please. Indulge yourself.''

Snake needed no further encouragement. Practically salivating, he dropped to his knees, grabbed a rock with both hands, and started hammering the lid. Aaron's hooded, predatory gaze slid to Silver. Every hair on her neck stood on end. When he released her, gasping, from his stare, she noticed that Rafe's right arm had shifted just behind his knee, where he held his knife in a white-knuckled grip.

''That oughta do it,'' Snake panted triumphantly, waving away a cloud of dust. He heaved his rock to the side.

The rim of the lid had buckled; he dug his fingers into the gap and grunted, his neck muscles straining. Slowly, he pried the chest apart. The hinges creaked. More dust puffed around him in flurries. Then the lid simply snapped off, clattering to the stone, unleashing a putrid, eye-watering smell. Snake didn't seem to care. He was too busy pawing rotted fragments of what looked to be cloth away from the insides.

Next came a handful of crude animal figurines, carved from antler or horn. Snake frowned in confusion. He dug out the crumbling remains of feathers, seed pods, snail shells, and what appeared to be three petrified corn husks. His face darkened, and he started to snarl. When he dumped the chest over, pawing through the ensuing mound of river pebbles and sand, nothing even remotely resembling jewels was unearthed.

Silver blinked. Was this Dancing Moon's legen-

dary wealth? This collection of spoils from Mother
Earth?

Snake grew positively livid. "This ain't no damned
jewels!" he shouted at Rafe. "This here's Injun
filth!"

"One man's trash is another man's treasure," Rafe
retorted quietly.

"Why you smart-assed, biggety, son of a—"

Snake reached. But he wasn't fast enough. His Colt
hadn't cleared leather before Aaron's .45 spit, blasting
a hole through the outlaw's back. Snake jolted forward, staggering, and Silver stifled a scream, desperately choking down bile as the Texican fell less than
ten paces from her feet.

The gunblast rolled again and again through the
chamber, triggering a small but ominous shower of
rock. Heedless of the danger, Aaron smiled his dry
little smile and drew once more on his cigarette. Even
though Aaron's bullet had most likely saved Rafe's
life, Silver didn't know whether to be grateful or mortified.

Until Aaron spoke.

"Witnesses," he drawled, "are such an inconvenience."

Rafe's eyes narrowed to glinting slits. "So that's
what happened to Loon?" he demanded acidly. "You
shot him in the back?"

"And Benson," Silver whispered.

Aaron looked amused by her accusation. "He out-
lived his usefulness, my dear. Surely you understand.
Rather like an old shoe one throws away. Or a contentious sweetheart."

"Aaron, no," she whispered, horror replacing her
momentary hope that he had spared Rafe out of an
attack of conscience.

"Surely you didn't think I'd let that little brick-wielding incident go unpunished?" He tossed his head, as if to flip his carefully styled hair away from his scar. "I must say, though, it will be a shame not to enjoy your millions. Perhaps I can get the ass who sired you to let me manage a memorial fund in your name."

"You spineless bastard," Rafe bit out softly. "Is that what you told your brother when you gunned him down? 'I'll manage a memorial fund in your name'?"

Aaron stiffened, his eyes glittering like a reptile's as he slowly, deliberately turned his attention to Rafe. "Ever the scene-stealer, eh, playactor? No doubt it will crush you to die in obscurity. In fact, I'm counting on it."

"Ah." Rafe's smile was sheer ice. "So the thought of me has been eating at you, has it? Rather like a cancer in your brain? Amusing, is it not, how your constituents think you clever, when you're really just stark, raving mad."

Aaron's face darkened. "I shall cut out your tongue when I'm through and feed it to the crows."

"Be my guest. I won't have any need for it to whisper from the shadows. To haunt your dreams, and stalk your sleepless hours. If you listen carefully," Rafe taunted in a macabre, throaty voice, "and even if you try not to, you'll hear me laughing with the others. In the darkness, we'll howl; in the moonlight, we'll shriek; we'll make your flesh crawl as we feast on your mortal soul. There are dozens of us. *Legions* of us. But then, you know that better than anyone, eh, Aaron? One corpse leads to two, two corpses lead to three, three corpses lead to four—"

"Shut up," he growled, perspiration dotting his upper lip.

But Rafe pressed his advantage.

"The blood can never quite be wiped clean, can it, Aaron?" he continued in that same hushed and raspy voice, causing even Silver's hair to stand on end. "And who's to say if you've poisoned them, plugged them, burned them all into *silence*? One little witness, yes, just one little witness runs away and *seals your doom*. You have no rest. You have no sanctuary. Tinstars and detectives and bounty hunters chase after you, hounding your heels like blood-sucking wolves—"

"*I said shut up!*" Aaron's gun hand shook as he stalked forward, kicking the chest out of his way and trampling its artifacts. "I've had enough, you cocksure son of a—"

The earth trembled.

Aaron must have felt the ground move too, because he halted, half-crouching. "What was that?"

"The . . . the floor is shaking," Silver breathed.

A long, low howl reverberated through the chamber. An icy premonition swept the length of Silver's spine.

"Aaron, we've got to get out of here," she pleaded, raising her voice above the whistling of a sudden, inexplicable wind. "This cave isn't stable."

Aaron bared his teeth. The wildly fluttering candle flames carved his face into grotesque shadow. "Then it's time to say good-bye." He cocked his weapon.

"Townsend, don't be a fool," Rafe snapped. "Another shot will bring the whole damned ceiling down on you too."

Aaron hesitated. Perhaps he'd heard the sense in Rafe's warning. Or perhaps he'd become aware of the dust and artifacts that were swirling in ever-rising eddies around his legs and no one else's. "What the hell—?"

He glanced down for only a second. But a second was all Rafe needed. He slammed into Aaron's arm, knocking it sideways. Aaron dropped the gun, but not before a shot zinged wildly off the rocks, creating another ominous cascade. Thrown backwards by the quaking earth, Silver yiked as she grabbed for a handhold on the wall. She slid down behind the chest. That's when she noticed the eerie, green glow pulsing at its center.

"Oh . . . my . . . God," she breathed, struggling to right herself. She was uncertain where to train her eyes next. The men had slammed into a wall. Locked in a grunting, flailing tangle, they were oblivious to the phenomenon rising from the chest. Roiling, swelling, the glow belched into a noxious green cloud. Sulphur and some other eye-stinging fumes assailed Silver's senses; her head started to spin. For a moment, in the feathery, fanlike plume of those gases, she could have sworn she recognized the headdress of the ghost from her nightmares.

Dear God. Could that be Dancing Moon?

Aaron loosed a triumphant bellow. She started, her heart speeding. The knife had slid from Rafe's fingers. Aaron kicked it out of the way and threw a punch. Rafe's head struck the wall. As he doubled over, Aaron dove for the gun and took aim.

"*No!*" Silver screamed.

The earth heaved again. Thrown off balance, Aaron's shot went wild. He fell to his knees, his eyes bulging as that green phenomenon closed around him. Suddenly, he was clawing at his throat, wheezing in pure terror. "The ghost!" he gurgled, his .45 spitting again.

"*Jesus Christ.*" Rafe lunged away from the cloud.

"Don't breathe," he yelled to Silver. "The gas is poison!"

He tackled her to the ground even before her stunned senses realized Aaron's bullets were ripping harmlessly through the cloud and striking the ceiling. A deafening roar shook the cave. Stones came crashing down as Rafe threw his body across hers, shielding her from the avalanche.

The rock slide was over in minutes. Silver quaked, hearing Rafe's labored gasps. Gunpowder mixed with dust and the lung-burning odor of poison. When she wheezed, his arms tightened around her. She wasn't sure how long they lay fused together, his heart hammering into her back, his forearm squeezing her ribs in such a desperate, lifesaving hold. All she knew was he lived. And she lived. In that moment, that was enough.

"Silver?" His voice, as scratchy as tree bark, sounded urgent. "Silver, are you hurt?"

She shook her head, daring to crack open an eye. She half-sobbed in her relief to see a feeble glow filtering through the haze. Aaron's lantern had survived the cave-in. But in the miracle of its survival, she recognized their doom.

The tunnel had been sealed shut.

Another ominous rumble greeted this revelation.

"Silver, we can't stay here," Rafe rasped. Loose stones pelted his shoulders, and he shielded his head, staggering upright and dragging her to her feet. "The whole damned ceiling's about to collapse."

She coughed. "I know, but the tunnel—"

"We have to dig our way out," he said more firmly, raising the lantern for a better view. "We need Snake's pickax."

She bit her lip, knowing full well Rafe was in no condition to dig them out of their would-be tomb. She turned right and left, squinting through the dust, trying to find some better solution. That eerie, pulsing column of green caught her eye. Beneath it jutted an expensive black boot. Aaron's leg was the only part of his body that hadn't been crushed by the rubble. Oddly enough, the gas hovered over him macabrely, triumphantly, as if it were fueled by some spark of intention rather than that inexplicable geyser of hot air that had risen from the floor to swirl the artifacts around his ankles. Chilled in spite of the heat, Silver hastily backed away.

Rafe, meanwhile, was heading for the tunnel where Snake had been prospecting.

"It's a dead end," she panted, trying not to notice that every gulp of air felt like a prairie fire in her lungs.

He muttered an oath, swinging her way again, his dust-caked face ghostly pale in the flare of the lantern. "Are you sure?"

She wished she weren't. "It's only half excavated. Let's look for a hole in the ceiling. Maybe we can climb our way to the next level."

He shook his head, grimacing as he raised a hand to his bloodied crown. "If the ceiling's caving, the floor above us will be no safer."

"Oh. Of . . . of course." Silver's throat constricted as she watched him battle his pain. She suspected the dust-laden air was the least of his problems. "Rafe, at least let me look at that wound—"

"There's no time," he panted, scrabbling back to the center of the room. "We have to get you out of here."

She quailed. *Just me?* "Rafe, please—"

"Listen."

She shivered into silence, desperately wanting to say the things she hadn't said, the things she should have said, but too afraid her confessions would sound like she'd given up. Because she hadn't given up. She just prayed Rafe hadn't either.

The seconds stretched. Silver strained her ears. Rafe was frowning, and she wondered what had alarmed him. She could hear nothing more than pebbles skating off the tower of boulders that blocked the tunnel.

Then she noticed steam rising from a newly formed crevice at the rear of the cave. Suddenly, something scrambled out of the hole. Her heart leaped. Spiders she thought, choking off an involuntary scream. *But no*, she consoled herself weakly. *Surely not*. She and Rafe were too deep even for the albino arachnids that dwelled beyond the light of day.

An exuberant bark reverberated off the walls.

Rafe dodged more falling rocks as he swung the lantern toward the noisemaker. "Jesus. Is that . . . Tavy?"

A very wet, very jubilant otter bounded out of the settling dust. Pausing to shake herself, Tavy sprayed half the room with water. Then she launched herself full-waddle into Rafe's arms.

"Good God." Rafe staggered, nearly dropping the lantern as he clutched the wriggling, tail-thumping pup to his chest. His features crumpled, and for a moment, Silver thought tears might erode his hard-won composure. "What's Tavy doing here?"

"She . . . she wouldn't leave you by the river," Silver whispered thickly. "Tavy crawled into your coat before Snake threw you in the wagon."

Rafe's chest heaved as he fought the pain and fear

that so insidiously gnawed at his reason. For a moment, Silver's mention of a river conjured old memories of picnic baskets, pack mules, and spiders. But there was something else. Something more important. He struggled to remember it through the fog in his skull.

Max's treasure map!

The memories flooded in then, of the millionaire smoking his cigar, swirling his cognac, and pointing at the parchment littering the desk in his study. *"Legend says,"* Max had confided eagerly, *"that Dancing Moon lived deep in the earth, in a crystal cave. The prettiest thing you've ever seen, with an underground river that leads straight to the surface and a waterfall..."*

The earth tremored again. Tavy popped out of his embrace like a greased watermelon. Dashing straight to the crevice, she turned, barked an encouragement, then plunged. Rafe's heart quickened. Grabbing Silver's hand, he hurried after Tavy. Together, they watched the otter skate down a rock slide, dodging in and out of steam, until she vanished in the yawning darkness below. Moments later, Rafe heard a splash.

"Come on, Silver." He tugged her closer to the edge. "It's our only way out."

She hesitated, but the walls were shaking all around them now, affording them little choice.

"You can do it," he encouraged above the rumbling din.

She nodded uneasily, and somehow they shimmied through Tavy's crevice. Scrambling, sliding, they skated down the bridge of rubble that connected the cave to the chamber below. Steam gusted up around them; sweat dripped from their faces and hands; still, they managed to hold on to each other until they reached solid ground. Once there, they could do little more than gape. The lantern light glanced off glittering spires of crystal. Luminescent with shades of rose, green, and blue, these spikes rose from the floor and plunged from the ceiling like fangs in some sleeping giant's mouth. The cavern was massive, perhaps the size of Silver's mansion, and the river that snaked through its center bubbled and seethed like some medicinal hot spring.

"It . . . it's beautiful," Silver breathed, watching the play of light across this otherworldly landscape.

Rafe nodded weakly, wiping his sleeve across his forehead. The stalagmite he braced himself against was moist and cool, and to rest there was an insidious temptation. The heat made breathing hard, even harder than the dust had above, and he felt light-headed, faint.

"Rafe, perhaps you should rest—"

"No," he said quickly, thrusting himself up and away from the rock. The last thing he needed was an argument about his condition. He didn't have the stamina for it. Besides, how could he tell her that if he let himself close his eyes, he might never wake up again?

Tavy's bark echoed somewhere to their left. Summoning his strength, Rafe caught Silver's hand and hurried her in that direction. He wasn't sure how long they stumbled and climbed, following the winding, hissing rush of the river. Somewhere along the way, he peeled off his coat. Further along, she stripped down to her chemise and bloomers. He knew he had to be in a sorry state, since he couldn't work up an ounce of lust. At times, he felt as if he were floating above his body, watching them struggle along the rocky bank. At other times, he was only too painfully aware of his laboring lungs.

And then, thankfully, they reached a dead end. A wall. Falling water could be heard roaring on the other side, just as Max had said.

"I'll be damned," Rafe muttered.

"The river seems to go through a tunnel," Silver panted, leaning as far over the bank as she dared. "I can't tell how far, but with the waterfall so close, the tunnel can't be too long . . . can it?"

Tavy's chirping rolled across the water. Once again, she climbed up on the bank, shaking her fur. She waddled to each of them in turn, giving them a snuffle and a kiss. Rafe's throat swelled. Even Silver looked misty-eyed. Then Tavy galloped to the edge of the bank. Holding their breaths, they watched in uneasy silence as the otter baby, fearless now in her element, dived, letting the current sweep her under the mountain.

Silver hugged her arms to her chest and turned anxious, luminous eyes to him. "She made it, Rafe. I know she did."

He nodded. There was nothing more to say. Whether Tavy made it or not, they had to make the same journey. They had no choice.

He kicked off his boots. "Don't give up, Silver. Whatever happens, you keep swimming, all right?"

She bit her lip. Even so, a tear spilled down her cheek. She'd been so incredibly brave, even though he knew she was terrified, and not just for him. "We can rest first—"

"No." He smiled. It was the sort of smile he'd honed over the years: cocksure, devil-may-care. He was afraid if he didn't convince her to swim now, she never would, because she wouldn't leave him behind.

He met her gaze evenly, another tactic he'd learned for his lies. "It's better this way."

Her fingers shook in his hand. "Then you have to promise me you won't let go—"

In answer, he kissed her. He combed his fingers through her hair, and crushed her hips against his, and made love to her with his mouth. He would have breathed his last breath into her if it would have guaranteed she'd make it to the other side alive. But she pulled away shakily, accusation glimmering through her tears.

"Don't kiss me like that. Not like it's going to be the last time."

He fought down a crushing desperation. *Guilty as charged.* But he couldn't tell her that. Not if he wanted her to fight her way to the surface.

"Come on, then." He reached once more for her hand and pasted on what he thought would be his last smile. "Tavy's waiting."

The water was hot. Unbearably so. But Tavy had survived, so they plunged in, gasping as the nigh-scalding liquid poured over every inch of their flesh. Muslin and denim were poor protectors compared to an otter's waterproof fur; human senses were even poorer navigators for the pitch void that yawned before them. Rafe prayed for the second time in as many days. *Swim hard*, he begged her with his eyes. *God, make her swim hard.*

Gulping head-pounding breaths, they dived, leaving the feeble light of the lantern behind. The current was fierce and swift; it propelled them, as blind and helpless as newborns, into the womb of Mother Earth. In the deepest, darkest heart of the mountain, an eerie timelessness prevailed. If not for his lungs, and their urgent need for air, Rafe would have had no sense of

the minutes ticking off his life. In that space, deprived
of all sound, all color, all gravity, there was nothing
but the elemental force that drove them relentlessly
forward to some unknowable end.

Then suddenly, there was light. They shot out of
the tunnel in a burst of black bubbles and foam. The
dull, muted roar of the waterfall pounded somewhere
before them. If Rafe could have breathed, he might
have sobbed. The waning moon shimmered like a
smile on the surface above them; a long, spindly
shadow jutted somewhere beyond that. Kicking frantically now against the current, he dragged Silver toward the sky and what he prayed was the limb of a
tree.

A shout rose, sounding dim and far away above
their splashing. "Over here, Silver!" Max called.
Two plump skirted figures—Cellie and Fiona?—
scrambled with Max down the riverbank. Then there
were hands, blessed hands, all around Silver as they
hauled her to shore.

Rafe mustered his failing strength. He grabbed for
the branch, determined to cling to consciousness just
a few moments longer. But as he waited for his own
rescue, an ominous splintering rose from the tree.

"Rafe!"

Silver screamed her warning as the branch snapped.
Suddenly, he was sinking, engulfed by boiling black
foam. He thrashed, gagging on water hot enough to
scald his throat. The current that had once befriended
him swept him helplessly forward. The waterfall and
the edge of the mountain loomed before him like the
precipice to hell.

No! he screamed silently at the God who had re-
peatedly let death snatch his one sacred desire away.

Don't You kill me when I finally have a chance for love with Silver!

Did God really care enough to answer prayers? It was a question Rafe had thought God had answered, the hard way, a long time ago. He struggled against the river, but it did little good. He'd used up his last dregs of strength to bring Silver to the surface.

"Hold on, lad!"

A mighty splash rocked the water behind him. A head as hairless as a rat's tail bobbed on the waves. Within a heartbeat, perhaps two, an arm like bulging steel tightened over his chest. Rafe coughed, reeling with fatigue as his spine collided with a mass of muscle.

"Fred?" he choked as his rescuer's legs began to churn. Slowly, doggedly, they swam away from the cliff and his doom.

"Aye, lad," the Brit crooned in his ear. "Breathe easy now. You're safe. Just like that night in the snowstorm."

Rafe shuddered, slumping against his foster father's chest. Fifteen years ago, when he'd nearly gotten himself killed trying to start life anew, Fred had rescued him. And now the lying, cheating windbag was rescuing him again, just like Fred always seemed to do when the chips were down.

Fred. Rafe's head lolled. A disjointed sense of irony washed over him. He smiled a little mistily. *Papa . . .*

It was his last thought before exhaustion finally drowned him in the peace of oblivion.

Chapter 17

According to Max, three days passed while Rafe lay unconscious, three days of abject agony for Silver—at least, that's what Max would have had Rafe believe. But the sting of Silver's handprint on his cheek was not a distant memory. And Rafe couldn't help but be worried when he woke to find Max's chubby face smiling down at him, not Silver's.

"You gave us all the devil of a scare, son, while you were traipsing 'round the Land of Nod. The womenfolk have been duking it out for three days over who would take care of you. 'Course, thanks to her crystal ball, Cellie had the advantage of knowing when you'd feel up to rejoining us, so she hurried down to the kitchen to rustle you up some soup. Fred went to fetch the doctor, and Fiona's getting Tavy."

"Fiona's getting Tavy?" Rafe repeated weakly as Max plumped up his pillows.

"Yep." Max chuckled, winking broadly. "Tavy's a heroine now. After she led you and Silver outta that cave-in, Fiona's had a change of heart about an otter's 'rightful place' as a hat. Fiona even donated a whole wig for Tavy to chew on—which is a good thing. 'Cause Silver's gonna hit the roof when she comes back from Leadville and finds Tavy gnawed on a half dozen of her shoes.''

Rafe was still pulling tufts of cotton from his brain, but he'd managed to free enough wits to register the most important of Max's news items.

"Silver's in Leadville?" His sense of disappointment grew sharper as hurt needled him.

"Well, she didn't go willingly, son. She practically had to be pried from your side. Still, you had plenty of nursemaids, and she was needed for business.''

"Business?'' Rafe repeated dully, the knife plunging a little deeper.

"There, there. It ain't how it sounds. I couldn't very well have a wedding while my best man was stretched out on his back, now could I? So, Cellie and me postponed the dang thing for a month, which is fine by me. But then Cellie's cousin wired and said he'd be presiding over a California trial on our new date. And with Judge Gates unlikely to make the wedding, Silver flew into a tizzy, 'cause she was afraid Marshal Hawthorne would arrest you for some back warrant. So, Silver went to talk to Gates.''

Rafe groaned, letting his head drop to the pillow. His self-sufficient heiress was going to be the death of him. No fugitive wanted to attract the attention of a judge, much less a *federal* judge with a reputation like Gates's. Around San Francisco, Gates was known for his unwavering honesty and his bulldog adherence to the law. Christ, Silver hadn't gone to *bribe* him, had she?

"Not to worry, son," Max said, settling in the winged chair by the bed. "Silver's got a lawyer with her.''

I'm doomed.

"And I told her to go ahead and pay off any debts

you owe. I reckon she can talk just about anyone into dropping their charges, once she offers 'em the kind of restitution they ain't likely to see from a jury.''

Rafe winced. Silver was going to make an honest man out of him—by indebting him to her father?

"Hell, Max," he said, shame lancing his chest, "I'd rather do my time than have you pay back all the money I swindled."

"I appreciate the sentiment, son. But it just ain't practical. 'Sides, you and me got a deal. You're supposed to stay around here, keeping Silver happy so I can chase my woman around the bedroom, remember?''

Rafe smiled feebly. "Yeah. I remember."

"And I expect a coupla grandbabies out of you. You can't very well raise my grandkiddies from jail, now can you?''

Rafe averted his gaze. His heart was growing sicker by the moment.

"And don't forget too," Max said less boisterously, as if he sensed he'd made one of his habitual faux pas, "I owe you more'n a couple thousand dollars. You saved my daughter's life. Got her outta that damned cave-in and nearly cashed in your chips in the process. One of these days, when you have a daughter, you'll come to understand: they're worth a sight more than a measly fortune.''

"That's kind of you to say," he murmured dutifully.

Max fidgeted, his chair creaking in protest. An uncomfortable silence stretched between them. "At any rate," Max said, "I'm glad to know Silver had the good sense to fall in love with you and forget Townsend. I still can't get over the things he did: murdering his brother, beating Amy, hiring Benson as a spy, siccing those two thugs on you—not to mention what he'd intended for my Silver. Cellie's crystal ball couldn't have been more right. Me and Fred might have drawn straws to see who got to plug the bastard, if Dancing Moon hadn't killed Townsend first.''

''Dancing Moon?'' Rafe repeated distractedly.

''Sure. Don't you remember? Silver told me how Dancing Moon appeared in a puff of green smoke, stinking as rotten as bad eggs, and rose up out of the treasure chest to strangle Townsend.''

Rafe eyed Max dubiously. ''Silver told you that?''

''Well, not in so many words.'' Max grinned impishly. ''I sorta read between the lines. The 'green gas' part of her story tipped me off. After all, everyone knows sulfuric gas ain't green. 'Sides. You can't tell me it wasn't strange how a howling wind swept through the cave at the *very same moment* Townsend stepped on ol' Dancing Moon's artifacts. Wind ain't normal underground.''

Rafe's skin prickled. He hadn't thought of that. In fact, he wasn't sure he *wanted* to think of that. It reminded him of a line from *Hamlet: ''There are more things in heaven and earth, Horatio, than are dreamt of in your philosophy.''*

Max grinned triumphantly, as if guessing his thoughts.

''Say,'' the millionaire blurted after a moment. He reached for his coat's breast pocket. ''I almost forgot. You got a letter the other day from a Miss Sera Jones. Is that your sister?''

Rafe nodded, unable to disguise his sudden wistfulness.

''Reckon it'll make you feel better,'' Max said more gently, offering him the envelope.

Rafe grasped the paper, the tremor in his hand betraying his eagerness.

Max climbed to his feet. "Tell you what, son. I'll, uh, be out in the hall, if you need anything."

Rafe's throat was too tight to respond. He barely waited long enough for the door to shut before he was ripping open the envelope and tugging out its contents: two pages of flowery scrawl. Sera, he'd learned over the years, was a bit of a dramatist herself.

"Dear Rafe," the letter began, *"I'm in love! But of course, Michael disapproves. I just know you would like my sweetheart, though. His name is Billy Cassidy. He's handsome and blond—just like you! And he's a gunfighter! Isn't that exciting?"*

Unease coiled through Rafe's innards.

"Michael is being positively beastly," Sera complained in typical eighteen-year-old fashion. *"I have to sneak in and out of my window at night. I declare, I would have run away by now, if Michael weren't so sick. Do you think you could come home now, Rafe? Michael thinks I'm a baby, and he won't listen to a single thing I say. Especially about seeing a doctor . . ."*

Rafe scanned the rest, his chest constricting. *Jesus.* Sera was behaving just as Silver had in Philadelphia with Townsend. Recalling the consequences of those moonlight rendezvous, he threw back the quilt—a mistake. The pain in his head nearly blinded him. Gritting his teeth, he sank back to the edge of the mattress.

Apparently, he'd be lucky to get to the kitchen, much less to Kentucky. For once, he thanked God that Michael was a belligerent, hard-headed donkey. What was the matter with Sera, letting a gunslinger woo her? And what the devil was wrong with Michael? Sera's letter was the first news Rafe had had of his brother's illness.

Slowly, persistently, guilt forced him to an unpleasant conclusion: he'd have to return to Blue Thunder as soon as he was well.

In the meantime, though, he had business closer to home. There was his own mixed-up, crazy romance to resolve. And there was a federal judge he had to answer to.

Sighing, he sank back into the pillows. He wondered if Gates would let him save Sera before enforcing the inevitable prison sentence on him. He wondered if he'd have time to wean Tavy from crab puffs and settle her in the wild before he was carted off to jail.

But most of all, he wondered gloomily, how many precious hours did he have left with Silver? Would she wait for him through all the months, maybe years, while he was locked up for his humbugs?

Silver nearly did hit the roof when she returned to Aspen, but not because of otter mischief. Arriving from Leadville on the evening stage, she'd rushed eagerly up the stairs to tell Rafe her good news, only to find him missing from the bed that, quite frankly, he'd been in no condition to vacate.

"There's no telling when this young man'll wake up," the doctor had told her, Cellie, and Fiona in dire tones the morning after the cave-in. "When he does, make sure he keeps to his bed for five days at least. A concussion is no trifling matter."

As a result, Silver had camped day and night at his bedside until an uncharacteristically militant Cellie had marched into the room. Armed with her crystal

ball and Judge Gates's telegram, she'd insisted that
Silver was wasting a golden opportunity to help Rafe,
and that she'd better stop moping and start packing.
Torn between her fear that Rafe might not live and
her fear that he'd be jailed if he did, she'd finally
relented, and spent nearly a week with lawyers, detectives, and Gates himself. To her amazement, the
trip had proven every bit as successful as the spirits
had promised.

Only now, Silver wasn't so sure she should have
gone. Rafe's bed was empty. More troubling still, his
traveling trunk and Tavy's cage were missing.
Stunned by the evidence of his departure, she tried
desperately not to believe the worst, until she spied
the female handwriting on the envelope by his cham-
berset. Intuiting disaster, she approached slowly, her
hand trembling as she forced herself to read Sera's
letter.

A heartbeat later, she was running down the stairs
and calling for Papa, Sera's letter fluttering to the
floor in her wake.

"Well, I'll be," Papa boomed, his voice rattling
Aphrodite in her alcove. "Silver's back!"

Stepping briskly out from the stairwell, he entered
the foyer in his top hat and cape. A slightly dishev-
eled, blushing Cellie hurried after him, dabbing her
lips. Silver tried not to imagine what they'd been doing in the coat closet.

"Papa, when did he go?"

"Who?" he countered jovially, flashing a naughty
grin at his fiancée.

"*Rafe*, for heaven's sake." Silver wanted to shake
him for being so obtuse. "He's gone! And he's not
supposed to be. I mean, the doctor said he shouldn't
leave his bed."

"Well, now, daughter, doctors can be wrong. Besides, he looked hale and hearty to me the last time I saw him."

"He did?" She knew a fleeting sense of relief. "When was that?"

Papa scratched his beard, screwing up his face in a parody of concentration. "Hmm. Can't say that I recall. Seems like it's been a couple days now, since he took Tavy back to Swindler's Creek. 'Course, I've been a bit preoccupied, you know, what with that Marzetti fella jabbing me with pins to fit my wedding tuxedo. Then, of course, there've been the burial arrangements for Benson and the negotiations with the Miners Union . . ."

He puffed out his chest, suddenly beaming. "Why, I reckon you don't know, daughter. Me and Cellie arranged a settlement with Dancing Moon. He's not so bad, once you get to know him. Said he'd leave the miners alone if they stop trout-fishing with dynamite. And he'll leave *you* alone if we plant a tree for every one we cut down."

"He said he'd be watching us, dear," Cellie said absently, shimmying her sash higher over the green and purple stripes of her tunic.

"That's right," Papa chimed in. "He wants us to keep his burial ground sacred. No wonder the poor devil was haunting us. He couldn't very well rest in peace with all our blasting rattling his stalactites, eh?" Papa glanced around the foyer, then lowered his voice conspiratorially. "Say, you didn't happen to spy any of Dancing Moon's *real* treasure tucked away in that crystal cave you were telling me about, did you?"

"*Papa.*" Silver was rapidly losing patience with

him. "Could we please talk about Rafe now, not treasure?"

"But he's *your* treasure, isn't he, dear?" Cellie interjected amiably.

"And the best treasures are always found where you least expect them." Papa winked, draping his arm around Cellie's waist.

Silver blew out her breath. Honestly, why did she ever bother asking them anything? Maybe Fred or Fiona knew if Rafe was coming back.

The sudden notion that he might not, hit her so hard that her knees buckled. What if he hadn't really taken Tavy to Swindler's Creek? What if he'd gone home instead to his sister and found someone else in the Kentucky backwoods? Someone like an old sweetheart?

"Well, so long, daughter," Papa said, giving her cheek a pat. "Gotta go. Dining and dancing tonight at the Chloride. Don't wait up," he added cheerfully.

"Papa, wait—"

"Oh, and dear," Cellie called over her shoulder as Papa bustled her over the threshold, "I did a little exorcism in your bedroom today. I hope you don't mind, but I had to pry the nails off the windows—"

The door slammed shut, muffling whatever else she'd meant to say. Silver blinked, dumbfounded, at the opaque glass. She didn't know whether to laugh or cry. Rafe was gone, and she had no idea for how long. Neither Papa nor Cellie had answered a single one of her questions. As for gathering information elsewhere, the clerk at the stage depot would be off duty by now, and God only knew where Fred and Fiona might be at this hour.

She felt like the butt of a conspiracy.

Dusty and demoralized, she fought back tears as

she gathered her traveling skirt and dragged herself up the stairs to her bedroom. Moonlight slanted in alabaster shafts across her carpet; tapers flickered on her vanity, their reflections gleaming in the mirror. *Strange*, she thought. Stranger still was the steam that slowly spiraled from the copper bathtub on her tarp. She wrinkled her nose, smelling basil, of all things, on the water. It was no secret she liked to bathe every night at this hour; perhaps Cellie had drawn the bath in anticipation of her homecoming. Silver shook her head at this consideration. The woman really was dear—*peculiar*, but dear. She wondered how much lavender she'd need to pour into the tub so she wouldn't smell like a salad.

Sighing, she unpinned her hat and tossed it across her bed. Next, she tugged off her gloves. She was just about to tackle the back of her dress when she realized her buttonhook was missing from its jar. Riffling through the vanity drawers proved fruitless. She frowned.

"You wouldn't be looking for this, would you?" a liquid baritone drawled from the vicinity of the window.

She caught her breath, spying her errant lover in white linen and swallowtails against the backdrop of breeze-stirred curtains. He smiled lazily, tapping the hook against his lips.

She half laughed, half sobbed, dashing away a tear. "I . . . I thought you'd gone away."

"I did. To see how Tavy was faring." His eyes captured the light, pewter velvet in the shadows. "But 'journeys end in lovers meeting, every wise man's son doth know.'"

"*The Tempest?*" she whispered.

"*Twelfth Night.*"

"Oh." Her heart took a dizzying leap as he strolled from his lair of muslin lace and shadows. "Is . . . Tavy happy?"

"She has three stalwart suitors. I daresay she's beside herself."

He halted less than an arm's length away. The heat of him licked her limbs like a tiny bonfire, and her legs wobbled, starting to melt. She wondered if Papa had known just how healthy Rafe *really* was.

Then another thought struck her. If Rafe was healthy, he would be leaving soon for Blue Thunder.

"I, uh, learned you might be going to Kentucky," she ventured, unable to keep the anxiety from her voice as she imagined him facing a gunfighter. Nevertheless, she understood why he must go. She understood it only too well. "Do you think you'll be gone long?"

"Hard to say. I did promise Max I'd be his best man."

"Oh," she murmured again, staving off a stab of disappointment when he neglected to mention their own wedding. Despite the sultry caress in his voice, despite the seduction he'd obviously planned, his manner struck her as guarded. If irony was his preferred armor, then he was fairly bristling with it tonight.

"You've said nothing of your own journey," he murmured, his lashes fanning lower to conceal the turbulence in his gaze. "But then, I suppose it must have curled your toes to learn your lover had committed so many misdeeds."

"Oh no," she whispered, finally understanding the reason for his restraint. "You mustn't think that, Rafe. You mustn't *ever* think that. As far as I'm concerned, your past is behind you. And as far as the law is concerned, you're no longer a wanted man."

"I'm not?" He sounded incredulous.

"No, you're not," she said firmly. "All but one of the charges brought against you were made by wealthy men who wound up in jail for embezzling, mine salting, or worse. The Statute of Limitations will run out on your larceny warrants before their jail terms expire."

"You don't say?" The corner of his mouth twitched. "Well, I guess the old axiom is true: it takes a thief to know one. And the remaining warrant?"

"It was dismissed. Apparently the gentleman died. You don't have to run anymore, Rafe," she added quietly. "You're free."

He was silent, no doubt letting the full impact of this news sink in.

"Not really," he said after a moment.

Her heart skittered. "Wh-what do you mean?"

"Well, there's this little matter of . . . us." He twirled the buttonhook between his fingers, much as he used to do with the quizzing glass. "Devilish inconvenient," he taunted softly, "not being permitted to touch the woman you love. The woman you're hell-bent on *marrying*."

Relief fizzed through her veins, bubbling as fast and frothy as French champagne. She clasped her hands, unable to hide her grin as that giddy warmth suffused her face. He loved her! She'd only dared to hope it was true through all those harrowing hours in the mine.

"Is that a fact?" she countered, adopting that same lilting tone he so delighted in tormenting her with. "I can see how that might be vexing for a man of your . . . inclinations."

"That *is* a comfort."

"So, tell me, Mr. Jones. All this marrying business aside, exactly what kind of touching did you have in mind?"

"Hmm." His eyes gleamed like polished silver in the shimmer of the candle flames. "I thought we might start with something sweet, but not entirely lacking in . . . spice."

She shivered as his fingers skimmed up her neck and brushed her cheek. "That *is* nice."

"So glad you approve," he purred, loosening her hair and smoothing the strands. Raising a curl to his lips, he captured her eyes with his own. The molten promise she saw smoking there kindled sparks inside her belly.

"Next," he murmured, drawing her closer as he wrapped her hair around his fist, "I thought we might progress to something a bit more . . . titillating."

"A kiss?" she whispered hopefully.

"Why, darling." His wicked flash of dimples couldn't dispel the tenderness of his smile. "I thought you'd never ask."

His lips sealed off her laughter, and she clutched him closer, reveling in the unabashed hunger of his kiss. He felt so good, so achingly good as he pressed against her, and her senses reeled as she considered how many times fate had nearly stolen him from her.

"Oh, Rafe," she breathed, "I would have died if I had lost you."

He raised his head. When she saw the intensity in his gaze, her throat constricted. "Promise me you'll stay safe in Kentucky," she said tremulously.

"My darling," he murmured, "could you think, for even an instant, that there exists a force in this universe more powerful than the love that would bring me home to you?"

A tear seeped past her lashes, and he caught it on his lips.

"You have my promise, Silver," he whispered. "My word, my heart, my soul."

His mouth lowered, brushing hers, and his hands skimmed down her back. Her gown slowly surrendered, parting with a silken sigh. Dimly she heard the clatter of the buttonhook near her feet. Fabric rustled to her ankles as her chemise chased her bloomers to the floor. Giddily, she fumbled with his own clothes: the coat, the cravat, the cummerbund. When she reached for his fly, he gave her a lopsided grin, one that made her blush like an unschooled maid.

"How I love a woman who knows what she wants."

She giggled, and he swept her up in his arms, clasping her effortlessly against his chest. She had a moment to revel in the sinewy strength of him, in the electrifying sizzle of flesh against flesh. Then she realized he was headed for the bathtub. She clasped his neck tighter, practically squealing as he climbed over the rim.

"Rafe, I thought we were . . . I mean, I hoped we would—"

He chuckled, and she gasped when he sank beneath her. Steamy liquid eddied over her limbs; clouds of heat snaked up from the waves that splashed the tarp. She grappled for balance, clinging to the copper edges even as his legs slid sinuously between her knees.

"Comfortable?" he purred.

She was still gasping from the sensuous shock of heat and man. "I don't think this tub was built for two."

"Well then, maybe you should straddle my hips."

A frisson of delight skittered down her spine as his

strategy became clear. Trying not to grin as shame-lessly as he was, she wriggled across his thighs. She was rewarded when a stealthy hand plumbed the depths to fondle her femininity. The sensation was exquisite: sinuous male fingers stroking the very places his smile had made throb. Her head drifted backwards. Her lashes fluttered closed. When his lips nuzzled her breast, drawing her nipple deep inside the velvet pressures of his mouth, the pleasure was almost beyond what her senses could bear.

She wanted more of him. All of him.

Sliding her palms over his thighs, she delved lower, pleasuring him with her hands. A pleased, throaty sound rumbled in his chest. He clasped her hips, guid-ing her lower, and a sweet shuddering need rippled through her. This was the way she'd always dreamed love should feel.

He melted into her, and she cupped his beloved face in her hands. Holding his gaze as he loved her, she poured her heart into his, letting time and place fade away with the spiraling steam. Rocking, flowing, they became the rhythm of life itself. In that moment, there was only the heat and the water, the flesh and the spirit, the elemental ecstasy of man and woman joining in body and soul.

And later, much later as their sacred bath cooled, he wrapped her in bed linens and cradled her before a crackling hearth. Sated and sleepy, she lay in the circle of his arms, marveling at the threads of fate that had bound them so inexorably together.

He smoothed her hair, turning her face to his.

"I love you, Silver," he whispered huskily.

The shining mirrors of his eyes hid nothing from her now. The playactor had taken off his mask, and at last, her scoundrel for hire was hers alone.

She smiled as his lips tasted hers. She felt blissfully grateful that destiny, not her own willful nature, had plotted the course of their romance. Raphael Jones was everything Cellie's stars had promised, and more. Who would have guessed that a devil with an angel's name could bless her with such a divine love?

Perhaps, she mused a little dreamily, there was something to Cellie's fortune-telling, after all.

**If you fell in love with Rafe
in *Scoundrel for Hire*, you won't
want to miss Michael's story . . .**

~~∽◯◯∽~~

When Eden Mallory walks back into Dr. Michael
Jones's life she's determined to forget the
dreams, now broken, that lured her away. But
Michael, haunted for years by her touch, has not
forgotten Eden and the kiss that branded her
memory across his soul. Now he must defy his
heart, for he hides a secret he is too proud to
reveal. Can Eden find the strength to make him
beileve in her? And will he allow her love to heal
his wounds?

All the answers will be yours.

*Available October 2000
from Avon Books*
or visit *www.adriennedewolfe.com* for more information
about this upcoming Avon Romance